Clare George

Clare George was born in Dorset in 1969 and had a
rural childhood in Essex, Kent and Cheshire before
moving to London, where she lives in Hackney with
her husband. Her first book, *The Cloud Chamber*, was
published by Sceptre in 2003.

Also by Clare George

The Cloud Chamber

Clare George

The Evangelist

SCEPTRE

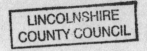
Copyright © 2005 by Clare George

First published in Great Britain in 2005 by Hodder and Stoughton
A division of Hodder Headline

The right of Clare George to be identified as the Author of the Work has been
asserted by her in accordance with the Copyright, Designs and Patents Act 1988

A Sceptre Paperback

1

A CIP catalogue record for this title is available from the British Library

ISBN 0 340 82424 7

Typeset in Sabon by
Palimpsest Book Production Limited,
Polmont, Stirlingshire

Printed and bound by
Mackays of Chatham Ltd, Chatham, Kent

Hodder Headline's policy is to use papers that are natural, renewable
and recyclable products and made from wood grown in sustainable forests.
The logging and manufacturing processes are expected to conform to the
environmental regulations of the country of origin

Hodder and Stoughton Ltd
A division of Hodder Headline
338 Euston Road
London NW1 3BH

For Ed

Part One

Darwin's Bulldog

I

This morning I got up, brushed my teeth, got dressed and took my dog for a walk, just as I always do. Our mission on these occasions is primarily to buy a newspaper, but it is my habit to eschew the shop on the corner in favour of a longer stroll across the bottom right-hand corner of Hampstead Heath, as both the mutt and I benefit from some pre-prandial exercise. We arrived at my favoured newsagent's in the usual fashion and Huxley waited outside, his lead tied to a lamppost, while I selected my breakfast reading material and paid the assistant. Normally the paper would remain firmly closed until we arrived back home, because the ritual of brewing my coffee, toasting my bread and serving Huxley his somewhat noxious repast must all be completed before I allow myself to dive into the forest of print. But on this occasion I requested the newsagent's permission to open it on the counter, fighting my way through the supplements, the advertising leaflets and the polythene to find the nugget I knew to expect today. And then I found it, and didn't go home at all.

We could have walked straight back onto the Heath, and in fact Huxley strongly expressed his desire to do so. But the Heath has become so beloved to me over the past decade that I couldn't bear to stain it with the poison of those words. I stared wildly about me on the pavement, looking for some refuge that would be both welcoming and unfamiliar, some-where I could be assured of never having to visit again. Then I saw it. Now that I look back to that moment, it seems both incongruous and inevitable that I should have chosen the grounds of a church. At the time I barely thought of it at all.

I let Huxley off the lead and threw myself onto the nearest bench before spreading the paper out around me. There, on the front page of the Review section, stared a photograph of myself from years before, an image I'd thought was forgotten and would never be seen again, a picture of a man sprawling and gesticulating and knocking ladies from his path. Above it was a headline, which had been blown up to stretch from one side of the page to the other: 'The Evangelist'.

My reaction should have been confusion. As a man of science and a defender of reason, there should have been no explanation for having been described with a word that smacked of religion and cant. But as I review the day's events, the fact that I already knew what it meant is the first piece of evidence against me. 'When the murdered man left his house at half past three—' says the suspect, and the detective responds sharply, 'How do you know that he left at half past three? I haven't told you that.' In my defence, I will say that the woman who interviewed me made it perfectly obvious that she was going to take that tack. I just didn't notice it at the time.

Then, the article itself. Nausea, as each deadly sentence harked back to memories of the words I'd actually said, now twisted into a tale of unrecognisable culpability and folly. I read and couldn't stop reading, even as my stomach convulsed, even as the blood filled my face and shoulders and hands.

'Professor Oldroyd.'

The priest's interruption was so soft that I slammed the paper onto the bench and jerked upright. He stood above me, a young man with a very large nose and a graceful slenderness beneath his cassock. As I am not in the habit of hanging around in graveyards, I had never seen him before in my life. But he knew me.

'I'm sorry if I've distracted you from your reading,' he said, kindly but not at all apologetically. He was craning his neck in an attempt to see the picture on the front of the newspaper.

'It's nothing,' I snapped back, blocking his view with my whole upper body.

'It's just that it's rather a surprise to see you here. I mean' – he cast his eyes up towards the spire of the church – 'in the grounds of a house of worship. Not really your scene, I would have thought.'

'I was looking for a bit of peace and quiet,' I said pointedly.

'I hope you've found it here. I can imagine that this morning's – news – has been extremely taxing.'

So he'd read it already. I supposed that an article with such a title must be quite eye-catching for a man of his profession.

'But surely,' he continued, 'solitude is something which is available in the privacy of your own home. When people come here they tend to be looking for something a little different. Not peace in the sense of quiet, so much. Peace of mind, more frequently.'

Do vicars gossip? An image sprang into my mind of a kind of weekly convention of clerics, with this young stripling holding forth to the rest. *You'll never guess who I had in my graveyard last week. That Max Oldroyd, the infamous atheist. I've signed him up for Bible classes and the Tuesday prayer group. We'll have him converted by Whitsun.* And the others humming and nodding in admiration of the catch made by this precocious fisher of souls.

'I can't imagine you can give the sort of peace I'm looking for,' I growled, and then wished I hadn't.

He smiled and arched an eyebrow. What a funny mixture he was, with his new-graduate sparkle, brim full with the habitual irony of his hapless generation, and the usual confidence on display from his navel like an umbilical cord to God. 'May I take a seat?' he enquired.

I grunted and mumbled, but shuffled along the bench anyway. I suppose it was his charm that made me do it, which was the outward manifestation of something genuinely attractive about

5

him. A freshness, an exuberance, an optimism, a deep, unconquerable certainty – oh, I thought, you are too intelligent for any of it to last for long. A decade, maybe. Perhaps two. But I don't give it much longer than that.

Then I realised what had made me move up to give him space.

Thirty years ago, the man with that certainty, that exuberance and that confidence in his ability to convert the world was me.

It is not true that I am as much a stranger to churches as we both pretended I was. The conventions of an ordinary British life prohibit any such purism. During last year alone, I darkened their doors on no fewer than three occasions. The first, appropriately enough, was a family christening. My niece, Sarah, had given birth to a boy, whom she and her husband named Jack. Had it been a girl, she would have been called Eleanor. To me these would sound appallingly staid, old-fashioned monikers, if it were not for the fact that every infant I've come across in the past few years has been given one of them.

Sarah herself was christened twenty-eight years ago with the most popular name of her year. She produced her first offspring precisely on cue, demonstrating that women are bearing children much later than they did in 1975, when Sarah's mother, my sister Rosemary, aged only twenty, inflicted the same ceremony upon her firstborn. In those days, of course, my presence in a house of worship was a less noteworthy circumstance than it is now, but even then I couldn't help thinking, as Rosy joyfully promised to bring up her baby according to the teachings of Christ, that it was a very wrong thing to make a child a Christian before it was capable of issuing a single word of protest. Fortunately, Rosy broke the majority of those pledges, as is the custom these days, and Sarah is unlikely to have seen much more of the inside of churches in those intervening years than I have myself. But this didn't prevent the daughter from spouting the same empty words as the mother.

Sarah is a robust young woman whose life has proceeded precisely along the lines of the statistical norm, and her only deviations from the template set by her mother and her grandmother are those which, on average, apply to an entire generation. If any of that female triumvirate – my mother, my sister or my niece – were asked whether they believed in God, the answer, unhesitatingly, would be, Yes; and the only variations would be in the degree of qualification as to what exactly God was. And although in Sarah's case the qualifications would have whittled Him almost down to nothing, that vagueness would have made it almost impossible for her to take her own beliefs seriously enough to tempt fate through rebellion. I know from my own experience of fatherhood how heartbreakingly fragile a thing is the newborn. Its perfection is at odds with all that surrounds it, its skin too soft, its limbs too tiny, its form too new. I can see that, when confronted with the emergence of a new person freshly delivered from nothingness, one might turn for protection to a force from the other side of existence. Especially if it's what's expected. Yet I cannot see that ritual as ordinary. It is spooky, it is sinister, it is surreal. The unknowns of infinity are tugged down from their spectral perches and tethered in a cage of suburban privet. There is no other world than this, spoke the smiles on each of the commuters' faces within that village church; the Ikea furniture and the Laura Ashley curtains stretch on forever. Surely, I thought, the tears pricking to my eyes, at this of all moments you can see that it is absurd. The unsullied creature was passed in its shroud from Sarah to the priest. Cold water was thrown onto its poor little face, mystical signs made above its forehead and supernatural powers invoked, and it screamed. It was a hard job to prevent myself from springing to its rescue and whisking it away to a future of freedom and knowledge. But no-one else noticed how strange it was, and after the service we all walked back to Sarah and David's executive home on an estate built over what had once been an ancient water meadow. I had the chance for a few moments to spend a little time communing with the newly Christian soul himself, and whispered into his burbling, gurgling countenance about the true mysteries of life, but soon enough he was passed onto the next person, and the next, until he retaliated with a wholly merited scream, and we all went home. The memory of that tiny face remained with me for days. Don't let it happen, I thought over and over again. You have the chance to discover the universe for yourself. Please don't turn out like them.

The second occasion was a wedding. Oh, Declan, you gin-sodden old fool. He is my oldest friend, a year my senior, and it is odd to watch a fifty-three-year-old man make an idiot of himself in front of an Almighty he's quite aware doesn't exist. It's not that I disapprove of the marriage. He's been with Georgina for more than a decade, which is quite long enough for her to have become accustomed to his lackadaisical approach to life and for him to have seen beyond her sexiness and sophistication to the Freudian claptrap which lies beneath. Apparently, the proposal was extracted from him on the condition that she would finally give him permission to have a vasectomy and, given his romantic history, plus his hysterical reaction to Georgina's acquisition of a kitten a couple of years ago, this would seem to be a firm foundation for a stable future together. But neither of them even pretends to believe in God. 'Oh, Max,' said Georgina with unaccustomed equanimity, her face glowing with the creamy satisfaction of the forty-year-old bride-to-be and her coffee table liberally scattered with glossy hardbacks on topics such as flower arranging and cake decorations, 'you're such a pedant.'

'Pedant? Look, Georgina, I'm aware I've got my faults, and I've had them listed to me often enough, but I can assure you that no-one has ever included pedantry amongst them. I would just have expected a bit more integrity from you two, of all people.'

Georgina has never been one to be cowed by my outbursts. 'You'll understand when you see the church,' she said. 'It's very special to me. You see, it's attached to a Carmelite convent, and it's on the top of a cliff—'

'A *convent*? With *nuns*? Those women go around wearing gold rings and convincing themselves they're all married to Jesus Christ. They're the necrophiliac wives of a dead bigamist, and they think that makes them good people. How healthy is that sort of approach to marriage?'

'You'll be as swept up by the sense of occasion as anyone else. You see' – she turned blushingly to her fiancé, who was in the process of unscrewing a whisky bottle – 'Declan, don't you think it's time you asked him?'

'I'm not sure this is the right moment,' said Declan.

I twitched. 'Right moment for what?'

With a shaking hand, he poured large measures into two glasses, passed one to me, and downed the other himself. 'Oh, all right,' he mumbled. 'I'd like you to be my best man.' Then he ducked.

Of course I didn't hit him. I was deeply touched. Regardless of wives and churches and mindless mumbo jumbo, being asked to be a best man is the greatest compliment that can be passed between two members of the male sex. 'Oh, golly,' I gushed. 'That's – that's absolutely fantastic.'

Declan's head tilted upwards in surprise, though the rest of his body remained in a crouched position. 'See,' said Georgina triumphantly. 'I told you he'd like the attention.'

I slung her a dismissive look. 'Of course I can't get involved in anything religious,' I said.

'God, no,' said Declan. 'You just have to pass me the ring. And make a speech, of course.'

'There will be rules about that,' interjected Georgina sternly.

There turned out to be rules for everything. My outfit was specified down to the last furbelow, and the spot on which I was to stand was virtually marked with a cross. There were at least three gods in the chapel that day, and whilst one might have been a loosely Carmelite deity, discreetly puffing out His presence from the candles and the censers, the second was English wedding etiquette, and the third was French *Vogue*. Georgina looked suitably stunning in a figure-hugging white lace creation, its lines showing off her Tai Chi'd physique, and Declan wore a purple morning suit which matched her oriental headdress and the spiralling festoons of flowers which lined the church. As the carefully selected music died away, and the priest launched into the service, I shoved tissues at Declan to stem the hayfever brought on by the floral decorations, and tried to repress an overwhelming urge to laugh. Never before had I been able to take the trappings of religion so lightly, because never before had they seemed so ostentatiously ridiculous. Declan and Georgina were ridiculously happy, and ridiculously well-suited, and the whole service was an unwitting tribute to the gorgeous absurdity of life. I watched Declan's eyes begin to goggle as the priest delved deeper into the intimacy of God's role in their future lives. *Really?* I saw him think as the voice pattered on. You mean that from now on I'm going to be fucking for Jesus?

'You must have realised that,' I said, when the service, the dinner and the speeches were over, and we were sitting on the end of the jetty of the hotel used for the reception, just as we might have done when we were boys, dangling our legs just above the breakers that crashed beneath our feet. Behind us the reception continued apace, but the darkness of the bay provided a screen, and Declan was afforded a respite from his mingling for a few minutes. I reached into my inside pocket, and pulled out the flask I'd filled with his favourite cognac for just this eventuality. 'You've been to dozens of church weddings.'

'I didn't have to listen to those ones,' he said, still shaking his head in dizzy disbelief.

But beneath the startled rabbit impression, he was calmer than I'd ever seen him. He'd handed over all responsibility for proceedings to his bride, and it looked as if it was a very good feeling. It did occur to me, as the entire shebang rolled out along its centuries-defined course, that it must be a very comfortable thing to be as sure of the rules of existence as was Georgina. She might have done a year's worth of organising, but apart from the style considerations, which were first nature to her, she'd done almost no deciding at all. From the wording of the invitations to the throwing of the bouquet, every detail of her nuptials had been laid out in advance by tradition. It didn't matter that her father's speech had gone unheard by all but those seated closest to him on the top table, or that the ratio of divorcees to virgins was skewed wildly in favour of the former, or that the groom was still a little bow-legged due to the after-effects of his recent operation. Every guest was able to relax into the expensive, overblown predictability of the occasion and concentrate on enjoying themselves. Even me, for whom it almost became a holiday from myself. How glorious it must be never to question what you think or feel. You don't need to believe in God to have that sort of certainty, as Georgina so deftly demonstrated, but it helps if you borrow him for the day.

And yet no-one ever really takes a complete holiday from himself. I was angry, beneath all the reflected joy. I would like to be able to say that my anger wasn't directed at the bride and groom at all, only at myself, but it would not be true. It was they who infuriated me. What right did they have to indulge in such starry-eyed complacency, after living so long, and experiencing so much? Didn't they know by now that twenty thousand pounds couldn't buy happiness, that no quantity of sea urchin ballotine could bind their friends to them forever, that the footsteps of dark-clad nuns along clifftop cloisters was no passport to eternal life? Even if there really had been a God to take charge of this ritual, so frivolous a display couldn't have got them one iota closer to any of those goals. I applauded their generosity and I rejoiced in their vitality, but I, the crusty old atheist, was deeply offended by the vainness in which they took the Lord's name. This is serious, my own voice kept muttering at me at intervals throughout the day, and in those moments I knew I was truly alone.

My third excursion into a church was for a funeral. This time there was no question of the main participant's devotion to his religion. He was my first boss, Professor John Hinds, and unusually for a biologist, he was a God-botherer. It had taken me years to discover this particular facet of his personality, but then I hadn't known he was a squash player either, despite playing on a weekly basis myself, and this fact was only delivered to me after his demise, when it was revealed that he'd died on the court. 'Really?' I'd said somewhat tactlessly when his devoted administrator broke this detail to me. 'God, who'd have thought he had the flexibility?' Tears rose to Marion's eyes, so I backtracked, and embarked on a long and caring speech about his kindness, his cleverness and his devotion to duty, and by the end of it had landed myself with an invitation to his spiritual dispatch.

Our relationship had not been entirely harmonious even at the start, and it had worsened over the years. Nevertheless, I was greatly troubled by his death. The service took place in the chapel of Erasmus College, London, where we'd worked and fought for more than three decades. He was only sixty-three, little more than a year away from vacating the position as head of department to which I would never be promoted. It is very distressing to hear time's winged chariot at one's back, and even more so when the platitudes used to cushion the blow are unavailable to oneself. As I listened with my head involuntarily bowed, it seemed unbelievable to me that they could have been available to John either. He must have known that when his ashes returned to ashes they would resume their position in the molecular scheme of things, and leave no residue of his mind. I couldn't deny that the mind had been a considerable one. Yet still he had believed, with more convincing firmness that I have encountered even in the professional evangelists of my acquaintance, that on his death his consciousness would be spirited away into the company of the imaginary friend in whom he'd been confiding all his life. And once again I thought, how easy. How completely obvious, that we would want it to turn out that way. A man of his intellect ought never to have allowed his desires to dictate his understanding of the world.

Now I sat in the chapel where he'd worshipped every Sunday, and I felt his presence very close to me. The recently deceased have a habit of lingering in their absence more vividly than they did when they were alive. I could feel all of him, the way his last remaining strands of hair clustered around his ears, the way his shirts clung to his inadequate chest, the way he breathed so surreptitiously, as if trying not to steal too much air or give back very much of himself. Suddenly his smallness, his unassuming neatness, his fastidious refusal to take up space, were huge. Because now I knew the thing that we always forget when we are dealing with a living human being: that he was himself. Whenever he'd been with me, there had not been one mind there, but two. Two pairs of eyes squinting out at each other; two pairs of ears vibrating to each sound; two bodies squirming their way around the objects that got in their way; two completely different views of the world. And the chaplain's oration, poking away at my brain, gave no hint of any of this. Yes, he had been kind. He'd been kind to me from start to finish, even when he was set against me, even when it felt as if he was doing his damnedest to destroy my career. His interventions in my life had not just been kindly meant: they would have done me good, had I been the sort of man who was capable of receiving them. And yes, he was a good teacher. His lectures had been so quietly presented that it was difficult to summon the enthusiasm to listen, but the best of them, once they got going, were flights across the wonders of the world, blessing his audience with wings. As a student I'd stumbled out of them, my feet tripping over one another in their haste to get to the library, less impressed by what I'd just witnessed than by the ideas sprouting in my own brain.

But none of this was the half of it. Didn't the chaplain realise that he might as well be describing a painting, or a piece of music, or an essay on the flight of the bumble bee? A robot could have done all the things that he was recounting, had it been programmed well enough, and then there would be no reason to mourn. Oh, no, the chaplain might argue, no-one could ever mistake John Hinds for a robot, because that sort of technology will never exist. But he'd be wrong. It already does. Computers can pass any Turing test we set for them. They can process more information than we can even imagine; they can command the sort of gymnastics that no body will ever evolve to achieve; they can learn; they can communicate in languages which not even their human creators can understand in the same effective manner. When we talk of Turing tests, we aren't really talking about being tricked into thinking that a computer is human. We're talking about being tricked into thinking it is conscious, that it *knows it exists*, and all such tests are pointless, because there is no test that can prove that even of a human being.

It's one of the few things that John and I ever agreed upon. As entomologists, the mystery of consciousness wasn't really on our patch, but we both strayed onto it all the same. 'A bird,' John said meditatively in an undergraduate lecture that I sat in on as a PhD student, 'has a brain. As such, it is a very mysterious thing, because we find it difficult to understand brains. For instance, it will not return to a nest that has been disturbed, despite the fact that its infants are dying within. How can it remember such a thing? Its memory of its nest's disturbance is not that disturbance itself, nor even the perceptions experienced by the bird during its discovery, any more than the pleasure dome at Xanadu in "Kubla Khan" is a real palace. Both are representations of things, real or imagined, somehow manufactured by and existing within the nerve tissue inside a creature's skull. And both abstractions have actual effects, whether it be the death of a nest-full of chicks and the termination of four of five unique combinations of genes, or the writing of a poem on paper and its quotation in a lecture more than two centuries later.'

I watched in satisfaction as the undergraduates around me tangled their brains over this thought, and tried not to notice that my own was getting a little messy.

'A bird's brain,' continued John, 'is only a little less mysterious than your own. Yet, if we stop worrying about the neurological mechanics of the thing, and look at it from an evolutionary point of view, it is not mysterious at all. There are sound reasons for that bird not to return to that nest, if you take reproductive economics into account, and it has developed mechanisms to enable it not to do so. It can receive inputs; it can remember those inputs; and it can act upon them. Consider the most familiar example of a bird's communication. It sings, another bird hears it, and a result is produced. We might construe that song as having some sort of meaning, in the way that we understand meaning, and therefore postulate that both the bird which emits that call and the one that hears it are fully aware of what is going on. But they don't need to be. The only meaning that song needs to have is its outcome: if the bird issued a warning, then the result is a life saved; and if it was a mating call, then it is a new life created. As long as the bird listening to the song is engineered in such a way that it responds correctly to those sounds, then it need have no awareness of hearing them at all.'

He had not raised his voice or lowered it throughout the entire speech. This was one of the things I eventually found most annoying about John Hinds: that his whole demeanour gave the impression of someone who didn't want to cause a stir, and that this in itself was all part of the effect. But in those days I wasn't thinking about him. All I was aware of was what he was saying.

'And if you think about it carefully,' said John, 'the same is true of ourselves.'

I thought then that he was an atheist. And so I thrilled to his speech, and my brain buzzed with its implications. Yes, I thought, we have no obvious biological need for consciousness. In fact, the only proof that we have it lies within our own minds. All else is extrapolation from ourselves. I can prove my own consciousness to myself, but I cannot prove it to anyone else, not even by thinking these thoughts, nor writing them down, not by anything in the world, because consciousness is experience, and no-one can experience my experience but me. How typical it was of evolution to make the thing we thought of as being the most integral part of ourselves the least necessary, probably a mere by-product of the complexity of our brains.

But at John's memorial service, I was thinking about the man, not just what he had said, and I knew that he hadn't been talking about evolution at all. He'd made out that he was stripping nature of its mystery, but he'd ended on a note of supreme mystery, because of course whatever we do or don't know about the birds, we know that we *are* conscious, even though we don't know how, or why, or what it means. And he'd done it because he loved mystery, and because he thought that the part of him which could only ever be private to himself belonged not to his genes but to God. How typical it was of John not to say so; how typical of him to take upon himself the mysteriousness of his alleged maker.

I had known him for so long that the pattern of his behaviour fell together like a neatly stitched quilt. There was nothing he could ever have done that would not in some way have been typical. Only this was no more than saying that a bird was typical, or a computer was typical. I had not understood him at all. It had driven me half mad at times. I had come to know what he would do and he would say, but I hadn't the slightest idea why. Why would he make his point and not drive it home? Why would he let me think that he was my enemy, when the slightest indication that he was my friend might have led me to take his advice? And most of all, why the fuck did he believe in God?

The chaplain had no answers to these questions. He clearly didn't even know that they existed. Instead, within the dark walls of that church, he performed a ritual which was supposed to deliver the essence of John to the Almighty. Oh, John, I thought, how could you possibly think it could work? The chance motions of the whole universe conspired to bring you here, in all your inscrutable uniqueness, and now those same forces have destroyed you. How can you possibly think that some supernatural power is going to reach down a hand and lift you into some bizarre new existence? You're *gone*.

'I did read that article this morning,' confessed the baby vicar, motioning his head towards the object I was hiding with my arm. 'It's naughty of me to dawdle on a Sunday, but the thing gets delivered, and then I start reading – And I have to say, I found it fascinating. In fact, I'm considering rewriting my sermon around it. Would you care to come along?'

'No,' I said, 'I would not.'

He shrugged genially. 'Didn't think so. But it is the most

marvellous coincidence that you should be here, reading it too. One would almost think—' And again he cast his eyes upwards.

He's taking the piss, I thought. 'No,' I said, 'one would not.'

'Well, there you go. But you see, one of the reasons it gripped me so much was that I've read your book, and I loved it.'

I have written almost a dozen books in my life. Nevertheless, there was no doubt in my mind which he was referring to. '*Genesis*,' I said.

His face relaxed. 'It's a marvellous book,' he gushed. 'Almost – spiritual, at times.'

'Most vicars tend to get annoyed by the title,' I said. Not just vicars, either. There were no complaints at the time of publication, but these days pretty much everyone seems to hate the name of that book. Especially me. 'It has been suggested that it would be possible to prosecute me for it under the blasphemy laws.'

'Oh, the blasphemy laws,' said the vicar dismissively. 'No-one would ever do it. It would just make them look stupid. There's very little in that book which disagrees with what the majority of believers accept to be true these days.'

That's as much as you know, I thought, and felt a wave of fondness for the all-embracing woolliness of the Anglican Church.

'I'm Matthew, by the way,' he said, sticking out his hand.

'Reverend Matthew, I presume,' I retorted, giving the hand a cursory shake and then withdrawing my own sharply.

He gave an embarrassing, self-deprecating chuckle. 'Reverend Matthew Watson, if you must. Takes a bit of getting used to.'

Now that he was by my side, I could judge his height in comparison with my own, and it was considerable. I am six foot seven, and there are few men whose heads reach much above my chin. His was slightly higher than my nose. This further similarity only sickened me more. 'You want to convert me,' I said dully. 'You're not the first. Though most of them wouldn't go as far as bothering to get me to believe in' – I gestured towards the walls of the church – 'all this stuff. Mostly they'd just like me to shut up.'

'I don't want you to shut up,' said the young man. 'It's always a good thing to hear the opposite point of view properly articulated, but you don't hear much of it these days. Our main enemy is indifference.'

I skewed a glance at him. The brightness in his eyes was entirely at odds with the gruesome piety of his smile. 'Well, indifference isn't *my* enemy,' I said roughly. 'Indifference is my absolute objective. If something doesn't exist, and you know that it doesn't exist, and everyone else knows that it doesn't exist, then indifference is the only option. It's absolute. But what you call indifference isn't indifference at all. It's complacent, blind, weak-minded acceptance.'

'Wow. You really are as angry in real life as you are on the page, aren't you? What brought you to a church?'

I looked at him for only the second time since he'd sat down. He was shrew-like in his intensity, the long triangular nose jutting out from the tightly screwed-up face. I wondered whether he really could be the younger self I'd glimpsed when he'd first assailed me. Did I truly think his beliefs would wreak as much havoc in his life as mine had for me? It was unlikely. He'd already entered a closed world, barricaded at its edge by people who would always tell him he was right. And even if the best happened, and the world emptied of believers and he chose to stay inside on his own, he'd still have God on his side. It's so unfair, I thought, the self-pity welling up in me. Possession of the truth had given me no advantages in life to compare with those of the young Reverend.

'Perhaps one day you'll learn that things aren't as simple as you think,' I said, hope making a valiant effort to get the better of experience.

His face lit up. 'Is that why you're here?' he whispered. 'Have you come to realise that science isn't enough?'

'You're a fool if you think it could ever be that easy to make your little conquest,' I snapped back. 'It's you who—' Then I heard what I was about to say, saw myself lunging for the bait just as I always had. I was playing into the hands of a nincompoop who would steal the intellectual rigour from my arguments and use it to make his own tired, flabby ideas stand up for a little longer. 'Forget it,' I said. 'It doesn't matter.'

A wave of disappointment spread across his face, and then it animated again. He jumped to his feet, and began waving his arms around. 'Of course you think it matters!' he cried. 'That's what I admire about you. It matters as much to you as it does to us. Surely, Max – you don't mind me calling you that, do you? – surely the fact of it is that *you* want to convert *me*?'

He made a ludicrously comic figure, bouncing up and down in the morning sun, his cassock brushing the daisy tops. 'No,' I said. 'Frankly, I don't.'

Because I am not an evangelist. I am just a man in search of the truth.

2

The interview took place several weeks ago. I had never met the woman before, though I had advance notice of her reputation. 'She'll eat you alive, mate,' said Declan, who writes for the same newspaper. 'Don't say I didn't warn you.'

But I was accustomed enough to the attentions of flesh-eating female journalists to disregard his warning. The occasion for the interrogation this time around was the forthcoming publication of a new edition of *Genesis*, 'revised and updated for the century of the gene'. Review copies had been sent out to those who might be supposed to possess an opinion about its republication, and press releases had been distributed, complete with a note at the bottom saying that the author was available for interview – a fact of which the author was, as usual, unaware.

The woman who turned up on my doorstep at the appointed time didn't strike me as the harridan Declan had built her up to be. It was a windy day, and the dusty brown hair blew around her face as she attempted rather ineffectually to push it away again. She must have been in her mid-forties at least, but unlike most London women of her age, appeared to have made no special efforts to preserve her looks. It was as if she'd carried her youthful prettiness into her middle years with careless disregard, and might leave it on a bus at any moment without noticing. She wore the clothes of a student and, when she turned to face me, the unguarded grin of a teenager.

'Hello,' she said. 'I'm Margot Hennessy. But I daresay you'd worked that out.'

The voice was quite different. It could have belonged to a

woman ten, twenty or even thirty years older: a Charlotte Rampling, a Joan Collins or even, at a stretch, a Miss Marple. She used it like an actress, and during the course of the afternoon I would witness the full range of its expressions: dark and sultry or warm and comfortable, abrupt and scornful or sweet and beguiling, but always, always replete with the sort of confidence that comes from having seen it all before.

She looked down at my feet, where Huxley was doing his guard-dog impression. 'Oh, Lord, a yapper,' she said. 'You two give the lie to the one about dogs growing to look like their owners, don't you? How tall is he?'

A snort of laughter burst out of me, because I was so unaccustomed to hearing that question directed at anyone other than me. We both regarded him. Huxley looked embarrassed. 'Eight inches?' I speculated. 'Ten, at a push.'

Huxley slunk inside, and we followed him in. It was only as we entered the sitting room that I anticipated the first of the problems of the afternoon. I live alone in a large house, and have never felt it necessary to burden myself with large quantities of furniture. There were only two items in that twenty-five-foot room, both huddled together close to the front window, and they were my chair and Huxley's sofa. She made a move towards the former, and through sheer instinct I nipped around her and took it myself. Margot slid me a look and settled herself down on the sofa, opening her battered leather bag and removing a huge pile of papers. Huxley crouched at the door and began to move towards her, growling.

'Aggressive little bugger, isn't he?' said Margot, and pulled a dictaphone from the bag. 'Now, before I turn this on, is there any scene-setting you'd like to do off the record? Anything you're antsy about, that sort of thing?'

I watched Huxley, my heart sinking. 'No, it's fine. Turn it on whenever you like.'

The button went click, and she stretched forward to place

the machine on the floor between us. Huxley seized his moment and leapt with a great snarl onto the opposite end of his sofa. There he took up position, his belly flat on the cushion, vibrating with intent. Margot attempted for a moment to outstare him, failed, and then turned to me.

'I should point out at this stage,' she said, 'that I'm not too keen on dogs. The feeling seems to be mutual.'

'Don't let him worry you,' I said dishonestly. 'He's too small to do any damage.'

'Hmm,' said Margot, and produced a pair of narrow metal-rimmed glasses, which she balanced on her nose. She took the top sheet from her stash of notes and perused it. Then she smiled, and her whole pose changed. 'Well, Max,' she said, 'I'm here, as you know, to talk about the new edition of *Genesis*.'

I nodded.

'The original is a rather wonderful work. I discovered it when I was twenty. You know, I suspect that many people these days think of you as being this old media tart who pops up every now and again to pontificate about science' – I stiffened, and Huxley's growls grew more intense – 'but in those days you were pretty hot stuff. Young, brilliant, Byronic, enormous – I fancied you like hell back then, you know. And what I really want to see is whether the old magic is still there—'

I coughed in embarrassment. 'I thought your newspaper tended to take a more intellectual approach to things than that.'

She laughed. 'Come on, Max,' she said. 'Even you must realise that your success has never *exclusively* been attributable to your beautiful mind.'

I frowned, and stared at the carpet.

'Or perhaps you don't,' said Margot. 'In which case, that's definitely one of the things we have to explore. But firstly, tell me why you've changed *Genesis*.'

'Changed it?'

'Updated and revised it for the century of the gene. After

23

all, you pretty much rubbish the whole idea of "the century of the gene" in your new introduction. I quote' – and there was a further rummaging in her bag, and the production of the book, festooned with the tops of post-it notes sticking out from its pages – '"The century of the gene is an anachronistic assumption. Just as the dawn of the twentieth century saw an outburst of gloom over the degeneration of the human race based on the fallacious interpretation of emerging evolutionary theories, the twenty-first sees an equally gloomy fever of prophecy that in a hundred years' time we shall all be sporting designer genes, simply because the cataloguing of the human genome has just been completed. We are in a better position now than we were in 1903 to judge whether the last hundred years constituted the century of degeneration; let our descendants in 2103 judge whether this has been the century of the gene."'

'Well,' I countered, 'that's all true.'

'Then why update *Genesis*?'

The real answer was, of course, that my publishers asked me to. I might have a reputation for being a difficult man, but there are times when almost anyone can be submissive. 'Biology has moved on a lot since 1977,' I fudged. 'As has the way people think about it. When I wrote *Genesis* I had no idea that anyone would take against anything I said. Now I do.'

'Yes,' said Margot, 'you do, rather, don't you? That's what I meant when I asked you why you'd changed *Genesis*. The great thing about the first edition was how confident it was in its views. You explained things so simply. I knew nothing about biology in those days, and there it was, all laid out for me. Yet your new introduction appears not to be prefacing a work of explanation, but something more contentious, controversial even.'

'You're right to say it was simple,' I said, warming to the theme she'd introduced. 'But you see, some people *did* see it as being controversial. And I've been fighting them ever since.'

We entered into a discussion of the religious opposition to

my work, during which Huxley attacked her. 'Oh, for goodness' sake—'

'I'll take him out if you like.'

'Please do.'

I stuck the poor displaced creature in the kitchen, made us
each a cup of tea and returned to the interview. 'You see,' I
said, bearing mugs, 'the creationists have made quite an industry
out of opposing evolution.'

'Yes,' said Margot, 'but you've made quite an industry out of
defending it, as well. You wrote a book which explained your
views on evolution. Then you wrote another book, and another,
and another, and at the front of each was an introduction which
appeared to be responding to the criticisms of the first. But there
weren't any criticisms of the first, at least not of the kind you
appear to address. It's true that you've got into a fair amount of
trouble with the God squad over the years. But it was you who
fired the first shot, with all those television appearances. When
people said that you were a crazed extremist, they weren't talking
about *Genesis*. They were talking about the fact that you went
around telling bishops they were evil.'

'I never said that!'

'Yes, you did. Several times. In fact, if one were to take the
evidence of those transcripts alone, then one would conclude
that "evil" was one of your favourite words. Rather an odd
stance for a man of your views, don't you think? Would you
say that you were a moral man?'

'Pardon?'

'In everything you've written, your objections to religion have
been fundamentally moral in their tone. You say that it is *not
right*. But morality can be a rather tricky topic for an atheist.
How would you describe your moral code?'

Her sharp intelligence was stimulating, but I was beginning
to find it a little exhausting as well. 'These things always sound
horribly trite.'

'What things?'

'Treat other people as you'd like to be treated yourself. That sort of thing.'

'Max, that's straight from the Bible.'

'Huh?'

'Do unto others as you would have others do unto you. Matthew, I think. The reported speech of Christ Himself.'

'Look, Margot, I don't have any argument with the individual sayings of Christ. From what I've read of the Gospels, he sounds to me like a man who spoke a lot of sense. But he was not a god. The whole shenanigans of putting the words of man into the mouth of something called God is an anachronism left over from a time when we knew almost nothing about the world around us. To continue to do so now, when the superstitions themselves have been superseded by science, is transparently cynical. It's perfectly possible for me to agree with Christ in his pronouncements upon moral matters, but when I do so, it's not because he's God. It's when he happens to be right.'

'When he's right? There you go again. Who's to say that it's right to do unto others as you would have others do unto you? Is there any scientific basis for that statement?'

I remained calm. 'You could say that to any scientist who also happens to be an atheist. Surely you aren't suggesting that every one of us is entirely amoral.'

'I'm saying the precise opposite. Max, you must be able to see that your rage is the most compelling thing about you. I've read most of what you've written, and I've watched every television appearance I could get hold of. From the very first one you were the strongest moral presence I've ever witnessed on the small screen. It was a panel programme from years ago, back in 1979. The topic under discussion was the *Life of Brian*. It was you, a television presenter and a bishop. The bishop was lucky to come out of it with his life. And now I can see you in the flesh. You're busting out of yourself. But the thing I still can't see is what your convictions actually are, other than an unusual antipathy to bishops.'

'I don't approve of the institutional propagation of lies. Nor am I prepared to stand by while films are banned on the basis that they criticise the state religion. The *Life of Brian* is a heart-breakingly sensible film. I still have a tendency to cry during the closing credits.'

'You cry watching Monty Python?'

I was suddenly embarrassed. 'Yes,' I said in a small voice.

'How sweet. What else makes you cry?'

'Injustice. Cruelty. Lies.'

'Ah, yes. Lies. The truth really does seem to be the corner-stone of your moral code, doesn't it? You say as much in the new introduction to *Genesis*.' She took hold of a post-it note with a nimble finger and opened the book again. '"The first book with the same title as this one was a creation myth,"' she quoted. '"And before science gave us access to greater knowl-edge, myths were the only things we had to explain our own origins. They still have their value as cultural artefacts. But now that we know the truth, to take them at face value is to trans-form them from creation myths into creation lies."'

'Well, it's true.'

'True. Right. Is there a distinction between right in the factual sense and right in the moral sense? I get the strong impression that you conflate the two.'

'You have no foundation for that statement—'

'How does telling the truth fit with treating others as you would like to be treated yourself? Sometimes people don't want to be told the truth. And sometimes they don't get it even if they want it. How much of the truth do you think you're prepared to tell me today?'

It didn't bother me. I was glad to be interviewed by someone who'd made the effort to do a bit of research into my work.

Her adroitness made me assume that she would understand what I was saying. I suppose I trusted her.

'Let's talk about your life,' said Margot. 'You were born in Plymouth in 1951. Would you say you had a happy childhood?'

'Oh, happy enough. Yes, I'd say it was definitely happy.'

'Your father was a naval officer. Would you say you got on with him?'

'We got on very well. He was away a lot of the time, of course. And this was the fifties, and fathers and sons didn't exactly go around having deep discussions about the meaning of life in those days. But I admired him a lot.'

'He died of cancer when you were in your early twenties. It's a tough time to lose a parent. Would you like to talk about it at all?'

I havered for a bit. I knew that I didn't have to say anything about it at all. But no-one had ever bothered to ask me before, and it impressed me that she had. 'You're right that it was difficult. I was just starting out in London, you see, and had so many other things to think about. My sister always thought I should have got more involved. Still does, in fact, but—'

'So you have a difficult relationship with your sister.'

It was the only moment in the afternoon when I saw the words she'd just said flash up on a newspaper page. 'You mustn't put that in,' I said softly. 'I don't, really. We're just different. It shouldn't be her problem that I go around being interviewed for the press.'

'All right,' says Margot. 'I'll leave her out of it. But you'll permit me to leave your parents in. They're rather fundamental to a discussion of the life of an evolutionary biologist. Which of them do you take after? Your mother, or your father?'

'It doesn't work like that. It's a great mistake to think that something as intricate as personality can be stitched together from the genes of the parents in an identifiable way. Lives have been ruined by those sorts of assumptions.'

'Really? You don't seem to have thought so as a young man. In 1980 you wrote an article which explicitly looked at the ways in which your three-year-old son took after you.'

'This is a very complex subject. It's different as a parent, as I'm sure you've seen yourself. You watch your children growing up, adding things bit by bit. So there's a much greater – atomisation, I suppose, of one's understanding of them. And one does think in terms of this bit taking after me, this bit taking after the mother, because you see each characteristic as it appears. Some of them might just as easily have been picked up culturally as genetically. But I'm sure there's all sorts of stuff that couldn't really be attributed to either, which is a new recombination of the two, or which has been introduced from outside the family environment. The thing is, you probably don't see those bits as clearly when you're a parent.'

'So would you say now that your assumptions about your son's similarities to you were wrong?'

'Some of them. Not others. It's difficult to say. I've known him too long. Other people would be better judges.' Huxley's scrabbling at the kitchen door was becoming frantic. 'Look,' I said, 'would you mind terribly if I let him back in? He's not used to being confined to such a small space, and he's probably getting thirsty.'

She looked very doubtful. But I could bear the noise no longer, and I got up to release him. Huxley whirled out, a small tornado of scampering paws and yapping. When I returned, Huxley was already installed in his usual spot, and Margot was gathering her notes.

'Thank you, Max,' she said. 'It's been a very pleasant afternoon. I'll call you if I have any more questions.'

I am not afraid of interviews, but the relief of having got through it without major mishap was there all the same. It always is, to an extent. 'Please do. I've enjoyed it too.'

The last thing she said was when we were standing on the

doorstep in the wind, Margot standing back out of the way of Huxley's gnashing jaws. 'I forgot to ask,' she said, 'why is your dog called Huxley? Is it after Aldous?'

'No. Thomas. Charles Darwin's associate.'

'Not—' She squealed with laughter. 'He wasn't the one they called Darwin's Bulldog, was he?'

I gave a reluctant nod. It had been a foolish joke, made originally by me and since then only ever used at my expense.

'How desperately appropriate. Except for the fact that he's a dachshund—'

'I suppose that's what you'll call the article now,' I said.

'We'll see.'

If only she bloody had.

'How'd it go?' said Declan when we met that evening for squash.

'I liked her,' I said. 'A very smart cookie. And she's been a big fan of *Genesis* since the age of twenty, which helps.'

He looked at me askew. 'That's as much as you know,' said Declan. 'You know she kick-started her career with an interview with Mother Teresa? Made her out to be an unprincipled bitch.'

'Well, Mother Teresa *was* an unprincipled bitch,' I said complacently. 'If Margot's got that much nous, then all the better. Why are you so worried, anyway? You've seen me make a fool of myself a million times before.'

'I feel responsible.'

I snorted with laughter. '*You*? You don't have a responsible bone in your body. Why start feeling responsible now?'

'Because I know her, I suppose. Max, she's good. And good doesn't mean nice. It means interesting. And interesting doesn't just mean interesting for the reader. It means interesting for you too. You have no idea what she's going to write.'

I shrugged it off, eager for the game to begin. 'Come on, man, get on with it.'

We scuffled around the court and played our shots, and the interview was forgotten. But now, with the article beside me, I begin to feel sorry for Mother Teresa.

'Max Oldroyd is a man who has failed. I visited him expecting to find that the big young beast of the seventies and eighties had shrunk and mellowed with the years, that the maverick of days past had merged into the establishment and that I would be greeted by a crusty, middle-aged professor. I was not. He is as big as ever and as bestial as ever, and in some ways even seems as young. Nothing within him has retreated. Nothing has relaxed. His presence is still on a biblical scale. But these days, so is his rage. And so is his loss.'

She told me that my rage was compelling. I was foolish enough to take it as a compliment.

'My first instinct on looking at him was to conjure up the images of the late Tommy Cooper and the late Ted Hughes. Together, they encapsulate his demeanour almost precisely. Add the fervour of Billy Graham, the startled disarray of Einstein and a dachshund scampering at his heels, and we have him. His hair obtrudes from every orifice in his clothing, a dark, aspirant fuzz with only the slightest suggestion of grey. The tousled mane is still there, as is the startlingly lavish clothing – a black velvet suit and a dress shirt, worn at home on a rainy Tuesday afternoon – and when I asked him whether there was any special occasion that had prompted his attire, he said as if I was an idiot, "It's the clothes I've got. It's what I wear."'

She may have asked me that. I don't remember.

'His house is a tall Victorian terrace on a street in one of those boundary postcodes of North London, the upward slope and the canopy of leaves a barricade to the view of the tower blocks at the bottom of the hill. It was a haven of suburban tranquillity in the midst of the town, and yet he greeted me with the visage of a solitary Neanderthal come to defend the mouth of his cave. The dachshund – a measly morsel of a thing, by comparison – emitted the howls of hostility his master was too human to be allowed to enunciate. Then the dog was pushed aside and Max Oldroyd admitted me to his lair, which turned out to be one of the coldest, emptiest and most uncomfortable abodes I have ever visited.'

I know that it is inappropriate to feel the indignation of a spurned host on such an occasion. That luxury is for the giver of cocktail parties, not for the writer publicising his work. But I *was* hospitable. I liked the look of her, and wanted her to come in.

'I remembered the column he wrote for this very newspaper in the eighties, which, in the gaps between the science, portrayed his life as a hectic whirl of activity into which his prodigious professional output could only be smuggled at rare quiet moments. What had happened to that life? Of course, it happens to us all. Children grow up, lovers depart, careers settle into predictability. But he is in his early fifties, and he is a man born to talk. As I settled down into the only piece of furniture available – a sofa which turned out to be the exclusive property of his dog – I wondered what had propelled his life down such a path. And of course, almost as soon as we began our conversation, I began to see what it might be.'

This, of course, is only the beginning of the article. An exercise in scene-setting, no more. But from the first devastating sentence onwards, the ingredients are there: the sense of failure and decline; the idea that this decline has been caused by my own failings; and the feeling that a failure in my work is inextricably linked with my failure as a man. All this, just from walking in the door and taking a seat. The specific allegations come later on.

'The way he talks about *Genesis* is all the odder if you consider just how phenomenal its success has been. A bestseller on publication a quarter of a century ago, it remains essential reading for every young person with a desire to be able to talk knowledgably about topics he or she knows nothing about. What, I asked, made him feel the need to write about it as if every sentence was the subject of the deepest controversy?

'"But it is," he said. "It always has been."

'I told him that I could assure him that amongst ordinary readers it wasn't. It might have raised some hackles in entirely predictable circles, not least because of the supposedly blasphemous title, but—

'He burst in, as if I'd just taken the lid off Pandora's Box. "What do you mean by an ordinary reader?" he demanded. "You probably mean someone who's just like you. But why should you be any more ordinary than someone who lives in the middle of America and reads the Bible to his family every evening after dinner? He probably thinks he's a lot more ordinary than you."

'I conceded that this was a fair point, but explained that I meant that I was probably a far better example of the kind of person who was *likely* to read his book. Why aim his work at people who were doomed to disagree with it, when—

'He continued as if I'd never spoken. "All people are fundamentally the same. They're all equipped with the basic tools they need to identify the difference between the truth and a lie. What they don't all have is access to the truth. Left with lies, they have no choice but to believe what they're told. And that's the issue I've been trying to address for the last twenty years. You know, there are times when I just can't understand the attitudes of people in this country. In Britain, I mean, not America. At least in America the debate's alive. But here there's this all-pervasive assumption that it's not *decent* to talk about religion. I mean, it's okay for religious people to talk about it, because they get these little boxes to do it in, like *Thought for the Day*, or they're people who sit in a box which allows them to do it, like the Archbishop of Canterbury, or the Pope. But however much people might disagree with a priest about whether there should be gay bishops, or whether it's right to abort a foetus, it never occurs to them to address the real issue, which is whether God exists or not, and that's absolutely bloody *ridiculous*, if you consider that that's what their entire opinion is based on—"

'I tried again to steer the topic back onto his book, but failed once more.

'"And it's the non-religious people who are the worst. People like you. It's all very well for you to say, yes, all right, there is no God, but we don't want to talk about that, we want to talk about something else, but can't you *see*, you're putting *yourself* into a box, you're cutting yourself off from your responsibility to the truth, you're letting them get away with it—"

'And so it went on. He might as well have been reading me the very introduction I was trying to criticise, over and over again, except that it was amplified by a factor of ten and turned directly towards me. I felt as if I'd stepped into a wind tunnel. In the end I had to shout just to make myself heard. "Max," I yelled, "you've said all this in your new introduction to *Genesis*. And in the introductions to every book you've written since. Why do you have to say the same thing so many times?"

'"Because people don't listen!" he shouted.

'"If you're so sure that they didn't listen last time, why say it again? What makes you think it'll be different?"

'For a moment I thought he was going to launch straight back into his tirade. Then the wind went out of him, and he gave a hopeless sort of shrug. I took what might be the only opportunity I'd get to change the subject, and we discussed the moral basis for his passionate convictions.

'But I was aware that we'd digressed from the real topic of the interview, both from his point of view and mine. For him, I was a potential mouthpiece for his views, and must be won over at all costs. He didn't seem to pursue this aim deliberately or even knowingly, and he certainly didn't do it well. But his need to be believed was overwhelming. And I had the strong feeling that this need was at the core of his being.

'It was when he mentioned the creationists that I suddenly got hold of the thing I'd been groping for. I saw a man shouting from a pulpit, terrifying his parishioners with visions of hell. And I thought, *that's you.*'

I don't remember having said the things which are printed on that page. As far as I was concerned, we had a brief and perfectly amicable discussion of the way *Genesis* was received by the more hostile sections of its audience, and then moved on. There were no raised voices and no tussles for the right to speak.

But then I am aware that I do have a tendency to get carried away, and so I might have sounded more vehement than I actually felt. I also concede that the opinions she records are ones that I hold. Given that she has the tapes of our discussion and I do not, I must assume that she has transcribed something that at least vaguely resembles what I said.

It is the conclusions she draws that are intolerable. She has extrapolated an entire state of mind from what couldn't have been more than a tone of voice. If this were all, I would still have relatively little to complain about, because it would be perfectly possible for readers to spot the discrepancy and make up their own minds. But she has prepared the ground so effectively with the images of the 'Neanderthal' in his lair, the cold uncomfortable cave and the all-penetrating odour of decline that her assumptions seem inevitable.

And then she goes on to do the really terrible thing. She starts making the same sorts of statements not about my opinions or my mannerisms, but about my life.

'I began to realise why Oldroyd's house was devoid of all but canine life. Dogs, I am told, are naturally disposed to accommodate their owners' habits, and this one was certainly as shouty and argumentative as his master. But what human could tolerate such an atmosphere for more than a few hours?

'Intrigued by this question, I asked him about his early years, wondering whether argument was something he'd been born into. And I soon discovered that this man, who had spent a lifetime studying development and inheritance, appeared to have no meaningful recollections of his own childhood at all. This was annoying for me, because I wanted to be able to build up a picture of it in my head, but it also rang very true. Evangelists are not inclined towards introspection. The fundamentalist preacher does not waste his energy asking questions of himself. He channels any doubts he may have into his never-ending quest to imprint his beliefs upon the minds of others. It could even be said that, for an evangelist, preaching is a defence against introspection, spurred on by insecurity. The idea that others might reasonably hold opinions different to his own is a threat to his whole identity, requiring the constant corroboration of others just to prove that what he believes is true.

'Oldroyd's difficulty in speaking about his own history didn't stop at his childhood. At one point he found himself unable to remember how many children he had. Each question I asked was greeted with confusion, resistance and more than a little pain. More and more, he appeared to me as a man whose refusal or inability to understand the dynamics driving his own life had cost him dear. He understood the loss, but not its cause. Driven half to distraction myself, I longed simply to tell him. But if there is one thing an evangelist will never accept, it is that the ills which afflict him are caused by himself.'

How does one respond to such allegations? They are fuel to anyone who has ever borne me ill will, and I cannot answer them. If I rage against them, I will be providing a specimen of that rage. Even if I reason against them quite serenely, I will be accused of being incapable of tolerating the opinions of others. I am trapped.

Yet no such attack would ever be made against someone who battled with communism, or fascism, or any other dogma. However entrenched their beliefs, they would quite correctly be considered to have the right not only to hold them but to fight for them to their heart's content. Margot Hennessy's article does precisely the thing she says I accused her of doing: it screams at me *Stay in your box!* because it cannot bear to have a word said against religion. And yet I would swear that there is barely a shred of religious belief within her. Like all the others, Margot stops her agnosticism at the gates of atheism, because the best of all possible worlds is to ignore God all your life and then have Him there as a backstop when you die. It's better even if it leaves us with no defence against any falsehood in the world as long as it's uttered by a priest.

What is it about the English, and why am I different from my own countrymen? That's the question she should have been asking. I can't say why she and I are different, because to me her way seems so obviously silly. But she ought to have been capable of answering that question. She accuses me of evasion and lack of self-knowledge and yet is palpably guilty of it herself. In an article which is about almost nothing but belief in God, she never once considers the question of whether He's up there or not.

Except that she has written her article about something else as well. I will say it more clearly than she does herself: she claims that my polemicism has driven my family away. I suppose this was the kind of thing from which Declan was trying to protect me. In a way I think that it shouldn't matter at all. I may have been naïve to suppose that the nature of my work would protect me from the sorts of indignities inflicted daily upon soap stars and game show hosts, but this does not mean that I should now consider her testimony to have reduced me to that level. (Nor, now I come to think of it, should I consider the actors and presenters who withstand such criticisms to be defiled by it either.) And yet – and yet—

It is not just that the Reverend Matthew, an obviously intelligent young man, clearly lapped it up, nor that a hundred thousand others will have done so too. If reputations are in such hands, then I don't care for reputation. The question that haunts me is: how does she know that my family have left me? Because, and I admit it now, they have. In their different ways, and to their different extents, they are all gone. But if she knew it from public reports – if it was contained in the voluminous stash of pages that comprised her notes – then she could have said so. She could have quoted dates, locations and circumstances, which would be both more informative and less harmful than what she actually has done. What she has written consists more of opinion than fact. And those opinions are far too familiar. If I could think of another explanation for them, I would hold on to it for dear life. But there isn't another explanation. She has been speaking to someone else. And whoever that person is, it is someone who has known me for a very long time.

Which leaves me with an underfurnished house, a dog baying for food and an empty page. Oh, if only at least one of her accusations were true: *Evangelists are not inclined towards introspection*. It may be true of evangelists, but it is not true of me. A little less introspection along the way and I might have been a far happier man today. And so I hesitate to do what I know I am about to do, which is to tell the true story. True stories are notoriously hard to tell. Life doesn't happen the way Margot's articles would have that it does, with their neat paragraphs summing up whole decades. I never meant to take a stand against God. It wasn't in the plan, but it happened, and I am where I am. Perhaps it's connected to the other things that have happened to me – everything is connected if you cast the net wide enough – and perhaps there is even a causal link somewhere down the chain. All I know is that whilst there are things I regret in my life, that is not one of them. I love my family. I always did and I always will. I would do anything to have them back. But when there is nobody else to make a stand, someone has to do it, and that person was me.

Part Two

*Portrait of the Scientist
as a Young Man*

3

I don't remember being reticent about my childhood, but she said that I was. And now that I sit down to write about it, it's obvious that no-one can talk about their childhood as they might about the rest of their life. People might construct myths to cover up the gaps, but if they do, those myths are faulty. A child's consciousness is a very different thing from an adult's; it does not spring, fully formed, from the womb. The reason why we are born nine months after conception is because if we left it any later, our heads would be too big to get through the uterus. But at this stage, the size of the human brain relative to the rest of the body is no bigger than that of a baby chimpanzee; nor is it strikingly different in structure, nor even genetic make up. The difference is that after birth, the human brain continues to grow at the foetal rate for another two years, and continues at an only slowly decreasing pace. As a result, throughout childhood our brains are in a state of constant flux. The story of ourselves is made up not just of what we experience and what we do, but also of what we choose to notice. And I find it almost impossible to describe a time when my ways of noticing must have been changing almost by the day.

Nevertheless, it would seem to be safe to start an account of my life at the age of ten, when my brain had finally stopped growing faster than my body, and almost all my mental faculties were in place. But just when our hectic neurological development has abated, puberty kicks in. In my case, this process was not dissimilar to that undergone by the Incredible Hulk when he gets angry. As a child I had been on the large side, but nothing exceptional. Then, quite literally, clothes began to split at the seams. I grew in all directions, by several inches a year, and continued to do so until I was twenty. At first I was delighted by my meteoric progress away from the marks which my mother made on the wall in the pantry, and I put my newfound advantages to good use on the sporting field. But though I was a promising fast bowler and had a prodigious reach on the tennis court, I was increasingly disconcerted by the ever-unpredictable length of my arms and legs. It was impossible to tell from one month to the next where my aim was coming from. And in rugby, though I was seen as a natural to be a prop, I found it so hard to keep my balance that I invariably ended up at the bottom of collapsed scrums, spreadeagled in the mud with thirty stone of pubescent male on top of me. These frustrations didn't prevent me from being picked for the first teams, nor did they destroy my love of sport, but they made things very confusing. As for the changes in my appetites – well, food was something I felt I never had enough of, and the peculiar things that happened to me when I glimpsed even the tiniest slither of naked female flesh scared me half to oblivion.

It wasn't an unhappy childhood – in fact, I would ask for very little more from it – but neither was it a closely observed one. This was, I accept, partly owing to my own nature as a child, but it was also the product of the society in which I grew up. No-one looked too closely at themselves in that time and that place. It was just the way people lived.

I was born in Plymouth at the beginning of 1951, and my sister, Rosemary, was born almost four years later. My father, as Margot has said, was an officer in the navy, a fact of which my mother was irrepressibly proud. His commission was displayed in the living room, which made both him and me uncomfortable, because we knew from mixing with real officer families that it was best kept in the library, or, failing that, the downstairs lavatory. My mother mixed with those families too, but her innate faith in the loveliness of the entire human race made her oblivious to all but the most heavy-handed sneers. I don't think it ever occurred to her that the fact that her husband had got his commission in the war was something she might want to conceal. This was why, as I grew into my teenage years, she was such an easy target for my left-wing or atheistic posturing – for all her aspirations, she was the least hypocritical bourgeoise ever. Whereas I would never have dared try the same speeches on my father. Though I never heard him raise his voice, his silence lent him a truly imposing authority, which was exacerbated rather than lessened by the fact that I had no idea of what he actually thought.

The house was one of those small red-brick semi-detached residences crammed into narrow roads named after English poets. Our road was called Spenser Avenue; it was sandwiched between Sidney Grove and Mallory Place. There was nothing about the neighbourhood that was intrinsic to Plymouth, or the West Country, or even the South. Those nineteen-thirties newbuilds had sprung up all over the country in the years preceding the war. Given the timing, it must have been just that sort of development which in 1939 inspired John Betjeman to implore Hitler to pay special attention to Slough. Which is odd. I first read that poem as a teenager in the early sixties and associated it with concrete. On the one occasion in recent years when I walked down Spenser Avenue again, in the deathly quiet of a midsummer Wednesday morning, I gazed around me at the neat lawns and trimly weeded borders, roses pushing pinkly at porches, and felt that I was trespassing on just that quiet, untroubled England that Betjeman thought was lost.

Hitler did, of course, go on to do his best to obliterate Plymouth. Once, in those gardens, little boys had scaled privet hedges to retrieve propellers from chrysanthemum beds; mothers ran across streets half-clothed, clutching babies to their breasts and pillows to their brows; and men in dusty helmets raked through the rubble to retrieve severed arms and broken wirelesses. But by the time of my birth, the suburbs had smothered all remnants of aggression or retaliation. The war was a time of distant excitement which we evoked constantly in our games, but which we knew was buried forever by the real world in which we lived. Our inheritance was a strange one. Plymouth was a nasty, dingy town in those days, its reason for being swiftly dwindling as the pink faded from the maps in our classrooms. The past was a land of giants. Kings magnified in mirth; emperors striding the sea; gold-giving lords. Then the rattle of rifles and the thud of bombs, our own living relatives wreathed in a glory we couldn't share. We didn't know which was supposed to be more splendid, the lost empire, or the fight they'd won to lose it.

I think my father was a hero. 'Be brave like your father,' my mother used to say when I hurt myself, though I doubt even she could guess how his courage had been displayed. There were no decorations other than the commission. Yet we knew it all the same. He carried it in his silence, and in the fragile, never-broached barrier of his eyes. Those eyes had witnessed the deaths of hundreds, and had confronted his own since before he was old enough to vote. They spoke of a wisdom too awful to be imparted, and of life as a thin hard blade. His achievements were too profound to need communication, and his death too permanently imminent to require contemplation. I suppose I have always hoped that some day I would reach the state he took wordlessly to the grave. But his entire adult life consisted of responsibility, hardship, duty, imperatives, urgency, and they never let up. He never knew the times I'm facing with so little courage now.

My father was my inspiration in most things, even though I didn't know what that inspiration was supposed to be. He was a distant figure, and most of the time literally, geographically so. When he was at home, the disruption to normality was such that it was like having a guest in the house. Not that he caused much trouble. He spoke rarely, preferring to leave that sort of thing to my endlessly sociable mother, meaning that his opinions on all manner of things were filtered through, or perhaps even fabricated by, her. His leaves were spent in the chair in the corner of the sitting room, which no-one else ever used even when he was away, reading and smoking his pipe. And just as my mother was able to attribute her opinions to him, he was the silent conduit for all my ambitions. Whether I was scoring a hat trick in cricket or sitting an exam, it was his approval I sought. Somehow his approbation was all the more accessible because it would never be voiced. I was free to choose my own goals; free to demand for myself that I lived up to them; free to blame myself if I failed. As a result, I very rarely did.

As children, my sister and I were regular churchgoers, because our mother was a devoutly conventional woman, and the Church of England was as important to her as napkin-holders, butter dishes and scones neatly arranged on a doily. It was part of the comfortable, well-ordered routine of our lives. But my father played little role in any of this. While he was away we went to church week in, week out, so his leaves were the only times when Rosy and I were ever allowed to miss it. His non-observance wasn't absolute – I always felt that religion was an annoyance to him, rather than an anathema – but when he came he fidgeted, and looked as if his mind was elsewhere. Such stony indifference was infinitely more powerful than the flowery acquiescence of my mother and the Sunday School teachers. I learned from my father that if God existed, He didn't matter. And if He mattered, then He didn't need me to believe in Him. How could I have followed a spiritual authority which was so desperate for tangible proof of my love? If God had created the universe, surely that should be enough to satisfy His ego. Yet nothing could be more human than His constant need for praise. That desire to be reflected back by his creations suggested that perhaps He found it difficult to believe in *us*. And such hopeless insecurity about His own achievements meant that He was far too pathetic to be worthy of worship. There was only one type of spiritual authority I recognised, and it was one which felt no need to boast of its achievements, kept its own counsel, and left the severe task of working out how to act to me.

Science, when I discovered it, was just such a master. It was a method, not a creed, and its simple disciplines were the key to all the mysteries of the universe. When I scribbled my sums in my room in Spenser Avenue, I saw the whole of creation as an ancient tapestry, obscured by the murk of human incomprehension. A scientist was a person who took a little corner of it and rubbed away until the splendour beneath was revealed. I was blessed to have been born into an age when the pace of this endeavour was hectic, and all over the tapestry, where geniuses had been at work, bright colours shone out from the dimness; but there was so much still to be done. And no God was needed; no Bible, no priests, no heaven or hell. All that was required to understand the universe was a human brain, and the energy and commitment to use it. There was nothing in the world I wanted more than to learn enough about the toils of those who had gone before, for me to take my place beside them, and get rubbing at my own corner.

At the age of thirteen or fourteen, when my mother tried to get me to go to church, I tried to explain this to her. 'That's lovely, dear,' she responded sweetly, and still expected me to trot along beside her, as if what I believed bore no relation to what I actually did. In the case of the Church of England, I came to realise that it probably didn't. It had more to do with England than with the religious conviction suggested by a Church. 'Mum,' I wailed, 'don't be so stupid.'

'Don't say Mum, dear,' she responded mildly. 'It makes you sound like an American.'

She gave up on taking me to church in the end. And from my point of view, it wasn't so very terrible for a teenager to be forced to consider his mother as an ignoramus. She was part of a bygone age and was blinded by its outdated assumptions. In the future, all people worth talking to would be like me.

Yet it wasn't just my mother who wasn't like me. My sister was different, messing around with her dolls and her silly giggly friends, and my peers were different too. I don't think I ever questioned the fact, or consciously desired anything different, except in my science-fiction-inspired fantasies of the future. In a way, it was a matter of choice as well as circumstance. From the minute I started at Plymouth Grammar, after passing the eleven plus with top secret but well-known marks, I was the acknowledged favourite of the staff. I could probably have gained acceptance from the other boys if I'd rebelled against their attentions, but this course of action never occurred to me, so instead I toed the line and put up with the inevitable distance from my peers. It couldn't be said that I was bullied in any way – I was always too big for that – but the boys in my class never really treated me as if I was one of them, and to tell the truth I didn't feel that I had much in common with them either. The teachers liked me because I was able to talk to them as equals, and the boys ignored me because I was incapable of doing the same to them.

And yet I did carry one friend with me out of my boyhood. To begin with, he was an unlikely prospect. Declan Harris was just a boy in the year above me, identifiable only as a member of a gang, and that gang contained some of the roughest boys in the school. In the case of some, the fact that they'd passed the eleven plus could only be explained by some freak error on the part of the examiners. Declan wasn't a prominent member of the gang, and he was rarely in serious trouble, but he was always lurking on the fringes of mischief, a sandy and sardonic little chap with a sharp tongue and an air of insouciance which appeared to deliver him power over even the most monstrous bullies.

But one day when I was in the fourth form, I overheard the teachers gossiping about the latest mock 'O' level results through an open door.

'Who came top?' said one.

'Harris, of course,' said the other, and they both groaned. 'If he'd only show signs of doing just a little work—'

'I think he does work. On the sly. Otherwise how could he possibly have such an extensive knowledge of the works of Virgil?'

'But when? And where? He never goes to the library. And at home – his mother—'

'Well, if he doesn't work, he cheats. And I'm damned if I know how.'

'He'd have to be as clever to get those results by cheating as by doing it properly.'

'I wish he'd just show even the slightest glimmer of ambition.'

'Have you spoken to him about what he's going to do after the exams?'

'He might stay on. Or he might not. He's talking about becoming a mechanic, which would be the most scandalous waste of his talents. When you think about what he could achieve if he really tried—'

I wasn't accustomed to hearing the brains of others being discussed in such terms. Nor could I reconcile this description with the person who bore the same name. If he was as clever as the masters said he was, I couldn't understand how he could bring himself to mix with the particular dolts in his social circle, nor how he managed to hide his intelligence so completely. He became the object of my fascination, which was partly prompted by rivalry – the teachers had spoken almost as if he was a contender for the status of the brightest boy in the school – but also by a hopeful sense of camaraderie. I suppose that despite my self-sufficiency, at heart I longed for a real friend.

That was the year in which I succeeded in breaking into the first teams in both cricket and rugby, and found that Harris was, typically enough, already well entrenched. In rugby I was in the front row and he was a winger, so we had relatively little to do with one another, but in cricket I was a fast bowler and he was the wicket keeper. As he spared no pains in pointing out to me, this put him in a vulnerable and frustrating position.

'Why can't you just throw it at the wicket instead of my head?' he stormed at me, after another delivery had gone for four byes.

'Why can't you just catch it?' I retaliated, equally furious.

'What with? My mouth? Are you trying to kill me?'

Which only served to wind me up even more. Yet despite our spats on the field, we got along well enough. Nostalgia is generally a craving for simplicity, and for all our vaunted brainpower, we were pretty darned simple in those days. We exchanged intense yet ultimately casual opinions about the batting averages in the various county teams and observed a cautious respect. One day we got talking about our respective Airfix creations, and I plucked up the courage to extend an invitation to come to my place after school so that we could work on them together.

'That'll be lovely, dear,' said my mother when I told her. She was only too delighted to have the opportunity to entertain a friend of mine for once. 'Where does he live? What does his father do?'

I coughed and tried to think of a way to dodge her questions. The answers to both were the two things I'd learnt about Declan since I'd joined the firsts, and neither was entirely respectable. He lived somewhere in the raddled warren of streets down by the docks which stank of centuries of syphilis and salt cod, with a mother who worked down at the fishery and was reputed to be a semi-retired whore. His father's identity was unknown. I had recently acquired an illicit copy of *The Communist Manifesto* from a second-hand bookshop, and decided that this was the right time to air my newfound views.

'Really, dear?' said my mother at the end of my lecture. 'Well, I'm sure your friend's very nice.' When Declan came round she fed him with rock cakes, and he devoured them like a starving man. My hopes of getting the conversation around to intellectual topics were frustrated every time, but whether for the rock cakes or because he genuinely enjoyed my company, his visits became quite a regular fixture for a time.

But in the later years of our adolescence, we drifted apart, just as naturally as we'd drifted together. The Airfix bug was borne away on the winds of ambition and puberty – the ambition mine, and the puberty his. He was a skirt-chaser from the off, and despite his average looks and poverty-stricken circumstances, was known to enjoy a fair degree of success. As I discovered later, a street such as his was the type in which both sexes had rolled around in the mud together from toddlerhood onwards. As soon as he had acquired the necessary equipment, his investigations became more intense, and he gained a reputation amongst his coterie for giving guided tours of what went on under a Corby Street girl's skirt.

I attempted to rise above it all. My envy of his experiences was submerged beneath contempt and disgust at the tawdriness of it all. The extent of my own urges was such that my aloofness from the topic of sex might have been difficult to sustain, except for the fact that I never met any girls. Whilst all sorts of unmentionable things might happen to my body in response to the sight of a skirt on a bus, I had never seen a woman who came close to matching up to my ideals. Nor did I expect to. It was not time. As I moved up the school, one thing and one thing only was urgent, and that was work.

My intellectual endeavours had, of course, always been important to me. But they had recently received an extra impetus. One Sunday lunch, over the collapsed sprouts and the lumpy gravy, my father had broken his customary silence to announce that I should think about applying for Oxford.

'Really?' I spluttered.

'Well. Your mother tells me that the masters are very impressed with your work. I would have thought it was the right thing to do.'

My mother looked so aghast at his outburst that I knew that this wasn't something that had been planted by her. And I too was in shock. I had been thinking along the same lines since I'd known what university was, but it wasn't an ambition I'd ever divulged to anyone. Now, instead of being another success which I would some day be able to present as a fait accompli, it was my future, lined up for me in advance. The pressure was immense. I waited for him to say more, but he didn't. That was all I had.

It was the first time in my life that I'd really been given the chance to fail, and the dread of it kept me awake at nights. The mountain I was trying to climb took on extraordinary dimensions in my head, and bore no relation to reality, because I'd seen far denser boys than me gain their place. But how could I really know how clever they were? Perhaps they were all like Declan, hiding their lights under bushels. What a humiliation it would be if I, who had never made a secret of my intellectual pretensions, should fail where they'd succeeded.

So from that moment on, almost every daylight minute was taken up with work. I stopped turning up to cricket practice, and though the games master still let me play in the matches, Declan slipped from my view. He defied the English master's fears by going on to the sixth form and gathering a clutch of sparkling 'A' levels, then confirmed them after all by taking a job at the ailing *Plymouth Argus*.

Eighteen. Surely by now I can begin to give a more coherent account of myself, and find some points of similarity with the man I am now. But the distance is so great. How could that introverted, physically unco-ordinated young brute be me? I have always thought of the years up to when I was twenty-one as a dress-rehearsal for my life, but it can hardly have seemed that way at the time. I passed the Oxford Entrance exam – oh, joyous day! – and my mother virtually expired with pride. There is a snap which would have been taken by either her or Rosy, of me striding up the High in my matriculation gown and mortar board, and I am glad when I see Rosy these days that she has rescued it from my mother's nursing home and still displays it on the mantelpiece of her house in Bristol. Because it shows what it ought to show, a strapping young blade marching forth into a bright future, and that's not how I remember it at all.

University should have been an explosion into manhood, and perhaps it felt like that at the time. All the other photos – me rowing at stroke for the college boat in Eights Week, me with seven other 'men', lopsidedly holding aloft the blade we'd won for our victory, me holding the trophy for rugby Cuppers, me posing after graduation with a spectacular First, me and my friends clinking pints at a pub on the river, surrounded by blonde girls with washboard-straight hair – they all attest to the same story. But what I remember is a nagging feeling that it was all more of the same. More sport, more exams, more doing what I'd done ever since I'd started school. I'd expected Oxford to be somehow loftier. Of course, it was certainly far loftier than Plymouth had ever been – the architecture was ravishing, the river a dream, the tutors almost spiritually intellectual, my fellow students people I could communicate with at last. And, needless to say, I was able to get my paws on female flesh for the first time. But it didn't help that my success with women was far more limited than the photographs suggest it should have been. I had no experience of talking to them, and my idea of love came straight out of Arthurian romance. The university bluestockings, amongst whom I might have stood a chance of finding a soulmate, laughed hopelessly at my attempts to woo them, and the girls from the secretarial colleges, who were much more willing to take me at my word, appeared flimsy and insubstantial. Neither the laughter nor the inanity stemmed my voracious, embarrassing lust, but this just made me all the more incapable of dealing with the situation, because it hadn't said much about that in Malory. On the rare occasions on which I actually managed to achieve coitus, it was physically and morally terrifying. I was so afraid of premature ejaculation, so frightened of hurting them, and so racked with guilt from the knowledge that these frenetic physical exchanges were nothing to do with love, that my sexual experiences were tugs of war with myself, my body racing ahead of my mind, my confidence in who I was slipping away with the semen on the bedsheets.

Of course my competence improved over time, but this only served to add to my sense of disillusionment. There should be something more, I thought constantly, and my disgust at my own physical urges began to get mingled with an equally puritanical suspicion of my whole way of life. Perhaps it was associated with the fact that my father had earned his own living from the age of seventeen, when he'd joined his first ship. It was the state which was paying my fees, not my family, but I couldn't help thinking that I ought to be *getting on with things* by now.

Yet the lure of science was very strong, and my waves of guilt never actually translated into plans or even daydreams of going out and earning a living. In my very early days at Oxford, it had become clear both to my tutors and myself that I was marked out for an academic career, and whilst I had no desire to turn out anything like the eccentric old dons who taught me, the dream of becoming another Newton, Darwin, Einstein,

Watson or Crick was inching closer by the day. The problem was that there were an awful lot more days in the way. Over the course of three years in Oxford, the place had slowly shrunk, so that towards the end I felt I could have been dropped blindfolded into any point in the town and, once my vision was restored, say the name of the next street on the left. I felt as if I was bursting out of it, and yet if I was to be an academic, I was consigned to three or four more years in the place.

I don't know where the idea came from. The television, perhaps, though I must have been thinking back to my teenage years, because the images I associate with my feelings at the that time date back to the sixties: Carnaby Street, the Rolling Stones, Swinging London. Books also played a part – particularly Dickens, whose entire oeuvre I'd munched through during the lazy summer of the second year in Christchurch Meadows. Whatever it was, it propelled me towards my first ever rebellion.

'I'd suggest Brightman at Corpus Christi as your main supervisor,' said my college tutor, as he glanced down the proposed outline for my PhD. 'I tell you what, I'll have a word with him tomorrow.'

'I'd rather not go to Corpus,' I said.

'Why not?' He looked up at me and smirked rather lasciviously. 'Girl trouble, eh? Bit of a rivalry with one of the students? You needn't worry, the MCR and the JCR have virtually nothing to do with one another.'

'No, I mean I think I'd rather not stay on at Oxford at all. I want to go to London.'

'That bad? Come on, old chap, time heals all wounds. You don't want to let something like that get in the way of your career.'

I tried to explain to him that it was nothing to do with my love life, but the real reasons were impossible to explain. How could I have told him that it was because I didn't want to turn into him? He huffed and puffed and made all sorts of dark predictions, but I took no notice. I knew that London was a perfectly decent university, and anyway, what difference could it make? I intended to succeed whatever happened to me.

Three weeks later I was in the heart of the metropolis, gazing up through sheets of rain at the dark turrets of Erasmus College, with its Victorian Gothic exterior, its dirt-grimed windows and its vibrating walls. It was the first time I'd ever been to the capital, and it lived up to all my expectations. As the wind whipped water around my ears and the horde of huddled businessmen hurried by, I could almost hear the Chancery Megalosaurus waddling through the mud. The noise, the confusion, the filth – I knew even then that these would be not distractions but inspirations, reminders of the headlong ambitions of our ancestors, who produced, produced, whether it was the pitfullest infinitesimal fraction of a product, until they had created not only themselves but a city.

Because the medieval calm of Oxford had never really suited me. It was the nineteenth century, Darwin's age, that drew me. The Victorians had buried almost as many children as they exchanged in marriage. They had dug the tube network and the sewer system that Londoners still, painfully, used, losing the lives of countless navvies along the way, boring recklessly into rock without any particular notion of its geological structure. The rock was unstable; it collapsed upon them; they propped it up again and then ran trains through it. I despised the fact that profiteers were prepared to suffer so many deaths to provide their own inflated fortunes. But I admired the fact that all of them, from capitalist right down to chimney sweep, felt, for whatever reason, that their work was worth it.

The man I had come to see, Dr Hinds, was young and quietly friendly. He wasn't the sort of dynamo I would have conjured from my dreams, but I was confident that I had enough energy for the both of us. 'Yes,' he said, smiling, at the end of our conversation about the cell structure of the dung beetle. 'I think this may just work out.'

'Well?' demanded my tutor when I returned from my expedition. 'How did it go? Bloody man's a bore, isn't he? I tell you what, why don't I have a word with Collins at Cambridge?'

But my mind was made up. London it was. And once I'd got that sorted out, I stopped feeling so equivocal about Oxford. The days began to rush past in a blur, until it came to the last rowing race, the last vacation, the last tutorial, the last exam, the last college meal, the last party, until I reeled into the porter's lodge of my college after finishing my stint as a barman at the Magdalen ball, bleary-eyed in the dawn light, my bow-tie askew and my head still light with the free alcohol I'd received as payment, and found the telegram in my pigeon hole.

'FATHER SERIOUSLY ILL STOP COME HOME PM TRAIN STOP MUCH LOVE MOTHER.'

It was the only telegram I'd ever received, but I did realise even at the time that it had been extravagant of my mother to add the 'much' to the 'love'. I tottered, incapable of reconciling the message with my circumstances. All around me were swaying partygoers in brightly coloured cummerbunds. Only the porter's funereal outfit and lugubrious countenance were in keeping, and no-one ever looked at him.

I left Oxford without getting changed, without saying goodbye to anyone, and it was only when I saw the spires retreating behind me that I realised I had left.

My father wasn't there when I got home, of course. He was in Singapore. At home I found Mum, and Rosy, and the vicar, and a vast quantity of cake.

'Oh, hello, Max dear!' exclaimed Mother, embracing me carefully. 'Would you like some fruit cake?'

I stared at the vicar, suddenly aware of the ridiculousness of my attire. But the set-up before me was even more inappropriate. In honour of the clergyman's visit, Mum had dug out the best crockery. There was a silver cake stand, and silver cake knives, and bone china plates, and Rosy and my christening cups. The vicar was drinking tea from a minuscule receptacle which would have served better as a thimble. I sat down. Mother and the vicar prattled on about parish affairs, and when he had polished off three slices of cake the vicar left.

'So nice of the vicar to come!' gushed Mum when he was gone.

'Mum,' I demanded, 'what's going on?'

She sat down, and for a second looked the grief-stricken, worry-racked woman she was. Then she brightened up. 'I'm sorry to have made such a fuss, Max dear,' she said. 'It seemed like the best thing to do at the time. I'm sure everything will be fine—'

'WHAT'S GOING ON?'

'It's Father. He's rather ill.'

I knew that much from the telegram. 'What sort of ill? Has he been injured?'

She shook her head. 'I believe it's – something to do with his stomach.'

Stomach? He barely had one. 'Are they sending him home?'

'Um – no.'

Rosy, who was sixteen and at the apex of her sulkiness, unco-operativeness and general misanthropy, piped up with a vicious-ness in her voice that was clearly aimed at me. 'He's not well enough to travel. They think he won't make it.'

'Oh, Rosy, I'm sure it's not as bad as that—' protested our mother.

'Yes, it is. That's exactly what Captain Burton said.'

'Travel can be very difficult if you've got a problem with your stomach,' I began to rationalise.

My mother looked up at me in relief, deferring to me as a man of science. 'Oh, Max, I'm sure you're right. That's exactly how it is. They're just waiting for the illness to blow over.'

This explanation didn't fit very well with the fact that I had been called home to wait with the women. But by the time I went to bed that evening, I had convinced myself that it was true, and I'm sure my mother had too.

Further missives from the navy didn't do much to reinforce our optimism, but Mum and I were so keen to cling onto it that we did so anyway. From my point of view, my presence was a bit of a sham. I was supposed to have spent my summer working at a research laboratory in Oxford before starting my PhD in London, and there I was, cooped up with my mother and sister, achieving nothing for anyone, not even for my father. My mother's state was too fragile for me to take it out on her, but Rosy and I each did our best to inflict our respective resentments on one another. From the start Rosy seemed to have decided that whatever was happening to Father was my fault, and she didn't hesitate to remind me that my duty was to her and Mum.

Then, at last, we received a communication to say that he was progressing better than expected, and that he would be coming home after all. It didn't mention that the journey was expected to be his final one, though subsequent missives gradually made this clear. He was due to arrive the week I was expected to register at Erasmus. After a summer of fruitless waiting, what choice did I have but to leave?

I did travel back from London as soon as I could. When I got there, I found a wordless skeleton whose only concern was to somehow bear the pain. I had never seen anything like it, and I have not since. Mum, still in her forties, bonny as ever, fussed around him as if her cushions and flowers could somehow relieve him. I suppose they may have done, in a way.

Perhaps I should have behaved as Rosy thought I ought, and put my life on hold. But I was a new boy at a London college and a stranger in one of the world's greatest cities, and to have thought only about what was going on at home would have been to surrender my future. It was important not only to plunge myself into my new situation, but also to enjoy it, otherwise I would have been overwhelmed. I believe that what appeared to Rosy as callousness was in fact a simple survival instinct, bequeathed to me by the very people she thought I was betraying.

I went back twice more after Christmas, and there was never any change, except that he got even thinner and more addled by drugs. I was twenty-two, thick and bristling with bulk and energy, my unwieldy size an insult to his frailty, my raucous breath drowning out his shuddering sighs. The horror of my own future passing was something I didn't let myself see. Nor did I dare weep for the past. I might have thought of myself as an adult, but I was too young to have forgotten my childhood self, and was not ready to take on the mantle of seniority.

Yet during that last visit, when Mum left us to ourselves for a while and he dozed, I did feel a certain closeness. I thought about all the things he'd seen and had never told us, and wondered what he thought of me. His strong silence was something I'd always wished I could emulate, but I had too much of my mother's garrulousness to even be able to try. Had I done okay? It was too late to ask him, and I doubted he would have told me even if he could.

'Bye, Dad,' I whispered when it was time to go, and tried not to cry. Then, just before I walked out of the ward, I suddenly turned back, and before I had time to think about what I was doing, I'd kissed him on the forehead.

I was very relieved that he didn't wake up.

I believe still that the most important duty that an offspring bears its parents is to live. By this I do not mean that we should cloister ourselves in the attempt to specifically avoid death. To do so would be the worst invalidation of the life that has been bequeathed. But the birth of a child, both emotionally and actually, is a new start. It is the chance to begin afresh, the opportunity to take a package of old genes and set out once more. I am sure that my father, who left his own family so young, would have agreed with me on this. What would the point have been of either of us staying at home and binding ourselves to lives already lived?

Because in the months since I'd travelled to London, the thing I'd been waiting for for so long, the thing which had fooled me with so many false alarms, had happened. My life had finally started for real.

4

I first saw her across a smoke-filled room. For a moment I thought I recognised her. There she was, standing a full six inches above the girls to either side of her, wreathed in a spiralling column of cigarette smoke. Her dark hair was cut into a harsh shoulder-length bob, and the bones of her face looked too big for their skin. She saw me staring at her over all those heads, and narrowed her eyes in a look poised between camaraderie and scorn before whipping them away again and continuing her colloquy.

I stood there at the edge of the room, my coat half on and half off, wondering what had happened to me. For some reason, Declan was bobbing up and down in front of me. I grabbed him by the shoulder and turned him around. 'Who's that?' I hissed.

He gulped and looked nauseous. 'Erm—'

'Declan, do you know her? Just tell me.'

'Sally Bowden,' he stammered, tottering backwards. 'Lucian Freud model. Aspiring artist. Christ knows how Tony knows her.'

'God, yes,' I breathed, staring back at her, misallocating the familiarity to a painting I'd never seen. I hesitated for no more than a second. Then I was off, marching blindly towards the bar. 'Two champagne cocktails,' I roared at the barman.

'And a pint of Pride for me, if you don't mind!' came an irate and petulant voice from somewhere behind me, which I didn't associate with Declan until the end of the evening, when he complained about my omission at great length. The barman prepared the cocktails at frantic speed, and I pressed some coins into his hand and turned in her direction. This time she did not catch my eye.

The crowd parted before me. I held the two glasses aloft, spraying champagne bubbles upon the heads of bystanders, and bore down upon her. The girls to either side of Sally Bowden stepped back to make way for me. I smiled beneficently at them all.

'Good evening,' I said, still clutching those cocktails. 'I'm Max Oldroyd. Who are you?'

Oh, you idiot, I say to myself, cringing and laughing as I write the words. But I don't mind cringing. Because at last that idiot is me.

Poor Declan, who had to put up with it. My phone call from Plymouth must have been the last thing he was expecting. It was, in fact, my mother who'd made me think of doing it. 'London,' she'd said thoughtfully towards the end of my summer at home, when, after all my certainty, I'd begun to fret about what I was going to do when I got there. 'You know, I'm sure when I was last chatting to Mr Tomlins' – Mr Tomlins was the headmaster of Plymouth Grammar, and goodness knows what she'd been doing chatting to him – 'he did say something about London. Now, what was it? Oh, I know! That terribly nice boy you used to have round for tea. He was very fond of rock cakes. Apparently he's working in London now. Perhaps you could make contact with him.'

It wasn't often that I took my mother's advice, but this was an exceptional case. 'Harris is in London?' I said. 'What on earth's he doing there?'

'I can't remember. You could ask Mr Tomlins.'

There was no way I was crawling back to my old headmaster to ask him for the contact details of someone as unlikely as Declan. 'Come on, Mum. You must be able to remember.'

'Well, I should think he'd be in the same line of work he was in before. He was a mechanic, wasn't he? Always terribly keen on cars.'

'No, Mum. He got a job at the *Plymouth Argus*. As a journalist.'

'Journalist! That's it! Now I remember! He's working at the *Daily Express*.'

Only my mother could be equally impressed by a local mechanic and a reporter on a national newspaper. I put a call through to the *Express*, and after much searching on the part of the switchboard operator, found myself talking to a bluff and astonished Declan. For the first few moments of the conversation I could have sworn that he didn't have a clue who I was, and his tone didn't change much once he'd worked it out.

'You see,' I burbled, 'the reason I'm going to London is that I want to get away from the ivory tower mentality, if you know what I mean.' His silence was expressive in communicating that he did not. 'So I really want to avoid student accommodation. I'd far rather find somewhere normal to live. The thing is, I don't know London at all. You know, like which bits are cheap and which are expensive, that sort of thing. I thought – well, that perhaps we could meet up, and you could – give me a few pointers—'

Silence. Then, in a tone of rather grudging magnanimity, 'Well. You'll have to sleep on the floor, but I see no reason why you shouldn't stay at my place while you look for somewhere.'

I was astonished. 'Really?'

'Really.'

'Gosh, that's most awfully kind of you.'

More silence. I felt like a grubby schoolboy about to gatecrash the world of men. We concluded the phone call awkwardly, and I felt even more panicked and excited about the new life I was about to embark on than I had before.

Declan was hardly more expansive when the time arrived for

me to move in. We might have been acquaintances since the age of eleven, but now that we were fully grown, it was clear that we didn't actually know one another at all. However, this wasn't too much of a disadvantage on my side, as it was my full intention to change. I spent my first few days in London on forays about the town, sniffing out places and people, and constructing a new grown-up image.

'Do you think the dons'll like this?' I demanded of Declan after my first trip out, producing a Peruvian-style neck-warmer I'd rummaged out of a shop in Carnaby Street. My new surroundings had inspired me to a sort of wardrobe assault upon the cosy assumptions of my soon-to-be teachers.

Declan shrugged.

'And this?'

A yellow-and-purple batik-style shirt with lapels that reached the armpits.

'I've no idea. I've never met an academic.'

'Except for me,' I said joyfully, fingering my new purchases. 'You know, this is exactly why I turned down the place at Corpus. Oxford is so insular. In London one is in the real world and can be whoever one chooses. It's a springboard. From here anything is possible.'

'Yeah, well,' said Declan, 'that's what I thought, a few years ago.'

'What do you mean? Don't you think that any more? But you're doing so well.'

He brightened, and consented to take me to a party, so that I could show off all my new clothes. It was over the course of those parties that we became friends. Because although Declan did his best to present the image I expected of him, that of a sophisticated man about town, it was soon clear that, despite the extensive opportunities for socialising afforded him by his job, he had more or less given up on partying long before, and had settled into the snugs of a few comfily seedy pubs in Fleet

Street. Now I was forcing him to put his dancing shoes back on, and he was none the worse for it.

I remember sitting sprawled on the floor of some posh bird's flat in Knightsbridge. The sofa we were leaning against would probably have fetched the price of Declan's entire block. There were waiters. We were wearing blue jeans and had brought along a six-pack of beers and a jar of pickled onions. I was toking on my first spliff.

'Will it damage my brain?' I demanded, wondering why the room was swaying so much.

'Jeez, Max, how come you never tried this stuff at college?'

I shook my head. Declan ducked. 'No-one ever offered it to me,' I said balefully. 'My friends were all either sporty or brainy. I did have a girlfriend who said she'd smoked marijuana. But no-one ever had any when I was with her.' I took another over-enthusiastic drag and giggled. 'Do you think she was lying?'

He attempted to carry me home. 'I am – never – fucking – doing this again,' he puffed, as I staggered, my arm across his shoulders.

But he did. Even after I'd found myself a rather disgusting one-roomed flat in King's Cross and had moved out, he still proved himself susceptible to my demands for a social life. And so it was that I found myself in that basement pub at a party held by someone whose name I didn't even know, holding two champagne cocktails and attempting to make small talk with Sally Bowden.

She was polite enough, but apart from that first fateful glance I couldn't delude myself that I had made a great impression on her. Most of the time she ignored me, all characterful elbows and elegant collar bones, while I was forced to make hearty conversation with a point between her clavicle and the face of her friend Antonia.

Still I wasn't deterred. 'You know, when I first saw her I

thought I recognised her,' I burbled to Declan as we walked back towards our bus stop.

'She has very striking looks,' said Declan glumly.

'And the fact that you'd said she'd modelled for Lucian Freud made me think that was it. That I'd seen her in a painting. Because in a way she does look like a painting. Doesn't she?'

'A bit less blotchy than most of Freud's stuff,' said Declan. 'But I suppose I know more or less what you mean.'

'But actually now that we've talked—'

'Didn't look like she was doing much of the talking.'

'—I've realised that it wasn't that at all. It was something else entirely. I did recognise her. She reminded me of myself.'

Declan stopped dead on the pavement. 'Now Max, that's bloody ridiculous. The only thing you have in common is your looks. Just because she's tall and dark doesn't mean she's your soulmate.'

'I wasn't talking about her looks!'

'Look at it this way. You're a scientist, she's an artist. She's posh, you're a yokel from Plymouth Grammar, whatever fancy manners you might think you've picked up at Oxford. And she stands minding her own business and talking to her friends, while you go barging across the room knocking over everyone's drinks and making a nuisance of yourself.'

He was wrong. However little she'd talked to me, I'd seen it in everything she did. The superficialities might be misleadingly different – the poise with which she'd held her drink, the dignity with which she'd shrugged off my more foolish impositions – but there wasn't a movement she could make which didn't make me feel closer to myself than I'd ever been before. I didn't care a jot for Declan's class barriers. It was the way she broke into laughter in the middle of a sentence, the way her friends fell silent when she began to speak, the way she took no word at face value. We were the same.

'You don't understand,' I said.

'Do you think *she* understands?' said Declan.

That was the problem. How could she fail to see something so obvious? But I was forced to admit, if only to myself, that it looked as if she had failed. Somehow, next time, I was going to have to make her see.

I cared very little for Declan's wishes during the time that followed. He was my route to Sally, and I was damned if I wasn't going to use him.

'Declan,' I announced triumphantly over the phone one day, calling him, as he had repeatedly told me not to, at work, 'I've got a date.'

'Marvellous, Max, marvellous,' said Declan. 'I'd just like to point out that I have a severed head and three fingers to deal with here.'

'What?'

'They were washed up on the banks of the Thames. And my editor wants me to find a photograph.'

'Declan,' I said again, trying to get my point across, 'you're coming with me.'

'What do you mean, coming with you?'

'To the Natural History Museum. You'll love it. They've got models of dinosaurs—'

'Jesus, Max. Sometimes you're such a teenager. Why couldn't you have bothered to have a proper adolescence at the usual time?'

'The date's with *Sally*, Declan,' I said, in case he still hadn't cottoned on.

There was a long pause. 'Max, I'm very pleased that you have a date, but you can do this on your own. You don't need me to help you. I'd only get in the way.'

'I do need you. You see – do you remember that you mentioned what a pretty girl Antonia was?'

'I said she had nice tits! That doesn't mean I want to make small talk with her in a museum.'

'She likes you. I saw it in the way she looked at you.'

'She never once laid eyes on me. Max, you can't go organising double dates without my permission.'

I did feel a little sheepish at that point. 'I didn't organise it. She' – I couldn't bring myself to sully her name a second time – 'did.'

Another pause. 'You mean she won't go out with you unless she has a chaperone.'

'Yes.'

'And you want me to distract the chaperone.'

'Yes.'

For a moment all our fates hung in the balance.

Then, 'Why do we have to go there?' Declan whinged.

I perked up. He'd capitulated, consciously or not. Only the venue was up for debate now. 'It's great, Declan,' I enthused. 'They've got fossils from every geological period. You can see the whole of evolution, laid out before your eyes. It's the next best thing to the Burgess Shale—'

'Do you really believe it's going to get her into bed?'

I suppose I did. My faith in Sally's spirit had not waned. If she had not seen that my own was equal to it, then it must be because she had not seen me in my natural habitat. In the Natural History Museum, she would have the chance to get a glimpse of the best of me. My brain.

There was a commotion at the other end of the line.

'My boss,' hissed Declan. 'Max, I'll speak to you later.'

He'd agreed to my plan. I have no idea what made him do it, but he did.

The girls arrived before us. I was in a terrible state. My outfit had failed catastrophically. I'd had a change of heart halfway through getting dressed, and then had run out of time, so those clothes which I'd managed to pull on disagreed with one another violently and still bore the signs of my struggle. And then there was my hair. Hair was a great preoccupation of mine in those days. It was my own special curse. I had got on perfectly well as a schoolboy, when my mother could be prevailed upon to give me a regulation short-back-and-sides every couple of weeks, but now I was a grown man I felt that I ought to keep up with fashion. The fashion at the time was to attempt to look as much like Marc Bolan as possible, whether one enjoyed his music or not, and the result was that I spent much of my time unable to see. On the rare occasions when I managed to get the stuff out of my eyes, I was fated always to catch a glimpse of my reflection, and be paralysed by humiliation. The tube journey had been an agony of trying to arrange my hair into some kind of order, then trying to hide behind it, and quivering. Declan had passed the journey by cracking a series of increasingly disconnected jokes, but nothing had succeeded in distracting me from my misery.

And now there they were, the women, leaning gently against the old stone balustrades and laughing in the sunshine. Antonia was spruce and virginal, her pink-and-white skin fragile in the heat, and her bright hair a beacon of youth and health. Beside her, the object of my devotion cut an altogether darker figure, a slash of midnight in the noonday sun. She wore a trouser suit the colour of dried blood, and a black scarf was knotted tightly around her long, long neck. I felt my limbs begin to collapse beneath me. My instinctive knowledge of her had only deepened in her absence, but though she was exactly, precisely, more even than the woman my mind had held, her skin now was a plate of armour. Suddenly I didn't know what I was doing there. The collision between my desire and her separateness was insufferable. For a moment I thought I would spontaneously combust. As we moved, I was borne simultaneously forward and back, and every step was an uneven mixture of bound and shuffle, accompanied by substantial huffing and puffing. 'Calm down,' muttered Declan. 'They're just women. There's nothing to be afraid of.' But I couldn't answer him.

Antonia was turned slightly away from us, chattering away. Sally's face was towards us, but though she acknowledged us with a lift of the eyebrows, she continued to give her friend her full attention until Antonia had finished a story involving a gas key and a plumber. 'My goodness,' she said to Antonia. Then she turned to us. 'Good afternoon, Max,' she said coolly. 'Good afternoon, Declan.'

Her voice was low and elegant, with that lightness that could come only from generations of effortless prosperity. It sent a shudder of pain through me, shaking sweat from my brow in a salty globular spray.

Declan gave a little snort of impatience. 'Top o' the day to ye, ladies,' he greeted them in his corniest attempt to be as Irish as his mother.

Sally blinked in slow disbelief. Antonia regarded him as if he'd emerged from a nearby drain. Then they looked at me, in expectation of some sort of speech, and I could only gurn in the attempt to eject some words. It was hopeless.

Declan tried again, unable ever to leave a silence be. 'Now,' he said, 'I hope we're all ready for the thrills and spills that lie before us. Roll up, roll up, for the ride of your life.'

'Do you mean,' said Antonia, 'that we should go into the museum?'

Declan glared at her, and began to stomp in the direction of the entrance. Released by his movement away from the epicentre of my discomfort, I shambled after him, and the girls followed at a safe distance. The walkway went on for ever and the building towered above us, its exhibition of Victorian egoism somehow inappropriate for the first time in my life.

'Oh, look!' trilled Sally as we passed into the cool of the entrance hall. 'The ladies' room. You will excuse us a moment, won't you?'

We stared after them.

'Out the bathroom window,' Declan forecast, in a tone of relief. 'Ah, well. At least we haven't bought the tickets.'

It was only slowly that I grasped his meaning. Surely he couldn't be saying – and I rallied. My brain rejected the idea completely. 'They haven't gone,' I said. 'They can't have gone.'

'Max,' said Declan, 'you saw the way they were behaving. Snooty fucking bitches.'

'But why would they go? Why would they come all the way here and then leave? It doesn't make sense.'

He looked me up and down sardonically. But my clothes didn't matter to me any more, and I saw that even for him they no longer had quite the effect he expected. In that lofty interior I was more at home already. The sweat had evaporated almost instantly. With fifty clear feet of space above our heads, it was I who was closest to being in proportion, surrounded by milling Lilliputians.

'Maybe they'll come back,' said Declan lamely.

'Of course they will,' I told him. 'They can't possibly climb through the window. Their clothes are too nice.'

I felt calmer than I had in a week. Declan assessed my appearance once more. 'You know,' he said grudgingly, 'I'm beginning to understand why you brought us here.'

Diplodocus was magnificent. I bounced around in front of it, as light and free as a boy, and pointed out its various features.

'How impressive,' said Antonia, all sarcasm expired. Perhaps the conflab in the ladies had been an attempt on Sally's part to soften their joint demeanour.

'Reminds me of my uncle,' said Sally, snorting a little and relieving me of any such illusions.

'Is he a very large character?' I enquired, trying to turn it into a conversation.

She stopped in her tracks for a moment, then gave a little

wave of her hand to signal that such a line of enquiry was not worth pursuing.

'It is the longest land animal that has ever lived,' I continued unabashed, gazing up at the old bones in respect. Sally followed my eyeline, then tracked back, for a moment casting her eyes along the length of my own frame. A shiver of pleasure juddered through me, as if I'd been touched. Then she whipped her eyes away.

'Is it really a true-life skeleton?' asked Antonia.

'Most of it is plaster of Paris,' I admitted. 'But it has been modelled largely upon the fossil finds of a single animal. This creature really lived and breathed, and went about its business just like you or I.'

'Not entirely like, I'd imagine,' said Sally.

She was sniping still. But that glance she'd given me could not be taken back. It had set up a crackling cord of communication between us, and however hard she hacked, it couldn't be severed. 'It's awesome enough as it is,' I said, and indeed it was, as long as a swimming pool and as high as a two-storey house. 'But imagine if it were alive. Imagine if it moved.'

I watched them imagine, and a collective shiver ran through us, as the pillar-like legs began to stir in the undergrowth, and the massive tail started to twitch.

'And yet,' I said, on the move, dancing down the length of the exhibit as the others hurried after me, 'just look at its head.'

They looked. In comparison to the bulk which lay behind, it was rather an elegant little thing, an elongated wedge of fragile bone such as one might see darting from side to side, beady eyes glinting, on a lizard on a rock.

'Are you sure it's really come from the same animal?' said Antonia.

'Oh, very sure. But it does seem extraordinary, doesn't it? That such a massive creature should have such a tiny brain.'

'I don't know,' said Sally. 'It has been known.'

She stood with her hands clasped and her face in utter repose. But her voice was tight with cattiness. I turned to her, knowing the meaning she intended, and feeling the hatred that lay behind her lie. Now that I had stopped moving, I realised that I was shaking still. 'Sally—'

I had said her name. The tables turned. She cowered, her perfect dark bob quivering slightly. My pain was overcome by a feeling of overwhelming tenderness, which seemed to be transmitted into the surrounding air. Now that she was so close, she didn't look so tall; an impossibly slight, almost fragile creature, those prominent bones as exposed as those of the relic beside her.

'Sally,' I said even more softly, 'are you not enjoying yourself?'

'I'm absolutely fine,' said Sally, looking anything but.

'I don't suppose the Diplodocus needed a very big brain,' interjected Antonia loudly. 'All it had to do was eat the local vegetation. Didn't it?'

I pulled myself together. 'Ah,' I said, 'but that's not such a simple proposition as you might suppose. A large part of brain function is concerned with co-ordinating nerve impulses throughout the whole body – whether it be the eyes, the stomach, or the feet. Even if one's only job in life is to eat, it's a complicated business in a body this big.' I began to stride back along the skeleton. 'And with the message being transmitted from such a small source, so very far away – well, it would have taken several seconds for the instructions to reach the hind legs, let alone the tail.' I picked up speed, looking back for a sign of Sally's interest, but she was staring in fixed misery at the dinosaur's foot. 'Which, of course—' Something happened around the level of my ankles. It was a metal sign explaining some aspect of the beast. One minute it was upright, the next caught between my legs, then, with a clatter, it sprang out again and, as I stumbled, I reached out for security, realising only just in time that I was about to grab the dinosaur's back leg, before swinging round, hopping over the toppled sign, and somehow remaining upright.

'Are you all right?' squeaked Sally.

I shook myself and rummaged in my hair. 'Which is too long for it to be able to walk effectively,' I concluded breathlessly.

Sally let out a hysterical giggle.

'I need a cup of tea,' said Antonia in exhaustion.

I had not, however, finished my explanation. My audience learnt that Diplodocus had compensated for its walking difficulties by developing a second nerve-centre at the base of its spine. Sally suggested that it might be wise for me to do the same thing, given my own difficulties with perambulation. This time a sprinkling of affection had forced its way into her humour, so in a burst of generosity, I relented and succumbed to Antonia's pleas for tea. After a short break, we proceeded to what I regarded as the highlight of the tour, which was the beetle collection.

Antonia and Declan were flagging, whilst also failing to find any pleasure in one another's company. But Sally seemed invigorated by her tea. She abandoned her jibes about my height and moved the discourse on to a livelier level.

'Look!' she cried from the opposite wall of the compartment. 'A praying mantis! I've heard the most wonderful things about those.'

I raised my eyebrows, and for a moment almost felt contempt, because this was the most hackneyed and inane snippet of schoolboy biology that existed. Nevertheless, my anticipation of the inevitable topic of her digression couldn't fail but give me a spontaneous physical jolt, which sent the blood flying simultaneously to opposite extremities of my body. 'And once the dung beetle has finished scooping the manure with its antennae – see how they're shaped like paddles—'

'What is it I've heard about the praying mantis, Max? I can't quite remember.'

'—it buries itself and the ball of manure in the earth, and feeds on it all summer. It can eat more than its own weight in twenty-four hours.'

'Very efficient, I'm sure,' said Sally. 'But shit isn't much of a food. Not half so appetising as a nice fresh post-coital snack of freshly-shagged mate.'

I spluttered in a rage of embarrassment and arousal. Antonia let out a small sigh of exasperation. The sweet old couple beside us stared fixedly at the beetles.

'Or am I wrong about that?' asked Sally.

'It has been known,' I mumbled.

'Is it the male which eats the female, do you know, or is it the other way round?'

'The other way round,' I muttered.

'Not much of a sexual incentive for the chap, is it?'

'It's irrelevant,' I objected. 'From the point of view of evolutionary survival, as long as his genes are transferred to the next generation, it makes no odds what happens to his own remains. And after all, they're put to good use on his behalf. His offspring will probably be all the healthier for the nutrients he's bequeathed.'

'Yes,' said Sally, not letting go, 'but if he hadn't been eaten, then surely he could go on to have more shags, and dispense a few more of his genes.'

'He doesn't have much of a choice in the matter,' I pointed out. 'Not if he wants' – I foraged for the correct phrase from a looming forest of obscenities – 'to reproduce.'

'Well, that settles it,' said Sally. 'Sounds like the most practical solution all round. The next time I have sex with a man, I'm going to eat him.'

I survived our encounter on that occasion. Though, like the

praying mantis, I would have stretched myself out as the most appetising snack in all cuisine if it would have meant getting beneath her unassailable skin. But I didn't get the chance.

'Look at the time,' Antonia said severely in the palaeontology section.

Sally looked at her watch and jumped. 'Oh, God,' she said. 'Max, we really must be going. Now.'

'But I thought we could go for a meal—'

'No meal. I'm sorry. I have to get home. We're going to be late already.'

'Late for what?' I pleaded. 'Surely you can—'

'I can't. Seriously, I can't. Thank you very much. We've had a lovely time. We'll meet again, I promise.'

I held out my hand, but she was already beyond reach. She waved feebly, turned, and was gone.

'Maybe she's left a slipper lying around somewhere,' conjectured Declan.

'Fuck,' I said sadly. 'Fuck.'

'I thought you did very well,' said Declan. 'Bored me out of my skull, but she seemed to enjoy it, in the end.'

'I love her,' I wailed, my words sucked up by the unfeeling air.

'Jesus, Max,' said Declan, glancing in embarrassment at the children and old ladies who passed us by. 'Just calm down. She's said she'll see you again. Take it as a triumph, and relax, for God's sake.'

But the next meeting was no more conclusive than the first. It was on neutral ground, at another party, and Sally spent most of her time talking to other people. Towards the end, Antonia kept me occupied, and she slipped away without me noticing.

'Oh,' said Antonia, 'didn't she tell you she was off?'

'I'm going to murder that woman,' I told Declan afterwards.

'Don't be so extreme,' said Declan.

'She's wherever I turn. It's almost as if – as if it was a plot, to stop me talking to Sally properly.'

'Max, it's blindingly obvious that it's a plot.'

'But why would Sally do that? You keep saying she seems to like me.'

'"Like" was not the word I used. I said she fancied the pants off you. That doesn't mean to say that she likes you at all. Anyway, I really wouldn't bother trying to understand women's ulterior motives. Just keep on going until you get her into bed. That's my policy. As long as she doesn't find you physically repulsive, it generally works in the end.'

It was true that this was his policy, and that he'd had a fairly impressive strike rate of late. But this was not the same thing at all. In Declan's pursuits, the stakes were kept deliberately low on both sides, and the satisfaction of little more than a few momentary physical urges was achieved. Whereas for me, the fulfilment of my desperate sweaty longings to desecrate and sublimate Sally's body would be as nothing if I didn't somehow succeed in also penetrating her brain. The sameness that had struck me with such blithe obviousness on our first meeting was mired now in swirls of difference. She was a dark and beautiful mystery, and if only I could start to find my way around the subtleties of her being, then I would be twice the man I was.

The next party – Declan had been forced to foster the friendship of Tony the socialite pretty swiftly in support of my suit, though he admitted that it had paid him dividends too – was fancy dress. The theme was 'Heroes and Heroines'. Declan borrowed my poncho and went as a Mexican gunslinger. We debated long and hard as to the sexiest persona I could adopt, and Declan drew on an unexpectedly profound knowledge of the works of Ernest Hemingway to suggest a bullfighter. This worked very well. Soon I had acquired a huge red velvet cape, size-thirteen high-heeled boots, and a Zorro-style black hat. I accessorised these items with a frilly white shirt, leather trousers and an excessively-buckled belt. All of them were obtained at minimal cost. I tell you, the early seventies was the best era in history to find clothes for a fancy-dress party.

'Darlings, you look marvellous,' said Tony's wife as she greeted us. The fancy dress had clearly been her idea, because no-one could have put together such an authentic Barbarella costume at short notice. Her breasts were ready for lift-off. 'Sally's in the conservatory, handing out Twiglets.'

So my pursuit of Sally was public knowledge. I didn't care. To my relief, I spotted straightaway that Antonia, dressed rather becomingly as a schoolgirl – Nancy Drew? – was cornered in the lounge by a man with a flowerpot on his head. The coast was clear. I girded my loins, decided that there was no more time left in me to be wasted, and went straight in for the kill, my cape swirling, the Zorro-hat hitting the hanging baskets. 'Sally,' I announced, breaking right across her conversation with Spiderman and Andy Pandy, 'I have to see you alone.'

She was Wonder Woman. There was no Lynda Carter in those days, so my imagination was free to translate the comic-book character into the flesh and blood before me. The gold underwiring of the super-bra, the star-spangled hotpants, the voluminous black hair bursting from the cardboard headband, the nuclear-powered bracelets, the endless bare legs, and most of all, the expanse of unadorned white flesh stretching from the top of her corsage to the tilt of her chin – all were perfect. Only the bowl of Twiglets was out of place.

'Hello, Max,' said Sally after a short pause. 'This is John Soper. He's a civil servant. And this is Douglas French. He designs car parks, apparently.'

I glanced at them, two displaced suburbanites in cornflake-packet costumes, transfixed by Sally's cleavage. They were utterly inappropriate to the urgency of the situation. I cleared them out of the way. 'Just one evening. I won't do anything to you, Sally, I promise. Please give me a chance.'

Andy Pandy's arm stretched between us to retrieve some Twiglets. I stared at it in disgust and moved closer to Sally. She backed herself against the cabinets and still I moved forward. Her cheeks flushed pink and she gazed up at me with wide eyes.

'Max—'

I should have been this honest all along. Her façade was cracking up before me, the rebellion slipping from her eyes, the lines of her face dissolving into what I at last identified as recognition.

The Twiglets remained an obstacle. I lifted them from her hands and placed them on the work surface behind her, and then, as delicately as if she might shatter, laid my palms on her hips. It was the first time I'd ever touched her. She shook.

'Sally, I have to—'

'I can't—'

Nothing now between us but her refusal, which contradicted everything my fingertips could feel. 'Please, my darling. Please.'

Somehow she didn't kiss me. The conversation was an eternity, containing almost no vocabulary other than that which I have already relayed. Yet as it stumbled to and fro, expressing her resistance and the need of us both, the universe retreated to leave us to a world that had been created at that moment. I knew then that neither of us would ever escape it.

Not once did I move my hands from the top of her naked legs. Nor did she make a single motion to dislodge them. Only hands, but though inches still separated the rest of our bodies, the soft, slight friction between our skin was enough to unite us. My cape hung from my shoulders and sheltered her from the banality outside.

'Max,' she whispered in the end, 'there are people watching.'

I looked over my shoulder and two dozen eyes were averted towards empty glasses. 'No, they aren't,' I said, turning back to her and smiling in triumph.

'You have to let me go now. It's so difficult for me. Max, I do understand.'

Of course she understood. Nothing could have convinced me otherwise.

'It's just that I'm going to have to explain things properly. Look. Why don't you come round to my place next Saturday? For dinner.'

I was aware that she shared a house with Antonia. 'Alone?'

'Of course. Well—'

The prospect of this being the end of this moment dawned upon me. And in anticipating its demise, I realised that it had already been broken. My hands fell from her hips. Distraught, I needed a movement with which to distract myself. I stepped backwards and flung the left-hand side of my cape over my right shoulder. Coughing back tears, I announced bluffly, 'Well. That's how it will be then.'

'Max, don't be so upset. It'll be just the same. I promise.'

I took another step backwards, pushing myself both away from and towards my grief. Saturday. A whole week. What sort of existence was I going to have in the void that lay between?

I found Declan in the garden. He was chatting up a milkmaid under a tree, and tried to ignore me. But the milkmaid switched her attention immediately to me. My cape and hat were both bedraggled appendages to my insufficiency. I wriggled in embarrassment.

Declan acknowledged me reluctantly. 'Hey, Max,' he said. 'You quite finished in there?' But then he saw the finely poised state of my emotional condition, and moved swiftly on. 'Meet Tess. Tess of the D'Urbervilles, that is.'

Tess laid down her pail, and stuck out her hand. The human contact felt limp and repugnant after what I had just left. I dropped the hand as soon as it had been shaken sufficiently. 'Declan,' I said, 'we're going.'

He snapped upright. 'We bloody aren't, you egotistical sod. You may very well be going, but I'm staying right here.'

I cried out to him. 'I want to talk to you.'

'You can talk to me right here. What happened? Did she knee you in the bollocks?'

The specified parts of my anatomy were still aching, in a desperate form of mourning. '*Declan*—'

'I'm sorry, mate. But the rest of us are having a good time. You can talk to me later.'

'Just promise me one thing.'

'What?'

'Take Antonia out for dinner next Saturday.'

'Good God, Max!' He was livid. 'Do you think the whole world exists for your own convenience? I happen to be taking Tess here out for dinner on Saturday. Aren't I, Tess?'

There was a small silence. Then, 'My name's Sandra,' piped up Tess. 'And I'm going to the cinema on Saturday.'

Declan let out an enormous groan. 'Just get out of here, will you, Max?'

So I got out.

The following week was a nightmare of lust. By Wednesday I had taken up smoking, though I gave up again on Thursday, having run out of both cash and lungpower.

Suprisingly, the date between Declan and Antonia was happening after all. 'Well,' he said, when I called upon him to explain himself, 'you blew it for me with Tess. She felt sorry for you, apparently. And then I got chatting to Antonia. Who does, it has to be admitted, have very nice tits. I thought I might as well ask her. And she said yes. Which, presumably, was a complete set-up. Still. I've never been fussy. Unlike some people I could name.'

'What do you mean?'

'You could have had any other woman in that room. Gagging for that Zorro deal, they were. Can't you just give up this whole palaver and lay some nice straightforward girls, like anyone else?'

I had been living so constantly in the cocoon of those moments with Sally that the suggestion sounded like adultery. 'She's invited me to her home,' I pointed out.

'Yes. Well, I just hope the pair of you get it sorted out, one way or the other. I don't think I can take much more of this.'

'There's only one way it can be sorted out.'

'Hmm,' said Declan, and a look of almost parental concern crossed his face. I was plunged once more into fear. The alternative was something I couldn't contemplate.

On Saturday evening I turned up at the door in as dapper an attire as I could physically manage, armed with an enormous bunch of lilies and a bottle of cheap methode champagnoise. She, at the threshold, was a vision of loveliness in full evening dress, draped in a floor-length jade-green creation which exposed her fabulous shoulders and intriguing collar bones. I staggered inside, suffused with joy, and found myself walking into the genuine romantic deal. Candle-lit table, crystal glasses, silver cutlery, the whole caboodle. She went into the kitchen to find a vase for the flowers, and I managed to arrange my backside in conjunction with the seat of one of the chairs.

It was as I sat there that the noise began to drift down from above.

'Oops,' said Sally, returning with the flowers still in her hand. 'Hold these, will you? I've just got to pop upstairs.'

The sound was so familiar that I ought to have been able to place it. But I could not. Then I heard Sally's voice. Talking to somebody. I felt I ought to sit tight and behave myself. But I could not.

I crept slowly up the dark stairway. Sally's voice was close enough now that I ought to have been able to make out the words. But she didn't seem to be speaking English. The other noise was gone now. There was a crack of light along the side of one of the doors that opened off the landing. I gave it a little push.

A cot. A pool of light in the corner. Sally standing there with a child in her arms and a look of great tenderness on her face. She smiled over its head at me.

'Max,' she said, 'meet Cassandra.'

I felt as if I had interrupted something of the most inviolable privacy. 'I'm sorry—'

'My daughter,' said Sally.

Afterwards, Declan told me about his discussion of this salient fact with Antonia in the Greek taverna in Camden. 'It was a great shock to me,' he said plaintively. 'The waiter nearly had to give me the Heimlich manoeuvre.'

'It was a shock to *you*?'

'Antonia assumed all evening that this was the last time any of us would see each other. She was very pleased about it. And I could see her point. Not that I was pleased about it myself – I couldn't even imagine how you'd react – but it seemed pretty terminal to me. She asked me what I'd do in the same circumstances. I said I'd run for the hills.'

'But you're not me.'

'Nobody is, Max. That's what we hadn't bargained for. Nobody's like you.'

'She looks just like you,' I said with tears in my eyes.

'Do you like her?' said Sally in hope.

I touched its little face. It opened its mouth and stared up at me with the widest eyes I'd ever seen. 'I love her,' I said. Then looked back up at Sally, the tears welling up rather perilously now. I wanted to say the same thing about her, but couldn't.

Sally's face crumpled a little. She managed to pull the muscles back into shape. 'Would you like to hold her?'

I nodded, and put my arms into what I thought was a cradle shape. 'No,' said Sally, 'she's too big for that now. You have to support her bum. Here.' And suddenly the child was sitting on my left hand, its back supported by my right, regarding me in horror. It let out a blood-curdling scream. I flinched and started to try to hand her back, but Sally stood firm. 'Eh, Cass, it's all right. Don't be silly. Talk to her, Max. She likes deep voices.'

'Hello,' I said. 'How are you?'

The child stopped wailing and frowned at me. Then she began again.

'You've got a nice room here, Cass,' I said. Small talk had never been easy, and with a baby I had no idea what she might be interested in. 'I like your rabbit. Have you ever seen a real rabbit?'

'Wawa,' said the child.

'Jesus, it talks!'

'A tad precocious,' said Sally. 'It's because she's got such a brilliant mother. I'm afraid that's the only word she has so far. Here, Cass. Here's Rabbit.' The bedraggled yellow toy was placed in Cass's hands and she took it eagerly.

'It's all a bit exciting for her,' said Sally. 'Do you mind if we take her downstairs for a bit while I finish making the dinner?'

'God, no,' I said, and as I was relieved of the child, I got round to wiping the tears from my face. I felt as if I'd entered a fairy tale, and didn't want ever to leave. The beautiful woman in green; the child with its guileless eyes; the warmth of this room.

I don't think I thought of any of the implications at all.

*

By the time Sally had finished preparing the starter, Cass had tired of my buttons, and was a small bundle of contented slumber in my arms. Sally stood for a second in front of us, transfixed, then said, 'Okay. I'll take her up now.'

Then she returned to me. Now that the news was broken and the distraction was gone, we were a little awkward with one another, like teenagers thrown together by their parents. For the first time I looked at her without an erection. It was a rather cleansing experience.

'I – wasn't expecting that,' I said.

'I know,' said Sally. She looked fearful once more. 'You don't mind, do you?'

'Mind?' I squinted in memory of the wonders I had just beheld. 'Sally, it's amazing. Incredible. You gave birth. You have a daughter. I can't get over it.'

She sat down abruptly, a flustered smile breaking at the edges of her mouth. 'It was rather incredible,' she confessed. 'One doesn't expect – to have experiences like that.'

'The birth?'

'The birth was terrifying. No. Afterwards. I kept thinking – I'm just a girl. Not this almighty being my daughter thinks I am.'

'I knew that,' I said proudly.

'Max, you didn't. You didn't know anything about me at all. Because I didn't let you know. I was very dishonest.'

I tried to reconcile her evasions with the essential image I had of her. It didn't work. 'You weren't dishonest,' I said. 'Just because I didn't know about Cass, that doesn't mean that I didn't know who you were.'

'Yes, it did. Of course it did. Oh, Max, I treated you so badly. From that first moment—'

My anatomical serenity was bowled away.

'You were like a thunderstorm approaching. I thought I owed it to myself to run as far as I could right then. I owed it to both of us. But I didn't. And I kept not doing. Antonia thought I was insane, and she was right. We were so *at odds*. There you were, threatening to sweep me up in your arms at any moment, and me unable to resist it – oh, it's been awful – and never telling you the truth. Then I'd come home to Cass, and she'd beam up at me, and it felt as if I'd betrayed the one person who ought to be able to trust me.'

'I trust you,' I said.

'Max, don't. You're just making it worse. I should have told you from the beginning. But I couldn't bear the idea of you going away.'

Our starters were untouched. I wanted to lean across the table and take her hand in mine. But her face was still too distraught. 'Why would I go away?'

'Well—' She stared at me in confusion. 'Surely most men would?'

'I have no idea.' Then it suddenly occurred to me that she had been basing all her expectations of me on her experience of others. The words came out so fast that I heard them at the same time that she did. 'How did this happen?'

She knew exactly what I meant. I couldn't take it back, because the jealousy was still aflame within me. But I was ready to drop to my knees at her feet if I saw that I'd hurt her.

She gave no sign of it. Instead she said to me softly, 'Max, aren't you supposed to be biologically programmed so that you'd have that reaction first?'

I thought about it. A dozen examples sprang to mind. Even male primates were capable of killing the offspring of a new mate if it wasn't theirs. Even humans, if the most horrible news articles were to be believed. But – news articles were news articles. They dwelled on the worst, and perhaps in our zoological analyses scientists did just the same for other species. I remembered Cass in Sally's arms in that small room. Did she know what a risk she'd been taking, giving me so stark a surprise? I shuddered with nausea. 'I think it depends on the person,' I said weakly.

'Yes,' she said, gazing at me very evenly. 'I think it must.'

'Sally – can I ask you—'

'Please do.'

'Who was it?'

She took a deep breath. 'He was Brazilian. We were both at the Slade together. My family were never very keen on me going to college, but I think they were happier that it was artistic than if there had been any threat of my becoming a bluestocking. They thought I might find a husband. As it happened, I did. I got pregnant in the first term of my second year, and by the time I was six months gone my mother had persuaded me to drop out and him to marry me. He left me two weeks before the birth. The assumption is that he's gone back to Brazil. I'm in the process of divorcing him, but it's quite difficult, given that I don't know where he is. I can do it on the grounds of desertion, but he has to have deserted me for long enough.'

'You're married.'

'Yes. Not that it means anything. We never even lived together.'

'Did you love him?'

'I certainly thought so, at the beginning. But I was very young. I was just glad to be away from home, really. To be away from my parents' expectations and do all these wild and uncon- ventional things. Like having sex with foreigners.' She caught herself. 'Not foreigners plural, of course. There was just the one. And I should have been more careful. But I went to a convent, and the woman who taught us sex education only told us about the rhythm method and had eight children. It was stupid. My family isn't even Catholic. They just liked the idea of me being brought up by nuns. But of course he was Catholic, and so there was no question of condoms.'

One half of me wanted to go straight out to Brazil, kick the shit out of him, then drag him back to face his responsibilities. And the other was only too happy to forsake vengeance on Sally's behalf to have him remain on the other side of the world. 'It must have been terrible when he left,' was all I could manage.

'Yes. It was. Thank God for Antonia. I was at my parents' place, and she came and rescued me. Of course my parents have known her since we started school, and have always been very impressed by her father being an ambassador—'

'*Is* he?'

'Yes. So they let her take me in. If it had been anyone else, they wouldn't even have let them in the door. I owe her every-thing. This is her house, you know. We don't pay rent. And with her being a student, I've even been able to do a bit of work here and there, while she looks after Cass. Not much, but enough to pay a babysitter here and there. Apart from that, she supports us, essentially.'

It became clear to me how little I'd thought to ask. I'd taken Declan's initial description of Sally at face value – *aspiring artist – models for Freud* – and had thought it explained everything. But for all I'd known she might have been living on air. 'What sort of student? What sort of work?' I bumbled incoherently.

'Max, do you really not know that?' She was smiling. 'Antonia always said you weren't interested in anything but gawping at me, but I thought she was exaggerating. She's at RADA. And I do a bit of design work for magazines. And a bit of model-ling.'

'For Lucian Freud,' I said, grasping at something I already knew.

'No. That's just a stupid rumour. I've never even met him. Someone once said I looked like a woman in one of his paint-ings, and it stuck. I model for the classes at the Slade. The ones I used to attend as a student. The pay's shit, but it seems to be all I'm capable of doing.'

I tried to take it all in. 'But – but how come nobody knows? About Cass, I mean? Tony, and his wife, and everyone else—'

'Everyone knows. It's no secret. Which was one reason why I didn't tell you. I assumed you'd find out in the end. But as Antonia says, you never actually talked to anyone except for me and Declan. And even Declan never found out, because whenever Antonia or anyone else tried to turn the subject to me or you, he said he was sick to the back teeth of it and wanted to be appreciated as a person in his own right, not as a friend of yours.'

For a moment all the jealousy and anger I felt towards Sally's husband, and her parents, and Antonia, and everyone in the world except for Sally and Cass, were funnelled towards my friend. 'Bloody Declan,' I said in fury.

'That's not fair, Max. He had a point.'

We sat there in silence for a moment, and then Sally picked up her fork and said, 'Are you actually interested in eating this starter?'

'Oh, yes.' I plunged a mouthful of prawns into my mouth.

'We don't have to. After all, it wasn't really why I asked you over. And I'm not feeling terribly hungry myself.' She laid down her fork, picked up her wine glass and stood up. Cascades of green silk fell about her slender body. I wondered how she'd kept her figure, and how she could afford that dress. Perhaps she'd made it herself. Everything I'd assumed about her was an illusion, but it couldn't be blamed on her, because I'd created it myself. I'd seen what I'd wanted to see, and no more.

And yet the reality – I blinked at her loveliness. 'Would you like to join me on the comfy seats?' she said.

I stood up, knocking the plate as I did so. She put my wine glass into one of my hands, took the other with her own, and led me to the sofa. We sat down. She kicked off her shoes and tucked her legs up beneath her, and turned her face to mine.

And then I kissed her. And the baby did not cry.

*

The lascivious plans my body had hatched in hours of darkness and light remained unexecuted that night. We spent a few hours of uninterrupted bliss, then fell asleep in one another's arms on the sofa, fully-clothed, exhausted by the emotion of the evening. When Antonia's key turned in the door at midnight, we woke slowly, and, still entwined, smiled at her.

'Oh!' said Antonia in unabashed surprise. 'It looks as if it went okay.'

There was the smallest touch of disapproval in her voice, but I forgave her for it. No plots of hers could sever us now. Antonia hung up her coat and bag, and switched the kettle on. 'You haven't eaten anything!' she exclaimed.

Sally ignored her. 'How was Declan?'

'A ratbag. But an amusing one. The food was disgusting. Do you mind if I cook one of these steaks?'

'Go ahead.'

The clonking of pans began. 'Sally,' I whispered, our hair still tangled together, 'I think I might go now.'

She looked into my eyes, and a dozen questions were asked and answered. 'Okay,' she mouthed back. I kissed her very gently, and she squeezed my hand, and I got up.

'Nice to see you, Antonia,' I said loudly.

'Great,' said Antonia in a burst of sizzling.

I wanted to go back to Sally again, but it had to end somewhere. This time I wasn't afraid. I opened the door, and left.

The door opened again behind me. Antonia stood at the threshold, framed by light, holding my jacket. 'I think this is yours,' she said.

'Thank you,' I said, and took it.

She stepped down onto the pavement and pulled the door almost shut behind her. 'If you dare fuck her around, Max Oldroyd,' she hissed, 'you'll have me to answer to. Because I think you know who'll be left to pick up the pieces. And if I'm not very much mistaken, you won't have the opportunity to run away to Brazil.'

It was not worth descending to the level of her opinion of me. 'I'll bear that in mind,' I said. 'Thank you for the loan of your living space.'

She snorted in anger, stepped back inside and slammed the door behind her. It didn't matter to me at all. Soon Sally would be beholden to her no longer.

This is how I remember it now. A series of memories wrapped in tissue paper and stored at the bottom of a drawer, rarely examined but never quite forgotten. I entered this chapter with a cry of joy at having finally found a version of myself that I could recognise, but now that those memories have been committed to the hard drive of my computer, I can see that it is not me at all. I recognise that man because I have kept him beside me for so long. The feeling that my life started at that moment was due to the fact that it was the first time I'd stumbled across a memory worth keeping. Because, of course, it was also the first time I realised that it was worth living for someone other than myself.

In practice, I should have learnt my 'theory of mind' between the ages of three and four, because it is at this stage that a child comes to understand that there are points of view other than his own, and learns how to put himself in the position of another. But this development is largely unconscious. If it came to our infant selves as an almighty revelation, it might overwhelm us. Understanding that there are beings looking out at us from within other skulls is not the same thing as getting an image of what it is actually like in there.

Such an experience must have been largely imaginary. It is not possible to see the world through a stranger's eyes from the other side of a crowded room. But she was real. That was what I couldn't believe, as the days turned into weeks turned into months. She was absolutely real. And hers was not the reality of the body, gloriously though it was expressed in every atom of her frame. It was something I loved even more: the reality of the mind.

Sally was not an intellectual. She didn't need to be, for me. Had our mental constitutions been more genuinely similar, then her effect on me might have been less strong. The jolt was not just that of recognition, but also a sense of the independence of the viewpoint within her head. Until then, the world might as well have been populated by ghosts, bare scribblings of human beings, their outlines conveyed by my own perceptions and their insides a blank. Now here was a person drawn in vivid colour, opaque and three-dimensional, her interior as real and compelling as that which I could see.

And though it was her separateness that attracted me to her, my compulsion was to eradicate it. This is what attraction means. We are creatures of action; there is nothing in us which is ever still; and the things which we value the most are often those which we are driven to change. Luckily, that particular quest is an impossible one, because if once it was completed and the other incorporated into oneself, then not only desire but even interest would be exhausted, and the thing which had been so treasured would be gone. Love is poised on the axis of familiarity and incomprehension, forever ready to topple off in either direction.

I am aware that the way I have described this period in my life has made a nonsense of science. I write of love now as I spoke of it then, as if it could be attributed to a spiritual essence within me, rather than being the function of a biological machine. Yet ultimately something wholly biological was at stake. I was aware even then that my desire for Sally was motivated almost entirely by the urge to reproduce. But this understanding had been delivered to me by education, and bore no relation to what I actually felt. Our genetic arrangements do not instil in us a knowledge of the joys and griefs entailed by child-rearing. It would be too ambitious an evolutionary strategy for a beetle or a snail, and too risky for a human, in whom such genetically programmed presentiments might be possible. Our basic drives are never long-termist in their motivation. There are simpler ways for our bodies to encourage the replication of their genes, and they are important to us right in the moment, not in some hypothetical future. We do not know how it feels for a beetle or snail to want to have sex, but I know how it feels in me. When I met Sally, it felt as if this woman and no other would do; it felt as if my heart would crack whenever she delivered a kind or harsh word; it felt as if my body would explode if I got too close to her. Then, it felt right; and now, as I relate it, it still feels right. Despite all apparent evidence to the contrary, my instincts at the moment I put my hands on her hips at the fancy dress party were correct. A world had been created, and would never be dissolved.

I wanted Sally for her body and her brain. It wasn't reproduction I was looking for, but communication. Never before had I seen such an opportunity to expand the field of my consciousness. It is there in the act of sex – a feeling of one's nerves extending beyond the perimeter of one's own skin – and it is there in the slow habit of companionship, the only thing I know which appears to achieve the phenomenon of an opinion forming in not one mind but two. Both may be illusions. It is possible that I never had any idea what was happening in Sally's mind, and that all we shared was the idea that we were thinking the same things. After all, consciousness itself may be an illusion, the combination of a million little mechanisms in the mind each doing its own thing to produce the momentary impression of a before, an after and a now. That impression is reconstituted as soon as it has come together; thirty years down the line it has been replaced so many times that it is all but untraceable. Yet in the realm of consciousness, illusions are realities. A thought is an act. Whether or not Sally and I ever knew a thing about one another, we thought we did; or, at the very least, I thought she knew about me, and I thought she thought I knew about her. Those thoughts, wrapped as I say in tissue paper, reconstructed anew as memories by every split-second generation of my consciousness, are some of the most precious things I have.

In recent years, the hypothesis has been put forward that many of the more elaborate features of the human brain, including perhaps even consciousness itself, have evolved through sexual selection in the same way as the peacock's tail. Sexual selection is as powerful a shaper of genes as natural selection, but it operates through organisms' relative success at reproduction rather than merely through their success at survival. It is responsible for many of the more flamboyant and outrageous works of nature which appear to have no utilitarian purpose, and works in straight, exponential lines which start out from the whimsy of sexual preference. According to this theory, our brains have been converted into amusement parks for the benefit of the beloved, in the hope of attracting a better partner. If that is so, and I owe my mind to sex, then I thank genetics for having accidentally stumbled along this path. Because sex produces the thing which most powerfully defeats the concept of dualism in our everyday lives. It unites body and brain, and we call it love.

5

I slept with Sally for the first time a week later. By that time I'd had more than a hundred and fifty hours to think about everything she'd said. About how hard she'd tried to resist me, and how frightened she'd been. The thought of it was enough almost to make me lose control, on buses, in the library, in supervisions with John Hinds. The skin of her face had been so soft against mine, her eyes so warm, her lips just the beginning of her – but she must not have any reason to be afraid, for herself or for her daughter. When I'd seen her with the child in her arms, I'd known that I was dealing with things I knew nothing about. She was a mother, the begetter of a whole new human being, and I was just a man. We must go softly, gently, carefully – oh, God.

The plan was that we would go to the cinema, but we got no further than the door to my flat. It was a night of joy trammelled only by my inability to find enough space within me to contain it all. We said very little of any significance, and moved no more than a few feet, but the world was expanding, vistas were opening up, a future of unimaginable gorgeousness was beginning to grow within us. Which just goes to prove my hypothesis that the world is fundamentally neutral. Because three hundred and fifty miles away, in a hospital in Plymouth, my father was drawing his final breath.

It was another two months before Sally found out, and that was only because she caught me having a phone conversation with my mother about the will. By then we were already making plans for her and Cass to move out of Antonia's house and into my flat.

It was hard to face her sympathy. 'He died.' I shrugged. 'It happens.'

'Oh, but Max,' she said, crumpling with unhappiness. It was so different from the way it had been with my mother, who was the only other person who'd ever cared so much about how I was feeling. Mum and I had been possessed of griefs which were shared and yet utterly separate, and we'd each been terrified of trespassing on one another's pain. Whereas Sally had no sorrow of her own to keep her away. Whatever she felt, it was entirely on my behalf.

'You poor thing.' She was tiptoeing towards me, her footsteps tentative with inadequacy. 'You've been so – stoical. It must have been very recent. Six months? How long?'

I said nothing, and her eyes flared with fear. 'How long, Max?'

I told her.

'But that's – that's— When was it, Max? When in relation to me?'

I told her, and she stood before me, perfectly still. I saw her replaying events in her head, saw them toppling one by one in her imagination, saw her staring at me in shock and incomprehension. It was clear enough what she thought. She thought that I wasn't the person she'd thought I was. But I was, I was.

'I'm sorry,' I said. 'I should have told you.' Except that I couldn't have done. The funeral had fallen on a work day, and I'd taken the long train down to Plymouth when she'd thought I was occupied by beetles in the lab. I'd wondered at the time whether I'd already done my grieving for my father while he was still alive. But it wasn't like that, exactly. The whole place had seemed a million miles away even while I was there. I couldn't afford to let it impinge on my new sense of myself for even a second.

'Why didn't you tell me? Did you not get on with your father, is that it?'

She was clutching at straws, and I knew that I must not lie. 'I admired him very much.'

'Well, then, why? Was it me? Did you think I wouldn't want to hear? How could you think that, after all I've told you about my life?'

It had never occurred to me that my silence might be a betrayal of her. 'No, no, it wasn't like that at all. I knew – that you—' I had to stop. I couldn't say anything about what I'd known she would do, because I hadn't thought about it at all.

'You must talk about it now, Max. I know it's awful of me. You've lost your father, and here I am, thinking about myself. But I can't share a bed – share my *life*, you must know it's got that bad – with someone who doesn't share his with me. All those times when I thought we were so happy, and you must have been—' She was crying. Oh, heavens. 'No, no, Max' – as I leapt up to embrace her – 'you mustn't comfort *me*, it's the wrong way round.'

We were both a terrible mess that evening, unsure of how to treat one another. I wanted to please her, to do the thing that would make her feel better, but though I was certain that I could have told her anything in the world about the way I felt about her, my feelings about my father didn't seem to exist in any form that I could actually express.

'I suppose you haven't really learnt how to deal with it yourself yet,' she said in the end. 'That's why you find it so hard to talk about it to me.'

'Yes,' I admitted. 'I suppose that's probably it.'

And though that was the most comfortable resolution we could come to that evening, it left me feeling hopelessly inadequate, as if I'd failed to match her ideals. 'I'm sorry,' I said again and again, and each time she said, 'Stop. Stop apologising. You've got nothing to apologise for. It's just—'

I tried to move the conversation onto more cheerful matters. 'Have you sorted out a moving-out date with Antonia yet?' I asked.

She looked at me, and terror gripped me. No. She couldn't decide not to live with me just because—

'Max—'

'Don't say it, Sally. Please don't say it.'

'I'm scared, Max. It's so soon. I mean, it's been obvious all along that it's too soon, but I didn't care, because we were so happy—'

'We're still happy. Aren't we?'

'I don't know. How can I know? You can't have been happy the week after your father died, and yet I was so sure that you were.'

The awful thing was, I had been happy that week. That was the thing I was still too ashamed to tell her. She hadn't seen anything other than the way I'd really been. Yes, there had been moments when the joy had subsided enough to expose the other thing which was lurking in my brain, and at those times it had almost overwhelmed me. But not when I was with her.

'We know one another so much better now,' I protested. 'If it had happened now, I would definitely have told you.' Perhaps everything would have been different if it had happened later. I would have been able to tell her about it, and I would have understood how I felt myself. It would have been another of the wonders of our love. Oh, bugger you, Dad, I thought suddenly. He'd hung on for so long. Couldn't he have held out for another two months? And then the shame, curling back on me and threatening to carry me away even from Sally.

'I think we should think about it for a bit,' she said painfully. 'About whether I should move in, I mean. It doesn't mean anything. You mustn't think that it does. The last thing I'd want to do is add to your troubles. We'll see each other just the same, it won't make any difference. It's just that I think that this is probably a bit of a warning. I mean, the stakes are so high, with Cass to consider and everything. I should have learnt by now not to go jumping into things. I'm not saying it's going to be like that – Max, I'm so sure, you must believe me about that, it's what makes it so difficult. But we have to take our time. There's no reason why we shouldn't.'

It was the promise I'd made to myself on the day before our consummation. Which had also, of course, been the last day of my father's life. For her sake and mine, I ought to be able to honour that promise now. But this was my first setback since I'd first taken her into my arms, and I was devastated. My brain could interpret the sense of what she said perfectly, but the rest of me couldn't make head or tail of the idea of postponing any happiness at all. 'You're right,' I said, burying the premonitions, forcing a smile onto my lips.

'Please don't look so tragic,' begged Sally, her own face creased in suffering, and then, beholding one another, we laughed for the first time that evening. Which cured everything. The words stopped and the togetherness came back, gently, softly, slowly, because we must take our time, because there was no reason why we shouldn't, except that once the barriers had been broken down it was very hard to keep hold of any intentions at all—

We did our best, and ended up breaking a coffee mug and hollering the place half way to Armageddon. Sleep was heralded by more laughter, except that just when I thought I was about to drop off, I didn't. That night, with Sally beside me, I thought properly about my father for the first time. What would he think of all this? Was our giddy, world-oblivious lovemaking a grave transgression of his moral code? Or had he been, as somewhere in my mind I believed he was, a man born out of time, who saw things not as he'd been told they ought to be, but as they truly were? The problem was that I would have had no way of telling even if I could have asked him. In a way, that was the reason for the absence of anything I could categorise as grief. The idea of my father was still a strong presence in my brain, but he was much the same as a dead man as he had been when he was alive. And perhaps that was the greatest grief of all.

It took her slightly less than a week to come to her decision.

'I'm hopeless, Max, I'm just hopeless—'

I swept her up into my arms and cavorted about the room. She squealed with laughter and batted at me with her hands in an attempt to make me put her down. 'Of course, I'll have to do some sorting out before we can move in properly,' she said.

'Sorting out? What kind of sorting out? Will it take long?'

'You'll see.'

Sally came to my flat with Cass during the day, when I was out at the library or the lab, and each evening I came home to a new transformation. By the time they moved in, paintbrushes, canvases, nappies and all, she had fashioned Cass her own quarters from a room which had a window but which had probably originally been designed as a cupboard. The walls of the single main room were a jaunty shade of primrose and there were hand-made drapes all over the place. Sally fixed the rickety table and decorated it with a mosaic of multi-coloured wall tiles. Despite the increase in clobber, the room seemed to have grown, and now seemed fit for its multiple roles as kitchen, dining room, lounge, bedroom, nursery, artist's studio and study. It resounded with our happiness. We were volatile with mirth, squelchy with sex, and alive to the possibility of fun round every corner. And whilst my own initial instinct was to pull her into my embrace and shut out the whole world, hers was the opposite. Now she had somewhere she could call her own, and she wanted to share it with everyone. I learned from her the happiness that can come from hospitality.

Antonia did not approve. Whilst she had by then come to

terms with my existence, and was perhaps even convinced that my intentions were serious, her year of virtual stepmotherhood had made her extremely protective of Cass.

'It isn't an appropriate place to bring up a child,' she said when she first came to inspect Cass's new living arrangements.

'Antonia,' Sally said mildly, 'lots of people bring up children without much money. They don't all have nice houses and gardens. And most of them are fine.'

'You didn't seem to object to the nice house before.'

'Oh, Antonia—'

It was the closest I ever saw them come to a row. But they pulled back at the last minute, and the friendship persisted. They told one another everything. I'd come in from the lab to find them sitting at the table, Cass on Antonia's knee, conversation hurriedly broken off.

'What do you talk about?' I'd demand of Sally when Antonia was gone.

'You, of course.' She'd wind her arms about me. 'Did your ears burn?' And she'd kiss them.

From my own point of view, it didn't bother me too much that they talked about me behind my back. Sally's opinion of me had survived Antonia's inquisitions when they'd been living together, and so I had no fear of her influence on our relationship now that we were a household of our own. But I wasn't so sure about the effect of Antonia's disapproval on Sally's opinion of herself.

It was the parties that really caused the strain. She couldn't resist them. Declan would drop in on his way back from work, and before we knew it, Sally had produced food, wine, and the kind of conversation that was quite capable of keeping us talking, in hushed voices, into the middle of the night. Or the sun would come out, and soon a hamper would be packed, Cass would be in her pushchair, and after a few phone calls, a convocation of everyone we knew would start to assemble in

Regent's Park for a picnic. Then, as often as not, as the warmth began to dissipate, the stragglers would drift back to our place to finish off the fun. As the hilarity escalated and Antonia's delicate blonde eyebrows began to twitch, it did sometimes occur to me that I was supposed to be acting in loco parentis. But Cass was such a quiet and obliging child, and never seemed to mind; and we always saw off the bigger groups when it came to her bedtime. We were also very fortunate on the babysitting front. Since she'd been very small, Cass's childcare had been provided in part by Mavis, an old retainer attached to Antonia's family, whose main duty was to oversee the maintenance of the ambassador's London residence, and she was only too happy to break up the monotony of this lonely work with the care of a docile child.

I would have forgone the parties if Sally had asked me to, but she never did. She cared for her child beyond anything, but the transformation which came with Cass's birth had not suppressed the innate outwardness of her personality. There was never a girl like Sally for having fun. When she entered her rare dark patches, it was this that surfaced. 'I'm so awful,' she berated herself, usually in tears, after parties that had got out of hand. 'I can never let a grain of excitement go past without being part of it. I should never have been a mother.'

It was at least partly true. By her early twenties life had already thrown a great many blows her way – unplanned pregnancy, desertion, divorce – and whilst she tried to accommodate them all, nothing could subdue her appetite for life for more than a few days. But I couldn't condemn her most precious attribute. It was what had brought her to me.

'It's fine,' I comforted her. 'You're young.'

'I know, that's what's been such a problem. I had to have my youth.' Then her mood passed, as instantly as it had come. A very small growl, and a foray under the covers. 'And you're the youth I had to have.'

The problem was that Antonia knew all about Mavis, and all about everything else. One morning she strode into the flat, grabbed an empty beer bottle, and flung it at full hurtle into the bin.

'This is bloody outrageous!' she shouted at me, even though Sally was sitting right beside me.

The impromptu party had, as usual, taken place at Sally's instigation. I could feel her begin to shake beside me with guilt. 'Shut up, Antonia,' I said. 'I'm fed up with you behaving as if you're Dr Spock. Sally's a wonderful mother.'

'Are you a wonderful father? The more I see you with Cass, the more I'm sure that your interest in her is not paternal but scientific. All you're interested in is watching the processes of inheritance at work.'

It was infuriating the way that she deflected all her concerns onto me. The beer bottle bore no relation to my preoccupations as a scientist, nor to any supposed lack of interest in Cass. She was Sally's friend, not mine, and any worries she might have about Cass's upbringing ought to be addressed to Sally, not me. I knew that this was the way that Sally would have preferred it too. 'She's fine when we're on our own,' she assured me when I railed at her about Antonia's behaviour. 'It just seems to be when you're there that she flies off the handle. I don't know why she does it. But I wish she didn't. When you're there, I can't answer her back properly.'

It ought to have been obvious to Sally that this was exactly why Antonia did it. Her fondness for Sally prevented her from being unkind to her face, but I was fair game. And in the lee of the outburst, as I prepared myself to reply, I could see that Sally was so torn by our antagonism that she would be able to stand barely another minute unless one of us left. 'That's complete rubbish,' I said briskly, impressing myself with my restraint. 'However, you women clearly need some time to talk. I'll take Cass to the park.'

Getting to the park involved a bus ride, and all the clanking of pushchair and child which that entailed. A man with a pushchair was not a common sight in those days, and I was soothed by the admiring glances of the women on the bus. Perhaps if I'd been a smaller and more innocuous specimen they might have questioned my masculinity, but as it was they fussed over us both. By the time we got off the bus, their combined opinions of me had outvoted any jealous accusations of Antonia's, and I pushed my girlfriend's daughter along the paths with my head held as high as any real father.

It was a sunny day, so I stopped the pushchair by a big flowerbed and took Cass out so that we could both explore it. Watching Cass discover nature was one of the most inspiring experiences I'd ever had available to me. She was still mainly crawling, but had started putting a few steps together a week or so before, and she couldn't wait to use her new combined means of perambulation to find out as much about the flowerbed as possible.

I lay in the grass, watching her bumble from flower to flower. Her features were so fine that people sometimes assumed her to have oriental blood, but that was just Sally's distinctive bone structure refined and softened by whatever she'd received from her Brazilian father. She took a bloom in her hand, and examined it with eyes and mouth wide open. Then she plunged it into her mouth.

'Oy, Cass!' I grabbed her, pulled her into my arms, and extracted the petals, wondering how the human race had ever struggled out of its infancy without being poisoned, given that the major method of investigation for infants appeared to be to ingest everything they found.

I thought of Antonia's tirade again. It might be true that I had a scientific interest in Cass's progress. But that didn't seem to be such a harmful thing to me. Would Antonia have preferred that I had no interest at all? And anyway, I had always cared for Cass in ways other than the purely observational. Being with Cass was a constant revelation of myself. No-one ever watched me with as wide eyes as Cass did. All babies do it to some extent, but I had never seen it before, and Cass's gaze was a constant monitor, following me around every room. Perhaps in that fatherless first year, she'd felt some sort of instinctive absence, and was constantly checking that I had not gone away again. I had begun to understand what Sally had meant when she had said that she couldn't believe that she was the person her daughter thought she was. It was even harder to believe that I could deserve such attention. But I had it, and I did my best to live up to it. Sally trusted me with her child, and so when we were together I felt myself gifted with responsibility. It was a strange but wonderful thing to hear myself talk to her, knowing that her perception of my words was utterly different from that of an adult. They carried little literal meaning for her as yet, but I knew that they were being stored, filtered, pieced together within whatever language instinct she possessed, and that soon some of my words would come tumbling out of her mouth on her own terms. And even now, whilst there was no real understanding, the meaning of my words was perhaps greater than it ever would be again. There was no possibility of contradiction or denial. She depended upon me not only for shelter and food, but also for information about what lay around her. From within her tiny but fast-expanding world view, my words were those of a god.

I hoped I'd teach her well. Right now, uncontaminated by folklore and superstition, she was the perfect little biologist, classifying everything she came across. She found a stick in the grass and laid it out beside another stick. Then she felt along their knobbles, and placed them in a different relation to one another, until she'd discovered their every property, and finally found an arrangement which suited her, at which point she tired of the sticks and moved on to the next new thing. In years to come, the primal scientific urge would subside, and she would have to be taught all over again how to see things with fresh eyes. How tragic it was that so many people failed to relearn it.

It was at that moment that I had the idea of writing *Genesis*. Materially, at least, we all owe Cass a great deal.

Doing a PhD was harder than I'd expected. The thing I missed most during the long uneventful days of research, reading and collation was exams. I'd never minded the monotony or the loneliness of academic work when there'd been the buzz of anticipation in my veins at the thought of the next three-hour mental assault course. I was good at exams – I could write faster than anyone else, structure my thoughts better than anyone else, and my memory was so accurate that in the intensity of revision I could remember not only the quote or the equation but the number of the page on which it had sat. I'd loved everything from the enormous clock ticking round on the wall to the ludicrous gown I had to wear while I wrote, and took pride in reading through my answers before walking out of the hall precisely quarter of an hour before the end. Now all such opportunities for exhibitionism were gone. Even the old weekly tutorials, at which I'd read out my essays to an appreciative don, had been replaced by infrequent supervisions with John Hinds. There were no essays to give him and no praise to be collected, just interminable arguments about methodology and scope.

'He's a bloody taxonomist, nothing more!' I raged at Sally.

'What's a taxonomist?' asked Sally.

That was one of the things I adored about her. She never prolonged her ignorance by hiding it. If she didn't know something, she asked; and the pleasure I gained in telling her was about the only reward for my work I got.

'A taxonomist is someone who sits all their life in the Natural History Museum and classifies beetles. Did you know, they've got twenty million insects in the cupboards on the upper floors? Or at least they think they have. No-one's ever counted. For more than a century, so-called scientists have been traipsing around places like the Amazon with fishing nets, and bringing back everything they've found to Kensington in crates. They've got Darwin's beetles in there. And Huxley's. And everyone's since. At least the ones from Darwin and Huxley have been classified. Most of the rest haven't. So they have an army of taxonomists up there, going through it all beetle by beetle. They'll never finish, because new ones are arriving all the time. I ask you, what's the point? What can possibly come of classifying the thirty-thousandth member of the Scarabaeinae family when we don't even understand how a cell splits? I'm glad I came to Erasmus, but I wish I hadn't got John Hinds. Then I wouldn't have had to do bloody beetles.'

'You were very keen on them once,' said Sally mischievously.

I gave her a look which acknowledged the memory but refused to be diverted from the topic in hand. 'I don't have anything against beetles as such,' I conceded. 'But I refuse to taxonomise. I want to take the things apart, see how they work, go back to basics, make it so that even a primary-school kid could understand it—' And I told her about the thought that had occurred to me in the park with Cass. That it ought somehow to be possible to make the whole of biology as clear to an unscientific adult as it was to a two-year-old child.

'Well, why don't you do it, then?' said Sally.

'Do what?'

'Explain it. Write it all down.'

For once, she'd managed to stem my normally interminable flow of words. I gawped at her for a moment, and then said, 'They'd never accept that as a PhD.'

'You don't have to do it as your PhD. That's your day job, and you should treat it as such. Do it in your spare time.'

The first thing I felt was a stab of terror very similar to the one I'd experienced when my father suggested I go to Oxford. She actually thought I was capable of doing such an outrageous, outlandish thing. Then I realised that Sally was not my father. There were no expectations, no imperatives. She just wanted me to do whatever made me happy, and was sure that I was capable of it.

'Bloody hell,' I said. 'You know, I think that's exactly what I'll do.'

And before she knew it I had dashed off to find paper and pen.

For all Antonia's protestations, it was she and Declan who provided the core of our social life, each of them tugging us in their different directions. While Antonia tidied up after us, Declan messed things up again; and while Antonia chastised us for our deficiencies as parents, Declan encouraged us to be as childish as possible. 'The reason why you two spend so much time with us,' he said once, throwing a provocative glance towards Antonia, 'is that we're the last spinster and bachelor in town. And despite all the lovey-doveyness, and the together forever, in your hearts you're both single yourselves.'

Antonia hated that, of course. It was always most comfortable to have them round together, because then they cancelled each other out, and their harshest judgments were reserved for one another. Even the thing they had in common – their singledom – was a point of extreme difference. Declan was single more or less by choice. If a woman had walked through the door who had the same effect on him as Sally had on me then he might have changed his views, but such a woman did not materialise, and in those circumstances he preferred to keep his options as open as possible. Antonia, on the hand, didn't want to be single at all. In 1976, after a depressing nationwide tour with an educational version of *The Canterbury Tales*, she announced that she was emigrating.

Sally was distraught. She had missed her friend enough when she was in the provinces, let alone California. 'But why Hollywood?' she wailed. 'You're a serious actress.'

'Sally, I've been going around for a year with my hand up a puppet's arse, sticking pokers up other puppets' arses. How much less serious do you think it's likely to get? I want to earn some money of my own. And I want to find some decent men. Okay, I'll come straight with you. I need to get myself a husband, and I think I've exhausted this country's supply of eligible bachelors. Is that all right? Or is that too calculating for you?'

It was true that she appeared to have snubbed, humiliated or otherwise rejected every single man in London. I told Sally that Antonia had only herself to blame for her situation.

'She's the nicest, sanest, most generous person in the world,' Sally reproved me. 'It's just that she has high standards. And rightly so.'

There were a lot of tears at Antonia's leaving party.

'I don't know what I'll do without you,' sobbed Sally.

'You'll be absolutely fine,' said Antonia, but her eyes were red too. 'Look, Sally. Why don't you and Max take this house? My parents would love you to have it.'

I bristled. 'Max says it's too far from the college,' said Sally, imploring me with a glance to keep quiet while she dealt with it.

'It's about twenty minutes on the tube!'

'He won't take charity. Anyway, he has a salary now. Our flat is fine. Thank you so much, Antonia, really, but we can't.'

Sally remained extremely emotional all evening. Towards the end, I realised that she had disappeared, and discovered her in the garden throwing up. 'I don't understand it!' she kept saying. 'I've only had two glasses of wine!'

It was three days after Antonia's arrival in Los Angeles that Sally discovered that she was pregnant again.

*

Sally's divorce had come through a year or so before, but I'd been so busy in my first job that it hadn't really occurred to us to do anything about it. With my child in her belly, I realised that it was time for us to formalise our responsibilities to one another. We married as soon as she was over her morning sickness, and the reception was held in the Admiral Hawke, the pub where I'd first laid eyes on Sally. My mother and teenage sister shared a battered corner table with Sally's parents, and they all drank sherry and exchanged awkward pleasantries while my mother did her best imitation of the Queen. Meanwhile, the rest of us got on with having a good time. We ate sandwiches made by Mavis, and by seven o'clock the families had retired to their guesthouses, leaving the rest of us free to party. A friend who played in a jazz band provided the music, and we danced ourselves into the ground. Even Sally, up to a point.

'You know, I can't keep getting pregnant and *then* getting married,' she objected loudly, swigging her orange juice. 'It means I don't get my fair share of the champagne.'

'You're not getting married again,' I told her. 'This is your last shot.'

'But what about the champagne?'

'You'll have all the champagne you want when you've given birth to my child.'

She grinned, and then said, 'I wish Cass hadn't had to go home.'

'It's way past her bedtime. Anyway, she had a brilliant time. She told me so.'

'Her dress was lovely, wasn't it?'

I nodded, and proposed another toast, full to overflowing with contentment. 'To our children!' I bellowed, one hand on Sally's stomach, her arm around my waist, and then danced the waltz to the band's classical interpretation of Gary Glitter's latest hit.

At one point, the excitement of it all became too much for me, and I followed Declan outside for a breather.

'Thanks for the speech, mate,' I said. 'Not sure about the bit about the praying mantis, but all the same.'

'No worries,' said Declan. 'It's been a brilliant day. Congratulations.'

'It's all fantastic, isn't it?' The totality of it had been dawning on me slowly all day. I was twenty-five. I'd just married the woman of my dreams and she was expecting my child. And there was more. Now that the alcohol was really hitting home, I felt the sudden need to express myself. 'Declan, I'm going to tell you something no-one else knows except Sally.'

Even through the haze of my drunkenness, I could see that Declan didn't look very excited about this. 'What?'

'I'm writing a book.'

'A book? I thought that was your job.'

'What do you mean, my job?'

'Which is it this time? Dung beetle sex, or that other stuff about sperm?'

'*Meiosis*. Which isn't just sperm. Anyway, it's about neither. Or both. It's about the whole show. The thing is, Declan, everyone's so bloody ignorant. Half the people I meet haven't even heard of Gregor Mendel. You know, I spoke to a girl at a party the other day who thought he was a composer?'

'And you're telling me he isn't?'

He was being deliberately provocative. I decided to put it down to his intrinsic personality, under the influence of drink. 'You see, no-one's explained how it all fits together since Darwin. Yet we know so much more now – there are things coming out every day – and it affects everything. It affects how we think about the world. Or it should, but it doesn't, because no-one knows. The scientists just spend their time digging further down their own little burrows, and the rest of the population doesn't have a fucking clue. No-one has the balls to take on the whole of creation and just tell it like it is.'

'And I presume that you do have the balls.'

'Bloody right I do.'

'Well, I wish you good luck with it. I think we should get back to the party. You're meant to be the star attraction, remember?'

'Aren't you pleased?'

'I'm pleased about everything, Max. I'm pleased about your wife and your child and your amazing career and your brilliant, inspiring book. I just have this sudden need to dance. That okay with you?' He dropped his cigarette onto the ground, pounded it into ash with his shoe, and went back into the pub. Whatever demons were gnawing at him, he exorcised them by dancing outrageously to 'Mamma Mia' and snogging Sally's under-age cousin. Later he came over to me and apologised for his behaviour. 'I'm sorry, Max. I shouldn't be such a cunt. It's your wedding day and I'm your best man. Basically, I'm just in need of a shag.'

I smiled in relief. 'Well, keep your hands off Harriet.'

'Oh, I will. I'm a gentleman. That's half the bloody problem.'

I hadn't noticed that being a particular disability of his before, but I let it pass.

I couldn't have written *Genesis* without Sally. It would never have seemed such a glorious exploit. Besides, she did quite a lot of the work. By the time I'd got to grips with what was involved, my PhD was finished and I'd embarked on my first job, as a junior lecturer. At first I thought it would be easy to do my lecturing, my research on meiosis and knock off a masterpiece in my spare time. But it turned out that all the thoughts I had in my head needed concrete examples, and those examples needed to be dug out of the literature. Sally was pregnant, and had no knowledge of biology outside what I'd told her, but she willingly lent a hand, squeezing her bump between chair and table in the British Library while Cass was in nursery school, scouring dusty texts for mentions of mate-exploitation strategies. It hurt her head, but she was soon sucked in. 'Max!' she cried one day, waddling at top speed back into the flat. 'I've found it! The most perfect example of parasitic castration!'

We conjectured that the baby in Sally's belly was destined to become a scientific genius, endowed as it was with my genes and fed by the biological theories coursing through Sally's blood. 'Do you think that really happens?' Sally asked.

'No,' I told her. 'Of course it bloody doesn't.'

She was the first reader of *Genesis*. Sally saw the examples on other people's pages before I whirled them up into my argument and weaved them into something new. She assumed that it was going to be an academic text, that this was the sort of thing all my colleagues were writing. 'My God,' she said to me with false modesty, because really I could tell that she was proclaiming her own astonishment at how clever she was to understand it, 'I can't believe how simple it all is.'

'That's the great cultural con-trick,' I told her. 'That the rules of the universe are complicated. Mysticism depends upon it. But the rules are not complicated. There is just one rule, out of which all complexity comes. Replicate, or be gone forever.'

At the academic parties – sherry and cocktail sausages in college rooms, or cheese and wine in professors' gardens – my colleagues always displayed a half-polite, half-paranoid interest in what I was writing.

'That's going it a bit strong, Max,' John Hinds said on one occasion, when I'd got to the end of a particularly fruity rant.

'Is it?' Sally pestered on the way home. 'Is it going it a bit strong, do you think? Will we have to change it?'

'Footnotes,' I said scornfully. 'Bloody footnotes. That's all they care about. If I'd been able to equip my speech with footnotes, he'd have had no problem with it. Unless, of course, it threatened one of his own precious theories. I tell you, Sally, academia is the bloodiest ecosystem in the world.'

I dedicated the book to her. In retrospect, I've sometimes

wished I'd thought of acknowledging my debt to Cass instead. But it would not have been right. Sally was my eyes and ears, my comfort and scourge, and most of all, my womb. Her belly made it real. And she believed in it and wanted it to work, when no-one else did, when my colleagues and even Declan were willing it to fail. She believed in it even when I started to lose faith in it myself.

With Antonia gone, Declan had become even more a part of the furniture of our flat, or, more accurately, he was like a human but rather badly disciplined dog, who romped around beside us, and only sometimes got in the way. Sally was better at drawing him out of himself than I was, and once, on a wintry summer evening, with the rain pelting at the window panes and the traffic roaring beneath our flat, one of those leisurely three-way conversions turned into something completely different.

'Why did you come to London?' Sally asked him.

'You've obviously never read the *Plymouth Argus*,' said Declan.

'You mean that it's a crap provincial paper. But you always say you're after an easy life. Surely it can't have been very easy to up sticks from Devon and make your way to London on your own. None of the rest of us did that. Max had Erasmus, I had Antonia and the Slade, Antonia had her parents' house and all her family friends. All you had was a year's experience on this newspaper you say was so awful and the clothes you stood up in. It must have taken an incredible amount of guts.'

'It doesn't take guts to run away.'

'What do you mean, run away?'

My skin began to prickle with the same embarrassment I'd felt when my mother had asked me where Declan lived and what his father did. It seemed enormously important for Declan's sake that such things should not be discussed, especially in front of Sally, who looked out of place even in my own mother's house. But Declan just stretched his legs out across the rag-rug, and leaned against the wall. 'I daresay Max has told you that my mother was a drunk.'

'No, he hasn't,' said Sally. 'Max doesn't talk about parents if he can avoid it.'

I began to splutter a protest, but Sally laid her hand gently on my knee. Declan smirked a little. 'I always wanted to have Max's mother,' he said. 'She's a honey.'

'Yes, she is,' said Sally.

'And mine was too, when I was little. There was only ever just the two of us, and she was such a live wire. I remember her racing me to the end of the street when I was just a kid, and though I ran as fast as I could, she beat me to it. It didn't matter that I lost, because I was so proud of how fast she ran.'

'That's a lovely story,' said Sally.

I listened to her in astonishment, shocked by the sheer well-practised technique of it, and thought back to the discussions we'd had about my own background. Since that first terrible wobble over my father's death, I'd managed to open up very well, and had talked more to her about my parents than to anyone else on earth. Yet perhaps she'd put as much effort into those discussions as she was doing now, prompting with the lightest touch, offering positive feedback wherever possible, and generally appearing almost invisible. Or perhaps she wasn't making any effort at all, and Declan just found it easier to talk about such things than I did. Which was a horrible thought, especially in view of what he was talking about.

'Things got worse, of course,' said Declan. 'You don't really notice it when you're a kid, because you don't understand. But – there came a time when I couldn't imagine that she could ever have run the length of the street. And when I couldn't remember the last time she'd come back from the pub and not hit me. Even then, it wasn't clear cut, because there were times when she'd get really lovey-dovey, and I used to treasure that, because it reminded me of when we'd been happy. But those moods were as unpredictable as her tantrums. Then I got a place at the grammar school, and it was brilliant, because it got me away from her. Which is when I really started to hate her. She used to say—' For the first time his face crumpled into something resembling pain. 'She used to say that I'd turn into her.'

'Oh, Declan.'

'She'd built herself a sort of fortress of self-loathing, and she wanted me to join her there. I should have got out when I first had the chance. When the English master said I ought to go to university. But I couldn't imagine it. It all seemed like such hard work. Really I wanted to work in the garage where I'd spent most of my time since I was a kid. I only said I'd be a journalist to shut Mr Thompson up. Then he produced that job, and it was a bit of a done deal, so I took it. And anyway, I thought I'd already got away from her. It wasn't often I went home, what with my job at the garage – I used to sleep there a lot – and the girls. One of them – her name was Mags – virtually adopted me. So did her mother. And her grandmother. We all slept together in the same room.'

I looked at Sally's face for signs of shock. There were none, and I realised that the person who was emitting such waves of embarrassment was me.

'And it was all right, because there was always going to be a future, and things were always going to move on. Only, once I started working at the *Plymouth Argus*, I suddenly saw that they weren't. It was a job for life. I was fine for a bit, because of the secretaries – much classier girls than Mags, though not half as nice, not really – and I hung around with them, and called one of them my girlfriend, and thought I was the bee's knees. Only then I got bored with the girlfriend, and started rowing with her, and it was then that I had no choice but to go back to Mum's every now and again. Which, of course, was a disaster.'

'She'd got worse?'

'It looked worse. Difficult to tell. She minded the fact that I'd deserted her. She screamed at me that she'd heard I was knocking up every tart in town, that I was a drunk and a slob, that I was a disgrace, and – of course – that people said that I was turning into my mother's son. The problem was, it was true. That night I hit her back. After that, there seemed to be nothing to do but leave.'

A long silence. Sally got up off the floor and poured him a glass of wine. He sipped at it thoughtfully, and said, 'She died six months later.'

'I'm so sorry.' Sally got up again, got another couple of glasses and the bottle, and settled back down again, pouring measures for me and for her. 'You do know that it wasn't your fault, don't you?'

'Yes, I think I do know that.'

'And that you won't turn into your mother.'

'Hey, I might. I don't really care so much any more. Things are better these days, not least thanks to you two.' He raised his glass. 'Cheers. Here's to friendship.'

A lump rose suddenly in my throat, and it was all that I could do to stop myself from bursting into floods of tears, though I had no idea what for. I clinked his glass. 'To friendship,' I mumbled.

'I'll tell you the fantastic thing about you, Max,' said Declan. 'You do it all, so I don't have to.' He waved an outstretched arm around the room, and then nodded towards Sally's bulging stomach. 'Just like when we were in the sixth form. You set your sights high and there was no margin for error. I set mine low and was free to over- or under-achieve as I chose.'

He left a lugubrious pause.

'I suppose the same has been true ever since.'

Early days in our friendship then. Too early for generalisations. But we rarely have a sense of the time being early, just as we never truly comprehend how late it's getting. Certainly Declan stuck to that characterisation of our relationship to one another through all the years that followed. Whether it would have been true if he hadn't, it's impossible to tell.

'I wish he'd get himself a girlfriend,' said Sally longingly. She loved the idea of there being four of us, just as there had when Antonia had been around.

'He has a girlfriend,' I pointed out.

'Really? What's her name?'

I couldn't remember. Declan had graduated from the multiple relationships of his early youth to a fast-paced form of serial monogamy, but it was no easier to keep up.

The first girlfriend of his I remember lasting any significant length of time was called Carolyn. 'She's like Rosalind Russell in *His Girl Friday*,' he announced before he introduced me to her. I spent several days waiting for him to say it again so that I could come up with the witticism I'd been too slow to produce at the time, which involved comparing him unfavourably with Cary Grant. But he didn't repeat it. I was always too slow for Declan.

She turned out to resemble Rosalind Russell in *His Girl Friday* so closely that I felt that her whole life must be based on a study of that film. It was an effort to remember to call her by her real name. I sat with them in a pub, and Carolyn smoked Lucky Strikes and drank whisky in her pin-striped suit while I flinched at the ostentatious aggression of their repartee. Every now and again she would send a glance over to me, and my instinct was to duck. But I was clearly too much of a dolt to be worth more than the occasional passing snipe. I excused myself early and made my own way home, feeling battered.

'What did you think of Carolyn?' Declan challenged me the next time we met.

'Um – I thought she was a bit—'

'Of a bitch,' Declan finished for me. 'Great, isn't it? Makes for fantastic sex.'

'Right.'

Afterwards Declan confessed that they had mistaken antagonism for passion and had bludgeoned one another into bitterness. 'She called me a wimp and a coward and aborted my
baby,' he mourned.

'Oh, my God—'

'I'm relieved about the abortion, obviously. But the insults
are another matter. She's in Vietnam now, did you know that?
Got a byline and everything. That bloody photo keeps staring
at me out of the foreign section. Exactly the same scowl she
used to have in the mornings. Makes me want to lash out with
a toothbrush. Her writing's a pile of shit, too. Stinks of adjec-
tives and egoism.' He abandoned his news-hound growl and
adopted a more elegiac tone. 'I'm beginning to think there are
no big breaks in journalism. Only out of it.'

The idea of Declan as an innocent robbed of his illusions
was hard to swallow. 'Did you ever think there were any big
breaks?'

'I just feel this sense of decline. Foreign correspondent's
suppose to be the top job, you know? It's what the real journalists do. If you want to be Ernest Hemingway – or Martha
Gellhorn, in Carolyn's case – that's what you do. But who wants
to go trudging through the jungle sniffing out napalm? No-one
reads those pages anyway. Not even *you* read those pages. Who
are they writing for, these people?'

I felt a little as the English master must have done when he
cursed young Harris for his lack of ambition. 'Perhaps reporting
isn't your thing. You should focus on writing as well as you
possibly can.'

'Do you know where I was yesterday? Reporting on the World
Conker Championships in Northamptonshire. It probably
won't even make it into the paper, so what's the point in turning
it into great literature? Even with the real stories it doesn't make
any difference. Standards in journalism are really very low. The

shit factor's all that matters. As long as it keeps you occupied while you're having a crap—'

I'd heard Declan's endorsements of the shit factor often enough not to need to hear them again. 'It does make a difference,' I said. 'When it's something interesting—'

'The content of the story might make a difference to you when you're on the bog. But what sort of difference does it make to me? I spend my days hassling the mothers of murdered children, bothering the wives of suspected criminals, and getting in the way of essential police work. At least in Northamptonshire they were glad to see me.'

'You should trust your readers more,' I told him. I was in the first throes of writing *Genesis* at the time, and had all sorts of opinions about readers. 'People do want to read good writing.'

'Not if they buy a newspaper they don't. If they want to read good writing, they'll go out and get a decent book. Actually, they don't even do that. They buy crap newspapers and crap books. And it all gets thrown out with the rubbish in the morning.'

It was at times like this that I wondered whether Declan was a happy person. But even when he was at his most scabrous I still enjoyed his company. He didn't seem to take his avowed misery terribly seriously. If even he, who had an ill opinion of the whole world, could deal with his doubts about humanity, I, with all the riches fortune had bestowed upon me, ought to be able to cope with any I had myself.

And I did have doubts while I was writing *Genesis*. I'd stare at Cass making the minutest adjustments to her misshapen Lego model, or Sally, big with child, sketching her daughter at play, and I'd feel overtaken by the reality of the process I was trying to describe. *All human life is here*. Not even just all human life. I was trying to capture the whole of creation. Surely I was failing. I ought to be working at my research or making notes for my lectures, building up a career that would support the people I loved, and here I was, messing around with something that everyone but Sally seemed to think was way beyond me.

And yet at other times the magnificence of it burst from my every pore. And at those times I knew I was worth a thousand times more to Sally and Cass and my unborn boy if I could only get those thoughts down on paper. They were my readers, and they were my passport to the rest. I had promised Sally from the start that I would give her everything I had, and most of what I had was locked up in my brain. She would read it, and so would Cass, and so would my son, and their universe would become bigger than it would have been without it, and it would be me who had achieved that expansion. And if it was good enough for them, it was good enough for the rest of the world.

So I wrote and wrote, and I finished the manuscript, and a publisher took it, and after many, many months they turned it into a book.

In the months of waiting something bad happened. Two other far more well-established biologists beat me to it, and achieved great success in the process. Their books didn't say exactly the same things as mine, but they were on the same turf.

'It's fine,' my editor told me. 'They've proved there's a market for this kind of thing. Publishers all over town will be commissioning copy-cat versions. We're one step ahead. We've already got it.'

But after all my work and all my dreams, it seemed that fate had deliberately struck to defeat me at the last moment. Perhaps the popular reviewers were bored with reading about biology now. I might not get any reviews at all. Or perhaps just one. There was now only one person in the world I could rely upon to give me column space.

*

'No,' said Declan.

It was betrayal. It was malevolence. And it was caused by his stupid, cussed inability to understand the important things in life. I swore at him a great deal. He remained calm.

'There are several things you're not grasping here, Max,' he said. 'Firstly, I am your oldest friend, and might quite rightly be accused of nepotism. Secondly, I am not a book reviewer. Thirdly, my newspaper does not review books about dung beetles.'

'It's not about fucking dung beetles!'

'No beetle references at all?' He picked up the book. 'What's with the design, then?'

I was very pleased with the cover. It was in jaunty, eye-catching shades of yellow and purple, and it was decorated with a double helix which might or might not be made up from shapes resembling those of insects. On the back was a very large photograph of me. 'Forget the fucking beetles! It's the only favour I've ever asked you. It's the only time I've ever needed your help. You can't let me down now.'

'Really?' said Declan. 'The only favour you've ever asked me?'

His fair point must have been meant to chasten me. It didn't stand a chance. All it did was remind me how I'd over-come his intransigence in the past. I shouted. I stormed. I paced up and down the room. But most importantly, I didn't give up.

'All right,' he submitted wearily in the end. 'I'll review your bloody book. Can't guarantee they'll take it, though.'

I collapsed in exhaustion into a chair. Declan looked at me rather plaintively. 'Does that mean I have to read it?' he said.

I threw it at him.

Two weeks before the publication date, Sally went into labour, a month early. 'Oh, Max,' she cried as I drove her to the hospital, 'I'm not going to make it to the party!'

'Yes, you are. Of course you are. You can both come to the party now.'

I sat white-knuckled in the corridor and annotated the proofs of a chapter I was contributing to an academic tome entitled *Molecular regulation of nuclear events in mitosis and meiosis*. Unlike *Genesis*, the print run was to extend to the hundreds rather than the thousands, and mine was the shortest chapter in the book. But my major review was coming up in a year and a half's time. It would decide whether I would be granted tenure at Erasmus or be turned out on my ear, and its success was dependent on publications such as this. *Genesis* didn't count, because it was written for the general public, not for the men who would sit in judgment on my career. It was vital that I got it right, and it was due back to the editor in only two days, childbirth or no childbirth.

'Centremere?' I shrieked aloud, to the consternation of passing nurses. 'Who are these jokers? Any fool knows it's centromere—'

And I scrabbled back through my own manuscript to check it was the typesetters' error and not my own. I was right. I'd written 'centromere' every time—

A pencil snapped in my fingers. Then another. I knew at heart that the source of my panic came from beyond the pages in my hands, but I couldn't afford to think about it. 'Meosis?' I wailed. 'They've missed out an i. How could they miss out an i? Can't they see from the text that they can't go around missing out i's? What if meiosis itself left things out, or added new things in, or randomly changed one letter for another—' And then I had to stop, because I had realised that, however rarely, that was exactly what meiosis did sometimes do.

Just like typesetting, meiosis was a process of copying. The aeons of evolution had honed it almost to perfection, but no copying process was free of errors. And meiosis was a particularly important copying process. It was the process by which sperm and egg cells were created, and it was responsible for the transmission of one individual's genes into the next generation.

The text I'd written talked in abstruse terms about anaphase in a species of vinegar fly. But behind it, before it, beneath it and above it lay a history whose culmination was taking place in a ward very near to me. Nine months ago, a single sperm cell amongst millions had set out from the warm haven of my gonads to begin an epic journey, swimming a distance through Sally's uterus equivalent to the Atlantic, in treacle, to be united with her egg. The resulting embryo was the unique product of a history of the swaps, cross-overs and shufflings of the DNA of a billion generations. My own genetic inheritance had been copied millions of times before I produced that happy swimmer. It was an unfathomably long series of replications: how could it be guaranteed to produce a foolproof recipe for a human being?

Of course, human cells were more efficient in their replicatory efforts than typesetters – they had a mutation rate of about thirty for every million sperm cells I produced, as opposed to the one word in thirty sentences which I observed before me. But given that I emitted three hundred million with each ejaculation, it was likely that there were quite a few mutants amongst them. And despite the positive influence of mutation on evolution over the course of a billion years, such effects never took place in the here and now. The chances of my publishers' bunglings actually producing an enhancement to the work were so remote as to be non-existent. In something as complex as a book, an error, even if only half-random, was always an injury. But at least with the book, they had succeeded only in mangling the sense. Paper, binding, ink all held together just the same. In a human being, the tiniest misspelling of the way to produce haemoglobin, or how to control muscular growth, would result in deformity, miscarriage or death.

I stared down at the copy on my lap. The mutations screamed at me from the pages. Some of them might have been there from the beginning; others were completely new. I remembered *Genesis*, and my cheerful thoughts of publication when I was putting the finishing touches to my corrections of the proofs. My intellectual offspring was now sitting in the distributors' boxes, waiting to be loaded onto the bookshelves. With any errors I'd missed still inside them.

Another pencil snapped. 'Doctor!' I howled as another medical functionary strolled past.

The doctor turned. I showed him the remains of my pencil. He lifted another from his breast pocket, and then he left me.

As his back departed down the corridor, my mind screamed after him still.

Please God, let him be whole.

He was the most beautiful child that had ever been born.

'I told you it'd be a boy,' I crowed at Sally.

She managed an exasperated look. I kissed her again, and then kissed him, and then tried to kiss both of them at once. 'Get off,' she remonstrated, but she was smiling and crying.

'Was it less frightening this time?' I demanded.

'No.' But I knew she was lying. I'd been out there in the corridor, willing her onwards every step of the way.

'You're marvellous,' I said, over and over again.

'Who are you talking to?'

Her. And the baby. And perhaps, just a very little, myself.

The party to which Sally had referred on her way to the hospital was our substitute for a launch party, which we'd decided to host ourselves as soon as it became clear that the publishers, an academic press, didn't go in for that sort of thing. I pushed it back a fortnight to take account of the interruption to our schedule, invited everyone we knew, and instructed them all to bring champagne. Sally, wan and wobbly from childbirth, was particularly zealous in its consumption. The guests, many of them Sally's artistic friends, were rather bewildered to be asked to celebrate the launch of what they saw as a scientific paper, but my euphoria brooked no dampening. 'It's going to be in bookshops,' I told them.

The child, whom we named William, was a prize exhibit. Even at little more than a month old, he was a caricature of me. 'Some have touted it as a deliberate evolutionary strategy,' I explained to those who started at the sight of his shock of black hair and his confrontational demeanour. 'It is a well-acknowledged tendency for children to bear a striking resemblance to their fathers in the few weeks after birth. It makes sense, except that it would be a very poor strategy for the genes of an adulterer. This means that we can either accept the phenomenon as proof that men's children are more commonly born to their own partner than to someone else's, or decide that it is a psychological fabrication of a collective mind inclined to seek tangible proof of rightful paternity. I personally have no opinion one way or the other.'

Declan sat in the corner, monopolising the vodka. 'Well?' I confronted him. 'Did you read it?'

He gazed at the child in my arms with bloodshot eyes. 'You've really pulled it off this time, Max,' he said, his mouth picking its way through the words with slow, bitter emphasis. 'You've just done the two things most conducive to peace of mind for a self-regarding organism in a universe with no possibility of an after-life and no room for God. You've published, and you've reproduced.'

The noise of the room seemed abruptly to cease, as if a lid had been put on it. 'What are you talking about?'

He said nothing. One of Sally's arty friends attempted to lift the mood. 'Are you going to review the book, Declan?' she asked.

'No,' said Declan.

'What do you mean, you're not going to review it?' I screeched. 'You gave me your word. I've told the publisher. You'll make me look a fool.'

'You won't need me to review it,' said Declan, his voice as dead as dust. 'And no-one is going to call you a fool.'

'Describes with lightness and skill the secrets of the universe . . . Will find a place in every educated person's library . . . The passage on the dung beetle is amongst the most lyrical pieces of prose I have read in the last decade . . . A true mystery story. By the end there is not a single jigsaw piece out of place . . . This astonishingly young maverick has established himself amongst the titans of scientific thought . . . No-one has made it clearer since Darwin himself.'

The applause clattered through my veins every minute of every day. It roared when I kissed my wife; it surged when I held my baby son. Then every now and again that strange silence returned, and I felt dizzy with fear. What on earth could be wrong? Life had never been more intense or more complete. Then I knew. It was the flipside of my mania. Nothing can last forever. To feel a sense of completeness is to know that you will die. I had no option but to find more noise to drown the silence out.

Yet what is life but a glorious and unstoppable noise, if you let it be? One day I looked at the balance of our bank account and saw something we'd never anticipated. We had money. On an impulse, I decided to buy a house. 'Where shall we live?' I asked a stunned Sally.

'I don't know. Somewhere cheap?'

We chose Islington, because it was unfashionable enough to be less expensive than most of the other places we knew, and also because it was only a short pram-push to the relevant estate agents. Soon we found ourselves in possession of a rambling and dilapidated house in a Victorian terrace, with a garden and a view of the canal. The French windows opened out onto a garden tangled with fruit trees. As soon as we saw it, both Sally and I were sure that the kids would adore it, especially the garden. It would be like having Regent's Park at the back of the house, I told Cass.

'With trees?'

'Lots of trees. I tell you what, I'll build you and William a treehouse.'

She looked suddenly wary. 'William can't go in the tree-house.'

'He's too little now, obviously. But when he's older you can play up there together.'

It's funny how a child can appear to understand something perfectly then turn out not to have taken it in at all. We explained to her about the move at great length. And for the first few days she rushed around the new house in a state of excitement, opening all the cupboards to look for secret passages and drawing pictures of herself in the yet-to-be-built treehouse. But then she started to look less happy.

'When are we going home?' she began to ask.

'This is home, sweetheart. We don't ever have to go back to King's Cross any more.'

'No, but when are we going home?'

'I suppose she thinks we're on holiday,' Sally said after Cass had gone to bed. 'After all, King's Cross is all she's ever known. It probably feels too good to be true.'

Cass didn't look as if she thought it was good at all. At Edenbridge Terrace she had a proper bedroom of her own, and after those first few days she virtually barricaded herself up there, coming out only for meals. When I was at work, Sally went to talk to her in her room, and tried to tease out of her what was wrong. At the end of the day she had bad news.

'Max,' she said, 'she thinks this isn't her house. She thinks we're going to send her away.'

'But where on earth would she get that idea?'

'She thinks that now we have William we don't need her.'

Of course there had been a great many changes in a short space of time – the wedding, the birth and now the move. And the baby got a great deal of attention, because he was a baby.

'Max,' said Sally, 'I think you should talk to her. I mean, it's all very well that we've always made it clear about you not being her real father, but we haven't said anything since William was born. I think she needs to hear from you that it doesn't make any difference. It's no good me telling her.'

So with a quaking heart I entered her soft little sanctuary in the attic. As I ascended the stairs, I could hear the sound of humming. When my foot landed on the top, creaky step, it stopped.

I bent under the beam. She was sitting on the carpeted floor, and around her stood a collection of Lego figures standing in front of their houses, some half-assembled, others with parasols or bits of fire engines sticking out of the roofs. She took her hands away from them and stared up at me with fearful, guilty eyes.

'Cass,' I said, then ran out of words.

How do you speak to a child? If only I could just sit down and explain exactly how it all seemed to me. For a moment I considered doing just that. But this was a person who was just at the beginning of piecing together her understanding of the world. A sentence whose vocabulary was beyond her would not just be misconstrued, it would be used as a reference point for that which came afterwards. I must keep it simple. This was not a time to expand her knowledge, but to reconfirm the basics.

'Cass, you know you're my little girl, don't you?'

Silence. Her tiny form was hunched over the plastic houses,

the protective mistress of Lilliput. I sat on the floor, so as to approximate something closer to her level.

'You do, don't you?'

'Max—'

And in that word, I saw half the problem. William was already learning to say *Dadda*. We should have thought about it at the start. But how presumptuous it would have been for me to go around assuming parenthood when I had only known her a few weeks. Now it was too late. I could not change my name.

'Cass, come here. Come and sit on my knee.'

'You haven't *got* any knees.'

I crossed my legs. 'Yes I have. Sit here.'

She crawled slowly over the houses and deposited herself carefully in the crook of my leg. I put an arm round her. 'Cass, you know you had a daddy before you were born. He gave your mummy a present, and that present was you.'

She wriggled and said nothing.

'But that daddy can't be with you any more. So I came along to look after you.' It didn't seem to be enough, not even to me. I wanted to describe how it had been when I'd first seen her, but I couldn't find the words. 'And you're my little girl, and I love you very dearly, and I'll always be here to look after you. You do understand that, don't you?'

Another wriggle. 'Yes,' she said doubtfully, and turned her face to look up at mine. It was creased with confusion, as if I'd missed something out. And I had. I'd missed it out because it wasn't true. I was not her real daddy.

'Give Max a hug,' I said. 'Go on. Max needs a hug.'

At that she suddenly flung her arms around me, and hugged very hard. The little fingers pinched into my skin through my jumper. I tilted her face so that I could see it. Still no tears.

'You know it'll never matter,' I whispered to her. 'You're my best girl. My own best girl.'

And at last her face lightened. 'Really?' she said. 'Your *very* best girl?'

'Absolutely,' I said. 'Come on, sweetheart. Let's go and see Mummy.'

I carried her downstairs. That evening, Cass sat on my knee while we watched television, and, just for once, William was not allowed to join us.

And despite such upheavals, within months, the four of us grew into our new shell as if the old one could never have fitted us. Though it threatened vaguely to fall down around our ears, the house in Edenbridge Terrace had corridors which turned in unexpected ways, rooms that ran into one another, cupboards built into the walls. The batik drapes and amateurish pen-and-ink sketches of King's Cross were all gone. Instead there were bare wooden floors, earthen-coloured rugs, chunky pine furniture and oil paintings by real artists. Sally's huge kitchen was dominated by the Aga, from which she produced voluminous lentil soups and experimented with jam-making, and Cass, who had always been quite a sombre little girl, blossomed into an apple-cheeked maid, who invented a series of stories about the creatures who lived under the floorboards and sang operas of her own composition in the bath. Her dreaminess was counterpointed by the sturdy, investigative presence of William, who dismantled everything he could lay his little hands on and could recite the definition of evolution to my colleagues by the age of two. We still had parties, but the surprise was that despite being respectable affairs they were even noisier than before, with the children running races in the garden and the adults indulging in heated small talk inside. Antonia visited us from America, and said that the emergence of William was making us start to face up to our responsibilities. In truth, we were growing up. And what they never tell you about being grown up is that it is even noisier than being a child.

*

The events piled upon one another. My major review came and went, and I was granted tenure. Sally fell pregnant again. My book was taken up by a publisher in the States, and I was invited there to do a book tour. These things happened in such quick succession that we ended up combining my tenure party with my leaving party and forcing Sally to abstain from the champagne once more. A flicker more of time and I was gone, and the American section of this story commences.

But there is one thing which I have been unable to fit into the spaces between all this activity. Declan attended that leaving party at Edenbridge Terrace. He turned up on our doorstep with whisky-stained breath, proffering a bunch of wilted carnations and a bottle of kirsch. But when I opened that door, my reaction was not what it would have been in the days when he used to drop round to our flat in King's Cross. My mouth fell open and the wine glass dropped from my hand. I screamed for Sally.

'Hi,' said Declan, just the same as ever.

Sally rushed to my side, stood stock still, and then threw herself into his arms. I just stood there. We had lived in Edenbridge Terrace for almost eighteen months, and it was the first time he'd darkened its door. The last time I'd seen him was at the launch party for *Genesis*, and we had not heard a word from him since.

I suppose the problem is that if I had told the story of his leaving in the proper chronological place it would have dominated proceedings, and the truth is that it did not. We were hurt, we were bewildered and we went to great lengths to track him down. After we'd found his address, Sally sent him a weekly letter just as she did Antonia, and kept going even though we never received a reply. But we simply didn't have time to worry about it too much. What wondering could we do, when there was so little indication of what had caused him to cut off contact so peremptorily? And how can I write about what I felt about it now, when there is nothing I can phrase but a series of questions?

I am as fond of Declan as I am of anyone outside my immediate family. But the fact is that when someone leaves with such an implied V-sign hanging in the air, there is little choice but to carry on without them. We did our best to find reasons. They never arrived. And after all, it was only eighteen months. Had he left for longer, we might have had to piece our friendship together all over again if it was to survive at all. But he returned exactly as he'd been before, with only an ostentatious air of mystery to show for his adventures, as if he'd come back from a holiday on the set of *The Third Man*. He never apologised and he never explained. I might have had it out with him if I'd had time. But I had to leave within a fortnight. And when I came back I was different, and he seemed more established in the rhythm of the life I'd left behind than I was.

Even after all the years of our continued friendship, and all the years of never thinking about it at all, it makes me angry just to start to try to explain what happened. I don't remember feeling this way at the time. Perhaps I did and I just made sure it didn't affect me too much. But he left without a fucking word. He insulted me at my launch party and then he just went. The first I heard of it was when I called him at his office and was informed that he was now the 'West Berlin desk' and that they couldn't give me a number on which I could contact him.

I still have an article he wrote during his stint in Germany. God knows why I kept it. Maybe I thought it was the last I'd hear of him. It certainly had a somewhat nihilistic tone.

'This is an easy town for strangers,' the newspaper said. 'No-one feels entirely at home in these streets. It is a city poised between vibrancy and resentment, never sure what it is or what it wants to be. My companions – I am not sure that anyone would admit to the ease of friendship – include Americans on the run from the draft and Europeans escaping from a dozen murky pasts. The drugs, the prostitution and the spies in every room are symptoms of a city on an endless quest for escape. Some of the younger German migrants are passionate admirers of the communism practised on the other side of the Wall, and talk endlessly about crossing over, but rarely do. Others are here in a statement of defiance against the evil Eastern Bloc, harking back to the Airlift and President Kennedy's visit, and strike a pose of heroism in justification of the vast subsidies that keep the place alive. Only the older native Berliners are quiet on the topic, living in the satellite of a nation most have never visited, and stranded within another that contains friends and relatives they have not seen in thirty years. All know that the situation cannot be sustained forever. And though experience prevents all but the young and wild from believing that any change can be for the better, the impermanence of the place endows its inhabitants with a liberty that is entirely out of keeping with the barbed wire on the walls of the fortress. Our freedom is not geographical or even political. In a city at the heart of history, drenched with it and scarred by it, we are nevertheless freed from the heaviest chains of all: those of the past.'

What the fuck past did he think he was escaping from? He was not, to my knowledge, on the run from the police. Nothing he had ever said to me, not even the conversation Sally had drawn out of him, had suggested any burden too great to be supported. All I could remember were his words to me at that launch party, when he'd refused once more to review my book, despite his promises to the contrary. He'd read it and rejected it, and it was in some ways the first really bad review that I ever received. But I had no idea what that review actually said.

When I'd written that book, I had no ideas of fame or increased reputation or enough money to buy a house. All I wanted was to explain the world more clearly to the people I knew. Now Declan had read it and he'd taken it not as a gift but as some sort of insult. Yet all there was in it was science. How could it have any bearing on the relationship between him and me?

I do not remember thinking these thoughts at the time, but I also have no sense of thinking them for the first time now. They are so obvious. And the idea that I cannot lift from my brain is that with Declan's re-emergence so fresh in my mind, I must have carried them with me to America. There he was, unrepentant, with no casual mention of – 'Oh yes, and well done about the book. Always knew it'd be a success. Bloody marvellous.' Nothing. If I couldn't get through to him, what the fuck chance was I supposed to stand out there?

And now I begin to wonder. Margot's article is beside me, as it has been throughout. There are a few words within it which have been niggling at me, not because of their content, but because their source is so clearly traceable. 'I am not saying that Oldroyd leads a wholly solitary life,' she has written. 'His friends attest to his faithfulness through thick and thin, even if he has not always understood quite how thin those times have sometimes been.'

Who but Declan could 'attest' to that? The plural must be journalistic licence, because there is no-one else. She is his colleague. It would be unnatural for her to do a profile of me without at least asking him for his views. No wonder he felt responsible. Perhaps he even knew what she had written before it was published.

And as I try to stem the tide of doubt – why didn't Declan tell me he was going to Berlin? What grudges has he been holding against me all these years? – I know it is him I should call, and yet I cannot. I don't know what to accuse him of. If he were responsible just for that one sentence, then it wouldn't be much. But there is so much more in the article. It presents a vision of my whole life, and I find it hard to believe that it is Declan's vision.

Yet there are so many things about him which I know I don't understand.

Why not that, as well?

6

There were hints before I went to America that *Genesis* was not as simple a book as I thought. The first, I suppose, came from Declan but, as I have explained, I found his response impossible to interpret. The second was easier: it came from the 'general readers' who, to my delight and surprise, bought the book in such large quantities. Despite the way I'd scoffed at the ignorance of the reading public to Declan on my wedding day, it turned out that I'd underestimated their ignorance. My aim had originally been to show how the scientific discoveries of recent years had deepened and modified a theory which had been in the world for more than a century. But though the phrase 'the survival of the fittest' had since become as easy a cliché as 'too many cooks spoil the broth', it turned out that most people had very little inkling of what it actually meant. When readers expressed shock or wonderment at what I had written, I was amazed to find that their consternation was caused not by the new truths, but rather by the old.

I should have taken these early signs as a warning. After all, Darwin's works themselves had produced quite a stir at the time of publication. A century of false opposition, even falser emulation and finally, ignorant assimilation, should have alerted me to the fact that a truth imbibed is not necessarily a truth absorbed. But youth is rarely inclined towards humility, and I assumed that all this astonishment was caused by my own exceptional powers of expression. Not once did it occur to me that it might be a kind of perpetual astonishment, an instinctive and evolved reaction to a genus of truth which the human species is ill-disposed to hear.

As the months went on, I had the opportunity to observe reactions more vicious than mere astonishment. My scientific colleagues at Erasmus College began to disdain me for daring to court a 'popular' readership; they claimed that their dissatisfaction was caused by the fact that I had written the book too young, and had failed to footnote it sufficiently, leading to potential misunderstandings on the part of the public. But I was sure that what they resented was that I had thrown open the doors of the ivory tower of science, enabling their rivals in other departments to converse with them on subjects within their own domain. In a way I could understand this reaction, because I myself was the primary victim of these pseudo-scientific commentators. Psychologists; educators; philosophers; sociologists; parliamentarians – each had their particular barbs to wield. I was not alone in becoming a kind of pincushion, because mine was not the only book of its kind. But I felt alone, because the scientists who should have been my staunchest allies became, in the midst of all this debate, my attackers too. They were my competitors for the public ear; it was imperative to them that they should prove my writings inferior to theirs; and when they struck at me, I didn't withhold from striking back. I was not the sole cause of what later became known as the 'Darwin wars', but I was intimately involved in their initiation. The battle is raging still.

But in the year and a half between my book's publication and my trip to the States, I held firm, taking issue with the scientific protectionism of my colleagues and insisting that the way forward was to explain further, explain more clearly, and explain again. And when it came, the invitation to America seemed like a vindication. It came garlanded with panegyrics to my eloquence that could never have been expressed by an English pen, and even before I left my own country, I had already begun to think of my curmudgeonly critics as being a local phenomenon that would be swept away by the fresh winds of thought that circulated in America. In a way I was right. But not in quite the way I expected.

In 1978 there were still Maxis and Morris Minors on the streets of London, with no irony implied. It took eight hours to drive in one of those rickety contraptions from Islington to my mother-in-law's house in Dorset, little more than a hundred miles away. No M25, no service stations, no traffic warnings on the radio. Black and white TVs were only just shading into obsolescence; there were three channels; and only common people watched the one with advertisements. Calculators, for those who could afford them, were much the same size as televisions. Telephones had dials that clicked as you dragged your finger round them, and digital watches were still a dream. The Queen's silver jubilee had been celebrated the previous summer with street parties from Land's End to John O' Groats, and every child in the land had been presented with a special coin. It rained a great deal, as it had for one and a half years, to make up for the unaccountably sunny weather of the previous two summers. The winter of discontent was looming. The stoical public erected its umbrellas, stashed its candles, bought British, and thought itself lucky.

I, however, had other plans. I left my family on the observation platform at Heathrow, and half an hour later was looking down through my first aircraft window. The cardboard houses of the West London suburbs passed beneath me, then the weeny fields of Middle England, and finally, the grand blue Atlantic. Nine hours later, I touched down in the New World.

It was my first trip abroad. How odd that seems, now that no twenty-year-old's education is complete without a lengthy sojourn taking in war zones, lost tribes and tropical oases. But my childhood was spent as a member of what must have been one of the least-travelled generations in centuries. The Empire, which I have always thought was the official British pretext for escaping the ghastly weather, was gone, and charter flights barely invented. When I was a child, my father avoided travel at all costs once he was at home, and my mother would not go anywhere without him. And whilst the cultural liberation of the sixties had enabled many of my contemporaries to rebel against their static inheritance by jumping onto trains and aping the Grand Tours of the previous century, or even by donning beards and kaftans and setting out to find new gurus in the East, such gallivanting had always looked essentially frivolous to me. The most exotic journeys I'd made to date were those from Plymouth to take up my place at Oxford, and then on to London, to discover the big wide world. It didn't occur to me to venture any further afield until I received the invitation from Columbia University to visit New York.

None of this prepared me for what I found when I got there. It should not have come as a shock to me that the buildings in Manhattan were tall or that the cabs were yellow. I had seen these things often enough in films. But I think that on some subconscious level, when the brain registers that the things seen on a cinema screen are different from the things outside the cinema, it attributes the difference to that between fiction and the real world. The fantastical is safely enclosed within the auditorium, and life afterwards proceeds just the same. Stepping off that plane was precisely like the moment in the Woody Allen film *The Purple Rose of Cairo*, when the hero of the movie Mia Farrow is watching stretches out an arm and lifts her into the screen.

It was November. I looked up from the cavernous New York streets to the glitter of glass, and beyond it, to ice-blue skies. The people who swarmed about me wore gaily coloured scarves and talked of snow at Christmas. They were joyfully, unself-consciously hospitable, and I entered home after warm gleaming home, speechless before the stylish modern furniture and the ubiquitous appliances. Then I called Sally. She held a candle, shivering, to the phone, and told me in a dull voice about the power cuts and the rubbish and the incessant rain. Britain was steeped in its own obsolescence, paused in freeze-frame at the moment before it was dragged screaming and kicking into a newer and harsher era. I saw the only world I'd ever known as if in the wing mirror of a car, smaller than it should be and receding at a great pace into the distance.

Because the tour itself was proving successful beyond any imaginings. I'd given a lot of talks about the book at home, and the audiences had shown a great deal of interest. But in England, promoting the book meant standing in draughty corridors waiting for audiences that no-one had remembered to invite, having esoteric discussions with strange middle-aged men with glasses and greasy hair who'd walked in off the street, drinking cold tea and being polite to sweet little old ladies who ran bookshops. In America success felt as success was supposed to be. At the end of my first lecture I received a standing ovation. When the audience first got to its feet I thought it was going to stage a walk-out, and when they started clapping I stared at them in alarm. Then it dawned on me what was going on. Something changed in me at that moment. It was as if a new valve in my brain had opened. Generations of my family had practised British reticence without a single known lapse, but acquired characteristics are not inherited and can be shed. I saw and heard a response, and instead of deflecting it as I had always been trained to do, I let it in. The applause grew louder. I smiled.

Professors twice my age booked personal appointments to ask my advice on making their own books accessible to a wider audience. My most difficult experience was a public seminar I was asked to give on the subject of the sociological implications of Darwinism, where an excessively bespectacled woman put it to me that all adolescent males should have their sperm extracted and then be castrated, for the future good of the species. Even this was invigorating. After I'd got over the shock of seeing all my best jokes fall flat, I came to admire and be stimulated by the great earnestness of the American student population. I might not always agree with them, but the fire which fuelled their beliefs burned as brightly as my own.

More universities booked me. Yale. Harvard. At MIT I was offered a job. 'It's a big decision, I know that,' said the enormous professor, smiling encouragingly. 'I know you gotta go home and have a think about it. Take your time. You just let me know if you wanna come out here and we'll see what we can do.'

I blinked and stuttered, too excited to be able to tell what I thought about it. Then Caltech agreed to fly me across to LA. Even Sally was pleased about that, because it meant that I could stay with Antonia, in Santa Monica. Antonia had been in California for more than three years by that time, and was running a reasonably successful aromatherapy business from an apartment which she assured me was modest but whose front wall turned out to be almost entirely made of glass. Each morning I stood before it with my mug of freshly brewed coffee, and squinted at the distant and truncated view of the sea.

It was during my stay with Antonia that a slightly different request came through. My agent called me from London and told me that I'd been asked to speak in a series of talks all over the South and Mid-West. 'Really?' I said. 'Which universities?'

'It's not universities. I get the impression you'll be the guest of the towns themselves.'

The towns themselves! My heart raced. I had been overjoyed to speak at places such as Harvard and Yale, of course, but this invitation struck a deeper chord. After all, my original inspiration for the book had been my frustration at meeting so many non-scientists who had no idea how evolution worked. I knew that in Britain my writings had become the topic of dinner-party conversations, but that was still a small and select audience. Perhaps here, in ever-adventurous America, I was breaking through to the masses.

'Three days till you're home!' exclaimed Sally on the phone. 'Oh, Max, I'm so dying to see you. I can barely believe—'

'Oh, Sally,' I said, and I did know even then that it was a betrayal. There was no dishonesty or ill-will, but I couldn't deny that I was putting my need to wring every last drop of success out of this tour above my need for her. 'I have to stay a bit longer, I'm afraid. It's not very long. Just two more weeks.'

'Two weeks? Why?'

It did seem awful. Then an outrageous thought sprang into my brain, prompted by the endless possibilities of the world around me. 'I tell you what. Why don't you and the kids come over? You can stay with Antonia, I'm sure she'd be delighted to have you. It could be a holiday. We've never had a holiday abroad.'

'Max, are you out of your mind? I can't fly. I'm pregnant. And it's term time. Cass has to go to school. I've never heard anything so ridiculous in my life.'

I tried to think myself to the place she was in, and could see how it would look from there, with the rain pouring outside and the grey prosaic streets a barrier to any adventure. We have to get out of that country, I thought, impatient with her Englishness and my own. 'All right,' I said. 'But I do have to stay for just a bit longer. There's a few more talks I have to do.'

She was silent for a moment. 'You will be back for Christmas, won't you, Max?'

'Of course I will.'

'There won't be a few more talks after this as well?'

'No. I promise.'

It didn't feel very good putting down the phone after that conversation. I felt as if I'd sinned, though there really was very little for which I could blame myself. Sally was supportive of my career, and this was part of it. It was just one of those things.

Now I wish she'd put up more of a fight. Then I might have got straight on that plane back home, and none of it would have happened.

'Dr Powell, I presume.'

The little man with the placard marked 'Oldroyd' put it hastily to one side. 'Dr Oldroyd! Swell to meet you.' We shook hands vigorously.

'So kind of you to come to the airport,' I said.

The little man looked at me oddly for a moment, as if assessing me, and then his smile became even broader. 'Here's my car.'

It was rather more battered than most of those I'd come across in California. I squeezed myself into the passenger seat and we set off. Within minutes the freeway had lost its lanes and was carving its course through the sort of endless openness I'd dreamt of ever since watching *Easy Rider*. The city receded into a small island of towers behind us.

'Jesus,' I said.

Powell twitched. 'You okay there?'

'Sorry. It's just – this is all completely new to me. I haven't really been out into the countryside before, or at least only the bit between Santa Monica and Pasadena, which doesn't really count—'

'This your first time in the States?'

'Yes. I think it's absolutely terrific. In fact I'm thinking of moving here – well, of course, I'll have to see what the wife thinks about it.'

'Here? To Shirley County?'

'Oh, goodness, no. To a university—' I realised my faux pas, and stopped short.

'We have a university.'

'I'm sure you do.'

'You haven't heard of it?'

Of course I bloody hadn't. 'Possibly – er—'

To my surprise, Powell looked even more self-satisfied than before. But the rest of the journey was passed in silence.

The first sign of civilisation was the trees. Then the occasional gas station or cluster of houses. Then suburbs, sprawling half-heartedly on and on, until almost without warning, we were in another city, smaller even than the one I'd flown into, but still marked with the inevitable high-rise downtown. Extraordinary, I thought. On the island of Manhattan there was a full evolutionary justification for building tall. But here, where the space was so endless – perhaps it was a matter of huddling against the vastness of America. It was impossible to tell. For the first time since I'd stepped onto the continent, I felt a truly sinister shiver of ignorance.

'Well, here we are,' said Powell, and we pulled into a parking lot.

Afterwards, I knew I should have seen the plaque at the entrance to the building; the posters on the walls; the people passing out leaflets; the coaches parked outside. At the time all I saw was my own name. I smiled at the leaflet distributors and walked in.

It was a sort of village hall, except bigger, and it was packed to the brim. Most of the audience was already seated on its rickety chairs, though some were milling around, exchanging sandwiches, chatting in excitement. On the whole, they were simply dressed, and ranged right through every age group. I noticed that there were rather a lot of children. Well, I thought, if they could persuade schoolkids from the back of nowhere to attend scientific talks, then all the accusations the snobbish English made about the United States being an uncultured society were just plain wrong. 'Goodness,' I said to Powell. 'They're already here.'

'Debate starts in five minutes,' said Powell.

'That's terribly efficient. No unnecessary hanging around.' And then, 'Debate?'

I felt a tug on my arm, and turned. The face of a bespectacled youth beseeched me urgently. 'Dr Oldroyd. My name's Dan Gorman. I loved your book. If I could just have a quick word with you—'

Dr Powell walked swiftly around the back of me and then right through the clasp between the young man's hand and my arm. 'Five minutes to go, Dr Oldroyd. We need to get going. Let's go up to the platform.'

Dan Gorman retaliated and darted to the other side. 'Seriously, Dr Oldroyd. It's important that you know—'

For a moment I was caught in a ridiculous tug of war between Dan's restraining hand and Powell's propelling arm. I shook both of them off and stared at them in astonishment. 'I have no idea what you're talking about,' I said. 'I'll proceed to the platform, if that's all right with you.'

Dan sank back into the crowd, and Powell darted after me, running up the steps to catch up. 'Your place is over there, Dr Oldroyd,' he said, as I made to sit down. 'That's Dr Vernon's chair.'

By now I was thoroughly annoyed as well as confused, and almost sat down anyway. 'And who is Dr Vernon?'

'I'll be doing introductions momentarily.'

With bad grace, I complied. Powell took a seat at the edge of the stage. My chair was at the other side. The chair reserved for Dr Vernon was right in the centre. The audience didn't seem to have noticed my own appearance at all.

Suddenly there was a whoop from the back of the hall. I strained my eyes and saw a man about twenty years my senior walking slowly down the aisle, pausing occasionally to shake a hand or share a few words with the nearest members of the audience. The whooping spread, then was overtaken by clapping. Dr

Powell stood up. As the man ascended the steps, Powell moved towards him, and shook his hand heartily before guiding him to his seat in centre stage. Powell held up his hand to the overexcited audience, and they gradually stilled.

'Brothers and sisters,' he said, 'thank you for coming here tonight, for what I'm certain will be a great evening. I introduce you to Dr Franklin Vernon, from the Academy of Scientific Creationism in California.'

The *what*? My brain did a backflip. I'd encountered the occasional religious fanatic in my previous talks, attacking my book on the basis that it contradicted the Bible, but they'd been so obviously demented that they'd given me a damn sight less trouble than the feminists and the black separatists. Surely this couldn't be some sort of – *organised* madness? This man was from an Academy. It was Scientific. The term 'creationism' must mean something else out here. Yet around me the whooping and clapping had broken out again.

'And,' said Powell, using his hand to quieten the crowd once more, but with more difficulty this time, 'our visitor from overseas, Dr Max Oldroyd. Dr Oldroyd has travelled all the way from London in England to be with us tonight.'

At last the audience fell into an awestruck hush. But there was something wrong with the quality of the silence. I caught the eye of a boy on the front row. He couldn't have been older than twelve, and he was actually rubbing his hands in glee.

'The form the debate will take is that Dr Vernon will talk for forty-five minutes on the topic of God's grand design for the universe. After that, Dr Oldroyd will offer a rebuttal, based on his arguments from his recent book promoting the evolutionist religion, *Genesis*. Dr Vernon will then be given five minutes to respond to this rebuttal, and Dr Oldroyd's final five minutes will allow him to have the last word.'

Forty-five minutes? Afterwards there were so many things I should have done at that moment. But I felt exactly like an undergraduate who had forgotten that it was his turn to give the paper at the weekly seminar. I stared down at my copy of *Genesis*, which I'd marked with pen and bookmarks to give my standard twenty-minute reading. Oh, fuck. Then rebellion rose up in me, just as it would have done in such situations when I had really been a student. If this was a bunch of religious crackpots, they were mincemeat, the lot of them. They had absolutely no idea what they had taken on.

'My friends,' said Dr Vernon. I regarded my opponent. He was a fat man with a bulbous nose and unwieldy features, his body squeezed into an expensive suit. There was an aura about him of bad health and extreme wealth. But a fine voice. Mine is finer, I thought. In Philadelphia someone had asked me whether I had ever sung jazz.

'Our distinguished guest here' – and I had learnt to hear by now the way the Americans frequently tried to ape an English accent when they addressed me. This man was conceding my enunciatory advantage already – 'has written a book which has enjoyed some measure of success, both in his country and ours. Some of you may have read it. Some of you may have been impressed, as I was, by its persuasiveness and its eloquence. Some of you may have even have been convinced by its arguments. If that is the case, then this is evidence of his seductive writing style. My friends, I am here to issue you with a warning. Do not be taken in by his arguments. They use every trick in the book.'

He was accusing me of lying. It was preposterous. I had never lied in my life, and no-one had ever suggested that I might. Yet it was beginning to make sense. This man was a churchman, whatever academic appendages he might have stapled to his name. He was a man of God, and he was afraid. The truths in *Genesis* were a threat to his dwindling congregation, and he was trying to get them back. But how foolish, to invite the wolf round for supper. Superstition could hold no candle to self-evident truth. Religion was dying in the face of science, and this man knew it.

'Dr Oldroyd would have you believe that we evolved from mindless chemicals that act according to the laws of chance and natural selection. He would have you believe that everything we are, everything we know, everything we understand has come about accidentally. Your eyes were not fashioned in order to behold the wonders of nature, your heart was not made to surge with love, your soul was not created to feel ecstasy. In fact you have no soul, your heart is no more than a pump, and you may as well not have eyes at all, because nature as you perceive it does not exist. Every thought, feeling and instinct you have is a fantasy. You were not created; you were not designed; you are a meaningless jumble of chemicals with no more right to be here than an ape. Or a rat. Or a maybug. Or a flu virus. Or a heap of horse shit. The depth, the insight, the passion of your spiritual life – it is all false. Our universe is a dead, flat, cold place. You were not meant to be born. Your death will be a reversion to your natural state, and you will take your place with the horse shit, because that is all you ever were.'

My depth and insight and passion were bubbling so hard I could feel them steaming out of every orifice. I knew what criticism felt like; I'd taken it, and I'd dealt with it. This was like nothing I'd heard on earth. 'Excuse me,' I protested at the blatant untruths. My stupid English voice bleated out against Dr Vernon's meaningful silence. Both of the other occupants of the stage turned to me with prim shocked expressions on their faces.

'Dr Oldroyd,' said Dr Powell, 'you must wait your turn.'

I subsided. What else was I to do? They had told me the rules of the game, and I had not protested then. Why had I not protested? For the same reason I couldn't do it now: I was on a stage, with an audience in cahoots, as securely bound and gagged as Thomas More at his execution.

'If I may continue,' said Dr Vernon.

I sat on my hands.

Dr Vernon lowered his shoulders, tipped his head on one side, and took a breath that heralded the depth of his calm. 'Some of you who have read Dr Oldroyd's book,' he said, 'may have been sceptical, but felt *obliged* to believe him, because of the feeling that evolution is something which scientists generally accept. Well, let me tell you something which you may not know. Evolution is not generally accepted by scientists. It has no claim to be science. And Dr Oldroyd's book is as unscientific, as wily and as *religious* a book as any you will ever read.'

Here it was again, the attack upon my so-called religion. It seemed very strange that a priest, of whatever sort, should criticise in such terms. If that was what he planned to do, then for all the creepy eloquence, and for all the compelling righteous doom-mongering of his speech, it should be very easy to destroy. Yet we were only a few minutes in. How could he sustain this for another forty?

'I will come onto evolution's false claims to be a science later on. For now, let me assure you that in the light of the great scientists of all the ages, these claims are widely accepted as holding no grounds at all. We will start with a more specific illustration, which comes in the form of the book which we are here to discuss, Dr Oldroyd's *Genesis*.'

Specific illustrations. Christ, I needed a notebook. I plunged my hand into my breast pocket. No pen. I scrabbled under my chair and retrieved my battered old briefcase, bought for me by my parents as a graduation present, and sprang open the clips. Inside was a terrible jumble of things: a creased shirt; a pair of Y-fronts; a book on embryology given to me by one of the professors at Caltech; a letter from Sally. Finally, a biro decorated with the words: Columbia. Leading-Edge Research in Cell Biology. I clicked the nib into action, and tried to find something on which to scribble. Sally's letter? It seemed like sacrilege, and anyway, I didn't want to risk her endearments fluttering off the stage and into the audience. I had another go. Aha. A few sheets of printed paper with blank backs. It was the flight details for the remainder of my tour, but it would do. I took out the embryology book, snapped the briefcase shut and shoved it back under my chair, and rested my makeshift notepad on the book. 'Evolution's false claims to be a science,' I wrote, and then, like a judge passing verdict, 'Unsubstantiated'.

I looked up eagerly, and realised that Dr Vernon was well into his speech.

'. . . which, like all apologists for evolution, repeatedly cites the fossil record. Yet the fossil record has nothing to say which supports the hypotheses which Dr Oldroyd so cavalierly calls to his aid. Palaeontologists are unanimous in this . . .'

'COMPLETE bollocks,' I scribbled, and then realised that I must write down what it was that was complete bollocks, as there would be little to distinguish it from what came before or after. 'Palaeontologists' unanimity . . . no fossil record for evolution . . .'

'You see,' said Dr Vernon quietly, 'the whole evolutionary myth is based on the supposition that life has evolved by minute steps, steps so small and yet so significant that a human being can arise from a fish. The absolute necessity for this theory to bear weight is that there must have been functional, living, reproducing creatures at every stage of this transition. This theory holds that there are no such things as the discrete, wholly unique and separate kinds which you and I perceive around us; they are all, as are we, transitional beings, on their way between being one thing and another, and never being anything at all. Incredible enough, you might say, as soon as you take the time to think this assertion through and imagine the grotesque intermediate forms that must have existed in order for a frog to evolve into a leopard, or a lizard into a nightingale. More incredible still, when you reflect that if ever there were such creatures, none is in existence now. No half-reptile, half-birds; no half-rat, half-wolves; and most certainly no half-ape, half men, unless you want to believe the theories of Dr Oldroyd's more vicious eugenicist precursors. So if you are to believe in the evolution of man from the simplest living forms, you must also believe in something which can only be historic, in creatures which existed in the past but which have all coincidentally died out now, with no new intermediate forms to replace them. And most incredibly of all, you must believe that despite the fact that millions of these beings once did exist, not one of them has left a trace in the fossil record.'

My scribbles had already worked their way all over one sheet and onto the next. 'EUGENICISTS!' I had scratched, and underlined it three times, in disbelief that a religious fundamentalist of the Deep South should dare to put *me* on the side of the racists. But I knew that I must not get side-tracked by Vernon's bile. I must focus on the omissions and the lies, not on the insults. Yet it was getting harder and harder to do, because they were so intertwined, and as my fury became inscribed in the loops and scrawls on the pages, winding over from one sheet to the next, I knew I was losing the thread of Dr Vernon's argument, let alone my own.

'. . . and whilst much is made of the dinosaurs, which actually co-existed with man during the first thousand years or so of our existence . . .'

Co-existed? For a moment I contemplated the wiped-out aeons, and then realised: this man was a young-earther. Someone who actually believed that the world had come into being six thousand years before.

'. . . Triceratops . . . A mighty creature, whose doomed existence might have been designed to make us wonder and make us fear . . . perverse contradiction of the evidence, held up as an example of evolution, when there exist no precursors to this kind in the fossil record whatever . . .'

And still onwards. Away from the hapless dinosaurs, who were no longer around to fight their cause, and on to optometry. 'William Paley, whose two-hundred-year-old wisdom predates Darwin and yet whose wisdom is incontrovertible still . . . no-one has yet found an answer to the question, "What good is half an eye?" Are we supposed to imagine that the first eye was a single mutation, which came into existence, as it were, overnight?'

Easy, I thought, easy, but now Vernon was on to Australopithecus, quoting real scientists out of context, giving the audience words those scientists had taken back when confronted with new discoveries, citing contesting theories as if their disagreement undermined the basis of evolution itself – 'Lord Solly', I wrote, and 'Gould', and 'PALEY WOULD HAVE CHANGED HIS MIND,' and 'Have you ever HEARD of Mendel?'

Still it was slipping away from me, the burden of half-cocked detail accumulating. The examples grew to ten, twenty, twenty-five. I had defaced my flight details and was now scrawling graffiti across the plane ticket itself. It was easy enough to think of devastating ripostes to each one of Vernon's arguments, but my confidence was beginning to ebb away. I didn't have the references to hand, didn't have the proof, was robbed by time of my colleagues' beloved footnotes. And though I knew that defeating him would be easy, the anger within me told me that the only fit response to his verbal assaults on my integrity was to demolish him completely.

Vernon was speaking faster now, methodical in his crackpottery, winding up the pace to a crescendo. 'Intermediate forms, the inseparability of kinds, designless design, the slipperiness of species – all chimeras. You will see by now how sophisticated Dr Oldroyd's arguments are, and I mean sophisticated not in the sense that the design of a butterfly is sophisticated, but sophisticated as in *sophistry*, which to you or me, friends, means lying.

And so what of Darwin's theory of evolution, which we assumed to be so watertight, yet which we now know to be so riddled with holes? Regardless of its demonstrable falsehood, its very nature fails all of the tests of science.

'The modern approach to science was originally proposed by the sixteenth-century philosopher Francis Bacon, and is based on the logic that theory is generated from experiments, which can be repeated to yield results which either confirm or challenge that theory. In this light, no theory can ever be conclusively proved, however many times a positive result is shown, as it is always possible that a conflicting result will be produced in the future, necessitating the modification or abandonment of that theory. Theories can act as no more than models for our understanding of Creation. Despite this, scientists ever since have been elevating theories to the status of laws, stifling the sceptical thought encouraged by Boyle. These anti-scientific scientists believe categorically in the ability of the human mind to understand every aspect of Creation, and hence subscribe to a faith system which is politically and culturally motivated by a sympathy with Humanism. At the Academy of Scientific Creationism we reject such "scientism".

'It is time to claim science back for truth. There is no need for you to force yourselves to believe in a religion which denies the goodness that lies in your hearts. You, my friends, are not accidents. You are not horse shit. You were meant to be here, and you were put here by Him in whose image you were made, who loves you more than you can ever understand. The passion and wonder and virtue inside you is no chimera. Never let anyone tell you that it is. My friends, you are human; God gave you free will; you have a choice.'

I could feel the applause brewing in the audience, bottled up over the three-quarters of an hour of Dr Vernon's monologue. The cork came off and the room exploded.

I stared around me in total incomprehension. The people in

the audience each appeared to be equipped with the usual quota of arms, legs, noses and mouths. They were recognisably human. And yet their reaction made no sense to me at all. There was no-one I'd ever met who would have cheered that speech. My mother wouldn't do it. Nor, I was sure, would the meek little vicar who'd eaten her scones so rapaciously when he'd come to counsel us in our times of sorrow. I hadn't had any cause to defend myself against religion since I was fifteen and trying to get out of going to church, and even then I'd had the disappointing feeling that there was nothing to argue against. God meant church garden parties and wardens' rotas and a sense of Englishness in a country slowly going to the dogs. It didn't mean that the universe was six thousand years old.

My experience of the country so far had done nothing to prepare me for this. It was supposed to be the most advanced nation in the world. Wasn't this the American people who'd kicked the British out, who'd fought a war to end slavery, whose protests had ended the war against Vietnam? I looked down at them and realised that it was not. I'd heard of Billy Graham, of course, but I'd always assumed he was one of those crackpots that all cultures threw out occasionally. Like Nixon, or Enoch Powell, or the Pope. And whilst crackpots of all persuasions could always find followers – Hitler had proved that for all eternity – I'd never expected to come face to face with them en masse. Yet here, in the middle of nowhere, Vernon had managed to assemble a whole hall full of them. Had he flown them in from all round the country? I knew already that he had not. One look at them showed that they were ordinary people, and the only explanation for their reaction was that the ideas which Vernon had proposed were deeply embedded within their brains.

Standing on that stage, I felt a nauseating wave of what felt like vertigo. These people already thought that I was a liar, and that Frank Vernon had told the truth. And such a mindset violated every concept of truth I'd ever known. I was suddenly acutely aware of how isolated my brain was in that room. It had never occurred to me before that my beliefs might even remotely depend on the agreement of those around me. I'd always assumed that they were independent of everything other than myself. But now, unhitched from all my moorings, I didn't know where to begin, because I had no idea what I was fighting against.

'It is now Dr Oldroyd's turn to respond,' said Powell, and a frission of expectation shivered through the still-hooting audience. I stared at them.

'Do you have anything to say, Dr Oldroyd?'

A ripple of laughter. And then sheer anger propelled me forward. I was on my feet, stumbling towards the front. Through the still-resounding noise of the crowd, I could hear Dr Powell's pointless voice, stricturing me to *go back to my seat*. I turned, and it wasn't until the expression on Powell's face sank into my brain that I realised that I was about to throw the invigilator off the stage. I threw myself around again, and directed all my force at the audience.

'*Shut up*,' I shouted.

A hundred indrawn breaths.

'Where I come from – indeed also where I have just come from, which is California, exactly the same place whence Dr Vernon has travelled – debate does not consist of an hour of untrammelled nonsense uninterrupted by good sense.'

'Dr Oldroyd,' piped up Powell, 'I would ask you not to be abusive.'

'Abuse? Did nothing Dr Vernon say count as abuse? Explain to me what you define as abuse, Dr Powell, or I'll show you abuse.'

There were the beginnings of motion from the musclier members of the audience. Rednecks, all. I realised I had better get on with the intellectual side of things. 'Despite the ludicrousness of the set-up I will abide by your rules. But I would ask for no more interruptions than Dr Vernon received. I would ask you to hear me out.'

They fell back, but the threat remained. I looked down at my hands and saw that there were no notes in them. Then I turned back and saw my travelling arrangements scattered around my chair. Damn it. I searched through my brain and came up with the last thing I'd written. HERRING GULLS.

'I'm going to tell you a story about some birds,' I said.

On the road from Santa Monica to Pasadena, a gull had hit my windscreen. The bird was enormous, and its impact had looked and felt catastrophic. I had screeched to a stop by the side of the road, expecting shattered glass. But the car was intact. I'd run back along the road to find the gull, and had lifted the damaged creature in my hands. Everything about it was still perfect; each feather laid neatly on top of the next, the beak still a sharp, hard scavenging tool, the wings more finely adapted for looping and whirling in the slipstreams of the air than any fighter plane. There wasn't even any blood. But it was dead.

'The herring gull of Great Britain is one of our commonest birds. It has adapted so well to the environment created by man that it has moved far inland of its old coastal habitats. The species has enjoyed great success in North America too. I am not sure whether you have them in Shirley County, but I have seen them in both Massachusetts and California and found them to be a very comforting, homely sight.' I remembered suddenly that in America homely meant ugly, but continued anyway. 'However, there are distinct differences between American herring gulls and their British cousins. Not enough to make them separate species, because our rough definition of species division is whether two individuals can mate and produce fertile offspring, and there is no problem of that kind between these two varieties of herring gull. But the differences are significant nevertheless, and noticeable to me, even though I am no ornithologist.

'If you continue to move westward, there are herring gulls all the way across the Bering Strait, in Siberia and beyond. These Asian birds differ once again from American herring gulls, though in small ways. Of course, this means that they look even more different from the British herring gulls; and as we cross Asia, the variations accumulate, until the comparison with the British bird is no longer quite so appropriate. By the time we reach Eastern Europe, to British eyes the bird has started to look rather more like a different creature, until we find ourselves all the way round the globe, back on my home turf, where a variation on the European variation of the Asian variation of the American variation leaves us with a bird we call the lesser black-backed gull. The Siberian version is pretty much halfway between the two. And in Britain these are two quite separate species, which exist side by side, exploiting different niches in the food chain, and which cannot generally mate together to produce fertile young.

'Which of these is the intermediate form? Of course I would regard every single variety other than those found in Britain as being intermediates between the British herring gull and the British lesser black-backed gull. But from here in America it looks rather different. I am sure that no American ornithologist would consent to American herring gulls being regarded as an intermediate stage between two inconsequential British birds. They are *all* intermediate forms. Now, I would ask you to think about what this means for the fundamental "kinds" of which Dr Vernon speaks. The term "kinds", by the way, has no scientific meaning as far as I am aware, and would appear to be of religious inspiration. Do the British herring gull and the British lesser black-backed gull fall within the same kind? Does their kind include all gulls, or even all birds? How much variation can be permitted? Or do each of the varieties of herring gull and lesser black-backed gull exist as a separate kind, individually designed and created by God?'

There was room enough in my brain while I was talking to think about what I was doing. And by my own judgment, I was doing rather well. I wanted to talk about Australopithecus and the revolution in physical anthropology which its discovery had heralded, rendering all of Vernon's quotes obsolete. I wanted to give a step-by-step refutation of Paley's assertions about the human eye, in terms which Paley himself would have understood. I wanted to range across every topic Vernon had violated, and rescue them all. But one of my talents had always been an instinctive knowledge of how argument worked, and my mouth sometimes knew more sense than my mind. Vernon's crowd-pleaser had drawn upon long centuries of design; who knew better how to rouse a human heart than an inheritor of one of the most successful religions on the planet? No-one who didn't already understand evolution would warm to a point-by-point destruction of Christianity's carrot-and-stick promises, even if I could do it in the time. Vernon's subtext had assured the audience of eternal life. Only a message as simple and positive as Vernon's own could stand any hope of winning them back. So I avoided confronting any of the more emotional issues, and stuck to the herring gull and the story of its long climb from the primordial soup. My attacks on Vernon were all veiled; I explained about Archaeopteryx, the toothed and feathered dinosaur that grew wings and took to the sky; I showed the small steps by which a light-sensitive patch on the skin could confer enough benefits to survive and be improved by subsequent mutations until the herring gull was equipped with a modern eye; I explained how, unlike the intermediaries between the herring gull and the lesser black-backed gull, which were protected from one another by geographical divides, the majority of the herring gull's ancestors had died out because of competition from close relatives with improved equipment for living long enough to reproduce. There was so much more I wanted to say, but I kept a firm eye on the clock, disciplined myself, and timed it to perfection.

At the end, I couldn't resist a strike at Vernon's biggest carrot: personal immortality. I returned to the story of my encounter with the herring gull on the West Colorado Boulevard. 'The collision was so hard I thought it had damaged the car,' I said. 'But my car was unscratched, and the bird's life was over. This might seem to indicate some sort of superiority of a designed machine over an evolved organism. Even if my car had been stampeded by a herd of buffalo, it could still have been fixed, though it might be economically pointless to do so. Nothing on earth could have revived that bird. All that history, all those tiny modifications, wiped out by a second of carelessness. On the gull's part, incidentally, not mine.

'Yet still I think the herring gull triumphs over the Chevrolet. When that car gets consigned to the scrapyard, it's gone forever, and it's up to the company that made it to build another. If I want a better one, they have to go back to the drawing board and design it all over again. But my herring gull may have lived long enough to rear chicks. If it didn't, it made pretty certain that the gene for flying into car windscreens is one step closer to extinction. Either way, the genes of the herring gull have been around for longer than any manmade configuration, and stand a chance of lasting as long again. When you leave this hall, look up. If you see a bird, you are seeing the ghost of Archaeopteryx, flapping its way into history.'

I stopped, and tried to make some indication that my speech was over. On the front row, an old man was slumped in slumber against the shoulder of the boy who had rubbed his hands.

'Bravo!' shouted someone from the back of the room. I looked, and saw that it was the youth who'd accosted me on the way in, clapping as if his life depended upon it. Around the

162

room there was a scattering of polite applause. Rigid with anger, I stormed back to my chair.

'Thank you, Dr Oldroyd,' said Powell. 'Now Dr Vernon has five minutes to give his response.'

Vernon stood up, smiling. 'I don't think I'll need five minutes for this one, Doug.' There was laughter. 'Dr Oldroyd has given us a series of brilliant examples of his argumentative style. I won't bother to go into the various proofs that Archaeopteryx was a bird which bore no relation to the dinosaurs. Nor will I correct his misunderstandings about the anatomy of the avian eye. His assertions may sound credible, but they carry all the hallmarks of pseudoscience: the assumption that a non-scientific listener will believe anything you say as long as they don't know it to be untrue. Well, anyone, however unscientific, can go away and check it out. And I advise you to do just that. I'll just point out one simple thing. The herring gull is a bird which can be found in Europe and North America. The lesser black-backed gull is a bird which can be found in Europe and Northern Asia. There are no transitional forms tucked away in Siberia. Unlike Dr Oldroyd, I don't expect you to take my word for it. Just ask any ornithologist. My friends, you don't need to believe everything you hear. God gave you free will. You have a choice.'

He sat down. I jumped to my feet. 'It's complete rubbish!' I shouted. 'How dare you call me a liar?'

Dr Vernon glanced at Powell. 'Am I permitted to respond to that one?'

Powell nodded.

'Because you lie, Dr Oldroyd.'

'It's a pile of *shit*. You are peddling ignorance and delusion. Don't you know there are children here? What are you trying to do to their brains? I'd like to see your arguments peer-reviewed and published in a respectable scientific journal. But they aren't and they won't be, because they are total fabrications. You accuse me of lying, of abuse? You've been doing nothing but lie and slander ever since you walked into this room—'

Powell stood up. 'That's enough, Dr Oldroyd. As you said yourself, there are children here. The debate is over.' He turned to the audience. 'Thank you for sharing this very interesting conversation with us today. As Dr Vernon has so succinctly put it, I leave you to draw your own conclusions.' He and Vernon walked off the stage. I darted after them.

'You charlatans! You monstrous scoundrels!' I was surrounded by people. 'What *is* the Academy of Scientific Creationism? How do you get a degree there? Do you buy it? How much does it cost? What does it teach you?' The crowd bore in on me. I pushed them aside, lost my balance, fell heavily against a young woman. There was a flash.

Later, Dan Gorman sent me the photograph. It was printed on the pamphlet published by the Academy after the event. I have it still. It is one of those embarrassing and uncharacteristic splinters in time, making me look like some antediluvian ancestor of humankind. I am enormous and unruly, my hair a dishevelled bush, my shirt buttons undone and my chest hair surging out, my face contorted with anger and my huge hairy arms flailing against prim young women in Stepford Wife dresses. 'MAN DESCENDED FROM APE', was the caption, in large bold letters, and underneath, in very small print, 'claims British scientist'.

I stood there, trying to regain my balance, blinking in the flashlight's glare. 'Dr Oldroyd,' said Dan Gorman beside me, 'I think you could use a drink.'

These days Professor Gorman bears little physical resemblance to the earnest grad-school student who pulled me out of that place and into the nearest bar. He is a burly, bearded, curly-haired bear, an enthusiast, and a scientific missionary of the most eccentric kind. Brought up in Missouri by a Seventh-Day

Adventist minister and his schoolteacher wife, he never did get along with his parents, and when it got to his first semester in university and he found out for the first time that the world wasn't made six thousand years ago by some relative of his daddy's with a big white beard, he got pretty mad. Dan has been mad, in his own special way, ever since. His mission over the past decade, in cussed defiance of the laws of his own land, has been the quest to clone a human being. For obvious reasons, this has required him to spend increasing amounts of his time in Europe.

The last time I saw him he was en-route from a conference in Italy where he'd been concocting further plans to undermine stem-cell legislation. 'I'm on the run from the feds,' he declared breathlessly. 'Can't stay long. Let's go visit one of your fine ol' British boozers.'

We reminisced about that first meeting. 'Three whores by the juke box,' chuckled Dan over his pint of London Pride. 'Four ex-cons by the pool table, not playing, looking for trouble. Dr Maxwell Oldroyd in his high school prom outfit big enough to bust the room and spouting indignance in Her Majesty's finest language at the top of his voice, as if none of it was ever there.'

He's right, I don't recall any of that. All I remember is the almost-physical sense of my wounds. When I think about it too hard, my heart beats faster and the weals ache dully, as if deep below the skin the scar tissue never quite succeeded in healing the fissures in my flesh.

The runty post-doc student manoeuvred me onto a bar stool and supplied me with something that might have been bourbon. He was relentlessly ebullient, a slim, slightly feckless youth with big glasses, hair that looked as if it had been glued to the top of his head and a grin that spoke of unconquerable optimism. I took the drink and finished it. He got me another. 'Well, Dr Oldroyd,' he said, 'I have to thank you for coming all the way out here today. It was just terrific.'

'Terrific?' I spluttered, and wondered for a moment whether this might be yet another word which had another meaning in the States. Perhaps when the Pilgrim Fathers set sail from my home town, it had still retained its original connotation of terror.

'Really swell. I've been looking forward to it ever since I heard about it. Just wait till I tell my professor I had a drink with Max Oldroyd. She'll piss her pants.'

'Who is your professor?'

'Loretta Weisz. Scary lady. Great teacher, though.'

'Golly,' I said, and felt a trickle of warmth to accompany the whiskey. If Loretta Weisz was impressed by me, I couldn't be a complete write-off.

'She always tells me I shouldn't come to these things. And I had given up, kind of. But when I got the details of this one, and I saw it was you – well, nothing woulda stopped me. I thought, if the author of *Genesis* can't lick 'em, no-one can.'

'I must have been a great disappointment to you. I suppose when you spoke to me before the debate, you were trying to save me.'

'Nothing coulda saved you, if that speech didn't. I never saw anyone do so well against Frank Vernon.'

'So you're a bit of a regular at these things.'

'Debated in a couple. I guess I've got something to prove.' He told me the story of his conversion to science.

'Jesus,' I said.

'The opposite. Alone in the universe. That's when I started reading Jean-Paul Sartre. Not a good idea for a kid from the sticks in a strange town. Anyhow, ever since I pulled myself together and faced up to the meaninglessness of existence, I've been on a mission to prove to the world that my daddy's wrong. Or that's what Professor Weisz says. Never managed it so far. Mincemeat every time. These guys, they're professionals. They've been practising this gig for going on forty years and they're just getting started.'

Dan's combination of joie de vivre and gentle cynicism was irresistible. I tried to pull myself out of my gloom. 'Who is Frank Vernon, anyway? What's his game? The Academy of Scientific Creationism – it's a disgrace. If they're not interested in the truth, then why go about arranging debates?'

He looked at me in astonishment. 'You mean you don't *know*?'

'Of course I don't know. He wouldn't get away with that sort of thing in London, I can tell you that.'

'But your book – surely it was deliberate?'

'*What* was deliberate?'

'You went straight for 'em. Straight for their balls. It was so *neat*. I woulda killed myself laughing if it wasn't so serious.'

'Look, Mr—'

'Dan.'

'Dan. I haven't the foggiest what you're talking about.'

'The *title*. Genesis. First book of the Bible. It's inspired. I couldn't believe anyone had the nerve. After everything Loretta told me about keeping out of it, I thought, here it is. Good against evil. The last battle.'

I floundered. 'I didn't mean—' In the darkness of that bar, I struggled to bring myself back to a world in which it had made perfect sense to name my book after the first chapter of the Bible. 'I didn't expect anyone to take it literally. It was just a fairy story they used to tell at Sunday School. I just wanted to show how much more exciting it was to hear the truth.'

'You mean you didn't think anyone *believed* that stuff?'

I thought about it. What had I thought? I supposed I'd expected to ruffle the feathers of a few scratchy old clergymen in places like Yorkshire, but no-one who mattered. 'Well, of course they do. But I would have thought that most intelligent people would be able to deal with the truth, regardless of their superstitions.'

Dan guffawed. 'Oh my goodness. That really is rich.'

'Dan. Please tell me. What was going on in that hall?'

He composed himself. 'It was a recruitment drive.'

'A *what*?'

'They want to ban the teaching of evolution in schools. So they set up a debate with a respected scientist, and the form is always like that. They insist on half-hour slots at the least, because that way they can get in so many examples the scientist doesn't stand a chance of refuting them all. If it's on their home ground, like here, they're onto a winner from the start. But even if the scientist specifies that it has to be in a university, the ASC and its friends slap an entrance fee on the debate, suppress its promotion, and then they bus in people from all the churches who want to hear that evolution is dead.'

'But then they're preaching to the converted. What can they gain if they never get into the mainstream?'

'They gain a lot. Because most people who want to believe that evolution is dead aren't very well-educated themselves, and so however strong their beliefs, they'd never have the confidence to contradict someone who they think knows more than them. But after they've watched a professional scientist being destroyed by the ACR, they think it's settled. So they go home, and they hassle a teacher. Even the children. That's why they bring the kids. The next time Mrs Appleseed starts explaining about evolution, little Johnny-know-it-all is going to stand up and tell her he knows she's wrong, because he heard it proved. How confident is Mrs Appleseed going to be about teaching evolution after that? Max, this is the Bible Belt. We're all Baptists and Seventh-Day Adventists round here. No-one wants to stir up trouble with the Church.'

'You mean – *everyone* believes all this stuff out here? *Before* Vernon gets going on them?'

'Not everyone. But a good percentage kinda think it's that way.'

'And how big is the Bible Belt? Is it just this state? Or others as well?'

'I'd say it was at least twenty times the size of your lil' old country. Maybe more.'

I sat there, flabbergasted, and for a moment wanted nothing more than to go home to Sally and the kids, to go back to my lectures at Erasmus College, and retreat back into the bubble of enlightenment that I'd thought constituted the whole civilised world. But the bubble was burst. Only ignorance had kept it intact, and there was no such thing as an ignorant enlightenment.

'What about all the people I've been meeting at the universities over here? None of them mentioned any of this stuff.'

'Hey, Max, why would they go doing that? I'm sure they're all nice guys you've been meeting with. Why would they want to poop your party when they thought there wasn't any need for it? Most of the East Coasters probably think pretty much the way you do. And plenty of the others. But a lot of guys will have had a similar experience to me. And most of 'em want to leave the past behind.'

'So it's all entirely calculated. Vernon's game. He's doing this for his own political ends.'

'Sure. But you're missing one thing. There's a reason why he has those political objectives. He thinks he's the instrument of God Almighty.'

I thumped the bar. 'I just can't believe that. If he's clever enough to dream up something like that, how can he be stupid enough to believe the shit he talks?'

'He doesn't want to be alone in the universe. He wants God to give him a pat on the head and say he lived a good life when he dies and goes to heaven. Max, you gotta remember that even Darwin wasn't very happy about believing in evolution. It takes a certain sort of temperament to cope with that idea, and these people don't have that temperament.'

'But surely there's no danger that they'll succeed in getting evolution banned from schools. The law isn't that much of an ass.'

'I dunno. I hope not. But you gotta realise that the judges and the governors and the committee members are all Baptists and Seventh-Day Adventists too. It's drip, drip, drip. They did it before, way back in the twenties. And feelings are much stronger now. Plus they've got this new trick. This Scientific Creationism deal. Every time so far anyone goes head to head on this one in the courts, it's the liberal churchmen standing up for evolution, and the people condemning it have doctorates in science. That kinda backs up their point about Darwinism being a faith.'

'But it's complete hogwash.'

'Yeah. Doesn't matter. Not if they win the argument.'

That was the worst thing. I had never been fond of losing. More than one of my friends had given up playing tennis with me because of my unflinching desire to win. The loss of a single set could be enough to set my skin jangling for days. This was beyond any such experience. I was a scientist, not a tennis player, and today I'd been not only routed on my own domain, but publicly humiliated. The audience had *laughed*, for God's sake. 'They won't win next time,' I said through gritted teeth.

'You're gonna do it *again*?'

'I've got two weeks of this lined up. I presume it's more of the same. But next time I'll know what's coming. What's the best way to get them?'

'Your way. I told you, I never saw anyone do so well as that.'

'But I didn't get them.'

'No,' said Dan breezily, 'and I don't suppose you will.'

I told Sally what had happened. 'He called me a liar,' I wailed. 'And they believed him.'

'Surely not,' she said.

'Really. It's fucking unbelievable, isn't it?'

'It sounds very weird. I mean, a couple of the nuns tried to get us to believe that sort of thing at my school, but though we all pretended to agree with them, we couldn't take them seriously, because of course we got taught the normal stuff in science lessons. Perhaps these people were like that too. You know, a bunch of teacher's pets. It sounds as if this Frank Vernon character was pretty much in charge of things. Maybe they'd have gone the other way if you'd been the top dog.'

'Sally, these people haven't even had the science lessons.' And I told her what Dan Gorman had said to me.

'How completely ridiculous. Well, you're well out of it then. You can get an earlier flight back now. Wait till I tell the kids. Cass hasn't been able to talk about anything except whether you'll be back for her carol concert. That and your book. She's been trying to read it.'

'Sally—'

The jolliness fell away. We both said nothing, neither of us prepared to acknowledge what I was about to say. She dared to break the silence first.

'Max, this is silly. There's no point in you staying out there now.'

'You have to understand,' I said. 'This is the most marvellous opportunity for me. America is where it's all happening these days in biology. I can't let these bastards grind it all to dust—'

'They *haven't* ground it all to dust. This has nothing to do with your tour. You've said yourself that they're just a bunch of god-squadders from the middle of nowhere. The tour has been a fabulous success. Just accept it, ignore those idiots, and come home.'

'Sally, can't you see? I thought I understood America. I thought it was easy. But I was wrong. The people I saw at the universities – they know all about this stuff, they have to contend with it all the time, and I just didn't know. I feel like an idiot, as if I was the last boy in the school to work out how babies were made, or something. I have to learn how to deal with this kind of stuff. How can I hope to be a serious scientist if I run away at the first sign of trouble?'

'You *are* a serious scientist. Max, please. Why does everything have to revolve around America? You're doing so well at home.'

But we're going to live here, I thought desperately. My daydreams of emigration had grown more and more vivid right up until the day I left Santa Monica, and now it felt like an established fact. After what I'd seen in the universities of America, the idea of returning to the stuffy parochial world of British science and never leaving looked like a pathetic small-minded retreat. Yet I still hadn't told Sally. Perhaps it was partly because when I'd mentioned it to Antonia, she'd said with dour amusement, 'Sally won't like that.' But probably mostly because I'd known it myself already. She just wouldn't be able to imagine living anywhere but London. I needed time to explain it to her properly, show her how England wasn't the entire world, widen her horizons and those of the children.

'I have to stay, Sally. Please understand. It's something I have to do.'

She accepted it in the end. The return flight was already booked, so she didn't have much choice. But it was very much harder for me to feel comfortable about my decision in the face of failure than it had been in the whirl of success.

Dan became my sidekick for those two weeks. He travelled by bus while I travelled by air, piecing together my directions from my vandalised itinerary. In the mornings we ploughed through the inadequate civic libraries for references to everything from Australopithecus to caddis flies. We created our own leaflets promoting the debates and posted them up all over any educational institutions we could find. Then in the afternoons or evenings, I stood up in opposition to a series of scientific creationists and failed to convince a single member of the American public to choose my truth over their lies.

'Just read my book,' I found myself pleading. 'Just read it and give it a chance. Give *yourselves* a chance. Don't believe this bollocks.'

I found a single bookshop that stocked my book and bought up every copy they had. Dan handed it out free to as many attendees as would take it. Most of them refused. 'I'm not reading that evil pack of lies,' they said.

'Morons!' I shouted after them. 'Imbeciles! Cretins!'

'Max, you gotta stop calling people those names,' Dan told me. 'They don't take it too well out here. They think you're saying they have a hereditary disease.'

'They have got a hereditary disease. It's called religion.'

As the weeks wore on, Dan began to find me harder to handle. 'Max, you gotta calm down,' he told me. 'Don't take it so damned seriously. Get rid of this crazy idea that you're gonna *win*.'

I lost my temper. 'There is no evil that can't be defeated,' I railed. 'Otherwise one would have to start believing in the Devil.' But as soon as I heard myself say the words, I knew I was wrong. There were lots of evils that couldn't be defeated. The laws of the universe did not differentiate on those terms.

'Survival of the fittest,' said Dan, echoing my thoughts.

'That's what I can't believe,' I said. 'Forget that Devil stuff. Nonsense. What I can't believe is these bastards are fitter than us. We're going to get them, Dan.'

But at the last debate I lost the will to go on. I sat and waited for my opponent to wrap up his speech. Then I stood up. 'I've had enough of this crap,' I said, and walked out.

When I boarded the plane back to New York, Dan said, 'Hey, we gave it our best shot. It was good knowing you, pal.'

'I'll be back,' I growled. 'I'd never forgive myself if I give up on this. Mark my words, I'll be back.'

But I never did go back. Not on those terms, anyway.

*

The problem I failed to confront in Missouri is the problem I've been struggling with ever since. The people I met out there had found an argument which was infallible in its fallacy. It was circular; worse, it was an inward spiral, always crossing the same ground and yet leading from something to nothing. The solecisms were shameless and exposed – using relativism to combat relativism, trapping liberal rationalism in its own open-mindedness whilst remaining airily free to dodge in and out of that openness itself, depending on whether it was defending or attacking. 'Your theory says that no theory can be proved right,' they said, 'and therefore you cannot deny what we say.' Yet by their own admission they were not themselves relativists: they believed in one true way, and used science's inherent objective-ness to force a lie upon the truth. They were no better than the neo-fascists or the holocaust deniers, who stabbed joyfully at liberalism's Achilles heel and stood upon a platform of 'free speech' to promote an ideology aimed at suppressing all inter-ests but its own. Those 'Biblical Christians' accused science of possessing a political and cultural agenda, whilst blatantly pursuing one themselves, beginning with Bacon and Boyle and ending with the imprisonment of homosexuals and the waging of Holy War.

I have never written about that trip until now, and to the extent of my knowledge, neither has anyone else. It was impor-tant from the start that I should not let Vernon's victory be a decisive defeat for me; I knew that if I really cared about what had happened, I would have to take up the struggle for myself when I got home; and I didn't want the stench of my first failure to pursue me through all the battles ahead. Yet now, after all this time and all this silence, Margot knows. She didn't say so in her article, but the evidence is clear enough. The grainy picture beneath the banner headline at the top of the page is the ape-man photo from that hall in Missouri.

*

This morning, I received an email from Dan. My first reaction was relief, because the last I'd heard of him since we'd discussed those long-gone days in a pub in Fitzrovia was that he'd been discovered by the media standing outside an abortion clinic in Seattle, holding a placard that read 'Abortionists against Murder' and wearing a T-shirt decorated with a gun sights' target centring round about his heart. In my own university, the ethics students ran an internet sweepstake on how long it would take before some lunatic took him out. When I heard about Dan's antics, I snorted with derision at the futility of his humour, and quaked in fear for his safety. But on reflection, I wondered whether our conversation in the Queen's Head had been the inspiration for his prank. Perhaps he'd found the only way out of the relativist trap after all. Stand up for freedom, and take the piss out of the enemy. Yet if that was the way out, I couldn't see how it could be extended from a rather context-dependent joke to being a creed that would allow us to confront hypocritical extremism head-on. No-one joined him on his picket line. Nobody else had the nerve. In the end the staff of the clinic asked him to go away, fearing that the whole place would be blown up. And, taking pity on them, and their day-in, day-out courage in the face of a danger he was inviting to their door, he did.

My second reaction was a mixture of suspicion and hope. The suspicion was caused by my realisation that there was only one person who Margot would be able to identify as being an associate of mine and who also possessed a copy of that photo-graph, and it was Dan. And the hope sprang from my certainty that though Dan might be perfectly capable of indiscretion, he would never deliberately sabotage me. So I emailed him a link to the web version of Margot's article.

'The photograph is one thing,' I wrote, 'but the other is the quote in the tenth paragraph. I can only assume that the surname of the source is not a coincidence.'

Margot had written, 'It is true that Oldroyd is loathed by the fundamentalist Right in America, at whom much of his rhetoric seems to be aimed. But their hatred is leavened by a rather more surprising emotion. "Max Oldroyd is the best thing that ever happened to us," chuckles Jeremiah Vernon, president of a student Christian organisation based in Missouri. "His books have awoken more unbelievers to the existence of God than any since the Bible itself." I ask him how this could be the case, and he says, "Most unbelievers don't spend much time thinking about their lack of faith. Oldroyd makes them think. And while they're thinking, they suddenly start to see how many gaps there are in his reasoning. Which is when they start to question their own."'

The article continues, 'This makes perfect sense to me. I would regard my own unbelief as being pretty unshakeable, but even I find myself making space in the universe for a God whilst reading Oldroyd's wilder passages. This is perhaps the tragedy that lies at the heart of his life. The harder he tried to defeat his opponents' cause, the more damage he does to his own.'

I have not given this part of Margot's thesis any more consideration than it deserves. After all, it is self-contradicting, because if I really were such a godsend to the fundamentalists, then it would be difficult to account for their loathing of me, or for the gallons of ink that have been spilt countering the threat I supposedly pose. But the *name*. It has to be, it can't not be. She had a million American fundamentalists to choose from, and she chose not an eminent evangelist but some obscure student leader. Coincidences happen, but this one is too neat. How could she have found one with the same surname as my first adversary unless she had a good reason to do so?

And then, further on, the strongest hint so far that she knows more than she is letting on. 'Yet *Genesis* itself was never an evangelical work. Something happened to Max Oldroyd soon after publication – probably in the period between 1977 and late 1979 – which awakened his latent insecurities. It was almost certainly the simple discovery that his arguments would not always be greeted with universal applause.'

The timing is too accurate for any other conclusion. I have been bewildered by the fact that she does not go on to tell the tale. But now that I think about it properly, I realise that she is abiding by the only code of honour a journalist knows: to protect her sources.

Dan didn't email me back. He phoned.

'Jesus Christ, Max!'

'Pretty bad, eh?'

'What fucking right does she have to talk about your family like that? I hope you've gotten yourself a good lawyer.'

I suppose it was the first time I'd asked for sympathy, and the warmth that rushed through me almost made me cry. Admittedly, Dan wasn't familiar with the particular idiosyncrasies of the British press, and was therefore more shocked than anyone else would be. But the fact that something is familiar doesn't make it right. 'Lawyers won't do it on this one, Dan. Libel doesn't cover opinions. She's allowed to think what she likes about me.'

'The bitch said she was a *scientist*. Said she was writing an article about creationists. And that *you'd* told her about the photo, and wanted her to include it. That's lying, man. It's gotta be illegal.'

'Look, I don't care about that. It's written now. If I dragged it through the courts it'd only get worse. The press in this country hates anyone who brings a libel case, even if it's against one of their competitors. They'd rip me to shreds. I just want to know what happened for my own sake. What did you tell her?'

'Nothing. She wanted the photo, I sent her the fucking photo.'

'Dan, seriously. When did you ever have a conversation as short as that? I'm not saying that you meant to drop me in it. Of course you didn't. But she could have latched on to anything. Did you mention Vernon? After all, that's who the debate was with.'

'*She* mentioned Vernon. Said she wanted the photo that was taken at the Vernon debate. Max, I was busy. I'd never heard of the woman in my life and hoped I never would again.'

The warmth dropped from my blood. 'She already knew? But how could she have known about Vernon? Who would have told her that?'

'Beats me, pal. But it sure wasn't me.'

In his own peculiar way, Dan is a marvel. Without a single prompt, he went away and found out as much as he could. The first revelation was that Frank Vernon is dead. The second was that Frank's thirty-two-year-old son, Jeremiah, has followed him into the family trade.

'She woulda gone out looking for a quote from Frank himself,' said Dan. 'And seeing how he's otherwise detained, the son'd be the next best thing.'

'But why didn't she say that Jeremiah was Frank's son? She doesn't mention Frank at all. If she went after Jeremiah for that reason, why wouldn't she say so?'

'Beats me. Hey, I found you a lawyer. A Brit. He's shit hot.'

'I don't want a lawyer. I just want to know who's betrayed me.'

There was silence at the other end of the line.

'Dan? Are you still there?'

'I'm here, Max.'

Suspicion reared its head again. 'Dan, do you know who it is?'

'Why d'ya think it has to be anyone? She's a bitch of a journalist and she's dug up some muck on you. If it was me, I'd go for her with the law. But you don't want that. You seem to want' – a weighty pause – 'something else.'

'Dan, can't you see? Whoever has spoken to her – they've fed her more than just the stuff about Vernon. They've told her other stuff. Stuff that they think about me. Stuff that I just can't believe is true. I feel like – I feel like I'm losing the past.'

'We've all lost the past, pal.'

'Dan, you can't—' Abandon me. Except that he wasn't abandoning me. He was as steadfast in my support as ever. It was just that he knew he couldn't give me what I wanted. And as I put the phone down, and reached for Huxley's warm, responsive and yet ultimately barren little frame, the loneliness almost overwhelmed me. There was no-one in the world who could give me what I wanted right then.

Part Three

The Descent of Man

7

I loved my wife. Nothing could be truer than that. I'd thought she'd be everything I wanted. She was more. I cannot pick the happiest days because there were too many of them. But I have the photographs, and they show a slow whoosh of time, blurred very slightly by small changes, ending up at – nothing.

The arch damsel poses against a streetlamp in the snow. She peers at me from under a table, the camera catching a big toothy grin and a glimpse of a short zebra-striped frock. Pregnant now, and in her vermilion wedding dress, looking up at me as I look down at her. Slowly softening, the hair growing a little longer, the shoes a little lower, the clothes a little more earthy, children at her feet, still kicking her heels in the air, still kissing me. Wrinkles begin to appear, the cheekbones ever more pronounced, the eyes creasing more comfortably into smiles, the hair still black but flecking a little with intriguing white strands, the archness never leaving her. Stretched out in the garden in a ridiculous yellow bikini, surrounded by flowers, the legs as elegant as ever, but their skin tone going, pouched a little and stained a little and wrinkled a little at the tops. And Sally heedless. Modesty was for other women. If there was one thing my wife did well, it was age.

It is difficult now to avoid regarding the tour of the States as a watershed. In so many ways, it was not. There were other events which changed our lives infinitely more: the initial move to cohabitation in King's Cross; Antonia's departure for Los Angeles; our wedding; William's arrival; the publication of the book; the purchase of Edenbridge Terrace; the birth of Steve.

Each of these was a change to the structure of our lives. The American trip was just a trip. I went away, returned, and carried on doing much the same things as before. I'd always been obsessive, irascible, impatient to the point of intolerance. Sally knew these things in me and, though they sometimes drove her to distraction, loved them.

In the first couple of weeks of separation, our longing for one another was a painful pleasure, an intensification of our feelings which in some ways transcended even the tumult of the very earliest days. The kids were always hanging around waiting for their turn on the phone, so we couldn't say very much, but that sense of closeness combined with the frustration of not being able to do the obvious and just *touch* was a very pure form of union, a more precise replication of our emotions in one another than even sex. Our telephone conversations usually took place before my breakfast, but on one occasion she called me after I'd finished my day's itinerary, in what for her was the middle of the night. I could feel the silence of the house, smell the lamplight from the window on her brow, see the warmth swaddled in the blankets that were wrapped around her. There were so many practical details which might have benefited from being communicated in such uncensored circumstances, but we talked about nothing but ourselves. We curled up together across the airwaves and touched one another with our words. Afterwards I lay spreadeagled on my hotel bed, my hands clutching its edges, willing myself not to defile the moment by submitting to the reflex towards frantic onanism. I wondered what we might do to one another once she was back in my arms. She ached at the edges of my skin and throbbed in my veins. I spent sleepless hours of torn pleasure, and in the last moments before slumber, as my fingers loosened their grip on the bedclothes and my mind surrendered its consciousness, I almost believed that I was her.

But though such moments of togetherness might be amongst

the best that life has to offer, they are so isolated in space and time that at some point the rest of life must intervene. In her case, the interventions came from the misery of a bad British winter and the boredom of being the one who was left behind. And in my case they came from my discovery of the New World. To begin with, I thought I could relay every impression via the wonders of transatlantic telephony and my huge enthusiasm to tell her what I saw. But she didn't always understand, and by the time I was offered the job at MIT and had started to weave dreams of relocating the whole family out there, I found I couldn't tell her about my speculations at all. The miles were too many, and I didn't want to introduce that distance into our phone calls. To tell her that I envisaged a future for us where I was would be a betrayal of the past we'd shared where she was. Only when we were in the same place would I be able to propose the idea of stepping out together.

After that, our phone calls changed for other reasons. It is hard enough to maintain communication when one person is happy and the other is not, but it is even more difficult when both are not. Neither were our conversations very helpful to my own state of mind. I'd rant at her before breakfast and get my blood temperature up to boiling before I'd even started the day. Then I'd go out, get ripped to shreds, come back to the hotel, toss and turn in bed, compose a narrative which was partly a riposte to my enemies and partly an exposition to Sally, dream of burning crosses, be woken by the siren of the alarm, get up in the morning and start all over again.

'I'm coming home,' I wailed at her at the end of it all. 'Sally, I'm coming home.'

'I should bloody well hope so,' said Sally. 'I've booked a babysitter so that I can come and pick you up from the airport.'

Two days later, I walked into the arrivals lounge in a daze. She threw herself into my arms, crushing the bunch of lilies against my breast, and smothered me with kisses. Through my stupor, my senses began to stir. I clasped her head in my hand and pressed my face and body so hard against hers that it felt as though the bones might break. For those long seconds, there was no America, and no England either. Only us, our minds subordinated to the immediacy of our bodies, with no past or future, no tyranny of contemplation, submerged in the reality of what our senses knew.

But the embrace broke apart, just as my hands had left her hips after that first moment of contact in the conservatory in Chelsea. A few of the petals detached from the flowers and fluttered onto our clothing.

'Hello,' I said.

'Hello,' mouthed Sally, magically, wonderfully, the community of all we knew about one another present in even the most formulaic excuse for a word.

Then I fell asleep. Right there, standing up, in the concourse of Heathrow airport. I didn't fall to the ground – I continued to function, in so far that I could be manoeuvred into the car park. But I remember not a bit of it.

Sally drove her unconscious husband home. She must have had forebodings for the weeks ahead, those desperate, Vernon-infested phone calls still ringing in her brain. And she would have had resentments of her own. She was four months pregnant, her body not her own, and for moments during the past month and a half she must have felt as much alone as she had when her first husband left for Brazil. But also, as she drove between the sleet-smudge lines of orange light that bordered the roads, and listened to the flick-flick-flick of the windscreen wipers and the uneven rumble of my snores, she must have been glad to have me back. America had been an interruption to our lives, no more. A night and day of sleep, a few long conversations and a lot of gradually de-intensifying sex, and all would be back to normal.

Much later, she woke me with a kiss. It was strange to drift into consciousness in my own bed, and find my wife seated on its edge fully-clothed, instead of naked beside me. 'Grmph,' I articulated, and rolled her over me onto the bed, Steve-shaped bulge and all.

She giggled and gazed at me. 'Afternoon, ragamuffin.'

I began to kiss her, and dived straight in under her clothing. She continued to laugh, and struggled free. 'None of that. Not now. We've got a carol concert to go to.'

'Umph?'

'It's six o'clock in the evening. And Cass is singing solo. She's desperate for you to hear her. Come on. Clothes on. Now.'

I sat up. 'Carol concert?'

'Cass told you all about it.' She reached to the dressing table, and thrust a cup of steaming coffee into my hands. 'Drink up. You'll have woken up by the time we get there, I promise.' Then she opened the chest of drawers, and threw pants, trousers, shirt and jumper onto the bed. As if on autopilot, I obeyed.

We walked through driving sleet along the streets of Islington, William trailing at the end of Sally's arm, skidding on short legs across the surface of the mire. I peered through the curtains of milling water and the scattered lamplight. Water in the air, plastic bags in the trees, wind whipping dampness into every crack of my clothing. Weather in England might not be as extreme as it was in other parts of the world, but it was certainly capable of a vindictive viciousness which could transform these toy-town streets into as barren a waste as any prairie.

A carol concert. There was some glimmering of a memory. One of those indistinguishable phone calls, in which I'd ended up promising my stepdaughter so many things that I had no chance of delivering them all. Something about singing solo. Ah, yes! There it was. Cass was singing solo in the school Christmas concert, and I'd told her to practise hard and not to be nervous, because I loved to hear her sing. How odd and how lovely it was to be back in a place where the prattlings of children turned into reality. And then I shivered, because more recent memories were creeping back too. I wrapped my scarf more tightly around my neck and squinted upwards.

Above us was a spotlit spire. The old stone thrust its assertive shape above the rooftops, swirled about with weather.

I don't think I made the connection even then.

Inside was a congregation of water, dripping from umbrellas, macs, skin, hair, collecting in dejected pools on the stone flags and leaving its previous hosts to shiver. The choir faced us from small chairs in the chancel, and the rest of the schoolchildren sat at the front of the audience. An unseen organist stumbled through the notes of an unidentifiable festive tune. Sally pushed a programme into my hands. It contained the titles of all the carols, and the words of those which we were permitted to sing ourselves.

The organist collapsed to a close, and silence fell slowly across the church. A ghostly pause, crackling with nerves, then a sound.

'Once in Royal David's City—'

Cass's voice was the background music to my life. Her songs were usually of her own invention, but last Christmas these same words had rung out from the attic and the bathroom.

'Stood a lowly cattle shed,
'Where a mother laid her baby,
'In a manger for its bed.'

Such a small sound, but so irreducible in its purity. It shivered against the stone arches above her, swelled in the frosty, rain-fugged air, then dropped with great seriousness, dampened by the hats and coats. I saw her lift her chin and continue, the spirit of the words rising in triumph with the pitch.

'Ma-ry was, that Mother Mild.

'Jes-us Christ, her Li-itt-le Child.'

The sound continued long after my little girl had shut her mouth, dropped her chin from its determined elevation, and cast her eyes to the floor in pride and embarrassment. It was innocence distilled, the hushed expectation of all beginnings. A child in a crib, a single star, a cloudless sky. And the ache of longing for that time *once* in royal David's city, for the time when everything was fresh and new, which is never, is always, now.

My pregnant wife blinked back a tear. William, squidged between us, gazed at his sister with rapt, spellbound eyes.

And then the choir broke the silence. 'He came down to earth from heaven, who is God and Lord of all, and his shelter was a stable, and his cradle was a stall. With the poor, the mean, the lowly, lived on earth our Saviour holy.'

They were older than Cass, and the rehearsed, drawling cadences of their voices began to wake me from my trance. God and Lord of all? Lived on earth our Saviour holy? The hymnsheet in my hand reduced in size and shape to a scrumpled ball. I looked down at it, then, realising what it was, flicked my hand away from it as if I had been scalded.

Sally cast me an urgent, mystified glance. But I was sinking. *For He is our childhood's pattern. And our eyes at last shall see Him. And He leads His children on, to the place where He is gone.* Past and present began to fuse. My body was still weak with the toils of sleep, and sodden with the indignities of the English weather. I was in yet another hall with crosses on the walls, and voices were taunting me with stock phrases. The *bastard*. Frank Vernon was here, he was in this church, he was poking at me, he would leap out from behind a pillar and start shaking hands with my friends and neighbours and family before launching into the story of all my failures.

I began to shiver uncontrollably. Sally's head was still turned towards me, her voice quavering with the tune. No, I thought, not you, please don't you do this to me too—

'Why aren't you singing?' she hissed.

I looked down at the crumpled hymnsheet on the floor. She thrust her own towards me, and I pushed it away. An expression appeared on Sally's face which I had only even seen her use on the children. Eyebrows shooting towards her hairline, the inner edges turned in towards her flaring nostrils, her eyes wide open and staring in disapproval, her lips pursed. It was clear now why it had quite such an effect on the kids. But for me, to treat me like a child after all my previous humiliations was the worst thing she could have done. I whipped my face around to stare straight ahead and tried to block my ears to Frank Vernon's taunts. Carol after carol followed. The cacophony of the man's mockery swirled around me. Finally, it ended. I shot to my feet and whisked William from the pew. 'Come on,' I snarled. 'We're leaving.'

'*Max*. For God's sake. We need to pick up Cass.'

A grinning vicar. Children dancing past with their bags and scarves. I stared up at the steeple and wanted to put a bomb under it.

'Cass! Darling.' Sally's voice made it into my head. 'You sang beautifully. It was lovely. Where's your umbrella?'

'I left it at school. Max—'

I flicked my gaze downwards. 'Very good, Cass. Well done.'

But nothing could keep me in the vicinity of that house of worship. I paced abruptly away from it, and my family followed.

Small footsteps, running to catch up. 'Max!' cried Cass from beside me. 'Max!'

I stopped and turned. Her heart-shaped face was tilted up towards me, streaked with rain, and her hair flew about in the wind. 'Max, I read your book!'

So had Frank Vernon, and that had not stopped him from grinding the facts to dust. *Christian children all must be, mild, obedient, good as He*. 'Not now, Cass,' I said. 'Not now.'

*

A carol concert, and Cass's first excursion into my book. The two were not connected from Cass's point of view at all. The one was something that happened every year at school, and the other had presumably been prompted by a desire to bring me closer in my absence. But they had both got tangled up with her infant desire to impress me, and with the failure of the first, she'd resorted to the other. Unfortunately, it was the worst possible combination of things she could have confronted me with that evening in the rain.

Sally closed the kitchen door behind us. There were Christmas cards pinned up all around the room, holly and mistletoe trailing from the picture rail, a sprig of mistletoe dangling an inch above my head. But the darkness in her visage was beyond anything she would have inflicted on the children. 'Explain yourself,' she said.

I couldn't get the carols out of my head. 'Oh, for God's sake,' I said. 'I've just been on a twelve-hour flight, and I'm knackered.'

'You have not just been on a twelve-hour flight. You've had sixteen hours of sleep since then. How much more sleep do you need before you're prepared to behave like a human being?'

It seemed as if I'd received nothing but abuse for months. I sat down chaotically. 'Oh, Sally,' I wailed, 'don't do this to me now.'

She frowned in severity and incomprehension, and walked around me. After contemplating me for a while, she said, 'It was because it was religious, wasn't it?'

Had she really not known that? 'Of course it was because it was bloody religious.'

Her frown intensified. She walked back to where she'd been standing before, by the dresser. Her hand reached to a rolled-up napkin, and she clenched it in both hands, the knuckles showing white. 'Have you lost your mind?' she said.

'I've done nothing of the kind. Sally, I've been through hell these past few weeks. I just want to forget about it.'

'You don't seem to have forgotten about it. I didn't think—'
She stopped.

'What didn't you think?'

'I do realise that you've been through a difficult time.' There
was something very dangerous about the tone of her voice, its
brittle restraint, the sense of words being chosen very carefully.
'I've sympathised with all of it. You talked about nothing else
every time you phoned me, and I gave you as much support as
I could. I didn't think it would carry on when you got back.'

'I haven't mentioned it at all.'

She stopped kneading at the napkin and slammed it back
onto the dresser. 'Max, there are other people in the world apart
from you, you know. Tonight was the first time Cass has ever
sung in public. Don't you think that's important to her too?'

'Of course it's important. I haven't—'

'She missed you, Max. Do you know how hard it was for me
to persuade her that you hadn't gone for ever? Especially when
the trip was extended. You know the way Cass is when she
starts being scared about something.'

I did know. But it hadn't occurred to me that anything like
that would have happened while I was in America. 'I'm sorry,'
I said. 'But you know she's going to have to grow out of that
in the end. I will go away, sometimes. I'm sure she must realise
by now that I'm always going to come back. After all, I phoned
almost every day—'

'And when you spoke to her, you told her that you'd be
coming to the carol service. That was everything she was
building up to. You'd come home, and you'd hear her sing, and
you'd think she was wonderful. Can't you see how important
it was? All day I've had to stop them both from waking you up.
It was the first time she'd seen you in two months, for God's
sake. What the hell does the fact that it happened to be in a
church have to do with that?'

For me, it had everything to do with everything. But I could see how it looked to Sally. Worse, I could see how it looked to Cass. 'I'm really sorry,' I said. 'I didn't mean to be dismissive. Shall I go up and talk to her?'

Sally sighed. 'It's school tomorrow. Leave it until the morning.'

'Would you like a cup of tea?'

'Yes, please.'

I got up and started fiddling with the kettle. 'You see, the thing is—'

'Max, I really can't believe that you're going to start on that again.'

I stopped, astounded. Did she really not care at all? Then I saw her place her hands on the small of her back, and lean back, wincing. 'Oh,' I said, realising. With all that sleep, followed by the carol concert, I hadn't had a chance to ask after her at all. 'You must be tired yourself. How are you feeling? Generally? Have the clinics been going okay?'

'I'm fine.'

'You sure?'

'I don't need hormones to be angry about the way you've treated my daughter, you know.'

My daughter. A slap round the face, never inflicted before. 'Sally, that's just not fair.'

'Yes, it is.' She lifted two mugs from the dresser, put tea bags in them, then took the kettle from my hands and poured the water. 'Would you mind passing the milk, please?'

I passed it in silence.

For a moment it seemed as if she would continue to submerge her anger beneath a veneer of frostiness, but she could not. 'It's as if you haven't given us a single thought since you went to that first stupid debate,' she said. 'As if we didn't exist. I mean, you might at least have brought the kids back some souvenirs, or something. Then they might see some point in you going to America.'

'Actually, I have,' I said suddenly. It ought to have been a vindication, but Sally's necklace, Cass's New York edition of Monopoly and William's baseball shirt had all been bought in the first few days of the tour, when I'd missed my family horribly and had felt good about both myself and the country I was visiting. I hadn't thought about actually giving them to their recipients for weeks. And from her face, I could tell that Sally saw straight through me. 'They're Christmas presents,' I added hastily. 'That's why I haven't given them to them yet.'

'I see,' said Sally tersely, and picked up her cup of tea. 'Well, I've had a long day. I'm going to bed. What about you?'

I'd been up for only a few hours. I shook my head.

'Jet lag,' said Sally, a little more sympathetically. 'Ah, well. Maybe you'll have adjusted to London time by tomorrow.'

Her attitude had made me feel as if I'd been in the wrong from the start. But now defiance surfaced. Why should it be just me that had to adjust? Yet there she was, on her way out of the door. It was nearly a whole day since I'd come home, and still we hadn't had a proper reunion. 'Sally,' I pleaded, suddenly desperate to try to reclaim my expectations of the moment, 'come here.'

'What for?'

'To say goodnight.' I glanced at the mistletoe above me.

She stayed still and gave me a quizzical look.

'Sally, I've been an arsehole. I have thought about you all, you know. I've missed you like crazy. But I'm just so mixed up at the moment. Can't you let me be mixed up, just for one day?'

She softened and came over to me, and put her hands on my hips rather awkwardly. 'As long as it's just for one day,' she relented.

We kissed. But it was a stiff and decorous kiss. The passion we'd brewed through all those lonely nights had fizzled into nothing.

*

Still on Mid-Western time, I wandered the silent house, its cargo of beloved sleepers oblivious upstairs, trying to reclaim it as my own. Everything was still there as I'd left it – the bookshelves I'd built, the furniture I'd helped Sally buy, my coats on the rack and my boots by the door. Yet there were differences. The rows of jars on the kitchen shelves, neatly labelled in Sally's handwriting; the wood in the basket by the fire, and the ashes in the grate. I remembered Sally talking about her struggles to master the art of preserve-making, in case food became scarce in the shops. 'Every woman I meet has an opinion, but they won't hand over their recipes,' she'd complained. 'Why did my mother miss out that bit of my education?' But the neat labels on the bottles were a testament to at least some sort of success. 'Gooseberry Jam, 5/11/78'; 'Pickled Carrots, 27/11/78'. And she'd talked about the fire, too. 'We're still not supposed to have them in London,' she'd whispered down the phone. 'Which seems bloody unfair, as the government is incapable of providing us with warmth themselves. Declan's bought a van. He says he's going to drive out and get some wood from Essex.'

Declan. And now a whole new source of resentment was tapped within me. I'd seen him just once since his return from Berlin, at my leaving party, and apart from a few haphazard exchanges over the fruit punch, which he'd monopolised, we hadn't really had a chance to talk. I'd watched him that afternoon, and had thought he was an anachronism, holding forth as uninhibitedly as he would have done at King's Cross, getting drunker and drunker, whilst all around him chatted amiably and kept an eye on their children. Yet, creeping around the dark sitting room, I could see signs that in the weeks I'd been away he'd become as much of a feature of the place as he had been in my old bedsit. A copy of *Punch*; a book on East End criminals; an ancient jumper strewn over the back of a chair. Doubtless such accessories had been necessary during those long cold evenings, when he'd tended the fire he'd built, and had shared its warmth with my wife. How dare he, I thought with a bitter surge of resentment, even though I'd known all about it, and even though I would have been the first to say that Declan not only could but should help out where he could. But the damned cheek of the man was that he'd slipped back into a home he'd never seen as neatly as if he'd never been away. Whereas I, who had bought the place and furnished it, and whose absence had been less than a tenth as long, was now the stranger.

It was Sally I couldn't see. I retraced my steps, searching for evidence of the woman I loved. But love wasn't the way I'd been pretending it was. The core of what I felt was absolutely private, unknown by Sally, and perhaps mysterious even to me. I found it frightening, and my more grandiose flourishes were a way of hiding from it. And I found the idea of Sally's love for me frightening too. Oh, I knew about it, up to a point. There had been glimpses. Her fingers entwined suddenly, urgently in mine, her saying, 'You won't ever, ever go, will you, Max? You won't go?' And the brief feeling in me of not being able to support such a burden, of being able to support forever my own passion, but never hers. This is the problem with the love of others. The minute we perceive it separately from our own, in some ways it is none of our business.

And yes, her coats were hanging on the hooks next to mine, her books were on the shelves, her sketches decorated the pinboard by her desk. But piled on top of her coat was a small pink one, and then a smaller blue one, and tiny hats and scarves, and the floor below was a muddle of infant shoes. Her old art books were interspersed with tales of Meg and Mog, and her own pen and ink was crowded out by drawings of smiling stick men and wonky houses. Even my postcards from Massachusetts and California were more prominent than what came from her.

She had not changed. I'd left a wife and mother, and a wife

and mother had greeted me on my return. Except that when I was away I'd somehow imagined something much earlier, and when I came back it was gone. I should have been able to accuse her of the same things she charged me with – that all she wanted from me was for me to solve the problems that had arisen while I'd been away. But she held the high moral ground, because it was Cass's feelings she was defending, and I'd never thought that anything would come between us that didn't come from ourselves.

Sometimes the heart feels like a bomb, heavy beyond support and full to explosion with all the love it is carrying. What happens, when things get mixed up like that? What happens, when you can't say a word to the child without injuring the mother, and when you can't see either of them for the bond that is between the two? In such circumstances, love becomes a web, a net, and there is no way either out or in. Where was Sally, in all this responsibility, in all this jam-making, in carol concerts and mustard and cress and bags packed for school? Where was the woman who could resist anything but fun? I knew she was there, but I couldn't find her; I loved her to distraction, but I couldn't go up to her. My abject ramblings through the house petered to a halt, and I sat at the moonlit kitchen table and moped.

8

In the morning we reconciled. How could we not?

'Sally,' I whispered, kneeling by the side of the bed.

Her eyelids opened on deep brown irises, and her skin breathed the fragrance of Eve on Eden's first dawn. She was mine, the only goddamned thing in the world that was mine.

'Sally,' I breathed, 'I'm a jackass. I'm an idiot. I'm a fool.'

She traced a finger across my brow. 'Oh, my darling,' she said. 'You haven't been to bed.'

'My system's all buggered up. Forgive me.'

'Silly billy,' said Sally. 'I'm so sorry I gave you such a poor welcome home. It was just – well, you know, I'd missed you so much. Do you forgive *me*?'

'Oh, Sally. There's nothing to forgive.'

She smiled the smile that needed to be kissed. And then I was back in the bed I should have been in all along, and we were all bundled together, Sally and I and the only one of our children that could still be held within us, and there was nothing but comfort, and the lightness of the morning, and love.

It was the weekend before Christmas, and the next few days were a whirl. Unpacking from America, packing to set off for Dorset and Plymouth, tripping over wrapping paper and suit-cases everywhere. Throughout all this, Cass drifted like a small, earnest, seven-year-old ghost, never mournful precisely, but somehow disembodied, as if her mind were away from us for the time being. I knew that I had to find a way to make amends.

'Cass,' I said as we tidied up the plates, 'do you want to come up to my study? You can tell me what you think of my book.'

Children are so endlessly forgiving. The joy sparked instantly in her eyes, and she nodded hard enough to make her head fall off. I knew that to her my study was a magical place, a den of stories and mysteries and Murray Mints, and it was a great treat for her to be invited into it. We scampered up the stairs together, and on my invitation, she pulled herself up onto the chair that my students used on the rare occasions I gave tutorials at home. She was a comically small figure in it.

'Well,' I said, pulling the book down from the shelf, 'what did you think of it?'

I pull it down off its shelf now, too, and turn to its first page, trying to see the words through the eyes of a seven-year-old child.

'Do animals other than human beings know that some day they will die? We do not know what meaning death has for any species beyond our own. The creatures which surround us spend their lives apparently divided between personal survival and perpetuation of the species, and may make no differentiation between the two. In this they may be closer to scientific reality than we are ourselves. Yet the human being's prior knowledge of death has had a profound effect on our history as a species. It has led us to deny the obvious with a thousand different theories: some of them scientific, and most of them religious. A century ago, Charles Darwin came up with the most convincing explanation of all. But even he had no detailed understanding of the mechanism by which living things attain life beyond that of their own bodies. It is only in the last twenty years that scientific discoveries have proven at last that our instincts towards denial were right all along. There is a part of us which has existed for a million years before our births and will, if we are lucky, persist a million beyond our deaths. It spirals through every cell in our body, spiritless, beholden to nothing and nobody. For the first time in the history of human thought, we have a firm foundation on which to base our understanding of life beyond death.'

She couldn't have understood a scrap of it. Yet I know that she read at least that far, because she went straight downstairs afterwards and grilled Sally about it. I was three thousand miles away then, and am further now in time, but I can see the pair of them in the kitchen of Edenbridge Terrace, Sally labouring sweatily and bad-temperedly over the Aga, and Cass, dancing around the table, attempting to distract her. Sally giving in, reaching for her glasses, sitting at the table and peering at the words. Then, between the two of them, making some approximation of what it meant.

I looked at her expectantly. Cass suddenly looked serious, and pursed her lips, as if the excitement of the study had completely put out of her mind anything she had thought. Then, just as transparently, a look of consternation came over her face. 'Max—' she faltered.

'Yes, love?'

'Max—' She came out with it in a rush. 'Mummy says you don't believe in heaven. It's in the book.'

'That's quite true.'

'But – Max, where's Grandpa?'

Sally's father had died the year before. He wasn't a great loss to anyone, least of all his wife, but since his death Cass had wrapped him up in all sorts of comfortable illusions. And suddenly I realised what a reversal it would be for Cass if I pronounced that the only place Grandpa existed was in the ground rotting. At his funeral the vicar had spelt out Mr Bowden's future in the sort of cloying detail that was the speciality of sentimental, Middle-England Anglicanism, with hints of angels and one-to-one chats with God. When we'd got home, Cass had buried one of her less-favoured soft toys in the garden, complete with a service consisting of what she could remember of the Lord's Prayer, until grief overcame her and she burst into our room after lights out to demand that it be exhumed. At the time I'd treated the incident with amused forbearance, but now I realised that I'd thoughtlessly allowed her young mind to be corrupted with the same sort of nonsense that had so blighted Dan Gorman's childhood. Looking at her face, screwed up in bewilderment and distress, I remembered the day I'd sat in the park with her, hoping that she'd always understand the world as well as she did then and dreaming up the idea for *Genesis*, and realised that it was about time I fulfilled my own ambitions.

'Cass,' I said, 'do you know what genes are?'

She'd been surrounded by them for long enough to know the answer to that one. 'It's a little thing in every bit of us.'

'That's right. And our genes don't necessarily die along with the rest of us. They carry on.'

'Oh.' She found a glimmer of redemption. 'So do our genes go to heaven?'

I laughed. 'I suppose they do, in a way. But it's not the sort of heaven the teachers tell you about at school.'

'But why do they say something different at school?'

'It's just a story they use because they think you won't understand the truth.' I wasn't sure whether this itself was true. Having met her teachers, I felt it perfectly possible that some of them were woolly agnostics who bailed out of answering the difficult questions by resorting to religion, but on the other hand the older and more formidable ones probably believed the stories themselves. Either way, I didn't feel that it was time to explain that some adults were morons. 'But they don't need to do that, because you do understand. Don't you?'

She nodded doubtfully. 'What sort of heaven is it?'

'It doesn't have any God up there with a big white beard.

And there are no angels or harps. Heaven is all around us. In the case of Grandpa, the heaven his genes went to was *you*.'

'Uh?'

'You were quite right when you said that our genes were in every bit of us. But they're not just *in* us. They come before us.' I stared around my study for inspiration, and found none. 'Look, Cass, can you get me your Lego box?'

Her eyes lit up. An experiment! She ran up to the attic and came back with the old ice cream box filled with plastic bricks. I scattered the pieces over the floor and pulled out a few interestingly-shaped nuggets. 'What's this meant to be, when it's built?'

'It's a spaceship. But William's put it together *wrong*—' She took the pieces from me and pulled them apart.

'It still doesn't look much like a spaceship to me. How do you know that's what it's going to be?'

'Well, because it's got this bit sticking out here, and this bit here—'

'I don't think that makes it obvious at all. How did you know the first time you built it?'

She looked at me as if I was stupid. 'Because that's what the *instructions* say.'

'Exactly right. Well, your genes are just like the instructions for the Lego. Except that instead of having all the pieces in one place and the instructions somewhere else, the instructions for building a Cass are in every single piece. So no-one has to put you together. Every little bit of you knows just where it should be, because your genes tell them what to do.'

'Oh.' Cass looked at her arms and shook them around a bit, clearly unconvinced by their capacity for self-determination. 'But how do the genes know?'

'That's where it gets very complicated. Essentially, they've evolved that way. Do you know what "evolve" means?'

'Sort of,' said Cass, in the kind of voice that meant that she knew the word but had no real idea of what it meant.

'It's when creatures change so that they suit what's around them better. For instance.' I rested my elbow on the desk, and then looked at it. 'When we were in King's Cross we lived in a small space, so we couldn't have very much furniture. But when we got here there were lots more rooms, and they all needed to have furniture in them. So your mother and I went out and bought some more furniture. By doing that, we were evolving, in a way.'

'Oh.'

It didn't sound that convincing to me either. 'But genes can do much better than we can. They can change things completely. You see, all animals have genes, not just people. If you think of a snail—' Why had I become fixated on furniture? 'A snail's genes have evolved not so that he can have more or less furniture, but so that he doesn't need a house at all. He's grown one on his back. And the way that's happened, basically' – I saw that it was necessary now to skip reams of science – 'is that his great-great-great-great-great-great grandparents – even greater than that—'

'Great-great-great-great-great-great-great-great-great-great-great?' suggested Cass.

'Something like that. Anyway, those great-great grandparents didn't look much like snails at all. They looked more like slugs. And they had lots of children, and one of those children was a bit different, so that it had a little bit of shell on its back. And that shell helped to protect it from birds which wanted to eat it, which meant that it lived much longer and had many more children than its brothers and sisters. And so it carried on, until more and more snails had more and more shell, until the snails looked completely different from the slugs.'

I came to a triumphant halt, relieved to have got to my destination without mishap and via a tale that sounded not unlike a *Just So* story. But Cass was looking at her arms again. It was true that I had not explained very much about her so far.

'Now, even the slugs themselves didn't always look like slugs. The same thing happened to make the slugs, and the snails, and even you and me. If you go back far enough in time, you can find some ancestors – that's the word for any parent or grandparent, however great – who belong to every creature that's alive today.'

'And all of that's because of genes?' said Cass, trying to get a grip on things.

'Yes.' I caught sight of my starting point, and made a mighty effort to return to it. 'You see, each time a creature died, its genes had a chance of living on, because they'd been passed on to its children. The genes that you and I inherited from the ancestors of everything have lived for millions and millions of years. In just the same way, Grandpa's genes live on in you.'

'You mean I've got Grandpa's genes, because he gave them to me.'

'That's right,' I said in breathless relief.

'How did he give them to me?'

'Well, he gave them to your mother, really, when she was born.' Please not the facts of life. Surely Sally or a teacher or *someone* had dealt with that one. 'And she passed them on to you.'

But there were no problems with understanding the facts of life. The problem was what they were. I saw the light dawn across her face, and it was terrible. She blurted it out. 'But Max,' she said, 'what about *your* genes?'

'What?' I stuttered, pointlessly, stalling for time.

'Did I – did you—'

'Oh, Cass—'

'You didn't, did you? That was someone *else*.'

I tried to be calm. 'Just as far as your genes are concerned. That's all. Cass, we can find out about your real father as soon as you're ready. Your mother's always said—'

'But you gave them to William.'

'Cass, I would have given them to you too if I could. But I didn't know your mother in those days.'

'And that's what your whole book's about?'

For a moment I wanted to say, *it's just a book, it doesn't matter, it has nothing to do with our lives*. But it wasn't, and it did. So I said nothing.

'Does it mean that I'll never be like you?' Her horror was turning into rage, demanding that I should contradict her and return things to the status quo. But as the rage mounted, I could see that she knew I would not. 'Does it? Does it?'

I tried to take her in my arms. 'You'll be like yourself, Cass. No-one is exactly like their parents. You're not just genes. There's more than that—'

She struggled free. 'That's all there is in the book!'

And she was gone. I knew that there was nothing I could say to make it better. All I could hope was that she'd get it into perspective for herself.

A week later, when we'd returned from our voyage to the West Country, our next-door neighbour came to our door with a slightly frosted, torn and muddy copy of *Genesis*.

'It was in our compost heap,' she said in laughing bemusement. 'I'm sorry about the state of it. I'm afraid it nearly got buried under the honeysuckle cuttings. Goodness knows how it got there.'

'Goodness knows,' I agreed innocently, and quickly took the book.

I hurried up to my study, which was immediately beneath Cass's attic bedroom. Leaning out of the window, I could see the compost heap on the other side of the fence that divided our garden from the neighbours. It would have taken a fairly mighty throw for someone of Cass's stature, but it was possible.

I gave it a good wipe and returned it to the bookshelf alongside the other complimentary copies. Not even Sally learned of its brief escapade beyond the perimeters of our land.

'Welcome back,' said John Hinds benignly when I crawled reluctantly to his office on my first day back at work.

I have often wished that I had not succeeded so young. Apart from anything else, it gave me a bad reputation. Most young lecturers take a couple of years just to get their heads around the job, but by the time of my major review, I had rave reviews from my students, a series of published articles under my belt, and *Genesis*. My superiors chose to see the latter as not a recommendation but a liability. They were still banging on about the paucity of my footnotes, and claimed that it would make me the butt of every hostile biologist in the land, rendering me henceforth unpublishable in serious academic journals. This proved to be more or less the case, but as the men who delivered this prophecy were well-represented on the editorial boards of the journals in question, I credited this more to their personal hostility than to their powers of divination.

At first, with the buzz of my book's publication still around me, I barely noticed that my articles were coming back for correction. And that then, when I made my usual perfunctory amendments, they came back again. But then I received an outright rejection. In the old days, before *Genesis*, John had been most helpful in putting a word out here, helping me to compose a letter to the editor there, and essentially pushing my efforts out into the light. Now this route to publication was closed. 'You've got your own reputation now,' said John. 'You don't want old duffers like me sticking their oar in.'

What I suppose he meant was that, having been so reckless with my writing, my reputation was my own responsibility. This didn't bother me very much at first. After all, the only way my reputation was going was up, and so it was clear that it didn't need John's help. Whatever obstacles were in my path, they would soon be cleared out of the way by my unorthodox methods of progression and my insatiable appetite for science. With great equanimity, I had invited John and all the other old duffers to the leaving party we held before I set off for America, and had forced them to give their sarcastic congratulations on my success.

Now I was back. And I knew that John could tell immediately from my demeanour that all was not well. That was the problem – I could have got away with passing off the first month of my tour as a dazzling triumph, if only I'd still felt triumphant about it. But to me the applause was now hollow, the acclaim superfluous and the accolades false. The people who'd praised me had already known everything I'd told them. I'd failed to infiltrate a single human brain.

'Hi,' I mumbled.

'I hear from Jeffrey Shay that you were very well received at Caltech.'

'Mmm,' I said in as absent-minded a tone as I could muster, wandering towards the window of his office.

John snuffled, which was his version of laughing. 'Come on, Max, modesty doesn't suit you. Tell me all about your grand exploits.'

'It was fine. It went very well.'

'Worth using up your sabbatical term for, then?'

Rage surfaced instantly, as I'm sure he meant it to. This had been John's principal argument against the lecture tour. He'd made it quite clear that there would have been no way he would have let me go if it weren't for the fact that I was due a sabbatical and he couldn't stop me. In his opinion I was damaging my career. A sabbatical ought to be used for research and building up a decent publication record, not gadding around foreign countries drawing attention to myself and publicising a book which was of no use to anyone other than pretentious young men who had avoided the rigours of a scientific education. And now I could see that in his own mean-minded, pettifogging way, he'd been right.

'I learned a great deal, as it happens,' I said through gritted teeth.

'Oh, I'm so glad. What did you learn?'

I should not have told him. But then, I shouldn't have felt ashamed to have come home so crestfallen; I shouldn't have needed so badly to prove that my trip had been worthwhile; I shouldn't have been tempted into a trap set by lunatics; perhaps I should never have gone haring off after an American reputation at all. It was so difficult at that moment to negotiate my way back to the innocent beginning of that avalanche of errors, and even harder to admit that I might have been wrong.

So I told him that I'd learnt that my book was even more important than I'd thought it was. I told him about Frank Vernon, and the Academy of Scientific Creationism, and the movement to ban the teaching of evolution in schools. I presented the Mid-Western debates as a preliminary scuffle in what was bound to turn into a protracted but ultimately glorious war. And as my oration progressed, and I heard my syntax and vocabulary becoming more and more extravagant, I knew that sentence by sentence, I was losing whatever respect John might have for me as a scientist. Because of course I was not a lone warrior in all this. Dan had drummed it into me well enough that biologists had been fighting this scourge since the publication of *The Origin of Species*. I was not so stupid as to suppose that John was ignorant of these facts. The only person to whom it had ever been news was me. Until that day in Missouri, I'd been too blinded by the rightness of the facts in my possession ever to consider the opinions of those who dissented.

Yet John didn't ridicule me, or even take issue with anything I had said. He looked at me thoughtfully, and said, 'Yes, Jeffrey did mention something about that.'

Jeffrey Shay. The previous time John had mentioned the professor I'd met at Caltech, I hadn't bothered to think about the implications. There had been nothing wrong with the man at all – I'd even asked him for advice about whether to take up the job at MIT. It had not occurred to me that he might be in cahoots with my boss. So John knew about the job, and he also knew how I'd been on the day before I'd left for Shirley County: super-confident, full of myself, and boasting that I'd been invited to speak by whole townfuls of people in the Mid-West.

'Shay *knew*?'

'Knew what?'

I was struggling, trying not to reveal that I'd been ignorant of my own mission, even though it must be perfectly obvious to John. 'That they were – they were—'

'Apparently he tried to warn you. But he had the impression that you didn't hear him. He asked me to find out how you fared.'

And now I was speechless. I hadn't said anything to John yet about how I'd 'fared'. The idea, however fuzzy, had been to avoid any mention of winning or losing at all. But now, so uncharacteristically, and yet in such a typical way, he was asking me.

'He was,' continued John, 'a little concerned about you. He felt that for all your brilliance, you might be something of an innocent in some ways. That you might take it to heart. But you shouldn't, Max, you really shouldn't. It's a long way away. A purely American problem. Even over there, I'd say that the majority of Christians are perfectly happy to embrace the teachings of science, just as we do over here.'

He hadn't even waited for a response. He *knew* I'd lost. He was talking down to me, calling me an innocent, trying to comfort me – and then, when I was halfway through assembling my riposte, the word bounced back at me in all its force. '*We*?'

'Yes, Max. We.'

I stared at him. Now that I look back on that conversation, it is difficult for me to separate the hostility I already felt for him from the knowledge I learnt only at that moment. In the following months and years, when Sally berated me for my antipathy towards Christians and used John as an example, I always fought back, pointing out that it was clear that I would have disliked him even if he hadn't been a Christian, because we were at loggerheads long before he told me. But is that really true? It is hard for me now to imagine him as an unbeliever. Perhaps what had always annoyed me about him was his complacency, his unspoken assumption that he was party to the moral rules of the universe; perhaps religion had always been the point of dispute between us, even when I hadn't known it. Because certainly, when I remember that moment, it feels like the scene in a cops and robbers film when the crusty old police chief who has always got in the way of the hero's maverick instincts is revealed as being the criminal mastermind who is behind the plot the maverick has been trying to foil all along. My breath was taken away from me. I was enraged beyond comprehension. But there was an unmistakeable rightness about the revelation. It was true.

'Would you like a sherry?' said John mildly.

Give me an *intelligent* Christian, I'd thought in America. Then I might start to understand what they're all so hooked on. John Hinds was the intelligent Christian I'd been delivered, and I didn't understand at all. I looked around his office. It was crusty with the paraphernalia of an old-fashioned British don. Heavy window sills, dark antique furniture, leather-spined books piled up everywhere, empty glasses slowly rotting between papers and second-hand envelopes and knick-knacks from abroad. In America they'd had clear desks, sweeping vistas, and shiny new test tubes. They'd also had the ASC. If I was to tolerate the fusty, self-satisfied dampness of an English university, then I was buggered if I was going to tolerate God as well.

'But you're a scientist!' I yelled.

'Sit down, Max.'

A stupid, spindly Chippendale chair was the only support available. I threw myself into it. Unobligingly, it remained whole. John pottered gently around the occasional table that served as his drinks cabinet, and provided a thimble-sized glass of sweet amber goo. Then he struck a pose by the window. It was not the sort of pose I would myself have struck, had I been inclined, but it was still a pose. Shoulders down, hips flagging, polyester trousers hanging fleshlessly around his thighs, eyes regarding the crumbling brick wall ten feet from the glass with misty intensity.

'It's not entirely impossible to reconcile the concept of a deity with the findings of science,' he said.

I tried to take a slurp of sherry. The far side of the glass collided abruptly with my nose, and the liquid sprayed all over my face. 'Reconcile it now!' I barked.

The merest quiverings of a smile floated upon his lips. 'If you ever take the time to speak to some mathematicians,' he said, 'you'll find that a significant proportion of them are deists.'

Maths. Yes, John's reputation was based on the fabulous statistical formula he'd discovered for the arrangement of insects' wings. No, I staked no claim to be the most mathematical of biologists. Yes, I knew that Darwin had been wrong in deciding not to read Mendel because he was too mathematical. No, I didn't agree that Mendel was the better scientist of the two. '*Why?*' I demanded. 'Just tell me why.'

He brought the glass of sherry to his lips, and sipped at it neatly, risking no confrontation between glass and nasal flesh. 'Mathematics is a language that was not created by man,' he said dreamily. 'It exists in all its immensity, and we discover it as we go along. Yet it is not anchored to any concrete reality. The moon may obstruct the light of the sun, and we may discover the way in which our equations predicted its course. But the sums exist alone. There are sums which have been performed on this earth which relate to nothing but themselves.'

'And?'

'I see no distinction between the relationships between numbers and the connections in the neural networks within the mind of God.'

'That's a non-sequitur! Relationships between numbers? Mind of God? How the hell do you get from one to the other, apart from by your own superstitious volition?'

He took a seat for himself, swivelled it round to face me, then placed himself between its arms and settled his elbows upon his bony knees. The forward-leaning stance was precisely that which he used to adopt in tutorials, when I was doing my PhD. 'It's perfectly obvious to me,' he stated. 'Mathematics is as beautiful as a body. It governs bodies, but it comes before them. What would it be but a body itself?'

'This isn't God!' I shrieked. 'It's just maths!'

'Really, Max? How can you tell? Why should something make sense, before any meaning? Our choices in these matters are predicated upon the construction of our own particular brains.'

This time I shoved my upper lip against the rogue edge of the glass and downed the sherry in one. The fire in my belly had the desired effect of cooling me down. 'Look,' I said. 'This is just semantics. I might call it maths, and you might call it God. But we're talking about the same thing. It has nothing to do with churches, or the ten commandments, or swearing your life away to the whims of a being which has no proven existence except in the imaginations of its inventors. Does it?'

'Churches are mathematical in their construction, in the same way that bodies are. Ten is a very wonderful number for the commandments. Nothing is invented, when you take it down to its roots.'

The man was mad, a theologico-mathematical obsessive. 'Well,' I declared, in a final fit of pique, 'I'd like to see you having that discussion with the vicar.' I threw my glass onto the occasional table. It tottered, but stayed upright. Then I vacated the room.

'Max,' he called after me. 'You're a talented scientist. Don't throw it all away.'

Would I have listened, had I known then what I know today? It is, of course, an irrelevant question, because the young don't know, and the old can't go back. But still I think, as I try so hard to identify with the sheer stupidity of myself at that time, that the only person I was damaging was myself. Why should I do such a thing? I had no long-nurtured stores of self-loathing to draw upon, as Declan did at the same age.

'Max, you're so spoiled,' said Sally, when I tried to let off steam about my continuing persecution by the academic establishment. 'Nothing's ever gone wrong for you before, has it? Everything's been so easy. Well, if it takes a bunch of religious crackpots in a town no-one's ever heard of to teach you that you can't always get what you want, then perhaps it's a good thing you came across them.'

My heart shrank with dread, and I saw the miles that had separated us coming back to lodge between us. 'Sally, I know it's been hard for you, coping on your own. It must have been very difficult, with being pregnant and everything—'

'Pregnant? This has absolutely nothing to do with pregnancy. It's about you. Just pull yourself together, for God's sake. I tell you what you sound like. You sound like you're one of those American evangelists yourself, as if there's only one truth in the universe and you're the only one with access to it.'

Where on earth had she got that idea from? 'That's ridiculous!'

'What did you expect, that people would keep praising you forever? Some people will always have different opinions, and the sooner you learn it, the better.'

But I couldn't learn it. These weren't mere opinions, like a taste for a type of food I couldn't stand, or a predilection for chintz curtains. They were falsehoods. I had trained as an educator – *John* had trained me as an educator – and now I was being told that there were some truths that I just couldn't teach. If I'd been a lecturer in history, or English literature, or even philosophy, then religious belief might not have been so much trouble to me. But the absence of God was so fundamental to my understanding of my own subject that it had never occurred to me before that anyone might want to refute it. What point could there be in the quest to solve the mysteries of the universe if it was doomed to end in nothing but the whims of a being whose consciousness we could never, by definition, comprehend? Why bother moving on from a flat earth under stars hung as lanterns from the midnight sky, if the thing you planned to end up with was equally bizarre? To close one's mind to the idea that the universe made sense would be to relinquish scientific endeavour altogether. I couldn't see how I could be expected to tolerate such ignorance and still try to teach the truth.

I tried to explain this to Sally, begging her to understand. 'But don't you see?' she retorted. 'I don't disagree. I think you're right. It's highly unlikely that any such thing as God exists—'

'Highly unlikely? Sally, those are the words of an agnostic.'

'I *am* an agnostic. You can't prove it one way or the other – even you've admitted that. I just don't think it matters. John Hinds is a nice man, underneath. You'll never change his mind about a thing like that, not at his age. So stop wasting your time worrying about it.'

I must have known that she was right. John's mind never would be changed, any more than I'd changed the minds of the people in that hall in Shirley County. 'But whose minds can I change, then?' I pleaded.

'Why do you have to change anyone's minds at all?'

'It's my job! What did you think I wrote *Genesis* for in the first place, for goodness' sake?'

'I thought you wrote it for me and the children.'

Which was what I'd always said. But now I could see that it had never quite been true. And that it wasn't just religious people who had opinions which disagreed with my own. Sally's were starting to look quite different too.

Oddly enough, one of the few people in whose presence I felt free of all these burdens at that time was Declan. We began playing squash together every other Tuesday, and this habit was initiated, as I later discovered, at Sally's request.

'Take him away,' Sally had implored him. 'Bash some sense into him. I can't stand it any longer.'

During their fireside chats during the power cuts when I was away, Sally had managed to delve a little into Declan's time in Germany. He had, she reported to me, almost fallen in love in Berlin. The girl's name was Johanna, and she was several years younger than him. She was young and blonde and hopeful. Since his mother's death, he'd had no particular roots in England, and could easily have started a new life for himself with her out there. He knew that he should throw himself into the affair the way she did, and accept her promise of the future for what it was. But Declan, as evidenced by the article of his we'd saved, was not in the mood for a future. The whole premise of his life there was its temporary nature. He couldn't help but tell her from the start that it would not last and that she would leave him. In the end she had no choice but to believe him, and so it did not and she did. When his newspaper cut back its resources and called him home, he left, almost relieved to have escaped being ensnared by the place.

I returned from my own travels to find his time accounted for, Sally's forgiveness bestowed and his reintegration into the household complete. It was an unsatisfactory situation as far as I was concerned, because there had been no confession or apology to me, and I was as offended and infuriated by his behaviour as I ever had been. But I couldn't cast him out, and I had no real desire to do so. There were enough irresolvable questions hammering away in my head without me bothering about the ones which concerned Declan.

'Squash?' I said when he made his unexpected suggestion.

'The game. Rackets. Squidgy ball. Walls. Lots and lots of running around.'

I was silent for a moment. Then, 'Is that the one where people smash one another into oblivion?'

'Oh, Jesus. If you want to put it like that, yes.'

Sport had always been an important part of our friendship. Ever since I'd been in London, we'd played cricket together in a dodgy team which consisted mostly of Fleet Street hacks, and had got appropriately drunk in the pub afterwards. But our hostilities with bat and ball were suspended in the winter. And that winter I wasn't sure whether I wanted to see Declan at all. But on reflection, a good workout would probably do me good. I dug out a rather disreputable pair of shorts, and the trainers I'd used when I was at university, put both into a Sainsbury's carrier bag, and turned up as instructed at the gym.

Declan gawped at me. 'Max, what *are* you wearing?'

I looked down. I'd come straight from work, and my clothes were the black velvet suit and white dress shirt I always wore for lecturing. It was true that they had not been washed or ironed for a while, but there had been no complaints from my students. In fact the odd thing was that Sally had not sorted them out for me.

'And your hair. And the bloody beard. Sally was right, mate. You're a state.'

I ran my hand through my admittedly vigorous stubble, and made a stab at flattening my hair. 'Look,' I said, holding up the plastic bag, 'I'm getting changed. It doesn't matter what I'm wearing now. Where do I hire this racket?'

We sorted out the basics, and went onto the court. I had not played squash before, and it transpired that Declan, deprived of cricket in Germany, had been playing regularly in the ex-pat clubs. To begin with I played tennis, serving overarm and hitting the ball into mid-air. Declan didn't bother to coach me, probably realising that my natural advantages would assert themselves in time. And, slowly, they did. The court was so small that I needed to take only a few steps to cover it. As I began to get the hang of it, something inside me released, and soon I was running like a demon, smashing repeatedly into the walls.

'Okay,' I growled after a pulverising winner, while the ball was still bouncing from one end of the court to the other. 'Let's play for points.'

I had the best of every rally and yet Declan won the first four games, exploiting my shaky grasp of the rules, tapping the ball gently behind my charging feet, looping it just beyond the reach of my towering racket. My fury mounted, until I was a hot-faced, quivering hulk. Just before the fifth game, I stopped and stood still, and had a bit of a word with myself. I had been playing every point as if Declan were Frank Vernon, and was going wrong in just the same way I had in my worst moments in the Mid-West. There was no point in striking out in blind rage. If I was going to beat either Declan or Frank, I would have to use my brain as well as my brawn.

'What are you waiting for?' I said to Declan, who was looking at me with an odd expression on his face.

'You,' said Declan.

I kicked the ball over to him. 'Let's get on with it.'

The match turned. When I won that game, Declan looked almost relieved. Then I took the next, and the next, and the next, and after the eighth game Declan himself stopped, and looked to be having an internal conference similar to my own.

'Four-four,' he said, dripping with sweat, a pink weal starting to emerge on his cheekbone where I'd caught him with my elbow. 'We should make this the decider.'

It was a battle to the death. I skidded across the court, tripped over my racket, trod on the ball and fell on my head. The ball whipped around and around and around. Declan played with icy, teeth-clenching calm as I whirled weightily past him, there before the ball, hitting it between his own legs, spreadeagled against the wall and reaching at full stretch. At the climax of the final point we collided mid-court, and Declan was thrown to the opposite wall and collapsed in a breathless heap.

'Mine,' I said. 'Bloody good game. I'll beat you properly next time.'

'Next time?' Declan panted.

'We should do this regularly.'

He looked more than a little scared, but agreed, and it turned out to be a good thing. Erasmus College seemed petty and provincial; John Hinds' slurs seemed more and more calculated to hit at the heart of my discontents; and even the charm of Edenbridge Terrace had faded, because I'd thought at the beginning of my trip that we'd soon be exchanging it for something else. Declan offered himself as a whipping boy for them all, and I soon forgot, as I bludgeoned my misanthropy into the dust of the court, that I had any special grievance against him at all. We were friends again.

The call from the BBC was entirely unexpected. 'Max,' said the researcher as if he knew me, 'we're having a bishop on the show to talk about *Life of Brian*. We need an opposing view. Couldn't get the Pythons 'cos they've done it before, so someone suggested you. Can you make it to the studio on Tuesday?'

I gasped in disbelief at the turn in my fortunes. It felt like a long time since the spate of newspaper articles that had followed the publication of *Genesis*. I longed for the excitement of those days. I suppose I must have known then what Margot would intimate a quarter of a century later: that where there had been photographs, I had not only sounded good, I'd looked good as well. One profile in particular had made Sally crease up with laughter. 'Oh, Max,' she'd giggled, struggling for breath, 'that soulful gaze! However did I end up married to such a creature?'

But I'd never been on television. The smarts of my failures were unfinished business, raw within me, and my vanity flared as it had never had cause to before. 'I'll take it,' I barked, envisaging an explosion of the newspaper profile onto the screen, words and vision merging into an utterly irresistible proclamation of the truth. And though I feared Sally's wrath for bringing it all up again, I somehow hoped that my performance would be so compelling that it would make it up to her too. Even if it didn't, it was better that I should take out my grievances on a television presenter and a bishop than bring them home with me every night. To my surprise, when I explained this to her, she seemed to understand, however reluctantly.

'I can't tell you how to run your career,' she said, with only a little ice in her voice. 'If it's that important to you, you must do it.'

But Sally's reaction wasn't my only fear. 'Don't let the kids watch it,' I whispered to Sally. Since the day I'd explained evolution, Cass seemed to have put her disillusionment behind her, and had perhaps been even more loving in her efforts to make it up to me for our tiff. The last thing I wanted to do was upset her all over again.

'Why not?' said Sally. 'If it's going to be screened in the early evening I can't really see how I can stop them. Anyway, why shouldn't they know what their dad does on the telly? Think how awful it would be if Cass heard it from someone at school and then found out that she hadn't been allowed to watch it. You'll just have to make sure that there's nothing to disturb them.'

I hadn't, of course, told her about the crisis over Cass's reading of *Genesis*. Cass had proved to be such a flashpoint between us that I hadn't dared to stack up yet more evidence against me. And if I told Sally now, then I was afraid that she would say that I shouldn't do the debate. Which I couldn't bear. So I went, trying to convince myself that Cass had got over her shock entirely.

It was live, and video recorders existed only in the R&D departments of Sony and Philips, so I never saw it. My impressions of the event are sketchy, overwhelmed by the heat of the lights and the invisibility of the studio audience. But I do remember people shouting, though I can't connect it with myself, and my astonishment when the bishop rose from his seat in anger. It was only when I got home that I learned from Sally that it was I who had got up first, and that I had towered over him by more than a foot, and that the presenter had been forced to get between us and insist that we return to our seats. 'Now I see how it was in America,' she said tightly, and though I didn't dare to probe further, I had the strong feeling that she wasn't expressing her sympathy.

For William, I think the experience of seeing his father on the screen was no more than a novelty, at an age when novelty was almost more common than familiarity. He pronounced the programme to have been 'better than Bod', and wanted to know when 'Daddy show' was next going to come on. But Cass, to my enormous relief, was truly enthusiastic. She was familiar with the ideas, whether she understood them or not, and was burstingly proud that I'd been transformed into a person on the television. 'You were very good, weren't you, Max?' she confided, her excited grin taking up the whole of her face.

I looked into her eyes, and saw a shadow of her mother in those hectic days when we were writing *Genesis*. 'If you think I was good, then I was good,' I told her, and crouched down to give her a cuddle. Oh, thank goodness for her sweet nature and the springy resilience of childhood. She was my number one fan.

Perhaps, for the time being, my only fan. In the end it was Steve who drew Sally and me back together. As the final months approached it turned into her only difficult pregnancy. The doctors made all sorts of ominous diagnoses, and the only one we understood was the high blood pressure.

'Do you think it's because we've been arguing?' said Sally, with stark, frightened eyes. 'Do you think he can hear?'

We stopped arguing instantly. And for the time being, Sally had no problem getting me to take an interest in my family. There was a number of scares, and for a month or so I spent all my time on the alert for another hospital dash. A caesarean was finally called for, and I watched the awfulness of my wife being cut into alongside the awesomeness of my son being lifted dripping from the wound. They were both fine, just about. Oh, thank God, thank not God, thank fate and luck and anything else I could bring myself to believe in. Sally's words about nothing bad ever having happened to me had hit home. For at least a week, I'd come close to believing that my time was up.

A frail woman looked up at me from her hospital bed, still too weak to hold her child. 'Oh, Max,' she said, her voice insubstantial, as if some of it had bled away. 'I'm so glad that – all that silliness – I'm so glad it's over.'

I wept, too close to seeing how it would have been if I'd lost her with the silliness still in the air. Yet now that I'd been reprieved I could also see that the 'silliness' was not gone. It was just that I must never talk about it to her.

9

Our children were all beautiful. They still are. William appears to be the most extravagantly endowed, possibly because he's the one who's most keenly aware of it. The legend was always that he was a mirror image of me, and as far as personality is concerned, that may be true. But the older he's grown, the more I've thought he looks like his mother. He inherited her slender frame and prominent cheekbones, along with the dark colouring of all sides of the family, and escaped my pestilent hairiness. And he holds a cigarette almost exactly as she used to, though in his case the poise is shrouded in careless masculinity. A foot resting on a stool, an elbow supported by his knee, an arm outstretched and the hand flicking smoke into oblivion. I can't tell whether the forthright jut of the chin is hers or mine.

He is an adult now, but I knew him for so long as a child that I still think of many of his attributes in those terms. And the egoism of children is a mesmerising thing. I know that an infant ego is not the same type of thing as an adult one. Yet, that child – when those crinkled eyes first squinted open from the depths of Sally's triumphant bed, they might not have known me, but they seemed very certain about knowing themselves. Something primordial glinted in their filmy depths, as if the soft little body encased a piece of shrapnel from the beginning of time. An illusion, a self-deception on my part, a projection of my own wishes upon my child – but he was so very like me, and so very like himself. And as he pieced himself together, worked out what he could do, found out how to exert influence on the world, my imaginings slowly segued into reality.

Onwards and upwards; never did a child put so much energy into assisting his own forward momentum.

I'm sure I too was a precocious youth, but it wasn't in the nature of my family to notice such things. Perhaps things came as easily to me as they did to William – perhaps I talked as early, walked as early, learned to read before I went to school, but if so I never knew it. Whereas William knew. And if everything was so easy, then nothing needed to be serious. Watching William as a child was a blessed release. I went to work and fought with all my might against the world, then came home and was pelted with apples from the tallest branch of the tree. Seeing his demonic little face peeping at me through the leaves, his small body twisted around the spindliest branch, I couldn't help but feel lighter inside.

'William, get off that branch. It's not safe up there.'

He slithered downwards, then – oh, Jesus – slipped off entirely, hanging by thin arms like a monkey. 'Blah!' he shouted in scornful joy, and took one hand off to wave it at me.

'Oh, William – bloody hell—' I was convinced he'd suddenly discover that he could support his own weight no longer, and began to scramble up the tree myself. But of course I couldn't reach him.

'Daddy,' said William, his bum safely back on the branch, kicking his legs towards me. 'When can I join the scouts?'

'You can join the cubs next year.'

'Can't I go to the scouts? They have proper football matches.'

'The cubs have football matches too. For goodness' sake, William, come down.'

To no avail. Sally worried about him incessantly, and not just about the physical dangers he scorned so lightly. But she need not have done. For all his anarchic energy, he wasn't really a rebel. He was too keen on coming top in everything.

Steve could not be more different from his brother. Or, indeed, from the rest of us. He's the only one with even the slightest touch of blondness, which I think must have skipped a generation from my ruddy, blue-eyed mother. In fact, in most ways, he resembles no-one so much as her. Shorter and stockier than the rest of us, his hair is nut-brown instead of the regulation Oldroyd black, and when he was a small child he was a soft, playful, roly-poly thing, the only one of the three of them who was ever referred to as being 'sweet'. From the start, his greatest talent was that of making friends. Sally used to push him round Islington in his pram, with the task of keeping William under control as often as not delegated to Cass, and wherever they went they were besieged by Steve's fan club. He was the most obliging baby, with a gurgle and a smile for everyone, and he grew into a cheerful and generous child.

'He's the most laid-back member of the family,' Sally used to explain. 'In fact,' she said as an afterthought, 'he's the only laid-back member of the family.'

Cass took to him instantly. Whereas William had been an interloper, Steve was a greater threat to him than to her, and aged seven, she was at just the age to discard dolls and teddies and move on to a real cuddly human being she could play at nurturing. Much of her attention was spent on the mission to protect him from William. Yet for all the childish battles fought over his head, Steve remained possibly the smiliest, bounciest baby that was ever born.

We were a little concerned about how William would react to Steve's entry on the scene, having already experienced Cass's reaction to the intrusion of a younger sibling. But we needn't have worried. William's spirit was far too robust, even at the age of two and a half, to be dented by such a mere squidge of humanity. His ingenuity was exercised in finding ways to derive entertainment from his brother. As they grew older, we were very glad to have Cass's extra pair of eyes about the place. Steve tied up with garden twine in the treehouse awaiting rescue by a Spiderman who'd got bored and moved on to other things;

Steve on the receiving end of William's Harold Larwood impression, having balls bowled at his head in the manner of the 1933 Bodyline series, which had just been turned into a TV drama; Steve sitting in the bath, patiently waiting to discover the results of William's latest electricity experiment until Sally grabbed the handwhisk, plugged into the kitchen socket by an extension we'd thought was safely hidden, out of his hands just in time.

In response, Cass and Steve formed a natural alliance in the household, a bulwark against the effortless superiority of William. When Steve was small, he and Cass would form a team against William in New York Monopoly, and William didn't care that he was outnumbered because it meant that there would be all the more glory for him if, as was almost inevitable, he won. 'The bank is feeling rich!' William crowed, and handed out bushels of cash to the opposing team just to keep the game going.

'Stop *cheating*,' said Cass.

'It's for your own benefit.'

'I mean you were cheating before. How can you have all that money when you've just put two hotels on Mayfair?'

'Don't worry. I'm a very benevolent landlord.'

Bicker, bicker, bicker. Yet Steve bickered with no-one. When William stole or even destroyed his toys, he didn't complain. Had he been born twenty years later, we might have dragged him down to the nearest clinic and received a diagnosis of autism. But in fact his problem, if he had one, was precisely the opposite. Autists lack possessiveness because they fail to make associations between themselves and anything else, including other human beings. They lack empathy. Steve had a surfeit of it. The only times I remember him crying, apart from when he picked up the usual injuries, were when someone else was upset, and he empathised with the feelings of others whether he understood them or not. 'Look, Daddy,' he said as we watched a particularly overblown episode of *Dynasty*, which was appointment television for Cass during her most obstreperous teenage years, 'that lady's *sad*.'

The lady in question was Joan Collins, the evil Alexis Carrington, and she was crying with rage at the failure of her latest scheme to destroy the life of her ex-husband, Blake. Cass was kind enough to interrupt her viewing pleasure and give him a brief explanation of the situation, but still he wasn't pacified. 'Yes,' he said, 'but she's *sad*,' and couldn't understand why Cass hated Alexis if she was always the one who came out worst. Surely it was Blake who was being unfair?

His kindness was the source of his charm, but as he grew older it was clear that it was also a curse. Towards the end of his years at primary school, the strain of trying to comfort everyone, protect everyone, be everyone's friend, began to show, and he became increasingly upset by the daily battles amongst his classmates. For most of us, the dilemma of being close to both people on the two sides of a dispute happens mercifully rarely, but for Steve it happened every day. So while we worried for William's safety, we worried for Steve's too-generous spirit, and yet if any of us had tried to picture what constituted home, Steve would be somewhere at the centre of it.

The summer before Cass went to secondary school, I launched myself on a quest to make the house everything we could have dreamed. I painted the outside, I painted the inside, and then, despite Sally's protestations that it would be much better to get a professional in, I decided to build a conservatory, just like the one she'd stood in that evening long ago, holding the Twiglets and knocking me dead in her Wonder Woman outfit. The children were beside themselves with excitement and, again overruling my wife's concerns, I allowed them to help.

William's interest proved to be transitory, and he was soon distracting himself by showing Steve the fascinating effects caused by pouring Ribena into the mortar. Steve himself was really far too young to do very much at all, and so I sent them away and told them to build an extension to the treehouse. But

Cass persisted. While she painted and I sawed, we had many fruitful discussions about all the fascinating things she would learn at her new school, until Steve fell out of the tree and broke his arm.

By then, Cass lived in a world of tunes. After I'd got back from America, one of my apologies for my misbehaviour at the carol service had been made by buying her a piano. She was already in the habit of rushing to any piano she could find in the houses we visited in order to bash out 'Little Donkey' by ear, so it seemed a natural enough step. Both Sally and I thought it would be a rather nice piece of furniture to have around the house, but we'd had no idea how perpetually it would be used. In the hope of alleviating Cass's obsession, Sally started taking her to singing lessons as well, but the activity merely doubled. The same phrase was played or sung thirty times, or a difficult tune taken so fast that it came out as a strangled mess. Then we heard the sound of the lid slammed onto the keyboard, the thud of feet on the stairs, and wild tears of despair as she lamented the fact that she would never, ever be able to play properly.

'But you play beautifully, Cass,' I told her, and it wasn't a lie. I don't think anyone who knew Cass and the rest of the family during that time can have escaped the thought that her musical ability must have come from her father. Even I, who knew that it need not be half so straightforward an inheritance, couldn't avoid it. I have often been complimented on my voice, and had it been possible, she might have inherited a certain strength of vocal cord from me. But it is my speaking voice which has attracted praise. As soon as I try to sing I am a corncrake. I simply cannot find the notes I hear. As for Sally, she could at least hold a tune if she tried very hard, but her singing voice was a weedy, insubstantial thing, too weak to continue without accompaniment. The point is that before Cass, our household was something of a musical void. Music was something you woke yourself up with in the morning, or danced to late at night, and that was all. Our tastes were the legacy of the music our friends had introduced us to in our teens and twenties, and so our under-utilised record collection consisted of a few jazz favourites, Manfred Mann, the Beach Boys, the Rolling Stones, and rather a lot of Simon and Garfunkel. I had one classical record left over from university, bought to impress a girl – it was *The Four Seasons* – but it was never played. The exuberant flowering of Cass's musical talent couldn't be accounted for by having been planted in such barren cultural soil. In fact, her ability was the purest proof I've seen that some things have nothing to do with nurture at all.

'*Was* he musical?' I brought myself to ask Sally in the end.

She was as bewildered as anyone. 'I don't know. I never thought to look.'

And so Cass sang, and William caused mischief, and Steve chattered to whoever would listen to him, and we were happy. Yes, I was horribly stressed during much of that period, and I am sure that I often brought it home, but life is like that. We all had our ups and downs. I just remember watching our three beautiful, brilliant children and feeling both humble and proud. Humble that in each case the whole was so much more than the sum of the parts we had donated, and proud that I was somehow helping to give them the greatest gift a parent can give, which is a happy childhood.

Yet I did it by pretending that God did not exist. Or rather, as both Sally and I were atheists, that the concept of God did not exist. I was allowed to talk to her about my frustration with my colleagues and my problems with being taken seriously as an academic, because those had been around before the schism of Missouri, but any grievances I had with the religious fraternity could be exorcised only on air. At the time, I managed to persuade myself that it was a good thing: after all, I was on a

Quest, and it was better if I saved all my energy for the real thing, rather than wasting it on my wife. But it was hard when I came back from the broadcasting studios with my mind still fizzing with resentment. I daresay Sally wouldn't have minded if I'd simply talked to her about how each interview had gone, but it was a short step from there to rehearsing the arguments all over again, and if I started I couldn't trust myself to stop. So I kept quiet, and it was nearly three years before that pact was broken. But when it happened, it wasn't I who did it. It was her.

At first it seemed as though she did it deliberately to taunt me. After I'd spent all that time being quiet and good on the one subject that threatened to ruin my professional life, she suddenly whipped it out again and flaunted it in my face. Shortly before Cass was due to start secondary school, Sally announced that she'd thought of just the place for her to go. It was her old school.

'I had a great time there,' she said cheerfully. 'And Cass won't need to board. She can be a day pupil. It's got a brilliant music department. She'll love it.'

'Sally,' I spluttered, 'it's a bloody *convent*!'

She looked so painstaking and patient that I couldn't help but smell a rat. 'Max,' she said, 'I thought we'd agreed that religion didn't matter.'

'Agreed what?'

She said nothing more, but merely waited for me to come to a remembrance of our supposed arrangement. The sense of betrayal was devastating. Did she really believe that I'd stopped fighting because she'd won the argument?

'Anyway,' she said with comforting cosiness when it was clear that I wasn't going to respond, 'you can see from the way I turned out that it isn't very good at producing religious people. Half of the pupils aren't even from Catholic families, they just choose it because it's a good school. And I can tell you, after being surrounded by nuns all that time, nobody ends up believing in God.'

'Sally, I can't believe you're suggesting this.'

The centre of her face crunched a little, and now the sense of betrayal appeared to be hers. 'Come on, Max. Don't over-react. You know how silly it is.'

'*Silly?*'

We stared at one another, and wondered whether we'd had any idea who we'd been living with for the past three years.

'Look,' I said after taking a deep breath, 'you've told me yourself that if the nuns at your school had bothered to teach you family planning you wouldn't have ended up—'

'Having Cass,' said Sally. 'When was that such a bad thing?'

'Oh, come on. Much as it's wonderful that Cass was born, you wouldn't wish that on her. Pregnant at twenty—'

'Girls from all sorts of schools get pregnant, you know.'

'Sally, I can tell you right now that there is no way I'm paying for Cass to spend the next seven years at a religious seminary.'

There was a hefty silence.

'All right,' said Sally with very bad grace, 'if that's the way you feel, that's the way you feel. I'll look again.' But the atmosphere between us had already been polluted.

Her next idea was an extremely select private girls' school in North London, with a reputation not for academic achievement or sport but for gentility. In fact, it might just as well have been Sally's posh convent, with the nuns taken out.

'Sally,' I exploded, 'this is just the same as the last one!'

'What do you mean, it's just the same? It's not a convent. If you think the nuns don't make a difference, then we might as well go for my school after all—'

'No!'

'What have you got against this one? It's a perfectly ordinary school.'

'It is not an ordinary school. It's a posh school.'

She stared at me. 'Max,' she said, 'since when did you become a socialist?'

I didn't know whether I was a socialist or not. But the idea of paying to take our children out of the real world made my hackles rise.

'Why do you feel that you have to send her to exactly the same kind of school that you went to yourself?' I demanded. 'Do you think she'll turn into an alien if you don't? I went to state school, and I'm not an alien. In fact I got a much better education than you did. There is absolutely no point in paying a fortune for a bunch of airs and graces she'll only get rid of if she's got any sense.'

'Max,' said Sally patiently, 'I'm sure your school was great. But it was a grammar school. There's no eleven plus in London. Surely you aren't suggesting that we send her to a comprehensive *in Islington*?'

I grunted, because she had a point. The children's primary school was fine, but the local secondaries were perhaps a little too real even for my liking.

'Look,' I said, 'give me a bit of time. I'll see what I can come up with.'

And prompted by that reckless, deal-breaking mention of religion, a new difference was looming. The gap between our backgrounds had never been as great as Declan first made it out to be – if there was any distinction, it was a foolish gradation somewhere between upper-middle-middle and lower-middle-middle – but it was always clear enough whenever our mothers got together, with mine putting on a strangulated accent while hers condescended gently. We were able to laugh at them together, regarding class to be a thing of the past. Now it seemed that it was not. We were each determined that our children would turn out just like us.

With the help of my colleagues at Erasmus College, I scoured the schools of London for something that looked as much as possible like Plymouth Grammar, with the added provisos that it must be mixed-sex and nearby. These were not easy criteria to fulfil, but I found something in the end. I said a private thank you to Margaret Thatcher for introducing the grant-maintained sector.

'Oh, Max,' said Sally, 'that's miles away. How do you think she's going to get there?'

'A lot more easily than if she went to your school. At least I'm not proposing that we send her to Hertfordshire.'

'Does it have a choir?'

'How would I know?'

'Can't you see that's the most important thing when it comes to Cass?'

'She can go to choir out of school. The main thing is that she gets a decent education.'

We both avoided playing our trump cards. Hers was that Cass was her daughter and not mine, and mine was that if she went to a fee-paying school, it was me who was paying. Those were the kind of things that weren't supposed to matter, and so we didn't mention them. But they did matter.

It turned out that the school I'd chosen did indeed have a choir. In fact it had everything else Sally might care to look for. The more we looked, the better I thought the school was. It had good results, it was well-funded, and it wasn't barricaded off from London's poor by fees. I was almost grateful to Sally for having forced me to look properly.

Still she wasn't happy. 'This is all very well, Max,' she said, 'but how are we supposed to get her into it, at this notice? It's not just a matter of passing an exam, you know.'

I threw all my principles out of the window and had a few words with people I knew in secondary education. Cass got a place.

'The point is,' I said, in a bout of retrospective justification, 'the beauty of it being a mixed school is that the boys can go there too. We don't have to split them up. It's so much fairer that way.'

I came to regret those words quite deeply.

I still don't think the school had very much to do with the way Cass was as a teenager. Whether she'd gone to the most bashed-up comprehensive in London or the most exclusive public school in the land, we had no right to expect a girl like that to stroll through adolescence unscathed. Cass entered it long before the boys followed her, and to make things more awkward she was a girl. There were long private and hostile sessions in the bathroom with a make-up case; hours in the attic with extraordinarily puerile music vibrating the ceiling of my study; heartfelt defences of popular culture, despite or perhaps because of her own immersion in the music of centuries past; and denunciations of her parents' snobbish, outdated tastes. She might as well have gone through the years between thirteen and sixteen with a 'Do Not Disturb' sign around her neck. But the one thing she never did was take me to task for my parental status. I expected it, at the time. It would have been entirely in keeping with her attitude during her worst moods. But though Sally encouraged her quite strongly to allow her to take up the search for Cass's father on her behalf, Cass would have none of it. 'I'm not interested,' she said. 'He left.'

She was less happy as a teenager than she had been as a child, and I suspected that this was because she wasn't very good at it. Cass was not a rebel, but neither did she have the flexibility of character to conform. And I could see that the real pressure to conform came not from us or from her teachers, but from her peers. Her beauty should have made things easy for her. At thirteen she looked her age or younger – those huge, startled eyes were for many years afterwards those of a child – but this didn't make her any less striking. Her adult face was already fully formed, a delicate triangle of eyes, cheekbones and mouth, and it was a badge of difference. A female William would have dressed it up to the nines and used it to taunt the whole world, but Cass only ever seemed to try to hide it. Shortly after she turned thirteen, she got all her lovely long hair cut off and the remains squidged into the ugly fluffed-up style of every teenager, male or female, of the eighties. Sometimes she came out of her interminable make-up sessions with the evidence of tears all over her face, the electric-blue mascara smudged in resentful streaks across her cheeks. I suppose she just wanted to look like everyone else. But she couldn't do it. She couldn't behave like everyone else either.

By that time it was clear that she was something of a prodigy. The last of the normal music exams beckoned, and the hours of practice lengthened, and then she flew through them with flying colours. Again, if it had been William, he would have used music as an asset with which to attract the opposite sex. But then he would never have committed himself to so much self-imposed work. And Cass was serious. We thought that passing her final exams with distinction would give her leave to relax a little and enjoy herself, but it rapidly became clear that she regarded herself as having reached the base camp of Everest, no more. It made no difference if we told her how well she had done and that no-one was expecting her to do any better. As far as she was concerned, we were both tone deaf and knew nothing.

I missed her so badly, in those years when she shut me out. The most difficult times of her childhood, the times when I'd had to go up to the attic and find a way of talking her through it just so that we could still go on, became treasured memories. Back then, I'd been the best and wisest and truest person in her world. Now I was irrelevant. 'Go *away*!' and 'Oh, stop being so *stupid*,' and 'I hate *myself*.' Then hour-long, whispered conferences on the phone with her girlfriends, the only people who could truly understand.

And me thinking, Cass, don't hate yourself, don't harm the little girl I love, if anyone else did it I'd have to kill them. But she was not a little girl any more. I did understand – the reason why there was no point in talking to me was that being my best girl was no longer enough. She had to find a way to be herself. It was as painful and frustrating for Sally as for me. Because there was nothing we could do to help her.

The years flicked by, happy, unhappy, fulfilled, unfulfilled. Sometimes home life was good and work life was bad, and sometimes it was the other way round. But what I found difficult to come to terms with was that on average, neither was getting any easier. I did my best with my work, and eventually had the word 'senior' tacked on to my job title. But this compliment and the accompanying pay rise bore no comparison with the reputation and earnings I enjoyed outside the college doors. For many years, I tried to sate my lust for recognition by doing the things my professor couldn't control – appearing on television, writing for the newspapers, churning out sequels to *Genesis*. But the futility of my efforts slowly became clear. Without serious academic work to back me up, even my reputation as a popular scientist dwindled, and I began to become known as the man who had said nothing new since he was twenty-six.

So in the end, to Sally's great relief, I took myself in hand. I pulled together all my rejected academic articles, took them to my publishers, and proposed that they print something serious. They were initially sceptical, but eventually complied. I gave up on the television and newspapers, and refrained from bothering God. By the Christmas of 1988, I was ready to get back to the thing I really loved, which was writing it all down.

Which should have made things easier for both of us. 'Thank God,' said Sally, when I told her that the academic book was ready to be written. 'Thank God you're taking your job seriously. Thank God you're being normal.'

But it was a taunt, not an encouragement, and though I

swallowed it and kept my mouth shut, I wasn't sure if I could do so for much longer. Because a dark cloud was hovering above us, threatening thunder, and it was only a matter of time before one or the other of us let the lightning rip.

In September of that year, William had followed Cass to the secondary school of my choice. And in his first week, he'd come home with a black eye.

'William, what have you done?'

'It was nothing,' said William breezily. 'You should have seen the other boy.'

'*What?*'

We went in to see his form tutor, who was as baffled as we were. 'He seems such a nice boy,' she said. 'However, from all we've managed to find out so far, it does seem to be him who started it. The thing is, you can't really tell from what the children say. We've let them both off, as it's their first week. But I'll keep an eye open, I promise you. If you hear any indication that he's being bullied, please do let us know.'

Two weeks after that he came home with bloodstains on his sleeve. There was not a cut on him.

This time we decided not to involve the school. Instead, Sally and I decided that I would ask Cass. 'It's better if it's you,' said Sally. 'That way she'll know it's serious.'

Another trek up the stairs to the attic. 'Sally, that doesn't work any more.'

'She'll be fine. At least it's not about her. And she's been much better lately. She's growing up.'

It was true, the moods and tantrums were beginning to abate. The workload of her GSCEs seemed to suit her. Perhaps she was finally able to feel part of a crowd, because her friends were working hard too. I waited until William was at Scouts. Cass was doing her French homework. 'Hi,' I said, and sat down on her bed.

She twisted round on her chair, the half-smile on her lips telling me that she knew what was coming.

'Cass,' I said, 'what's going on with William?'

The smile grew a little, and she swayed in time with the music on her stereo.

'Tell me,' I said.

'Well,' said Cass, 'of course I don't know for sure. It's all gossip.'

'What gossip?'

'Well,' said Cass slowly, 'you know there are quite a few rough kids at our school.'

There had been rough kids at my school too. One of them had been Declan. 'I'm sure there are,' I said. 'Why is that a problem?'

'William hasn't realised it yet. And he keeps, well, lecturing them.'

'Lecturing them?'

'Yup.'

'What about?'

'Oh, I don't know. What does William normally spout on about? Karl Marx, probably.'

'*What?*' said Sally when I told her. 'He's getting beaten up because he talks about Karl Marx?'

'Well, not exactly. He lectures them about Karl Marx, then they start to tease him, and then he beats them up.'

'That's bloody ridiculous.'

'I think we should leave well alone,' I said. 'He's clearly capable of looking after himself. They'll soon learn not to mess with him.'

'That's just so wrong. He can't go around hitting people.'

'Sally,' I said, 'he can. It's all part of being a boy.'

'I refuse to accept that. We can't let him get away with it.'

So we gave him a lecture. William scowled throughout.

'Are you happy there?' Sally asked him at the end.

'They're a bunch of pricks,' said William.

'*William!*'

Three weeks after that, we received a phone call from the form tutor, and went back in to see her. 'I'm sorry,' said the teacher. There was no talk this time about him being a nice boy. 'I'd be very grateful if you could do something about your son.'

Another conference was called. 'William,' I said, 'what is it that makes you so angry about these boys?'

'They're just bloody thick,' said William viciously.

'Don't you dare swear!'

He squirmed in resentment.

'William,' I said, 'you can't go through life expecting everyone to be just like you. Can you?'

'I don't.'

'Then what justification did you have for hitting them?'

'They deserved it.'

We got no more out of him. By December the decision had been taken. If we didn't take it, then we risked seeing him excluded, and then who knew what downward spiral beckoned.

The school he was due to start in January was single sex, highly academic, and expensive.

We took Declan with us that Christmas, and the reason, ironically enough, was that we thought he had finally found love.

The story of his relationships was a series of endings. After Carolyn there was Johanna, the mystery woman in Germany whom he had mentioned only to Sally under duress, and who was out of bounds to me. But after Johanna they were pretty much public property, a string of funny incidents whose ends were predicated in the ridiculousness of their beginnings. Sometimes I thought it was only the names that changed.

Beth. Cheryl. Janice. Pauline. Megan. Liz. Rowena. They got marginally older as time went on, but not as much older as he did, so that he did a slow slide back down the generations, and whilst his first girlfriends in Plymouth had been able to talk to him about T Rex, by the early eighties they were only interested in Duran Duran. I used to gawp at these slices of modern history in astonishment and wonder how he ever found anything to say to them. He displayed no preference for any particular type, and so some were tall, some were short, some were rake-thin, others were blowsy, some were posh, a few were as common as dirt, some were intellectuals and others could barely string a sentence together. This variety was so relentless that it did nothing to help me distinguish between them.

'Hey,' said Declan one evening in 1988, plonking his arse on the stool and his pint on the table, 'I've met a new woman.'

I nodded. 'What's she called?'

He sniggered. 'Altruista.'

I spluttered into my beer. '*What*?'

'I know. Fabulous, isn't it? I thought if I went out with a woman with a name like that, you might at least be able to remember it.'

Altruista actually turned out to be a very nice girl, with none of the bohemian pretensions her name suggested. 'I'm an oil trader,' she told me shyly from under her fringe, in answer to my question.

'Really? Erm – what does that involve?'

'I buy and sell oil stocks.'

'Oh, I see. In the City.'

'Actually, my office is on an industrial estate in Hemel Hempstead. Bit of a pain in the bum. But it's not too bad a journey by car.'

I found myself hoping that Declan would stick with this woman. 'What's with the name?' I ventured.

'Nothing, really,' Altruista confessed. 'Just one of those random things your parents do to make your life more difficult.'

Excellent. She had a streak of cheerful stoicism, which was an essential qualification for any girlfriend of Declan's.

I took the plunge, and invited them both to dinner with us. Sally was immediately as captivated as I was by Altruista's pleasant ordinary looks and her unassuming manner, and did her very best all evening not to intimidate her. 'So how did you meet this idiot?' said Sally fondly.

'At an oil conference in Milford Haven,' said Altruista, with a loving glance towards Declan.

Declan wriggled in discomfort. 'I wasn't there for the oil conference,' he said. 'I was there to interview that woman who was trying to have nine babies—'

'But, you see,' said Altruista, 'he was staying in the same hotel. I was meant to be networking with all the oil people, but it's terribly difficult, they really aren't very interesting, so I ended up talking to Declan. And then in the morning he was so hung over I had to give him a lift home—'

'You left your car in Milford Haven?' Sally demanded of Declan.

He scowled. 'The photographer drove me there.'

'And you see, by the time Declan got up, the photographer had already left—'

'So you've already seen his worst side.'

'Oh, it was a lovely side. I laughed all the way home.'

Sally and I both stared at her in bafflement. Declan smirked.

To our astonishment, the relationship survived our interrogation. 'She's absolutely perfect,' said Sally. 'Oh, I do hope—'

That Christmas, Sally decided that she wanted a break from rushing round the grannies and staying with my sister in Bristol, and she booked us a cottage in Somerset, within easy enough reach of both Plymouth and Dorset so that we could pick the grannies up and bring them to us. This also meant that Rosy would be spared cooking Christmas dinner for once, and that we need suffer her husband and children for one day only.

'Max,' said Sally cautiously, 'there's bags of room in the cottage. If we invited Declan and Altruista, do you think they'd come?'

I considered it. Christmas for me was problematic, given the first syllable of its name, but it was at least a festival with pagan origins, and I had no objection to its celebration, even if some of its trappings were offensive. But for Declan it was the celebrations rather than the trappings which were off-limits, and though we'd invited him to spend it with us countless times before, he'd always declined. Instead he retreated into his usual ritual, which was to spend the early part of the day in the pub with his printer friend Dave, have Christmas dinner courtesy of Dave's wife, and end up by snoozing through all the television programmes at their house in the evening. It didn't sound like much fun to us, but it seemed to suit him.

But this year he'd spent eight months in one relationship, and perhaps times were changing. 'We could give it a try,' I said.

'Of course, they might want to spend it with Altruista's parents.'

'Can't see it. He can't stand them. And they live on the Costa del Sol.'

'Oh,' said Sally. 'Well, I'll invite them, then.'

They accepted.

It was the first time Sally had ever had the chance to do the whole Christmas thing herself. She got immensely excited, and vast quantities of food and drink began to accrue in the kitchen and utility room.

'Sally,' I said, 'how are we going to take it all down?'

'We'll have to take both cars. We'll probably need them anyway, for ferrying the grannies.'

I left her to it. For me, the advantage of the 'cottage' was that it had so many rooms that I might be able to commandeer one of them as a study, and avoid being cooped up with a gaggle of women all staring at the telly and discussing sprouts.

*

In the event, Declan arrived sixteen hours late, not long after dawn on Christmas Eve, while we were still having breakfast. The taxi driver grumbled and paced while we took the half-dozen bags out of his boot.

'Declan,' said Sally, 'where's Altruista?'

'She dropped me off near Tisbury.'

'Tisbury? Where the hell's Tisbury?'

'Middle of the bloody Salisbury Plain. Fortunately it has a station. Unfortunately that station has no trains which go anywhere near here. I had to get a night train from Exeter and a taxi from Taunton. Now I remember why we got out of this sodding part of the world. Here, Steve, make yourself useful.' He handed one of the lighter bags to our eight-year-old, who beamed and struggled manfully towards the house.

'But why didn't you just tell us? We could have come and picked you up.'

'That would have been boring. You're on holiday.'

'Declan, have the pair of you had a row?'

'You could put it that way.'

'Oh, Declan—'

'It wouldn't have worked. You should see the stuff—' He gestured at the bags and turned to the driver, who was loitering in a style that suggested he might get a pickaxe out of the boot if his fare wasn't paid soon.

The full story came out in dribs and drabs, while the pair of us were consigned to the outhouse chopping logs. I kept the axe firmly in my own hands.

Apparently the journey had started badly, when he'd seen how much she was bringing. 'You wouldn't believe it, Max. She had presents for everyone. Even your sister's bunch, and they're only coming for lunch. And a Christmas cake, and a box of oranges, and some bloody pot pourri stuff, and jars of chocolates, until the car smelt of Santa's Grotto. I told her she didn't even know these people, that she'd look silly, but she wasn't having it.'

'Women are like that about Christmas,' I told him. 'You'll have to get used to it.'

'No, I won't. Will I?'

Things had taken a turn for the worse once they were on the road and she'd installed her chosen tape in the cassette player.

'Frosty the frigging Snowman. Little Saint Nick. Winter frigging Wonderland. Do They Know It's arse-wiping buggering Christmas.'

I managed not to snigger. 'Surely she would have changed the tape if you'd asked her.'

'I was being *nice*. Only then "A Spaceman Came Travelling" came on and I couldn't take it any more. She started bloody singing along—'

This time the snigger came out. 'Sorry,' I said hurriedly.

'I pressed the eject button. It was a mistake.'

'You must have come across her music taste before.'

'Well, it's usually pretty tedious, but I can ignore it. But this—' He collected himself. 'She was terribly hurt, but she agreed to change it for a carol tape. Which was only marginally better—'

I gave an involuntary shudder.

'Anyway, I just couldn't bear her sitting there being hurt. I'm afraid I got pretty steamed up. Then she started playing this guessing game about reindeer—'

'Declan,' I said, 'if you feel that way about it, how come you've managed to go out with her for so long?'

He sighed. 'Altruista's a lovely girl,' he said.

'I know. But she annoys you.'

'She doesn't, really. Not normally. I mean, she's so long-suffering, I kind of feel I have to be long-suffering too. Which is quite a good feeling, in a way. I suppose I've just got bored of – things ending. It seemed worth trying things carrying on for once.'

I felt suddenly sorry for him.

'Give me that axe,' said Declan.

I hesitated. He took it from me anyway. 'You see' – smash – 'I think we might have made it, if she hadn't – well, she asked me what I normally do at Christmas.'

'What was wrong with that?'

'Nothing's wrong with that. But she thought it was a sign of a deeply wounded soul. She said' – crack – 'she said, "Declan, I know you've had a very hard life"—'

'Ah,' I said.

'And I told her that I'd had a perfectly good life, and that I didn't want her meddling with it.'

'I see.'

'It unravelled between Andover and Amesbury. I didn't want it to, but once it was started, there was nothing I could do to stop it. You see, we'd always had quite different ways of looking at the world, but until then we'd managed to get along by never contradicting one another. I assumed she could live with my way, and she thought I'd come round to hers. But that was all nonsense. We clutched at straws, and tried to build bridges, and did all those things which only exist in cliché because they have nothing to do with the real world—'

'Declan,' I said, 'I think those logs are small enough now.'

He stared at them in confusion. I put the logs in the basket, brought over another batch, and took the axe from him.

'She started talking about sacrifice, and compromise, and all that sort of painful, pre-war rubbish,' said Declan. 'I told her it sounded like she was talking about a marriage. And she said she was, in a way. At which point I told her that she was deeply mistaken if she thought I was ever going to marry her. For a moment I thought she was going to let it pass. She started talking about how lovely Stonehenge was—'

'Why Stonehenge?'

'It was there. Right in front of us.'

'Oh, I see.'

'We went past Stonehenge. She carried on driving for a few more miles. Then she asked me what I wanted.'

'What did you say?'

'I said things had been exactly as I wanted them until a couple of hours before. She said she thought it ought to move on. I told her not to try to turn me into someone I wasn't. She said she wouldn't. Then she pulled in at the verge, and told me to get out of the car.'

'Oh, God.'

'It took me a while to realise that she was serious. It's weird. We hadn't had a single major disagreement in all those eight months, and it turned out that was why. For Altruista, arguments aren't a way of passing the time. They're terminal.'

'And she—'

'She unloaded the luggage – all the bloody luggage – and drove off. It was frigging freezing. I hitched a lift to the nearest station. Thought I'd better bring the parcels with me. Couldn't leave them on the A303.'

We stared at one another. I was pretty cold myself, shivers running uncontrollably up and down my back. Somehow the scenario he'd described was just too close to the bone.

'Come on,' I said. 'I think we've done our duty now. Let's go and light that fire.'

It was a great comfort to me to have him there. At least there was someone with more of an axe to grind than me. Which had, I suppose, been his role in my life all along.

'Hey nonny no, fa la-la, deck the halls with boughs of holly!'

I stared at Declan in disbelief. He was putting all those presents which Altruista had chucked out of her car under the tree and, as far as his demeanour was concerned, he might as well have been Altruista herself.

'Lovely,' said Granny Bowden. 'What a terrific display of presents. How very clever of you, Declan.'

'Absolutely charming,' trilled my mother, not to be outdone.

Since her arrival, the house seemed to have got horribly crowded. And suffocatingly hot. And we still had Rosy's crowd to come in the morning.

'I tell you, Sally,' said Declan, 'you are a culinary genius. That salmon roulade we had for tea was beyond compare.'

'Thank you,' said Sally, trying to smile. Her face was taut with exhaustion.

Steve began to bounce. 'Dad,' he said, 'can we do Rudolph now?'

In the background, I saw Sally twitch, and I almost backed out. But this was a bargain we'd made long ago. For nearly a decade, I'd wanted to banish Father Christmas to oblivion. 'If we start teaching our kids that sort of nonsense—' I'd said.

'But Steve's still just a kid. Let him have his childhood. The others did. And anyway, all children stop believing in Father Christmas in the end, quite naturally.'

'Really?' At that stage, halfway into the decade of dissent, William most definitely did not, and Cass still went through the old rituals. 'When does this happen, would you say?'

'Oh, by eight at the most.'

After much argument, the truce was agreed upon on the basis that all references to Father Christmas would stop when Steve reached the age of eight. Now he had.

'Steve,' I said, 'we're not doing Rudolph this year. I've already told you that.'

'But we can't not have stockings.'

Declan was making bemused faces. I tried not to let him catch my eye. 'You're going to have stockings. We're just not going to have Rudolph.'

'But that doesn't make sense—'

Suddenly, out of nowhere, a figure burst out from beneath its book and dashed into the kitchen. Everyone tried very hard not to look at Cass's retreating back. She returned with a mince pie on a small plate, and a carrot. 'There you go, Steve,' she said. She set them down by the fire. 'Now, shall we write our notes?'

Steve seemed suddenly aware of the audience. He glanced around nervously. 'It's all right.'

'Come on, let's write them.' She grabbed two gift tags from the pile of wrapping paper, and a pen. 'Dear Father Christmas. What do you want from Father Christmas, Steve?'

Steve just stood there, tongue-tied.

'Thank you for your presents. I hope you like your mince pie. Lots of love, Cass and William and Steve.' With a shaking hand, she laid it on the plate with the mince pie. Then she took the other gift tag. 'Deeee-er Rudolph. Happy Christmas. Munch, munch—'

'And don't get your hooves too cold in the snow!' burst out Steve.

'Lots of love, Cass and William and Steve.' The carrot was placed carefully on the mantelpiece along with the gift tag. 'There you go. Now Rudolph won't go hungry.'

Steve sniffed a little, then dashed back to his spot on the sofa next to my mother. Cass stood up straight, collected her book and went upstairs.

Sally had said nothing. Which was a very bad sign.

There was a great volume of hissing, both of us hoping that the walls were thick. I was all too aware that Declan's bedroom was next door.

'You ban carols. You ban Father Christmas. What do you think this is, the Cultural Revolution?'

I knew it had been a mistake. 'I'm sorry,' I said. 'There are so many people here—'

'Numbers have nothing to with it. The only person going around upsetting people is you.'

I thought of relating the story of Declan's treatment of

Altruista, and thought better of it. 'You're tired,' I said. 'We've got a big day tomorrow. Let's get some sleep.'

'I will not let you wriggle out of this. It was appalling. Admit to me that you were wrong. Just for bloody once in your life, admit you were wrong.'

That eternal refrain roused me from my apologies. 'I don't know what you're talking about,' I lied savagely.

'The most robust of our children ends up with the best education. I suppose it'd make sense to you. Survival of the fittest.'

'That school's right for Cass,' I growled back, 'and it might have been right for William. You just can't tell until they get there.'

'It *isn't* right for Cass! You've seen what she's turned into—'

'Cass is fine. She's just a teenager. We can't guarantee that William won't get into fights at his new school as well.'

'Then why are you bloody paying for it? I'll tell you why. It's because he's—'

Your son. The reason she didn't say it was that it just wasn't true. '*Fuck* this,' I breathed very softly, and left her to her sobbing while I went to solve one of the trickiest equations in my very best book.

The next morning was Christmas Day. Perhaps I was right about Cass, and her sulkiness was just that of a girl at an awkward age. But that was not what Sally thought the next day, when it came to serving up Christmas dinner and Cass could not be found. Never before had I felt such visceral panic and guilt. I stormed up hills, trawled the woods, splashed out to sea, terrible pictures looming at the edge of my mind. By the time I got back to the cottage Cass had been back for more than an hour, and the expressions of all told me that the episode was very firmly closed. I was furious. But no-one would tell me what had happened. Not even Declan.

*

Six months later, William was doing brilliantly at his new school. Cass plonked away on her piano, and Steve drifted about making friends, still an innocent, still the boy who had brought us back together when he was in the womb, still untouched by our sins. Sally, who had decided that her usefulness as a housewife was waning with the advancing ages of our children, started a professional life of her own, illustrating children's books. As for myself, I had produced the best piece of science I am ever likely to achieve. My new book opened up a whole new area of exploration in relation to the energy exchanges during meiotic anaphase, and is now standard reading for all those doing higher degrees in the area. It will never cause my name to be shouted from the rooftops, but there is a particular kind of immortality which comes through science, and which can survive even the world forgetting who you were. Science is a chain of achievement, winding through a matrix of phenomena and time, and once your piece is in place, it will be there forever, the link between what came before and what happened next. When I could be assured that this had happened, I knew for the first time that I had 'made it' in a more secure way than any other opportunity would afford. On publication it won me acclaim even from my staunchest enemies in the university, and finally got me a serious academic reputation. John Hinds could ignore the facts no longer, and I was promoted to Professor.

Yet those were dark days, darker even than those that came afterwards, perhaps the darkest. The darkness crowding in, crushing out the light, and still I didn't know that there was any way out, that things could ever change. I thought that my relationship with Sally was the one true thing I could hold onto, even when it was no longer there.

And everything I did was suspect, and everything I did was scorned. When we were together in public, Sally told me in front of everyone not to shout, and not to interrupt. In the end

I couldn't open my mouth without feeling that she was about to stick a sock in it. Afterwards there were always accounts of how much I'd upset so-and-so, or forced so-and-so out of the conversation. She told me that people were laughing at me. But I was sure that they were not. All they were laughing at was the contempt in which I was held by my wife.

I knew that it must always have been very difficult having me around. She was right when she said that I dominated. But why did that mean that I had to change? She hadn't changed. Sally was still the party animal she'd always been, working the room, finding the most interesting people to speak to and discarding the bores. The only difference was that now she seemed to think that one of the bores was me.

I supposed that it must have got a little tiresome, being a spouse and hearing the same stories over and over again. Hearing the same response each time the same button was pressed, seeing the same signals lead to the same alarms, feeling the same dangers over and over again, day after day, month after month, year after year. But that was what marriage was like. It was what family was like. My mother repeated the same stories into oblivion, and I didn't mind. What was so wrong with mine?

Once, worn out by a particularly vicious struggle, I returned to the argument we'd had on that awful Christmas Eve. 'Sally,' I pleaded, 'what's the problem? What's changed?'

'Nothing's changed,' she said bitterly. 'You were like this all along.'

'But you never used to mind. What's different?'

She stopped and leaned against a lamppost. Her poise was as perfect as ever. Once she'd stood like that and our embrace had threatened to bore a hole in the earth. 'I just get so tired,' she said. 'Sometimes I want to be the one with opinions. Sometimes I want to be the one with something to say.'

'But you are. You do. You're the life and soul of the party.'

She shook her head wearily. 'Only as long as I don't stand next to you.'

Was that all it was? An objection to the way I behaved at parties? I knew it was not. All my decisions were distrusted, whether they were over our choice of insurance company or the book I read in bed. 'But it's not just when we're out. It's at home as well.'

'At home?' Her voice was bitter. 'You're never at home. You're too busy working, trying to beat John Hinds. Trying to beat – *God*.'

Once it was the worst swear word I could have thrown at her. Now it was the other way round. 'Just shut up about that, will you?'

'Tell me it isn't there. You just stand there and tell me it isn't there.'

I couldn't, and I didn't, because it was. Except that I no longer knew whether I hated God on his own merits, or hated him because of Sally. He took my wife away from me, and I have never forgiven Him for it.

The last decision we made together was that of where to send Steve to school. We had a shortlist of two: Cass's school, or William's school. I, jangling with guilty nerves, was not prepared to go through all the arguments again about why our decision for Cass had been the right one, and privately concluded that it was inevitable that he should follow William. She, strangely detached from our old disputes, decided that William's school was too much of a hothouse for Steve, and proposed that he should follow Cass. Astonished, I agreed at once. I think I might even have agreed if she'd suggested that he go to a monastery. The fuel for our antagonism, which was love, had run out.

When Declan and I used to sit in the pub, his neck would slowly swivel each time an attractive girl walked by.

'You're disgusting,' I reprimanded him. 'And bloody rude. If I did that in my job, I'd be sacked.'

'It's natural,' said Declan. 'A normal biological instinct. You should know all about those.' He looked at me curiously. 'Don't you? Or does your world-conquering love for Sally extinguish even that?'

Of course I looked at other women. As Declan suggested, it was a reflex, something that could no more be blotted out than breathing. In the summer the girls wore v-necked vests and shorts to my tutorials, and embarrassed me with their gleaming, breathy flesh. Sometimes women tried to chat me up, gazing up at me with star-struck eyes and waggling their tits. But no woman ever stood the way that Sally had in that bar. No-one else but her ever matched up to that dream.

Then one summer I discovered that the dream was no longer an obstacle. My appetite for perfection was exhausted. Slowly, creakily, lust began to prickle back to the surface of my flesh. I was fallen, sodden, rotten, decadent, debauched. And something gave way. If she didn't think I was a good man, then I didn't want to be one. The effort of maintaining my self-image in the face of all her disdain was no longer something I had the energy to do. It was time to ruin the man I thought I was.

Her name was Vicky, and she would have been a victim had she not been so thoroughly capable of looking after herself.

I was careful enough not to choose a student, but she was the next best thing. She was a junior lecturer, appointed a year before straight out of her PhD, and whilst I wasn't her direct boss, she was scheduled next term to run a number of lecture courses within my remit, and it was necessary for us to meet up so that I could give her advice.

She shared two things with Sally, and those were her height and her slender build. The rest was all different. She was blonde, she had big tits, and her face was badly put together, as if her Maker had been having a lazy day. Her voice was adorned with a swashbuckling South African accent, and she had a habit of slapping her thighs. She called me 'Professor Famous'. I knew she was taking the piss.

That scratchy July she came to my office in the regulation v-necked vest top and mini-skirt, and while she drawled out her enquiries about the best way to teach the cell signalling and regulation course, she leant down her long legs to scratch her ankle just below the gold chain, tilting her head up towards me and displaying a pale cleavage in between. I thought it was the dirtiest thing I had ever seen.

'I like your nail varnish,' I stammered out, my flesh turning to pulp.

She sat up and even blushed a little, but soon recovered her usual uncomposed posture. 'Do you now,' she said thoughtfully, and leaned down to scratch again.

It took her several days to think about it. The next time she came to see me it was colder, and she was forced to cover up some of that yellow-pink skin, but the neckline plunged even further, and her tights were pale mauve. I'd been on agonised tenterhooks for a week, and I began to shake.

'I like your tights,' I said this time. My voice sounded both juvenile and ancient. I had no idea what to do.

A smile quivered at the edges of her mouth.

'But not as much as the nail varnish,' I pressed on, propelled by the dirty, burning juices circulating in my groin.

'Are you,' said Vicky, 'proposing that I remove the tights?'

'Yes,' I spat out above the thundering of my heart.

Her eyebrows rose and she gave a slow contemplative blink. 'If I didn't know better, Professor Famous,' she said, 'I'd say you were trying to take advantage of me.'

'I would never take advantage. I would never do that.'

'You're a gentleman, are you? Then perhaps you should watch more porn.'

She was undoubtedly right. However, I was now beyond porn. 'Please,' I said. It was the most pathetic thing I had ever heard. 'I want to see your body.'

And slowly, tauntingly, she leaned down and gradually loosened the heel of her left shoe. All the while she kept her eyes fixed on me.

Communication couldn't have been more absent. Why on earth would she do such a thing, submit so easily to such a low and wretched request? Outside that room, I might have found reasons on her behalf. My position, my fame, my power. Perhaps she even fancied me. Inside that room, it was all irrelevant. I desperately didn't want to know what she thought. All I wanted was to—

'You gotta take your clothes off too, Famous.'

She was naked. I smacked the blinds down, and ran to my door and locked it. Then, fumbling, moving far too fast, I scrabbled at my clothes. She didn't attempt to help me, just watched from her chair.

'Jeez, Max, you gotta lotta hair.'

I looked down at my rugged body. 'Do you mind?'

'Hell, no. Always fancied having sex with a gorilla.' She stood up. So much skin seemed unnecessary, overdressed, almost. I reached out to touch it.

'What do you want, Maxy boy?'

I wanted to hurt her. Hurt Sally. Hurt myself. I fucked her across the table, and achieved all three.

Sally knew. She knew straight away. We'd had half a lifetime of accustoming ourselves to each other's every mood, and as soon as I returned home that evening, my infidelity was rank in the air between us.

I wanted her to know. We hadn't had sex in months. Perhaps years. I'd long since given up counting. In some ways it didn't matter, because I'd always thought that there was more to our love than that. But Sally was still beautiful. When she came back from her meetings with her authors she wore trim coloured suits and knotted silk scarves, the perfume still lingering around her, and she sat down, crossed those elegant legs, and held her head in as unconsciously coquettish a manner as she had when I first met her, and her body was as familiar and impenetrable as her mind.

I wanted her to know, because it seemed to me like the first truthful thing that had happened between us in years. She thought I was a sinner and now I had sinned. Her disapproval could become tangible, something I was capable of understanding, and though what I had done could never be reversed, there would somehow be a kind of cleansing, a reunion brought about by our joint knowledge of what I had done.

Did I really think it was the way to win her back? Surely I can't have been that stupid. But I wanted it to be the way it once was, when our thoughts were so intermingled that we couldn't bear our skin to part, when our time together was so precious that any separation was a theft. I didn't know why it had stopped being like that, or when. Perhaps when we spent our first nights apart, because I had gone to America. Maybe I should have kept her by me always, and then our brains and bodies would never have diverged.

But I don't think I really thought that. I didn't think much at all. Most of all, I wanted her to force me to leave, because I couldn't bring myself to do it myself, and living with the ghost of our former love was more than I could bear.

We might have possessed all the intuition in the world regarding one another's moods and actions, but by that stage in our relationship, facts were the only things we were prepared to deal with out loud. So, whether by design or not, the facts emerged. She found a condom in a briefcase when she was looking for a gas bill, and it clearly wasn't intended for her, because she ensured her infertility by other means.

'Max—'

She held it delicately between thumb and forefinger. In that brief silence quivered what hope either of us had left. Perhaps I would deny it. Maybe I would confess and be forgiven—

'Max,' she said, and her voice came out in a strangulated whisper, 'what have you been doing?'

And suddenly I saw Antonia on the doorstep, hissing threats at me, telling me how I was going to behave. I'd left that night in a haze of love, sure that Sally herself would always trust me. Now we'd come full circle. The girl I'd left on that sofa was still there in my mind, but the door was slowly shutting behind me.

'Just say something, Max. Say anything.'

'I thought the problem was me talking,' I heard myself say.

Slam. 'Get out!' she screamed. 'Get the fuck out of here. Now!'

There was nowhere to go but Declan's. I said I'd had a row with Sally and nothing more. In the morning I went back. We sat down in the living room and attempted to have a discussion. She cried, unbearably, her body swaying from side to side, and I, finally, having no right to comfort her. 'Antonia told me,' she sobbed. 'I never believed it. I never thought—'

It was nothing to do with anything that Antonia had told her. Things had moved far, far on from there. But there was no point in saying anything at all.

'Do you love her?' she squeezed out between sobs.

'No.'

'Will you go to her?'

'No.'

'Are you going to leave?'

I paused. 'Do you want me to?'

'Max, that's not *fair*—'

She was right, it wasn't. 'All right. I'll leave.'

And that was it. Over.

*

We told the children together when they got home from school. I left Edenbridge Terrace that afternoon. Because I couldn't bear to stay another day. Love is a very hard thing to part from, and I wanted rid of every shred of it.

I took the Northern Line away from the people I knew, and then got off as soon after Camden as I felt was safe. Tufnell Park. Then I walked until I found an estate agent. My budget was the balance in my savings account. The estate agent showed me a house in Gospel Oak which corresponded to that figure, and I arranged to pay the full sum that afternoon, without even commissioning a survey. The family who lived there were somewhat bemused, but the house had been on the market for a while, and they didn't feel they could turn down a cash offer. The following weekend, I helped them move their belongings into storage myself.

'Max,' said Sally's distant voice over the telephone, 'there are things we need to sort out. The house. The furniture—'

'Keep it. You deserve it. I've got everything I need.'

'You have to have something—' Her voice cracked.

'No, I don't.'

Imagine no possessions. The family before me had painted the entire house white in the hope of speeding up the sale. I would have bought it if it had been green and purple, but white was good. Even the silence was cleansing. I lay on my back on the bare wooden floor of the lounge, and let eighteen years of tension seep away.

In the pub, the smoke fogged up the air as it always had done.

'Max,' howled Declan, 'what have you done?'

I blinked, uncomprehending. Did he mind? What did it have to do with him?

It took about a year for me to fully realise that everyone minded. That I'd done something that was to do with more than just me. That I'd left nothing behind at all.

And it was then that I finally let Vicky go. She screamed at me and called me a bastard, things Sally had never done. It was a great relief.

After that, I had all the time in the world to work. And I worked very hard. Without the distractions of family, I managed to combine my public life with decent, published scientific work. I even got on better with John Hinds. I still got into fights and I still made enemies. But now there was no-one waiting at home to hate me for it.

The person who was kindest to me when I left Sally was Cass. She was only eighteen at the time, but in the two years since she'd run away on Christmas Day, she seemed to have well and truly grown up. Perhaps she'd realised how foolish she'd been; perhaps Declan, himself a fatherless child, had said something which helped. Or maybe it was just her hormones calming down. I never found out. Either way, there was no more slamming of doors or piano lids, no more ostentatious self-hatred, no more tear-streaked mascara. She'd grown her hair long again, eased up on the make-up and produced a boyfriend. Suddenly we'd had a third adult about the house, smiling, asking us if we wanted a cup of tea, and discussing the merits of a play or a book as if it might actually be worth listening to our opinions. Which was a good thing, as there wasn't anyone else behaving like an adult in that household at the time.

And when I'd gone, even though she was on the verge of leaving home herself to study singing at music college, she'd seemed to worry more about me than herself. 'Max,' she said earnestly, when she first came to visit me in Gospel Oak, 'aren't you going to get yourself some furniture?'

I made some vague promises, but as had happened so many times before, they were not kept. 'Perhaps Vicky can help you,' she said hopefully the next time she came round.

It was wonderful that she could mention the name so easily,

when everyone else could do no more than spit it, at best. But Vicky was already on her way out. When she was finally off the scene, Cass felt that I needed cheering up, so she bought me a dog. The choice of breed was influenced by Sally's mother, who'd always kept dachshunds. No-one but Cass noticed that I needed cheering up, or if they did, they didn't care. All they'd noticed was what a ridiculous idea it was to get me a dachshund. I most heartily agreed, but I couldn't let Cass see it, and so I was forced to give shelter to this absurd little scrap of nothing. The scrap of nothing grew, and began to exhibit all kinds of interesting animal instincts, and before I knew it, I'd become as foolish an anthropomorphic dog lover as Sally's mother. During her college vacations, Cass came round quite often to make sure that Huxley and I were doing okay, and one day she brought the sofa with her from Edenbridge Terrace in the back of Sally's Volvo, so that she'd have something to sit on when she visited. Huxley never minded sharing the sofa with Cass.

I made a decent enough life for myself. 'A mid-life crisis,' Declan called it once I was back on an even keel, and I let the idea stick without thinking about it, because it was easier to let him congratulate me on how well I'd recovered from its ravages than it was to reflect on how much I'd lost. But now, almost fifteen years later, I cannot agree with that verdict. Oh, my behaviour may have showed all the hallmarks: I had slept with a twenty-six-year-old and struggled free from the restricting chains of family life. But the usual motivations for such actions feel far truer of the way I feel now. Claustrophobia, as the future shrinks to a smaller and smaller size in relation to the life I have already lived; shock, as I watch my older son grow to an age at which the power he wields in the world challenges my own; rebellion, as I resist the realisation that the trajectory of a life is not an upwards curve forever. Back then I was barely forty. My children were still children and more than half my career was still head of me. I didn't end my marriage because I wanted to feel young again. I ended it because it had already ended. And even after all this regurgitation and all this analysis, I still don't really know why.

Except. There was a reason then, and there is a reason now. It was there when Sally and I made our wordless pact over the bed where Steve was born, never to speak about God again. It was there when she broke it, by suggesting that Cass should be schooled at a convent. It was there in that cottage in Somerset, with the mince pies and the reindeer's carrot; there on the pavement outside that cocktail party, when Sally screamed at me about trying to beat God; there from the beginning of the end to the end of the end, and even more there once it was over. I knew all along it was because of God. Yet how could it be because of God, when He didn't exist? Even Sally knew He didn't exist. How in heaven or on earth could it be because of God?

Which brings me back to Margot's article, and the insults it turfed up from beyond the grave of my marriage. Margot called me an evangelist, and said that it was the source of all my troubles. It was the same accusation that Sally had thrown at me when I came home from arguing with John Hinds, twenty-five years before – '*You sound like you're one of those American evangelists yourself*'. But it had not been new even then. The first person to come up with that one was someone who'd known me for even longer.

Declan.

Am I right or am I wrong? The memory has come back to me only now, and so I find it hard to trust. But it is so strong. I can see him sitting on a wooden bench and lounging against the wall with a pint in his hand, and there is a woman to his left. Carolyn? It's possible, because Carolyn would certainly have been more likely than most of his girlfriends to join in such a conversation, but I have the feeling that this girl wasn't joining in. All I know is that it wasn't Altruista. He would have been more restrained if she'd been at his side, and it was earlier than that. Before America. Because—

'So you want everyone in the world to read this book.'

'Well, not *everyone*, obviously, but I'd certainly like it to be read by most educated people—'

'Educated people? Why are you getting *me* to review it, then?'

That was it. We were arguing over whether he was going to review *Genesis*. Yet my other memory of that conversation is located in a different place – in the sitting room of the flat he lived in before he went to Germany. It would not be unusual, of course, for us to have repeated an argument, perhaps many times. But this one must have come first, because I definitely remember that the other one concluded with his submission.

'Oh, come on, Declan. You *are* educated.'

'So you're not satisfied just with people with a university degree. You want it to be read by everyone who ever went to *school*—'

Now the field of my vision shifts, and I can make out the girl. A blonde. Her name was – no, I definitely can't remember her name. In my memory, her face has a kind of fuzz in the middle of it, as if the police have pixillated it on the video tape in my brain to protect her identity. But I remember her voice. 'I think I'd like to read a book like that,' she said meekly.

Declan twitched with annoyance. 'Oh, *Janice*,' he scoffed. There! It was Janice. She was a travel agent from Tooting, and she was wearing a scarlet top. Most of the fuzz has gone from her face now, though I'm still not sure about the shape of her nose. 'Don't bloody encourage him. He's trying to found a new religion, and he'll mark you down as his first convert if you're not careful.'

What I remember is my bewilderment. A sense of not understanding why he was so annoyed with me. Of course, he was often belligerent when he had a girlfriend with him, and I put it down to the fact that he felt threatened, just as he had when he'd been chatting up the girl dressed as Tess of the D'Urbervilles the evening Sally invited me to dinner. But there was really no need this time. I had a wife at home. Janice knew that I wasn't available. And it didn't seem to be about that anyway.

'What do you mean, trying to found a new religion?' I objected, hot with injustice. 'That's just total nonsense. My book's about as far from being religious as you could possibly imagine—'

Only, the memory is confusing me. Because this is before the publication of *Genesis*. It's the end of 1976, or at the very latest, the beginning of 1977. And I didn't go to America until nearly two years later. If I'd already had to defend myself against Declan's accusations of my messianic zeal, then why did it take me so completely by surprise when it happened again in Missouri?

And he continued. 'It's just the way you are, Max,' he said, his bitterness softening into great weariness, as if he'd been a martyr to my monstrousness for a hundred years. But it was too soon for that. We were too young. There was no way he could have thought of me as a monster when I was only twenty-six. 'The whole human race was created so that you could give it the benefit of your wisdom. We're all blank slates for you to write upon. I tell you, Max, this book of yours is a lose-lose situation as far as any of the rest of us are concerned. If it's a failure, you'll be insufferable. And if it's a success – well, I think I'll just have to leave the country—'

Janice comes into focus properly now, even her nose, which was a beaky thing perched in the middle of an otherwise pretty face. Her expression was as confused as my own must have been. Poor woman. In only a few weeks' time, her boyfriend would vanish without a word. She probably remembered that conversation in every detail once the time came to wonder why he had gone. But I didn't remember it. Until now.

With the exception of a few breaks here and there, Declan and I have continued our bi-monthly squash matches, which we started after my return from America. Over the years, our post-match conferences have provided the ideal forum for airing our dissatisfactions and our triumphs, and for discussing the world at large. We've pondered on girlfriends and wives, bosses and colleagues, presidents and prime ministers. But there's one thing we've never talked about.

'Why did you go to Berlin?' I asked him this Tuesday.

He choked on his drink. This is rather a characteristic of his, and I've often wondered whether he does it for dramatic effect. 'Max,' he said, 'it's a long time ago now. Why do you want to know about that?'

I picked up my sports bag, pulled out the infamous Sunday Review section from the paper the week before, and laid it on the table in front of him.

My suspicions had already been deepened by the fact that he hadn't mentioned it before our match. After all his worries before it was published, it seemed unnatural. I watched his face as he glanced at it. There was no particular change in his expression. 'I've read it,' he said. 'Looks like you came off pretty lightly, doesn't it?'

'That's not what Dan thought!' I protested, preferring to attribute the reaction to someone other than myself.

'Dan?'

'Dan Gorman. Come on, you've met Dan.'

'Oh, the clone guy. Well, he's American, isn't he? Anyway, you should read some of Margot's other stuff if you want to see how lucky you've been. Sounds like she fancies you like crazy. Just look at all this stuff about how sexy you are. You haven't made such a big impression since the seventies.'

'I don't give a damn whether she thinks I'm sexy. Didn't you read the other stuff? The evangelism shit?'

'Max, people always say that about you.'

'Do they? Who has ever said that, other than you?'

He looked at me oddly. 'I really don't know what you're talking about. Why would I say it? It's just the sort of thing people drag up when they want to give you a hard time in print.'

'Declan, they don't. Believe me, I'd know if they did. The people who give me a hard time are all believers or scientists, or both. I mean, the creationists call me *religious*, because they're so bloody deluded that they think it's me who's peddling fantasies and they who are dealing with the hard truth. But they don't call me an evangelist, because they aren't exactly going to slag me off by comparing me to themselves. The same applies to the wishy-washy Christians over here. And the scientists who aren't believers are too busy attacking my science to bother about anything else. The only sort of person who would ever make that comparison would be an agnostic, because it's only agnostics who are perched high enough on the fence to have the luxury of hating both sides.'

'Well, Margot's an agnostic. There, you see, you've just explained it.'

I frowned at him in confusion and distrust. It wasn't at all like Declan to abandon his original point of view in order to slide out of an argument. 'But you just said that people had said it before. And they haven't. Except for you. Declan, I can *remember* you saying it.'

'Can you? Well, I can't remember it.'

He didn't even ask when or why. I squirmed. It had seemed like such a good idea to get to the bottom of this when I had been alone in my study with my notes. But now that I felt I was getting closer, I didn't want to know.

'Why did you go to Berlin?' I demanded again.

'Because the guy who used to work there retired. They asked around the office whether anyone spoke German. I had my "A" level. I volunteered.'

'That's how you went to Berlin. It isn't why. There wouldn't have been any need for secrecy if it was just to do with work.'

'Max,' said Declan, 'what's got into you? What are you accusing me of?'

He knew that it was an accusation. He'd resigned himself to it, and he was waiting for it. For a few moments, I couldn't speak. My memories were knitting together into something much nastier than a few words of abuse in a pub with Declan's girlfriend. Because now that I really thought about it, my suspicions of Declan were too numerous to count.

I sat there with my glass and remembered Janice, sitting there beakily, listening to the conversation of the men. Those poor women. He seemed to hate all the girls he dated before he went to Germany. But why would he despise them so much? None of them ever did anything to deserve it, except Carolyn, and she was spared his scorn until after they'd split up. Perhaps it was to do with his mother, but he didn't hate all women. Sally was one of his best friends through all that time. And after I came back from America it was as if he never managed to conjure up quite the same contempt again.

The dates were thudding into place, as if triggered by the

submerged image of Janice's face. His bitterness towards me. The threat to leave the country. His departure. His return. My trip to America—

I could bear it no longer. 'Why can't I ask you about Berlin?' I spat. 'You told Sally about Berlin.'

It was four decades since I'd first met him. He was sandier, balder, thinner, sharper. And now we were like two cats in an alley, backs arched, fur standing on end.

'You think I fucked her, don't you?' he hissed.

An almighty pause, as if time had been suspended.

'How fucking *dare* you, Max Oldroyd? After all these years—'

But I'd thought it for years. Not from the beginning, it was true – at the beginning I'd been too wrapped up in myself, too 'spoiled', as Sally had put it, too confident that nothing in my life could go wrong. I might have had inklings that night after I got back from the States and saw his stuff littered about the place, but I hadn't known what those inklings were. It was only when things really had started to go wrong in my marriage that such a thought had attained the power to surface, occasionally, suddenly, unexpectedly, always unthinkable, always repressed, always in the past. What if – they'd spent all that time together in front of the fire, while I'd been thousands of miles away, being destroyed, ruining my life. What if Declan had always been in love with Sally, had gone to Berlin to escape her, had come back to find me gone? I'd let her down while I was out there. She'd been tired, cold and lonely. What if—

'Why do you think that's what I think?' I batted back, frigid as ice.

'Max, Max—' He put his head in his hands, then looked back up at me. 'You little *shit*—'

'Why do you think that?' I repeated. 'What put that thought into your head?'

He was backtracking now, slippery as a fox. 'You said – you

said' – he put on a squeaky, ingratiating voice – '"*You told Sally about Berlin.*" Like you were a little kid. "*You told Sally about Berlin, you gave Rosy more cake than me—*"'

'Shut the fuck up,' I snapped.

'You, jealous of me. That's a bloody laugh.'

I sat up as far as I could on my stool, trying to regain some dignity. 'This is obviously a bit of an issue with you,' I said.

'It's an issue with you! Look, I'm sorry if Margot's article has upset you, and I'm sorry if I said anything to her which might have given her ammunition. You're probably right to hate what she wrote. I wouldn't have hated it if it had been me, because it wouldn't have been news to me that I was a failure. But—'

'Are you saying that I am a failure?'

'Oh, God, what does that mean anyway? We're both idiots to think in those terms. So's she. But Max, I was *relieved* when I read that article. Because of the things it *didn't* say. She's usually so scrupulous in her research. And – stop it, Max, sit down – I don't mean *that*. It didn't happen. I swear to you, I did not fuck your wife.'

I remained where I was, my arse halfway off the seat, still looming. 'But you think I think you did,' I said. 'And you've thought so for years. Why did you go to Berlin?'

'Sit down. Sit down, Max, and I'll tell you why I went to Berlin.'

I sat down. He stared at his empty pint glass. 'I need another one of those,' he said. 'You?'

My glass was three-quarters full. 'Yes,' I said vindictively, not prepared to let him get away without paying for his round.

'Back in a mo',' said Declan, almost his old insouciant self. I trusted him not an inch.

It was all there in my mind, even though I'd never dared piece it together. He'd loved her from the start, perhaps from before

I'd even seen her. But he'd known he hadn't stood a chance, not with the beautiful, cut-glass Sally Bowden. His insecurities about class, so quickly displayed to me as soon as I'd shown an interest in her, were far too pervasive to permit such an idea. Yet maybe he'd seen that I was blind to such differences, and had feared that I would succeed where he was so sure he'd fail. That was why he'd bobbed up and down in front of me when I was trying to catch her eye; to prevent me from seeing her.

Then, of course, he helped me to win her. But he was never cheerful or willing. What had been his motivation? Weakness, perhaps, because I was pretty insistent. And then, once the deed was done and she was by my side, a weakness for her. It never mattered to me in those early days that the pair of them got on so well. I expected it. She was the best woman in the world, and Declan was my best friend. And so it made perfect sense to me, even if it didn't to Antonia—

Oh, God. Another memory blinking out from under the rubble. Antonia walking into my bedsit and casting a disparaging glance at Declan, slumped on a beanbag. 'You again,' she'd said. 'I told Sally not to start feeding you. Like stray dogs. It's always a mistake.' Then she gave Sally a look. It was a private look, which referred to conversations that Declan and I hadn't been party to.

I thought it was just Antonia being Antonia. She'd been nasty enough to me, and so I was hardly likely to take her side against my friend. But that look. What had she and Sally discussed behind our backs? I'd only ever worried about what Antonia might have had to say about childcare. But if they'd talked about Declan, then it wasn't just the conversations between Sally and Antonia that had happened behind my back. It was the conversations between Sally and Declan as well.

I clutched my glass, and reminded myself that I had no reason to be suspicious of Sally. Not then, when our whole lives revolved around one another. Perhaps she'd had no conversations with Declan to report, and it was just Antonia, in her absolute cynicism, observing the things which were obvious and yet which were visible only to her, warning her of Declan's growing dependence. Or even if there were conversations with Declan that worried Sally, they would have worried her rather than doing anything worse. But—

She got pregnant. What had that meant to Declan? I searched for more images, and found none. We'd told him – had we told him, or had he just found out along with everyone else? I couldn't remember. Had *she* told him? No, that was ridiculous – my memories of that time were of the four of us, me, Sally, Cass and the unborn child, huddled together, writing *Genesis* between us, and if there were memories of Declan scattered amongst them, I couldn't place them. Perhaps he'd begun to withdraw. Which would make sense. It might have been all right when the family he'd latched on to was a lopsided unconventional entity, whose loose ties admitted entry to almost anyone. And he might well have identified with Cass, because she was as fatherless as he was himself. But then – the prospect of another child. My child. The proof, if he needed it, that Sally actually had sex with me; the imminent emergence of yet another person who was mine and not his. And then we married, and Declan, best man, life and soul of the party, was charming to everyone but me. *I'm sorry, Max. Basically, I'm just in need of a shag.* Which he was; and only the barest threads of self-regard prevented him from defiling Sally's fifteen-year-old cousin in a suicidal bid for the only pure love he knew.

The hatred was accumulating, and occasionally surfacing. Like that night in the pub with Janice. That night it had already been in his head to leave everything because of me. He'd actually said so, to my face. But of course he hadn't been able to say why. So he'd pinned it all on something else, some rubbish about my book, some cock-eyed idea he'd dreamt up that minute about me trying to found my own religion—

Except that I knew, remembering it, that he hadn't thought it up that minute. Because if it was true that I had infiltrated the brains of others, it was truer of him than anyone else. What was he in those days if not a twisted kind of disciple? Ever since I'd come to London, the direction of his life had been dictated by mine. My social life, my home, my wife. When he said, 'We're all blank slates for you to write on,' there was no 'we', not really. He was talking about himself.

Then, the launch party. He met my progeny for the first time. It was a miniature version of me, and had sprung from the womb of the woman he wanted for himself. Declan looked at it through a haze of vodka and rage, and something snapped. He uttered the words which were supposed to be the last he'd ever say to me. *You've just done the two things most conducive to peace of mind for a self-regarding organism in a universe with no possibility of an afterlife and no room for God. You've published, and you've reproduced.*

Then he left. How blinkered I was to see none of it at the time.

The drinks sploshed onto the table. Fastidiously, I moved my second pint behind the first, and attempted to mop up the mess with the beer mats. Declan took a hefty slurp from his glass, and gave me a glance from beneath what looked like terrified eyebrows.

'All right,' I said. 'So you didn't fuck her. But you were in love with her. Weren't you?'

'Things just aren't as *simple* as that,' he said, the panic starting to rise in his voice.

So there we had it. The first admission.

'I can understand it,' I said, trying to keep my own voice steady. 'She was amazing. Anyone would have loved her.' But understanding it meant nothing. He'd had no right to love her. She was mine.

'Max, I didn't love her. She was your girlfriend. Your wife. I would have been insane if I'd even let such a thing cross my mind.'

'I don't think sanity has much to do with these things,' I said. 'I can't remember being very sane about her myself.'

He managed to rouse himself to some sort of defence. Which was, as was typical of Declan, the evasion of an attack. 'Why does everything have to revolve around you?' he shouted. 'Just because you loved her, that doesn't mean that everyone else has to! Can't you look at it from my point of view for a change?'

The evangelism jibe. I registered it for future use, but didn't allow myself to be deflected. 'What is your point of view?' I said.

'Look. I know you think I didn't read *Genesis*. And it's true that I didn't want to. But you made me do it. And – well, I thought it might be a complete mess, all non-stop numbers and beetles. But of course it wasn't. It was brilliant. Even *I* thought it was brilliant, and I wasn't exactly kindly disposed towards it. Max, you were *twenty-six*. I was the one who was supposed to be the writer, not you. You were doing well enough as it was, as a scientist. What right did you have to write a book like that, on top of everything else?'

On top of everything else. We were getting warmer. Perhaps the book had been part of it, after all. The final straw, adding insult to injury. But not the only straw. *You've published, and you've reproduced.* 'You would never have got that worked up about your career,' I said. 'Not worked up enough to leave the country. You didn't care about it enough.'

'What was there to keep me in the country? I hated my job, I hated the women I slept with, I hated everything. What did I have to keep me there, except—'

Now that it had come to it, he couldn't bring himself to say those words. And neither, for that matter, could I.

'Excuse me,' I said. 'I'm just going to the loo.'

I was sure now. Declan went to Berlin as people used to join the Foreign Legion: to forget. In order to achieve this aim, he left instructions that no-one except his closest colleagues should be given his contact details. But he reckoned without Sally, who was the product of an upbringing that neither Declan nor I fully understood, and never let an invitation go without an RSVP, or a party without a thank-you letter, or a friend slip back into the ranks of strangers. She found the address, and she wrote. And though the letters were supposedly from me too, Declan would have known that I'd played no part in their writing other than to huff and puff and swear at him for his treachery, before going off to do something else.

How would that have felt for a man who'd run six hundred miles to escape from his own lust? In a way, those letters must have been the most intimate correspondence that had ever passed between them, straight from her to him with no-one else in the room. I tried to imagine what she would have written, and how he, in his self-imposed isolation, might have read it. They would have been full of chatter about me, my career, William's progress into toddlerhood – all of it poison to him. But I knew from the many cards and greetings that she'd written and I'd signed that she couldn't have put pen to paper without allowing her spontaneity to shine through. She would have told him about the weather, what she'd had for lunch, the telephone conversation she'd just had with her mother – whatever popped into her mind. Those reflections, however mundane, would have brought a blast of her whole personality, and with them probably the memory of her physical presence as well.

Perhaps he didn't read them; perhaps he destroyed them. But that would have been no better. You can choose not to open a letter, but you can't prevent it from being delivered, and she didn't stop sending them. 'Oh, God,' I said one week, when she'd finished her letter to Antonia and had appealed to me, as she always did, for anything I might want to say to Declan. 'Why should I say anything to the man? Why should *you* say anything to him? He's made it quite clear that he doesn't want us in his life. I don't know if I'd want to say anything to him even if he wrote back, after all this time.'

'He's our *friend*,' said Sally. 'We can't desert him now.'

'Even though he's deserted us?'

'Especially because he's deserted us. There's obviously something wrong, Max. He has to know that we're still here for him if he needs us.'

I probably felt a stab of jealousy even then. But I assumed she'd do the same for anyone, and I wasn't sure that I wanted Declan to disappear permanently either. It was the easy way out, to let Sally write to him. It meant that I didn't have to work out whether I still wanted him as a friend.

And so the letters kept on coming, the ties he was running away from still unsevered. He did his best to free himself; he went out looking for love. But though his later account to Sally suggested that he came closer than he ever had before, he didn't quite manage to let himself go, and when he failed and the girl left him, the letters from Sally still kept coming. The path back to the old life was still open, just as she'd intended it would be.

There was probably nothing sinister about her actions. If there had been, it was unlikely that she would have been so open with me about them. Even if I hadn't imagined the memory of Antonia's meaningful glances, even if Sally had known all about her own role in Declan's departure, then she might still have made those dogged overtures in a spirit of pure friendship. After all, there could be no harm from my point of view in returning to the status quo.

Yet harmless motives can conceal dangerous ones, even from those who hold them. She might have begun her mission of communication out of a sense of honour, an appreciation that the only true courtesy towards a friend is the kind that persists even when his own courtesy has been withdrawn, but to have continued for so long was beyond courtesy. It could only have been driven by some fugitive sense of pleasure. What woman wouldn't have been flattered by the adoration of the two men she held closest in her affections? I could see now that her fondness for him had been founded upon the same attractions that drew all Declan's women – by his laconic sharpness, his wit, and the mystery of a suffering that no-one was allowed to share. She wanted them back. For her own sake, not mine.

God, I'd been as stupid as a priest. The timing of Declan's return had seemed so random at the time, his reappearance as sudden and unexplained as his vanishing. But as a scientist, I should have known far better than to accept the unexplained as unexplainable, when just a little further investigation might have provided the answer. It wouldn't even have taken any investigation. I'd known that Sally was still writing to him; I'd known that she would have told him that I was about to leave for America. The only thing I hadn't known was the thing I didn't want to know, which was how Declan might react to receiving the news.

Which was perfectly obvious, now. He'd held out for so long, he'd failed to break free, and the only thing stopping him from giving up was the horror of returning to the very same situation that had driven him away. When he opened the letter that told him I was going, all of that changed. This was the first chance he'd ever had in his life to go back to the past and actually change it.

As soon as he read those words, he would have returned. Of course he would have returned. If I'd thought about it properly,

I would have known it even before it happened. I didn't think about it properly. But the woman who wrote that letter *must* have known it herself.

Water on the floor, the stench of piss rising in steam from the urinals outside. There were feet visible through the gap under the door, and the shuffling, hissing sound of casual urethral evacuations. What if those feet belonged to Declan? A knock, a mildly worried, 'Max? You okay in there?' Just don't, I thought, as the footsteps passed my door. Just don't.

Because this, I knew, was the bottom. Crouched in a locked cubicle, voyeurising the imagined voyeurism of the man who'd once wanted to bed my wife. Declan was married now, and I was not. All my nostalgia centred on a time when he'd wanted what I had, and not the other way round. The only person I'd ever been able to let myself desire was so far barricaded into the past that this was my only way back to her. By fantasising about the ways in which I might have been betrayed.

And yet once unleashed, the story reel just wouldn't stop playing. After all those months of dissecting long-forgotten conversations, reimagining, recreating, spinning myself into other people's minds, it wasn't only that it was tantalisingly easy to do. It was also that it was becoming the only way I knew of assembling anything that remotely looked like truth. I wanted to leave, I wanted to go back to the table and remember that it was possible to live in a world that contained squash matches and pub conversations which would be forgotten a week later. But the story was only part of the way through. And the whole point of a story, the thing which makes it feel real, is that it has an end.

He came back to London because the paper recalled him. It was an easy excuse – there always had to be an excuse. When he turned up on our doorstep, the excuse for the whisky on his breath was the carnations he thrust towards us: 'Flower shop next to the pub. Would've seemed rude not to.' And the excuse for the poor state of the flowers was the bottle of kirsch he'd brought us from Berlin: 'Had to stick 'em both in my pocket on the tube. Not much room in pockets.' The kirsch itself needed no excuse, except that it had come from a country he'd never told us he lived in. But whatever excuse he had for that one, he didn't make it to me.

I know I was angry at that moment. Red mist angry. Perhaps, just as Sally must have known underneath why she kept writing to him for so long, I knew at that party why I hated him so much. I wanted to pick him up by his dishevelled collar, pin him against a wall and scream questions at him until he had made it up to me. But I did none of those things. Tight-lipped, I watched Sally throw herself into his arms, and then avoided him until he had gone away again. And then, apart from a bit of enraged crockery-throwing when he popped into my head while I was doing the washing up afterwards, I didn't give him another thought until I got back from the States.

Whereas for those two, that headlong plunge, that awkwardly charged clash of flesh on flesh, would have been the beginning of something new. Even if Sally didn't know it; even if she was the most innocent woman in the world. Because I had never voluntarily left her side before. And she was pregnant. I remember now, the things she used to say to me when she was pregnant with William: 'Oh, Max, I'm so glad you're here. I'm so glad that you're going through it with me, not leaving me to cope with it all on my own. It was so lonely last time.' And I used to hug her very close, and tell her again how happy I was, and that I would never leave her to cope on her own. Why didn't I remember those promises the second time around? Why didn't she *remind* me, when I was so full of my plans for America, instead of loading her letters to Declan with bait to bring him to her side?

And the luck was with Declan all that winter. My call to America, Sally's pregnancy, even the state of industrial relations in the UK. I can't, obviously, find any causal link between Declan's desires and those power cuts. Some things just happen at the same time. But he was prepared to go to fairly extreme lengths to exploit his good fortune. Why, for instance, on returning from Germany did he choose to buy a clapped-out builder's van instead of a perfectly ordinary car? There never was a reason other than its oh-so-fortunate suitability for carrying logs to Edenbridge Terrace in the winter of discontent.

Discontent? He must have been on cloud nine, snuggled between the cushions in my place beside the hearth, reading his books and magazines, hearing at second hand the story of my descent towards doom. 'He's had some sort of fracas with some Christian fundamentalists,' I could hear Sally telling him archly, peering over the spectacles she'd acquired the summer before. 'Seems to think he has to vanquish them. It means he has to stay out there for another two weeks. I can't imagine what's got into him.'

Oh, what manna from heaven that must have been. But there was more. There was ammunition. A chance to actually change things between us.

He would have taken it gently at first. Chuckling affectionately. 'Well, well,' he would have said. 'Sounds like our Max has finally met his match.'

'Met his match?'

'I don't know about you, but ever since we were boys he's always reminded me of some demented evangelistic preacher whenever he gets into his stride.'

Perhaps she bridled at the implied criticism at first. But he'd known me longer than she had, and she was angry and upset. With Declan, it would have felt like less of a betrayal to voice her emotions than it would with anyone else, and any insight he could offer into my behaviour might have sounded plausible.

'Don't you see?' Declan would have said, as soon as he could see that she was ready to let him go further. 'His passion isn't for beetles, not really. It's too big for that. What he's really after, what really drives him, is the desire to take over other people's minds.'

Easy for him to say that, ensconced in my armchair, drinking my wine, his eyes wandering over the curvaceous and yet still elegant form of my pregnant wife. Easy for him to comfort her when the tears came, easy for him to take everything that was mine in the loneliest hour of my life—

Perhaps it didn't happen straight away. Yet there were so many more opportunities. Sally didn't spend all of my time away in misty contemplation of my return. When I came back she was different. Guilt-ridden, perhaps, as well as full of the need to justify her awful transgression. She called me an evangelist. The word never sounded right coming from her mouth. Who could have put it there, except for the man who had known me since he was thirteen, who had every reason in the world to exploit it? He'd been in the right place at the right time to provide Sally with the word she knew would hurt me most, and he'd been in the right place at the right time twenty-five years later, when a journalist called Margot Hennessy had said them again.

I was out of the cubicle. That much had been achieved. A face stared back at me from the mirror, peering into the depths of my own eyes, wild and hair-stricken, pale and dark and contorted and enormous. A monster. I ran the tap and splashed the water into my eyes. It flew up in cascades, falling in slow motion around me. Then I straightened.

There was absolutely no point in killing him. If ever I had been going to do that, it should have been years ago, when the logic of the truth was still scattered amongst my illusions, when there were still dreams left to be saved. Now there were none, and therefore nothing worth killing. All that I had the right to expect now was a confession to me, to follow the one he'd given to a stranger.

I made my way back to our table, swaying slightly as if drunk. Declan was crouched over his pint. I sat down.

'Big shit?' said Declan.

It took me a moment to realise that the phrase wasn't an admission of his own true nature. 'Some things take a while,' I said, and was astonished to hear words coming out of my mouth in the normal way.

'Look, Max. If you want me to say it, I'll say it. Though I can't see what good there is in dragging up something like that. Yes, I did fancy Sally. Still do, in fact.'

Fancy? What a nasty, childish little word. How could he even pretend to show a woman like Sally so little respect?

'But then I always do fancy attractive women,' Declan continued. 'So do you. It's normal.'

'It's not normal to run away to Germany to escape from *fancying* someone—'

'But it was such a small part of it—' He shifted backwards as I began to rise. 'Okay, okay, not a small part for you. But can't you see? It's as I said before. I didn't go to Berlin to escape from Sally. I went to escape from *you*.'

I said nothing.

'Of course I wanted her,' said Declan. 'But she wasn't the only thing of yours I wanted. I'd wanted your family since I was thirteen years old. After I went to your house and your mum fussed over me, I used to dream that there'd been some sort of mistake in the maternity ward and we'd accidentally been swapped. And that some doctor would turn up at school and announce what had happened, and we'd be ordered to go home to our real parents—'

He was playing the sympathy card, just as he had when the

pair of us had sat on the floor of my bedsit with Sally and toasted friendship. 'That's pathetic,' I spat.

'Max, I'm not quite sure what you think I actually did. How would either of us have lived with ourselves if we'd had sex? She was pregnant, for God's sake. You came back. Life went on as normal. Where does our supposed adultery fit into that?'

I shuddered, my mind staggering, as if he'd landed a heavy blow. '*You think I fucked her*' had been bad enough. But the coarseness of the word 'fuck' at least afforded a little distance from proceedings. Whereas '*if we'd had sex*' was intimate. It was the way Sally and I would have referred to what we did in bed. And the collective pronoun implied consent, the two it took to tango. He'd probably never referred to himself and Sally as 'we' in my presence before. It half-confessed that there had been a 'we' to talk about.

Life had *not* gone on as normal after I got back. Sally had initiated a screaming row with me the first day I was home. Declan had run around doing her errands, taking me out to play squash because she couldn't bear to have me in the house – how long had it carried on? When and where would they have conducted their affair? I had no idea, because I'd been far too busy at the time running around after God. The long, slow decline of Sally's respect for me, the ever-escalating rows, the trip to Somerset with Altruista abandoned en route – Jesus, how long had it continued? The only evidence I had that it had ever ended was that they were both with other people now.

'You wanker,' I began to say, and then couldn't stop. 'You wanker, you wanker—' And then his face above mine, his mouth weaving words, tugs from behind me, and a strange noise as my arms crumpled and Declan fell. A low howl, which seemed never to stop, until I realised it was coming from me and I tried to stop it but couldn't.

It was such a bizarre sound, unearthly, like something

dragged from the bowels of the universe. Grunts, and squeaks, and huge, phlegmy sniffs that resembled the most raucous of snores.

'It's all right,' I heard Declan say. 'Leave us. I think he's been building up to this for a while.'

I was sitting on a chair, trying to hide my face in my hands, and getting very messy in the process. Declan prised them apart. He was crouching on the floor beside me. 'Max,' he said, 'we have to leave. I'll hail a black cab. They think you're an escaped lunatic. Seriously. Let's go.'

'Oh, shi-i-i-i-it—' I wailed, the word coming out in disjointed fragments between the heaving of my diaphragm. Declan stuffed a beer mat in my face and grabbed my elbow in an attempt to haul me to my feet. I found the means to co-operate. The air outside was a blessedly cool hit upon my senses. But still I couldn't stop sobbing.

'Max,' said Declan, 'I know it's hard, but you have to stop doing that, or there's no taxi driver in London who'll take us. Come on. Ease up now. There we go. That's better.'

As if I were a child, or a dog. The shuddering slowed, and I peeped over my beer mat at his face. '*Did* you fuck her?' I said.

'No,' said Declan. 'But I think we should leave that one just now.'

With his usual nose for alcohol, Declan sniffed out my whisky within seconds. 'Hmm,' he said, drawing it towards him from the cupboard under my sink. 'Ardbeg. Not bad at all.'

My head throbbed and every part of my body ached, as if I'd been beaten up. Which I knew I hadn't been. I sneaked a surreptitious glance at Declan to check that he was unharmed, and was relieved to see his face intact. 'Oh, shit,' I said, putting my elbows on the kitchen table and resting my head on my hands.

'You've said that,' said Declan.

I was too tired even for embarrassment. He sat down opposite me, and pushed a tumbler towards me.

'I'm not sure that's a good idea,' I said.

'It's medicinal,' said Declan, and downed half of his generous portion in one go. 'We're going to have to find a new pub for after squash, you know. I reckon that's the last time they're going to let us into the Coach and Horses.'

I took a sip of whisky, and the fiery effect on my throat was very soothing. 'I'm sorry,' I said. The words sounded odd. They weren't ones I'd been expecting to use that evening.

'I probably deserved it. Pretty damn stupid of me to say I fancied your wife, if you think about it.'

'But it was true.'

'Not the way you took it, it wasn't. And it wasn't your fault you took it that way. I would have done the same. Well, I wouldn't have had much luck trying to dangle you in the air like that, but you know what I mean.'

'Did I hit you?'

'No. You looked as surprised to see me up there as I was to see you down below. There was just the waterworks after that. Why? Did you want to hit me?'

The answer was yes. I knew now that I'd wanted to hit him for a very long time. But the feeling seemed to be passing now. I hoped it wasn't just the whisky. I felt strangely light-headed. 'Declan,' I said, 'how did things get so fucked up?'

'Beats me. But Max—'

'Mm?'

He pulled hard at what was left of his hair, his eyebrows rising to push the creases in his forehead to the top of his temples. 'I'm trying to think of a way of putting this that doesn't make you think you've got to stick my head through that window.'

'I'm all right. I'm not going to get out of this chair.'

He leaned back a little. 'You've got to get over Sally. Get over all this one-true-love bollocks. You met this great girl, you married her, you had kids with her, you spent nigh on twenty years with her, and then it ended. Finito. It happens all the time. You two had a great time while it lasted, but it's over now. It doesn't mean you have to live like a monk.'

'I don't live like a monk.'

'Oh, come on, Max. The number of times Georgie's tried to fix you up—'

I saw the flaw in his argument. 'You're talking shit,' I said. 'How can you say that there's no such thing as romantic love when you've got Georgina? Your life was as buggered as mine is now until you met her. And you had to wait about forty years for that.'

'It just isn't like that. Life isn't like that for anyone except you. I mean, the rest of us have those dreams, but it's only you who carries on as if it's actually happened to them. That's what you got wrong about the way I felt about Sally. That if I'd thought about something, it must have happened—' His chair skidded backwards as I reacted. 'I didn't think about it. I *didn't*, Max. You've got me wrong, it was just never like that for me—'

'You just said you did!'

'I didn't mean it like *that*. Oh, God, it's like trying to communicate with someone who speaks a different language— What I'm saying is that I didn't spend forty years waiting around for Georgie. I spent fifteen of those being a kid, and the next twenty-five being an arsehole. Timing is everything. You've got to want something before you can have it.'

'It's not just timing. I can't see what there was that happened' – I made a rather long-winded calculation: he'd met Georgina at an Erasmus College bash to which I'd flogged him a ticket after Vicky dropped out – 'ten years ago, that made you suddenly stop being an arsehole and start being ready for love, except for the fact that you met Georgina.'

'Can't you, Max? Can you really not see it?'

I frowned.

'Stop being dense,' said Declan.

'What has me splitting up with Sally got to do with it?'

'Ten years ago I was feeling somewhat homesick.'

'Homesick?'

'I never had a family of my own. Having a family was always a fantasy. One I thought I'd never live up to. I thought if I was going to meet a woman who'd make me part of a family it would have to hit me between the eyes the way it hit you. I thought I'd have to be talented and charismatic, I thought I'd have to *grow up*. And given that I knew I wasn't going to, the best I could do was rely on your family to be mine. Then even your right woman turned out not to be the right woman after all, and the family wasn't there any more. I was devastated. I probably felt as uprooted as Steve did. But then Georgina turned up, and this time there was no fantasy to compare her with. For once, I could do away with fantasies, and make do with real life instead.'

He paused, and took a long draught from his glass.

'You could do with trying the same thing one of these days, mate,' he said.

So many stories. Some of them mine, some of them his, overlapping and diverging, competing and converging, barely distinguishable and yet utterly at odds. As we peered at one another over the whisky, something occurred to me. That last story, the one about how his horrible childhood had made way for a dysfunctional adulthood until he'd finally been forced to confront the past and make way for a bright new future – it was improbably coherent, and weirdly familiar in its structure. 'Declan,' I said, 'you would never have said all that stuff in the past.'

'What stuff?'

'About how shit it was not having a family. When Altruista said you'd had a hard life, you dumped her on the spot.'

'Yeah, well.' He looked shifty. 'Maybe it wasn't just timing with Georgie. Or even that she was the most fanciable woman I'd met in ages. She has other advantages too.'

'Uh? What advantages?'

'They say you shouldn't sleep with your shrink. But it works for me.'

That was it. Despite all appearances to the contrary, Declan had been psychologised. I felt manipulated. His whole history had been neatly parcelled into an official version, a reinterpretation designed around Georgina's Freudian training and engineered to culminate in the happy ending of his marriage to her. 'So that's all I have to do,' I said in a rather hysterically high-pitched voice. 'Find myself a sexy psychiatrist.'

'Erm, I'm not sure it'd work for you, mate. You've already got your own views on life. I was a blank slate.'

My confusion was absolute. 'Declan,' I said, 'I'll believe you that you never slept with Sally. I'll believe you about anything. But the evangelism thing—'

'I didn't talk to Margot about Frank Vernon, or about your family, or anything else in that article.'

'And you never said to Sally that I was an evangelist?'

'Uh? *Sally?* I thought it was Margot who called you that.'

His bemusement looked genuine. Which meant nothing, because there was no reason why he'd remember it even if he had. 'Okay, Margot. Did you say it to Margot?'

'I promise you I didn't. If it's worrying you that much, why don't you ask her who said it to her?'

I stared into my glass, knowing that I couldn't. Because he was telling the truth. And at heart, I'd wanted it to be Declan. He would have been by so far the easiest person to blame.

'Do you think it's Sally who said it to her, Max? Is that it?'

I didn't know. It seemed very unlikely. I'd lost her so long ago, and she wanted very little to do with me now. Stirring up trouble with me was the last thing I could imagine her doing. But though Declan might have called me an evangelist first, it was Sally who'd really meant it. It was she who had banned me from talking about God, who had pushed me away, who'd accused me of never listening to anyone else's opinions but my own. Margot had explicitly drawn the parallel between my failures to defeat the creationists and the problems in my private life. If it wasn't Sally who had spoken to her, they were still Sally's words. And they could only have been spoken by someone who'd known her as well as I had.

'It's—' I began.

'What is it, Max? What are you afraid of?'

We'd knocked down so many barriers during the evening. One more couldn't do any harm. 'The kids,' I said, in the most craven voice I'd ever heard.

Something flashed suddenly in Declan's eyes. Dread, or comprehension, or— But before I could begin to interpret it, it was gone. He finished his whisky. 'That's just paranoia. Your kids love you. It might not seem like that all the time, but that's just the way it is with kids. Stop worrying, Max. I can understand that this article's got you into a stew, because it's dragged up a lot of bad memories. But you don't have to have your life dictated to you by the likes of Margot Hennessy. Forget the whole thing. Please. You owe it to yourself.'

He stood up.

'Are you going?' I protested in panic.

'You may only have had half a pint and a few sips of whisky, but I have to tell you that I got quite a lot of alcohol down me while you were sulking in that toilet. If I don't catch the last tube I'll get home rat-arsed in a taxi, and then there'll be hell to pay.'

'But you—' There were still things he had to tell me. I didn't know what they were, but I was sure they were there.

'It's been a big evening. Look after yourself, Max. I'll see you the Tuesday after next, if not before. Okay?'

I said nothing. His hand hovered for a moment, and then he patted me awkwardly on the shoulder. 'G'night, Max,' he said. 'I'm not very good at this sort of thing, but – we all care about you. Remember that. You know where I am.'

I stayed exactly where I was. When the door clicked to, I poured myself another whisky.

He was hiding something. After everything that had passed between us, he was still hiding something. And if that was so, I couldn't trust a thing he'd said after all.

II

One of the books that came out just before the publication of *Genesis* was Richard Dawkins' *The Selfish Gene*. I was doomed to hate it anyway, not least because it was so damned good, but I must also have been one of the first of a select group of people whose reaction to the title was to flinch.

It was just a metaphor, and a very good one. Dawkins' 'gene's-eye' account of evolution changed the way that the reading public thought about natural selection. It even changed the way that scientists thought about it. And by using a metaphor, Dawkins made some severe mathematical facts digestible to struggling human brains. Our brains have evolved to communicate using language, which itself has evolved by a strange type of natural selection. To survive, all language must do is have the ability to make an idea take root within the thought patterns of a brain, and metaphor is a particularly effective adaptation to this purpose. It takes an image with which the brain is familiar and demonstrates its parallels with something new. This is a kind of shortcut, because the new thought can be slotted into our network of associations along-side the old image, where we can store it until we learn more about it. Such a shortcut is so much more palatable to our untidy but relentlessly ordering minds than a series of equations; and once we have the new concept firmly in place, surely we can learn the sums later.

But though science must use language if it is to be passed on from one person to another and survive, it has another master too: objective truth. One of the great achievements of science has been to be faithful to this second and difficult master, and to develop methods of communication which forsake ambiguity. On the surface of it, these methods should be easier to absorb than the more slippery linguistic techniques we use every day, because they are simpler. Each set of symbols corresponds to only one meaning and, if you do the sum, there can be only one correct answer. But in fact this simplicity is its own undoing. These symbols are free of the myriad of associations attached to other kinds of word, which means that there is only one way to get them into the brain, and that is by learning each one separately. In early youth, such systems may appeal to certain types of brain, particularly those which prefer the order of science to the confusing world of social interaction, but it still takes a lot of work to master them. And in later life, when human behaviour has become easier to decode, even for the most isolated individuals, and the facility for learning new languages is less strong, it is even more difficult for those unfamiliar with science to find a way in.

I am a scientist who managed to learn the language of society. When I was a young man and full of the joys of my own comprehension, it was impossible for me to contemplate keeping the two separate. I could understand perfectly well that a page full of numbers and diagrams was barren to a mind brought up without them, and I wanted to explain the truth that lay behind those sums in a way that the unscientific could understand. This was perhaps the biggest reason for that flinch when I saw the title on the cover of Dawkins' book. I saw what those words had done, and though I didn't admit it to myself, I think I glimpsed the hopelessness of my desire to be both completely comprehensible and completely accurate at the same time.

Because a gene is not really selfish, and Dawkins didn't mean that it was. To take it literally that it is selfish is to assume that it knows what it is doing and where it is going – in other words, to ascribe to it a mind. And it knows no such things at all. One gene's structure may result in its certain extinction, and another's for its billion-fold replication over the aeons, and yet the first is not stupid any more than the second is clever. The only distinction between them is that those aeons later, it will be the descendants of the second that we see around us. It is a simple mathematical fact, and mathematics does not have a mind either.

Yet those who do not understand mathematics do understand the concept of selfishness. Is it really so harmful for science to work with the structures of the brains it is trying to infiltrate, rather than against them? As a popular scientist I am horrified to confess that yes, perhaps it is. A single word is a Pandora's Box. The word 'selfish' already sits in the reader's brain, and this is why it is something onto which the concept of the gene can be hung. But it sits there with its network of associations already formed. 'Selfish' and 'gene'? If genes determine everything we do, and genes are selfish, then selfishness is at the core of us, and despair or fascism are close to hand. The reader may not have turned a single page of Carlyle, Nietzsche, Maudsley or Galton, but the phrases are there, sitting beneath the surface. Heroes and Hero-Worship. The Will to Power. Degeneration. Hereditary Genius. And beyond them lie their own unintentional corollaries: Hitler, Stalin, massacre, holocaust, the monsters of our minds made flesh and most especially blood.

Genes cannot be selfish, but people can. We are bound up within our own beings, and we relate everything around us to ourselves. When I was young, I thought that love would protect me from the worst crimes of the ego. But now I am inclined to believe that nothing can. The problem with selfishness is that it cannot be denied. However much we suppress it, it always pops out somewhere else. What are we to do with it, this huge amount of self that we have within ourselves? Our lovers accept it if they are strong, but they must balance it with their own. Our children have no choice but to bear it at the beginning, but we have handed it down to them, and theirs will be more important in the end. Perhaps the only people who can take it are our parents, but we leave them far behind. I do not know the answer. But the one thing I know about parenthood is the thing I now realise I failed to do. We must stop being selfish, and let our genes do it for us instead.

Perhaps it was William who spoke to Margot. If he did, then my recriminations would be at an end. He is, after all, not a man who is averse to expressing his opinions. A little bit of flattery from Margot, followed by a few leading questions – I know myself too well to suppose that my son would choose discretion over the opportunity for a bon mot.

He was always the most selfish of the children. He imbibed the message of the genes at an early age, and used it throughout his childhood to justify whatever he couldn't argue for in any other way. And occasionally he used it for even worse motives, as the intellectual equivalent of pulling the wings off flies. One day when he was twelve or thirteen, in the twilight days of my marriage, he deconstructed the barren life of Sally's maiden aunt in genetic terms over the dinner table and almost reduced her to tears. As I was heading for the toilet, his mother grabbed me by the wrists and hauled me into the kitchen. 'Stop encouraging him!' she hissed.

'I wasn't encouraging him.'

'Yes you *were*. He has it too easy. Sometimes I think he's turning out just like you, except without any of your redeeming features.'

'Which would you classify as my redeeming features?' I bounced back, extremely sceptical as to whether she still thought I had any.

'You're serious, at heart. For William, it's just a game. And you just laugh along with him, as if it doesn't matter whether he's rude, as long as he's funny.'

She was right, though I couldn't admit it then. As he grew older, I no longer had Sally by my side to do my worrying for me, and I was at a loss to know what to do about it. I remember him aged nineteen, sitting on a pile of books in the study I'm writing in now, and gaining maximum annoyance from me by taking the opposite tack to the one that had amused him so much as a child. 'You always say that complexity is the result of natural selection,' he said, half-pissed on the lager I'd got in so that we could play at being men together. 'But natural selection has only two tools: infertility and death. And complexity doesn't arise from the creatures who *died*. You, and I, and the rat under the sink in the kitchen, and the thistles in the garden – even Steve—'

'Oy!' protested Steve.

'—we are all the latest in an unbroken line consisting entirely of organisms which lived long enough to reproduce.'

'If you're trying to make the facile point that sterility can't be inherited—' I intoned sternly.

'Dad, you've got completely the wrong end of the stick. I mean that everything that's alive today was impervious to natural selection all along. When did the grim reaper get his paws on us? Never. Not once did he beat us to it in the whole history of the universe. Every turn we've ever made was the right one. From the big bang to Chernobyl, we got there first every time. How did natural selection give *us* a hand-up with inventing an eye? We never even needed its help. Our ancestors got there first with that old light-sensitive patch, then when the other fish were still bumping into stones, we got ourselves that weird hump of see-through skin and had a lens to focus the light better, and when the others still thought black-and-white was the state of the art, we were going around with colour televisions in our heads – and you tell me, Dad, what death had to do with any of that.'

He was deliberately missing the point. 'William, that's naïve rubbish. You're fundamentally underestimating the sophistication of the selective process. It's infinitely more—'

'I'm not understimating anything. From everything you've ever drummed into me, you don't get selected in, you get selected out. But we *didn't* get selected out. The fish that went down all those stupid dead paths are just irrelevant. They had nothing to do with us at all. We didn't evolve an eye. We just grew one.'

'You just listen to me for one second—'

Of course he didn't listen. He just liked to hear himself weaving elaborate rings around me. It was like one of those riddles you get told when you've had too much to drink, in which Harry raises ten pounds each from Jeff, Lucy and Nancy, spends it buying lunch, and gives them more change back than he has left in his pocket. You know that the rules of maths haven't stopped working, that there's a sleight of hand somewhere, but even if you get a sideways glimpse of the solution, all it takes is a restatement of the original cock-eyed algebra and the beguiling illusion leaves no room for the unwieldy truth.

On this subject at least, I was quite capable of exposing the error. Evolution was not a sculptor, I told my sons. It was not an animate and intentional agent which used death to carve intricate structures from the passive formlessness of chaos. William, I conceded, had ably demonstrated the fallacy of that one. It was dynamic, and its dynamism was that of war. The dead had as much to contribute as the living, just as they did on a real battlefield.

Yet William wasn't even out to prove me wrong. He knew I was right. Rebellion was too dull for him, and even when it came to ideas, fun was what mattered most. And in a way he had a point. All the biological arms races in the world couldn't disguise the fact that each time, we'd been on the winning side. William was the precise psychological opposite of the religious freaks I had to contend with in the outside world. The luck that had got him born didn't frighten him. It contributed to his unquenchable sense of personal immunity. The three of us in that room had beaten universe-defying odds to be there, and possessed flawless lineages stretching back to the beginning of time. It didn't worry him that the same was true of the rat under the sink or the thistle in the garden. They were quite welcome to see their good fortune with the clarity he did if they wanted to.

When he was a child I used to marvel at the opportunities that would be available to him in later life. Would he be a prime minister, or a great writer, or a captain of industry? I had chosen science early on and had stuck to it. He persisted in excelling in all subjects, and when it came to choosing a university course, opted for maths with philosophy, so that he'd have an answer to everything. I never heard much about his work while he was there, or even about his sporting activities, though he came out with both a First and a half-blue. (The blue was for water-polo, which had the double advantage of being played by very few people and in mixed teams, but they won the match, so there was some merit in it.) Then he left, and started his job in advertising.

'Advertising? What the hell's the point in that?'

'Many men,' said William, raising an arch eyebrow, 'would be proud to have a son embarking on such a highly sought-after career.'

I'd have said it was the money, but there was far more money to be earned in merchant banking or management consultancy. Even accountancy would have paid more. If he'd wanted glamour, he could have gone into television or film. And if he was after an easy life, he could have chosen something that required him to work shorter hours. The only conclusion I have ever been able to come to is that it was a compromise between the three.

William has done very well in his chosen field, which was

the least that could have been expected, and despite the low starting pay, has been promoted so quickly that he is well on the way to beating any academic salary I have been able to command in this country. He owns a luxury flat on Bankside, in which is installed his flatmate, a no-hoper graphic designer and would-be musician, and they live in grime and booze so stereotypical of their generation that I wish the stereotype had not been invented. His life, from what I can make out of it, is spent in one long social whirl amongst a vast gaggle of friends, male and female, who sleep on one another's floors and swap sexual partners as my own generation might have swapped babysitters' phone numbers.

Yet I am forgetting, am I not? It is in the nature of parents to forget. Declan and I, stoned out of our heads at that party in Knightsbridge. Sally and I, dancing on the tables at a gig in a pub in Camden, and getting so drunk that we missed the last tube, had to walk home and face the wrath of the babysitter. Declan, Antonia, Sally and I, celebrating our engagement over numerous bottles of wine until four in the morning, keeping our voices down so as not to wake Cass. Yes, we slowed down sooner, but that was because we had to. It is odd that in a generation which was supposed to have been liberated by the contraceptive pill, all the most glamorous people seemed to have children. My own children's generation appears to have been a little more successful in staving off the demands of reproduction. And so they are free, to drink and to have sex and to push all manner of things up their noses, because there is no-one to harm but themselves.

Anyway, I accepted it, as I accepted the decisions of all the children as soon as they came of age. I was always on hand for advice and opinions when they wanted them, or even when they did not, but it was a point of principle for me not to interfere. The deep respect I'd had for my own father had sprung at least partly from the intellectual freedom he gave me, and all I had to do was remember the terror that gripped my soul on the one occasion when he set me a goal, and it was enough to make me desist from doing the same.

But then one night about five years ago, shortly after William started his new job, I awoke to find Huxley barking in my face. He was begging me for protection rather than offering his own, because as soon as I heard the smashing of glass and leapt, sleep-grimed, out of bed, he darted beneath it and stayed there. I had never had to deal with a burglar before, and whilst I'd always hoped or feared that I would be fairly proactive in deterrence, this movement happened without thought. Adrenaline grabbed a mallet from the toolbox in the bathroom; adrenaline propelled me, two steps at a time, down the stairs; adrenaline lunged towards the attacker in the darkness of the sitting room, weapon whirling. My antagonist was a wiry figure almost as tall as myself, dressed like a white rapper and covered in blood. He reached backwards, and it was only when he came forward again and it glinted in the light of the streetlamp that I recognised that he was wielding a large, dagger-shaped shard of glass. My mallet thrust forward to smash it into his face, and at the very same moment I looked into those dilated pupils and saw the sprinkling of stardust that had once squinted up at me from his mother's arms.

I behold that scene now, as I couldn't then, and it sinks in my heart with the tragic inevitability of a Greek myth. The son confronts the father. Is it rivalry, is it greed, is it revenge? I am in no position to understand that it is the consequence of a pathetic series of events, fuelled by too much drink and too many drugs, involving a girl he does not want to sleep with and a house key he has dropped down a drain. All I know is that my first born is ready to plunge a stake into my heart, and that in retaliation I am about to end the life I myself engendered.

'William!' I gasped, swung the mallet down towards my knees, ducked, and reeled away. Squatting almost, I tottered backwards, just out of reach of his own deadly swipe, and ended up on my back on the floor. He took another step forwards, and I slithered, trying to get to the door, trying to get to my feet. *'William!'* I screamed. *'Drop that!'*

For a moment it was as if a twenty-one-year-old man had been caught having a five-year-old's poo fight. He looked up at the glass, frowned at it, and set it calmly down on the sofa. 'Oh, sorry, Dad,' he said. 'I got confused.'

I clambered to my feet and switched the light on. 'William, you arsehole! What the fuck do you think you're doing?'

William wiped the blood from his eyes and pushed it into his hair. 'Lost my keys,' he said. 'I knew you'd be okay with me kipping here. Had to break the window, I'm afraid.'

Shaking, I laid the mallet on the floor. He'd made a mistake. But he must have known that it was my house he was breaking into, he must have known that it would be me who would come at him out of the shadows. I stared into his bloodshot eyes, which were alert but flickering, and couldn't tell whether he knew anything at all. 'Don't you understand what you were doing?' I shouted at him. 'I could have killed you!'

He laughed recklessly. 'Hey, Dad, don't be melodramatic. You would never have killed me.'

For a moment I almost had the impulse to lunge at him again. 'You're not fucking immortal, you know! Things matter. Things *count*. You've got to take things seriously—'

I was almost sobbing, an old man crying for the sins of his offspring, and the humiliation was almost as great a grief as the knowledge that without that streetlight it might have been a corpse I was contemplating now. He had unfathered me as effectively as he would have done if I'd followed through with the swing of my mallet. I collapsed into my own father's armchair, unable to meet his gaze any longer. 'William,' I said, my voice artificially deep, 'I don't know what you've been up to, but—'

His own voice was even and rational. 'Look. I'm really sorry I broke the window, and I'm really sorry I gave you a shock. As I said, I lost my keys. All a bit of a fuck-up, really.'

'You've been taking drugs,' I said, intending to sound imposing, but losing control of my intonation once more. 'I thought you were too intelligent for that.'

'Oh, come on,' said William, frowning in amused perplexity. 'You're not going to give me a drug lecture, are you? I thought *you* were too intelligent for *that*.'

Witty, even through whatever daze he'd inflicted upon himself. I longed then for a moral code as rigid as Frank Vernon's to allow me to rant at him without hypocrisy. But there was no speech in me that began with 'After all I've taught you'. The only thing I'd taught him was to steer his own course. And this was where it had led him.

I had to do something to restore my authority. 'You've cut yourself,' I said weakly. 'Let me look at that.'

He blinked, wiped his face again, and gazed at his hands. 'Oh, yeah,' he said.

I took him into the kitchen and he fidgeted but was quite passive as I examined his face for traces of glass and then dabbed ineffectually at it with a damp tea towel. It was like Sally patching up the cuts and grazes from the garden at Edenbridge Terrace, except much less effective. As I looked down at him, the tears rose behind my eyes again. His blood-smeared beauty was too much for me.

When I'd finished I looked at my watch. 'Oh, shit, it's nearly six o'clock. William, I've got a lecture in three hours. I'm going to have to get ready for work. You can sleep in your old room if you like.' The 'boys' room' wasn't much better furnished than the rest of the house, and had not been used for years.

'No, it's all right, I've got to get to work too. Can I use the shower?'

I stared at him. 'You're going to work? Dressed like that?'

'I've got a suit in the office.'

'How the hell are you going to explain what's happened to your face?'

'I'll say I was glassed.'

It was the absolute assumption of normality that floored me. As if it was a perfectly everyday occurrence to go to work drugged up, with no sleep, bearing the evidence of a violent confrontation.

'Look, William,' I said, and I didn't know whether I was finally succumbing to the desire to lecture, or forcing myself to do it against my will, 'you're twenty-one, and your body feels like it can take anything. But it can't. You have no idea how few years it'll be before you start to feel the effects of what you're doing now.'

He cocked his head very slightly onto one side, as if amused. 'Would you rather I *didn't* go to work?'

No, of course I wouldn't. I had to confess to myself that his commitment to his job gave me some comfort. Perhaps he really could take it, now at least, and when he could no longer manage both the work and the – other things, it would be the work that took priority.

'I'm like you, Dad,' said William, smiling slightly, though not at all conspiratorially. 'It's just different stuff. Different stuff, that's all.'

That little speech has haunted me ever since. What did he mean? It felt like an accusation at the time. He knew well enough that I never did serious drugs. Yet he seemed to think that I was a living excuse for his irresponsibility. Of course, he'd lived through the trauma of the dissolution of his family, and it might well have left scars I had never seen. But he didn't sound scarred when he said it.

I tried talking to Declan about it, and he was useless. 'You take it from me, Max,' he says. 'Your boy has a very low boredom threshold. And sooner or later, he'll get bored.'

'But what will he do then? He won't be able to start again once he's blown his brains out on drink and drugs.'

'He won't blow his brains out. He's far too fond of them. I haven't a clue what William will do with his life, but if there's one thing I'm sure of, it's that he'll be fine.'

I hoped he'd be more than 'fine'. Fine was not good enough for William. Oh, God, I wanted so much for him. More than for myself. I wanted him to meet a woman the equal of his mother and have her bash into him some sort of respect for the preciousness and fragility of his condition. But when he consented to have steady girlfriends at all, they were either sweet girls who were too much in his thrall to avoid quickly falling by the wayside, or foreign beauties whose main recommendation other than their exotic looks appeared to be their insanity. I was beginning to come round somewhat to Sally's point of view about William, if indeed she still held it herself. It was possible to have things too easy.

Yet it is almost impossible for me to think ill of my children. And of William, though he is undoubtedly the worst of them, the most impossible. Even I see that me-ness in the tilt of his brow and the jut of his chin, whether Sally's in there too or not. And then, from the same mouth, such related yet alien sentiments. If I could limit my responsibility for him to the language of the genes, then it could be tempered, because inheritance is so much more and less than copying. But I know that a William who had been fathered by me and brought up by different parents would not be the way he is. That unknown person, given a few twists of fate, might even be more like me. I was brought up in a household with strict rules of behaviour, and I cast them off myself. Those rules might have been irrational and even unhealthy, but they were there. Whereas William has cast off nothing. He has just followed his upbringing to extremity. Taught to rely on rationality, he rejects any rule that does not measure up to it. I am bewildered by the outcome.

William is the most accessible of my children. He lives in the same city as me, and consents to see me. Yet I find it frightening to meet him. I am too aware that our encounters are more for my benefit than his, and so I must make them as palatable for him as possible. But what sort of meeting would be palatable for a twenty-six-year-old advertising executive in the company of his embarrassingly eager-to-please father? If I were his mother, I would invite him round to Sunday dinner and gossip at him relentlessly until he warmed into communicability. But I am not, and neither of us knows how to gossip. I always say 'the pub', and leave the choice up to him, knowing that he will choose some tucked-away place which offers no danger of bumping into his friends.

'The Compton Arms,' said William this Monday. 'Old geezers' pub down an alleyway on the other side of the roundabout from Highbury and Islington tube. Blink and you'll miss it.'

William and I do not go in for surprising one another. Only, this time I knew that if I had the courage, I was going to have to do so. The Sunday Review, ever more dog-eared, was tucked into the pocket of my greatcoat. We met one another with our usual gruff handshake, two dark giraffes stooping to avoid the beams of a miniature hostelry, and took a table in the snug. After I'd set up my tab at the bar and brought the drinks to the table, he regarded me with the accustomed air of resigned patience, waiting for me to think of something to say.

'How's work?' I said, as I always do.

At these moments love screams within me. It is an emotion that could never have any expression. There is nothing I can name that I want from him, except to know that he has what he wants for himself. And I don't understand what he wants, so I must just smile and nod. Or grimace and shake my head; whichever seems most appropriate. I usually get it wrong.

William doesn't like talking to me about work. The more impressive things – those that aren't connected with his daily grind, like trips abroad and invitations to film premieres – are dropped into conversations about other things, because to list them as achievements would be to allow that they were worth getting excited about. As for the work itself, he takes it as a given that I can't understand the nuances of advertising, so on the occasions that he favours me with a reply, he approaches his summary with the foreknowledge that I will misinterpret it, and twitches with annoyance before I have even responded.

On this occasion, he lit a cigarette and cocked a sceptical eyebrow.

But what else is there to ask? Sally, I know, would have had a list of the names of all his friends at her disposal, together with their occupations and their latest romantic attachments. Women are like this, squeezing whole databases of information from the least communicative of offspring, and so they are never at a loss for a leading question, which results in the garnering of even more data. But I have never seen it as my place to delve into the lives of people I've never even met. If William chose to tell me about them, I'd listen. The fact is that he does not.

'How's Nick?' I asked in desperation. This is one person I've met, because Nick was around when William was at school. He and his family moved away to Scotland when the pair of them were in their early teens, and they met again only by chance, because they ended up in the same 'industry'. The history of their relationship has always reminded me a little of mine with Declan, and its continuation is not unlike either, with Nick the impecunious sponger who occupies the spare room of William's 'loft apartment' and applies himself to the business of earning a living with only half-hearted commitment. William, meanwhile, is the man with the career. However, there the similarities end.

William leant back. 'Nick's a pain in the arse,' he said. 'To tell you the truth, I'm getting pissed off with the whole thing.'

I jumped with surprise. 'What whole thing?' I asked. 'With Nick, you mean?'

'Oh, God, no. I mean, he was born to be a pain in the arse. Complaining about Nick is like complaining about the English weather. No, it's the *whole thing* I'm pissed off with.'

I was clearly supposed to know to which entirety that enigmatic phrase 'the whole thing' referred. 'What, you mean work?' I hazarded.

He began to look impatient, and threw his hands around a little. 'Work. London. Tossers in nightclubs. Women who start worrying about their body clocks at the age of twenty-nine.'

The specifics in that speech were impossible to decipher. So I concentrated on panicking about the generalities. Was he about to decide that his career was getting in the way of the more disreputable parts of his life, just as I'd feared the night he broke into my house? And was he so sick of London that he was preparing to follow his younger brother into the unreachable place which young people called 'the world'? 'But you're so good at your job,' I protested, unable to face the idea of losing him too. 'It would be such a shame to give up on it now.'

He looked scornful. 'Dad, it's a bit rich you getting worked up about my job. When I started, you hated the fact that I'd gone into advertising. Why don't you just say, "I told you so", like anyone else would?'

Because when he'd started he'd barely entered adulthood, and I'd thought that there were so many better paths for his life. Now that he was fully grown, I could think of no alternative that didn't look like a slide downhill. I knew that it was unfair to have so little faith in someone with so much of his life ahead of him, but I was being selfish. The only person I could allow to have a grand transformation now was myself. 'I never hated you going into advertising,' I said, convincing myself for long enough to get the words out. 'I just didn't know anything about it.'

'Yeah, well, I do.'

'What's wrong with it?'

He flicked the ash off his cigarette. 'It's too *easy*.'

Oh, God. Sally's gestures, followed by Sally's words. 'There's no such thing as too easy,' I said, fighting against the neatness of it, wanting prophecies not to be fulfilled. 'It just depends on the level you take it to.'

'Oh, I realise that I'm not allowed to talk about it being easy. I am, after all, a board account director of one of the biggest agencies in the world at the age of twenty-six.'

'Well, there you go,' I said, leaning towards him, trying to suppress him with my words, avoiding the eyes of the other people enclosed with us in that very small space.

'But what people don't realise is that there are countless account directors on dozens of pissy little boards around the world. An account director is someone who's been out of college for a respectable number of years, and a board account director is just another account director who's had another promotion in lieu of a pay rise. Of course, the pay's good anyway at this level, and I have a four-figure monthly mortgage payment which I can easily afford—'

Didn't we bring him up not to say that sort of thing in public? It wasn't the kind of thing I could imagine Sally ever permitting. But then I wasn't Sally, and we weren't the only influences on his life.

'—and so people say, if it's so easy, then why doesn't everyone do it?'

'Well, then,' I said, suppressing my embarrassment and my shame, 'why don't they?'

'Of course not *everyone* could do it.' If anything, the volume of his voice was rising. I was aware from my own habits that this was a diatribe he'd already delivered at least once to himself. Sometimes family likeness is a curse. 'There are all kinds of things you need in order to get ahead in advertising. Average intelligence, for instance, and physical attractiveness, and unshakeable confidence. Once those have been taken into account, however, it really isn't rocket science. So the question remains of why not everyone who could do it does do it. And the easy answer to that one is that they wouldn't want to.'

'But you just said—'

'There's nothing moral about it,' he said, as if I'd made a point I hadn't. 'Most people just couldn't endure the hourly compromises required. Like believing for minutes at a stretch that the most important thing in the world is the successful photocopying of a pitch presentation onto acetate in case the PowerPoint projector breaks down, while some poor woman with boyfriend problems and a bad case of technophobia scurries around you in fear of her next pay rise. Like sitting through a three hour meeting about point-of-sale promotions and listening to half a dozen smarmy twats, each one as arrogant as you are yourself, pontificating in bad English and unspeakable jargon about their own pet idea, which is of course entirely political and designed to further their own course up the career ladder, each prefacing every interruption with a heinous glob of insinuation, all repeating themselves and each other and making sly digs at their rivals and aiming every word at the person they have rightly or wrongly judged to be the most influential person in the room. Like reading a document prepared by a subordinate about the merits and demerits of animation versus live action and going through it with a fine-tooth comb for errors and miscalculations as if it actually mattered. Which of course it does, because it must matter, if the job is to be done. None of my friends could do any of these things, none could play up, play up and play the game, and come out with their haloes shining and their circle of power expanded without first vomiting or expiring of boredom or committing murder.

So yes, I am special. I've got what it takes. I know what it takes, and I do it knowingly, and I know why I do it. There is, as they say, no such thing as a free lunch.'

Oh, how he loved the sound of his own voice. During the course of the oration, the two other groups in the snug had gathered drinks and possessions and moved elsewhere. William was oblivious, glowing with vitality. His nihilistic assault on his own raison d'être had become its celebration, through the sheer force of his rhetoric. Yet nothing could soften the barrenness of what he'd said. And despite my misery on his behalf, somewhere in me was a protest that on the one night when I'd really, really needed to talk about myself, William had taken it upon himself to be in a confessional mood.

'So what do you want?' I said in a low voice.

'I want for nothing,' he said with a flourish, as if that proved his point. 'What could I possibly want?'

A reason to live, I thought in despair. I remembered his words when I'd been patching up the cuts on his face. *I'm like you. It's just different stuff, that's all*. Perhaps this was what he'd meant then, and perhaps it was what he still meant now. And though I longed to empathise, I couldn't bear to let him feel the way I did, so young, so soon. If he did, then he was like one of the cloned sheep whose short lifespans had done so much to threaten the prospects for Dan Gorman's experiments. He'd inherited the knocks and bruises of a lifetime along with his genes, and was born with arthritis of the soul.

Then I thought of a way to move the conversation on without contradicting him. It was a technique that had been used on me often enough. 'You're right,' I said, knowing that he'd never resist agreement, even if what I said next had nothing to do with what he'd said. 'Advertising isn't that much different to anything else.'

He stopped in his tracks. 'Uh?' he said.

'Work is just work. It doesn't matter whether it's discovering the gene to save mankind or directing the next Coke commercial. The wrong things become important. They have to, if we're going to feed ourselves. We're selling our time for money. But there has to be a reason for feeding ourselves. What's your reason?'

I'd expected him to continue his bombast, and find justifications so strong that they would sustain my belief not only in his spirit but also my own. But he didn't. 'There doesn't have to be a reason for the hills or the stars or our friends to be there,' said William, in a voice as cold as the darkest recess of hell. 'They exist, that's all.'

It was a quote from *Genesis*. And panic gripped me. I realised that it wasn't going to be a relief if it had been William who'd spoken to Margot. He was far too bright to have been unaware of the likely impact of anything he'd said. 'William,' I said, doing my best not to speak with any special emphasis, 'have you been talking to any journalists lately?'

'Journalists? I know lots of journalists. So do you.'

'I mean, have you spoken to any journalists you don't know.'

'Dad, what are you talking about?'

'I'm not saying that you meant any harm. Just – well, there was an article that came out a couple of weeks ago which said a few things about the family that I wasn't comfortable with.'

He frowned at me. And staring at that familiar face, I could barely see his features at all. They were like notes in a song too often played, or words in a text too often read. Had they fallen into an expression of genuine perplexity, or had he simply arranged them into a habitual approximation of plausibility, designed to make accusations impossible?

'Oh,' he said, the light of comprehension drifting slowly – too slowly? – across his face. 'You mean the Margot Hennessy interview. I didn't read it. Cally told me about it.'

I wondered briefly who Cally was, then pursued my point. 'Did you talk to Margot?'

'No,' said William very firmly.

There it was. A denial. I could take it or leave it, but the one thing I couldn't do was argue with it.

'Why?' said William. 'What bothered you about it?'

And I couldn't tell him. Parenthood is the greatest restriction in the world. Perhaps the image of my own father was too strong in my mind. He would never have embarked on such a conversation with me. Yet I was not like my father, or William might have turned out more like me. In my father's day, when even a wife was someone who should be protected from the awfulness of life, the loneliness of being a man must have been appalling. Was there any point in extending my pretence that I was such a man, who never faltered, who never asked for help, when it was so clear to my son that I was not? And if I did pretend, what sort of example was I setting in a world very different from the one my father might have liked me to have inherited? I didn't know where the mistakes started, or where they would end. But there was one thing which felt as if I held it in common with my father. I felt responsible. For everything.

William had an excuse for leaving – something to do with a friend who'd flown in unexpectedly from New Zealand that afternoon. It was feeble, but I was happy to take it. Then I found myself back at home, with a good portion of the evening still waiting for me, and so I wrote my account of our conversation, and arrived at its end.

After which, there just didn't seem to be anything more to say. Was this really where it was all leading to? Utter confusion, an absence of answers to anything, a history unravelling towards a conclusion devoid of any meaning? I shivered. There was, after all, nothing in my philosophy which suggested that it should be any different.

'William,' I said, when, on the third attempt, he finally answered his mobile. It was very late, but I'd known that he was pretty much guaranteed to still be up.

'Yeah?' he drawled.

'William, it's Dad. William. Where are you exactly?'

In the background was what sounded like the sort of music they used to play in lifts, except slowed down and with a beat added. I was treated to it for quite a few seconds, and then William's voice returned. 'That's not really an appropriate question right now,' he said.

'Okay, okay. But William. This is important. Do you have a phone number for Steve?'

'What, here?'

'I don't know whether you have it there. Not least because I don't know where you are. But don't you keep your entire life on your mobile? And more importantly, *do you have Steve's number?*'

'If it is on my mobile, I'll have to look it up and call you back.'

I didn't trust him. 'You don't have to ring off. I've seen you playing computer games on that thing while you were on the phone. Just look up the number and give it to me.'

He gave a long-suffering, patronising sigh. 'Give me a few seconds.' The sounds from the phone muffled, and I dimly heard him say, 'Kara. Don't move a muscle. I'll be back soon.' Then, when he resumed conversation, his voice echoed, as if he was speaking from a bathroom. Which he probably was. 'All right,' said William. He recited a very long string of numbers, which I attempted to scribble down on the edge of the newspaper. Then he said, 'But Dad, why don't *you* have Steve's number?'

'Because the last one I had for him was in Bangkok. And he isn't there any more.'

'What's so important? It isn't that article again, is it?'

Did William think I was obsessed? Perhaps I was. 'I think it's fair enough for me to want to talk to my son every now and again,' I said.

'At this time of night?'

'It isn't this time of night in Chicago.'

'He isn't in Chicago. He's in Missouri.'

'Well, the same applies—' And then I stopped dead. *Missouri?*

There was an extremely evasive pause. 'Look, Dad, it's great to speak to you and all that, but I've got things to get on with—'

'I'm sure you do.'

He rang off. And I stared at the phone. *Missouri?* I picked up Margot's article and leafed to the relevant page. There it was.

'"Max Oldroyd is the best thing that ever happened to us," chuckles Jeremiah Vernon, president of a student Christian organisation based in Missouri.'

Back to the beginning. To a time when Steve wasn't even born. Shit. And then I realised that I'd done something very strange. For all my paranoia, the one person I'd never suspected was Steve.

It is time for me to pay a visit to my younger son.

12

The plane wobbles somewhere between the runway and thin air, then shakes, and then steadies itself on a cushion of nothingness, defying all my inborn beliefs and confirming those I have learnt by experience. A lozenge-shaped piece of metal weighing several hundred tons can float at a height of thirty thousand feet and a speed of three hundred miles an hour. I don't know how it is done, but it is possible.

My laptop is on my knee. Its manufactured memory contains all the words of this story that I've written so far. Crunched up across two seats – I foolishly chose to fly economy class, making no allowance for my size, though fortunately I have managed to find an empty row – I feel as if I hold my whole life in my hands. The flight to St Louis involves a change of planes in New York, and so the route is the same as the one I travelled when I took my first plane. Yet I would not be able to tell the difference if it were otherwise. Air travel is fundamentally unreal. We move from A to D without passing through B or C, and there is something as illogical about that passage as travelling from the age of twenty-seven to fifty-two with none of the days between. As I look down at the beginning of this book and then up out of the aeroplane window, this is effectively the journey I am taking. Except that while I am spared the physical wear and tear of crossing the world under my own steam, there is no airy shortcut over the heartache of the missing years.

Steve, as I have said, was the most laid-back member of the family. But it couldn't last like that forever. Sally and I separated when he was eleven, and for a time everyone, with the possible exception of William, was upset. The pair of them used to come to my house on Saturdays, and for the first time Steve was a resentful, sullen child. I used to try to cook them lunch, and whilst William was perfectly happy to exist on whatever mangled scraps I managed to piece together, Steve lost his patience with me every time. 'Dad,' he complained, staring disconsolately at his plate, 'that's *hopeless*.'

'Eat up, there's a good boy.'

'If you can't cook yourself you should come home and let Mum do it for you.'

I couldn't explain to him that Mum didn't want me to come home. He probably knew it anyway. But he didn't understand it in the least. He was a natural peacemaker, and could never see why people shouldn't just be able to get along.

It must have hit him particularly hard that Cass left home for college at almost exactly the same time. Once she was gone I suppose Steve had to fight William on his own or submit altogether. But left alone with their mother, they did develop a greater solidarity over time. And Steve didn't manage to keep up his truculence with me for very long. In the end he found a solution to our bodged meals. He learned to cook himself. Those Saturdays when it was still the three of us were my last real taste of family life. We brought the television into the kitchen and watched the football while Steve cooked one of the four dishes in his repetoire: spaghetti bolognaise, Swedish sausage casserole, chicken in tarragon sauce, or toad in the hole. They reminded me tantalisingly of the early days of my marriage, because they all came from an old seventies recipe book that he'd commandeered from his mother. Each one was cooked in turn, so that I'd know what shopping to do beforehand, and as he grew older he began to experiment, so that by the time William had left for university and it was just the two of us, he was ordering peppers to go into the bolognaise,

Cumberland sausages for the casserole, wild mushrooms for the chicken and Dijon mustard for the toad in the hole. If I got one of the ingredients wrong he was furious, but other than that we spent very equable times together playing interminable games of Dungeons and Dragons or Risk. I'd never spent so much time alone with any of my children until then. The sight of Steve's brow, furrowed in concentration over the board behind his heavy brown fringe, is one of the happiest pictures I have in my brain.

Steve never seemed to mind that he couldn't match William's academic achievements. He had no more interest in coming top in maths tests than he had in supporting the same football team as his brother. Instead he was a diligent worker, who struggled somewhat with science but fought his difficulties to get pass-able results, and whose dedication paid off in the art studio. In those days, perhaps the greatest minefield for Sally and me was our joint attendance at those school parents' evenings, and we had some humdingers of rows as we emerged from hearing William's reports, glowing though they were. But we never disagreed about Steve. The school was very apologetic about his lacklustre science results, assuming that we would expect him to have inherited my own ability. Sally and I were united in attempting to disabuse them of their misapprehension. We were very happy with our son, as long as he was happy himself.

To my surprise, Steve didn't choose to study art after leaving school. It was one of the times when I felt the absence of Sally most keenly, because I had no idea what she thought or what conversations had gone on between them. 'Are you sure you really want to do anthropology?' I said. The last thing I would have expected from him was that he would follow in my own foot-steps, however remotely. 'I thought art was your favourite subject.'

'Dad, you have to have real talent to go to art school. Just because I enjoy it doesn't mean I'm good enough to make a life of it.'

Your mother went to art school without any particularly outstanding talent, I thought rather rudely. But then she hadn't exactly made a life of it. Perhaps he'd been put off by her failures. 'Everything worthwhile is difficult,' I said. 'That's no reason for not trying.'

He shrugged off the suggestion. 'It's social anthropology I'm applying for,' he said. 'There's no biology in it, so there's a chance I won't be completely crap at it.'

'Steve, that's not what I meant at all—'

'I'm actually quite interested in it, if you want to know.'

'Really? You never mentioned it before.'

'I don't necessarily mention everything.'

He succeeded in getting a place at his top choice university, Hull, and was pleased that he'd be reasonably near to his girlfriend, who was heading for Leeds. Of course that didn't last once he'd got there, but he soon produced an equally charming replacement. Even by that stage, when both Cass and William were into their twenties, he seemed to be the only one of the children who was capable of holding down a serious relationship.

Yet for all his lifelong steadiness, it is Steve who is now wandering around the world, with neither a home nor a job to call his own. To begin with it seemed perfectly logical. All the children travelled in their university vacations, and Steve's hankering after remote places was at least linked to his course. He used to telephone me weekly on a Saturday, wherever he was, just when we would once have been sitting down to our spaghetti bolognaise.

Then, after graduating, despite the fact that his 2:2 had ruled out an academic career, Steve announced that his heart was still in anthropology, and set out for New Guinea overland. I'm not sure what I thought would come of it, but I gave him the money to get him started anyway. And when he first went abroad, his Saturday telephone calls were replaced by emails, sent at just the same time. 'I have arrived in Rome.' 'Took train to Istanbul yesterday. By next week I'll be in Asia.' 'India amazing. Very smelly.' Only emails weren't the same. However conscientious he was, Steve was not a voracious communicator, at least not with me, and without my prompts to draw him out, my idea of what he was up to began to fizzle away. Then, as he voyaged deeper into Asia, the regularity of his correspondence declined. Yet I couldn't help myself, each week, from checking my inbox; and the crushing disappointment of finding nothing there was mingled with the dull, thudding panic of concern. Cass was gone; William was impossible; Steve was all I had to rely on. That hour on a Saturday when he would once have called never failed to pass without a twinge of dreadful, fateful loss, until, like a sleeper waking from a nightmare, I pulled myself into reality and forced myself to believe that he was still out there somewhere, being Steve in just the same way he always was. Yet he was not. Time and distance changed everything, and I didn't know enough about the new reality to be able to keep hold of it. My gentle nut-brown boy vanished every time, and the next week I was ready to lose him all over again.

I don't think he ever made it to New Guinea, but I can't be sure, because I've received nothing but cursory email messages from him in the last year. The last one was over three weeks ago, from Chicago, which suggests that he has been diverted somewhat from his original mission. I have no idea how he survives, because he has never asked for money after that initial instalment. If he asked I would give it.

William, who is on the receiving end of a series of more detailed circulars sent to all his friends, assures me that there is nothing to worry about. 'Leave him alone, Dad,' he says, when I pummel him for information. 'At least he's doing something of his own for a change.'

'Does he have a girlfriend?'

'I'm sure he does. Steve always has a girlfriend.'

Perhaps he lives on his charm, beguiling himself into the

hearts of strangers just as he did when he was a toddler. But my worst nightmares picture him as skin and bone, the hair unkempt and the eyes blank or raving. When I hear of the murder of backpackers I don't know whether to be afraid that he is the victim or the perpetrator.

'He's *fine*, Dad,' says William. 'It's perfectly *normal*.'

Why am I always being told to trust that my children are fine? I don't know enough about them to know whether they're fine. It may be normal for them to create so much distance between myself and them, but it doesn't feel normal, and I don't think I can afford to accept it any more.

The plane has begun its descent. Or at least, so the pilot informs us, but otherwise we would not know. Just like certain periods of my life. If only there had been a pilot on board to warn me then.

I feel a little insane, to be finding so many parallels between my life and this aircraft. Yet when one is stowed away like this in a metal box, far above the earth, immune most of the time from motion sickness because there is no sense of motion, then one's mind is encapsulated, somehow, shielded from anything outside, reliant only on what it already knows.

Just as my mind has always been.

This must stop. Not least because the announcement has come through that we must turn off all electronic devices. So: a few rebellious final sentences, just to show that I'm not intimidated into thinking that my computer will interfere with air traffic control just yet. Then, a packing of my laptop back into my holdall, a general tidying of myself, and a long, crooked wait to file off the plane onto a runway in a real place thousands of miles from where I started. Somewhere near to here is my son. But these words must remain stowed in my bag.

I am on my own.

*

None of the nightmares of my mind's eye were true. He was just Steve, a broad-backed, tawny youth, though his hair was both longer and blonder than it had been, one shade lighter than his tanned skin.

'Dad,' he said, fixing me with a firm handshake and brushing his long fringe out of his eyes. From the sunny lightness of his manner, the last time we'd met might have been the previous week. 'Look, I've got you a present. Been carrying it with me ever since Laos.' He heaved his enormous rucksack onto the stool next to his own, and began to undo all the elaborate clips and zips down the side. Eventually, after a spray of underpants and empty toiletry tubes, he pulled out a large object covered in plastic bags.

'You were in Laos?' I stuttered.

'Oh, yeah. Awesome place. That's where I met Michelle.'

'Michelle?'

'My girlfriend.'

'Ah.' I took the package from his proffering hands. 'Thanks. I wasn't expecting a present.'

'I don't think you'll be expecting one quite like this, either. Hope it doesn't cause you any problems with baggage control. You won't be able to take it in your hand luggage.'

I began to unwrap, and was none the wiser. It was about two feet long and carved from wood. When it was revealed in all its glory, I could make out that it represented a vaguely humanoid form, with some rather explicit genitalia which should rightly have only been found on two separate carvings of opposite sexes. I glanced round at the other occupants of the diner, but fortunately their attention was elsewhere.

'It's a fertility symbol,' explained Steve helpfully. 'Thought it might bring you luck.'

'Er – it's great. Very unusual.' Then, unable to stop myself, 'What on earth do you mean, bring me luck?'

'With women,' said Steve.

I stared at him in total incomprehension. Jet lag, excessive concentration over the past sixteen hours, an overwrought emotional state over the past two months – what came out next was as uncensored as it was illogical. 'I don't want new children,' I said. 'I just want the old ones back.'

Steve sat perfectly still. So did I. An anxious-looking waitress brought us both cups of coffee, even though we hadn't ordered anything.

'I haven't gone, Dad,' whispered Steve.

Oh, God. I felt absolutely out of my depth.

'It's great to see you,' he persisted. 'I'm sorry I haven't been back to England. But, you know, I want to see as much of the world as I can while I have the chance.'

I stirred my coffee. This was ridiculous. Flying all the way to Missouri for what couldn't possibly be more than a few days, playing hooky from college, letting my life go hang just to sit here in a diner, tongue-tied before a twenty-three-year-old boy – only I had just realised something incongruous and inexplicable. This twenty-three-year-old boy was quite possibly the person I admired most in the whole world.

'What are you doing in Missouri?' I burst out. 'There's nothing to see in Missouri.'

'Well, you see, Michelle had to go back to Chicago. Her contract in Laos ran out. And I'd never been to America. So I thought I'd go with her.'

'Chicago isn't Missouri. I can understand your staying in Chicago. It's a very fine city. But why Missouri? Is your girlfriend here too?'

'No.' He peered at me from under that fringe. More handsome than William, I realised, the way you only do when it's too late to change your opinions. 'I – Dad, why are *you* in Missouri?'

I could have said, *To see you.* Or, *It's about time I saw my son.* Had it been William, I would probably have said something more noncommittal than either. But then, had it been William, I probably wouldn't have dared fly out there at all. Instead I said, 'Surely you know.'

He was still looking me straight in the eyes, as if he could cope with any danger I provided. Where did he get it from, this security, this strength? Not from me, that much I knew. From Sally? But if Sally had been this strong, it would have been enough for both of us. And then there would never have been a reason to leave.

'The article,' said Steve.

I met his eyes.

'William told me,' said Steve.

This web between my three children is something which I must accept and cannot. Of course, Cass and William don't speak to one another. They never did, if they could avoid it. But Cass speaks to Steve, and William speaks to Steve, and thereby the three of them are connected. They say things to one another that they could never say to a parent. I have no idea what opinions are shared amongst them about me.

'What did William tell you?' I said.

'He said you were upset about that article that was written about you. Dad, what's so bad about it? I've heard the things people say about you. I've seen the customer reviews on Amazon. I mean, of course your books still come out with four stars overall, because so many people love them, but all those *mad* people. Calling you Hitler, Stalin, Osama bin Laden – it's horrible. And all those books that've been written to contradict what you've said – those religious fundamentalists calling you the Antichrist, inciting Holy War against you. But – why now? Why this? She didn't write anything like that.'

'That's different,' I said. 'It's over here. The religious right in America are a very strange bunch of people. But Margot Hennessy doesn't believe in God. And neither do her readers. I'm happy to take insults about my opinions. It's part of my job. But not about my personality. That's not fair. It's not fair to me, or to you, or to – any of us.'

'Hey, guys,' said the waitress. 'You wanna order, or what?'

I stared at my inert cup of coffee.

'Thanks for the drinks,' said Steve, looking up at her with that bewitching smile.

'Those are on me. But you gotta order something now.'

Steve perused the menu with the leisured intensity of a true gourmet. 'I'll have a Gooberburger with fries and a Cherry Sprite, please. Dad, what about you?'

'Gooberburger?' I repeated. 'What's a Gooberburger?'

'It's their speciality. A normal burger, but with a layer of peanut butter on top. In a bun. Bloody marvellous.'

I frowned and had a look at the menu myself. But there was nothing that sounded any less outlandish. 'Erm, I'll have a Gooberburger too, please.'

'And a Cherry Sprite?' said the waitress.

'Oh, God, no. I'll stick with the coffee, if that's okay.'

She left us. Steve said, 'Dad, why aren't you going out with anyone?'

So *that* was what the boys said about me. Hence the fertility symbol. It wasn't children he thought I should be getting more of, but sex. Just like Declan, in fact. 'Steve, that's not exactly—'

'No, but seriously. Everyone else I know whose parents are divorced, their fathers have remarried at least once. Not their mothers so much – I think it's harder for an older woman, but for a man of your age it should be pretty straightforward. Especially for someone like you.'

'Steve, will you stop—'

'Stop what?'

Behaving like an adult, I thought. Making me feel like a kid. But that was hardly a request I could make. 'These other fathers,' I said, 'well, maybe their first marriages—' I stopped. It just wasn't something I could talk about to him, of all people.

'I know you always used to say that you would have gone back to Mum if she'd wanted you to. But—'

'I never said that!' I'd only thought it. Except, how could Steve remember my thoughts?

'Yes you did. And I got very upset about it at the time. Because Mum said exactly the same thing, and it just seemed so wrong if all either of you wanted was to be back together, and if the only thing stopping you was that each of you thought that the other one didn't want it—'

'Oh, Steve, I'm sorry if we said stupid things. It was very silly of us. You were just a kid.'

'No, no, that's not what I mean. I *was* a kid. And I was bound to think stuff like that. But the thing is, it wasn't true. You wouldn't have gone back even if she'd let you.'

I blinked hard, and tried to think of something to say. Would I have done? It was such a dark deep distant question that I felt to unravel it would be to unhook the clips that held my soul together.

'And probably Mum wouldn't have had you back if you'd tried. But the thing is—'

'Well then. We were both right. Steve, I'm not sure this is something it's very useful to talk about—'

'No, but *Dad*. The difference is that Mum's carried on as if it was over. I know it was very hard for her in the first few years. Very hard. But she picked herself up, and made a new life for herself—'

'I suppose by that you mean that she's with Giles.' It was a hard word not to spit. I had nothing against the man person-ally, except that when I'd first seen him at William's graduation ceremony – a gaunt man who was pushed around by Sally in his wheelchair, and with whom she'd flirted outrageously – William had confided that he had six months to live. Four years had passed since then, and there was still no news of his demise.

'Well, I suppose so, in a way. Except that Giles isn't exactly

– well, anyway, she hasn't gone on saying she'd have you back if you'd come. Whereas you have. Or at least, if you haven't said it, it's the way you think. And it's the way you *live*. But I just don't think it's true.'

'Steve—' He was lecturing me. Telling me how to live my life. And suddenly William's extended adolescence didn't seem like such a terrible thing. If there was one thing William was unlikely ever to do, it was judge me.

'You wouldn't go back, Dad. Would you?'

Was he behaving like a child after all? Pushing me to confirm his statement in one last desperate hope that I would deny it? After all, what all children wanted was for their parents to get back together. Wasn't it?

'You wouldn't have gone back then, and you wouldn't go back now. I mean, I know I haven't had many serious girlfriends—'

He'd had more than me, I realised.

'—but I do know that once it's over, it doesn't make any difference how wonderful it was when you were together. You have to let it go.'

So he wasn't being childish. He didn't want his mummy and daddy to get back together after all. He just wanted Daddy to start behaving like an adult. And I couldn't bear it. If Steve, who'd been the heart and soul of Edenbridge Terrace, could write it off so easily, then was it, as Declan had said, a fantasy of my own making? Did it matter to anyone other than me? Yet I knew that it was natural enough for him to move on, just as I had. Would my own father have wanted me to cling to the memories of my childhood, rather than striking out into the future?

'All right, Steve,' I said, trying to sound authoritative and paternal. 'I'll do my best to find a girlfriend, if that's what you want.'

'Well, you're not likely to get very far with that attitude. But the thing I want you to know is that you must never, ever think that it would bother any of us. I know it's the kind of thing parents do – Mum was very shady about Giles to begin with – and we probably gave you quite a shitty time over Vicky. But we've all grown up a bit now. It's your own happiness you should be looking out for now. Okay?'

'Okay,' I said hesitantly, feeling about three feet tall. If only there had been some woman I could produce from the ether, to fulfil the magic formula everyone seemed to have composed for me.

'Great,' said Steve, and that smile broke out. 'Hey, excuse me!' he said, hailing the waitress. 'That Gooberburger was bloody marvellous. Can I have a strawberry shake now, please?'

The waitress brought the shake. It was enormous, burdened with what must have been a fruitbowlful of bananas and strawberries, and topped with a tower of whipped cream. Steve ate it with a spoon, savouring every mouthful. At the end, he wiped his mouth with a paper napkin. 'Are you going to finish that?' said Steve, eyeing the remains of my Gooberburger.

'No,' I said.

'Can I have it?'

'Yes.'

He scooped it up onto his plate, munching happily and washing each mouthful down with a slurp of strawberry milkshake.

'Do you really like this stuff?' I asked. 'You're such a good cook. I would have thought—'

'Yes, but this is great food, in its way. You've got to take each culture as it comes. Like, when I was first in Laos I thought sticky rice was pretty disgusting, but then I found the best sauces, and it was brilliant. This is the same. What you've not got to do is expect that every burger or every bowl of sticky rice is going to be edible. You've got to find the places that really care about their food, whatever it is.'

I was seized by the conviction that my son would one day become the leader of some New Age cult. No. Stop it. 'I can see why you had to get away from us all,' I said.

'What do you mean?'

'Trying to keep us all together. Trying to get us to see eye to eye. You couldn't put your family back together, so you got shot of the whole lot of us.'

He looked startled, and also uncomfortable, and I felt relieved. 'I wasn't trying to get rid of any of you,' he said.

'Yes, you were,' I said, his evasion liberating me at last to play the father's role and tell him something he didn't want to know about himself. 'Weren't you? It seems like it was a very sensible thing to do. Everyone has to do it, at some time. I understand, Steve, I really do.'

And, his silence giving me more room still, I finally got to the point. 'What do you know about Jeremiah Vernon?' I said.

He cast his eyes down to his empty plate. Then he looked up again. The serenity was gone entirely. 'I came to Missouri to find him,' he said, his face rigid with defiance. 'And I succeeded. If you're looking for someone to nail, it's me.'

I think the first thing I felt was relief. A sign of clarity, at last; an indication that the light of meaning might break through the darkness of confusion.

Then a terrible mind-wrenching dread. 'What do you mean, you came to Missouri to find him?' I demanded. 'Did Margot come to you, or did you go to her?'

'I haven't spoken to Margot Hennessy,' said Steve. 'He did.'

'I know he's spoken to her. She quoted him in her article. But how did she know to speak to him? Him, of all the people she could have chosen?'

'She didn't know, Dad. It was Jerry who got in touch with her. He's a fundamentalist campaigner and he got wind that you were publishing a new edition of *Genesis*. So he decided to use it as an opportunity to win over more people to God. He wrote a press release, and sent it out to all the British papers. I daresay Margot Hennessy picked it up and decided to interview you on the strength of it.'

I stared at him, trying to process the information he'd given me. And as I slowly got my head around it, I began to realise what a simple explanation it was. All this time I'd been wondering how Margot could possibly have known of my link with the Vernon family, and the explanation was that she hadn't. Jeremiah Vernon had simply followed in the footsteps of his father, and had taken the battle one step further, onto my home turf.

Yet – 'What about all the other stuff?'

'I don't know about any other stuff. All I know is that Jerry Vernon sent a press release to the British newspapers.'

So it had all been a wild goose chase, a figment of my imagination which had chewed up thousands of words of exegesis and thousands of miles in aviation fuel. 'But Steve,' I said, 'how do you know all this? How did you know it was Vernon who started it all? What made you come to see him?'

'He—' His face twisted horribly, and then he burst out, 'I should have gone home. I'm so bloody stupid. I shouldn't have let you come all the way out here. It's not—'

'Why, Steve?'

'Dad, I just want to say' – he was struggling badly – 'that I haven't gone away. I'm sorry I haven't kept in touch better. I'll come home for Christmas this year, I promise. Maybe Michelle can come too. We can go for walks on the Heath—'

It was a blatant attempt to change the subject. But it was also a real promise. The tiny idyll flashed before me, of having Steve back home, happy and with a girlfriend. And if Steve was home, the others might be able to face me too. Oh, if I could have something like that, just the peace of mind of having something resembling a family once every year or so, then nothing would seem quite so much in vain. But a dream spoken out loud is a dream made real. And the nightmare which lay behind it was more real still. *I haven't gone away* – he'd said it twice now, and it was a confession of sorts. That he had gone away. And that it was going to be very difficult for him to come back. That the promise he'd just made was in reparation for something worse even than his not coming back, something that was torturing him, something he just didn't seem to be able to tell me.

'Steve, Jerry Vernon doesn't matter to me. If it was all because of him, then I haven't got anything to worry about.' Except that I knew I did have something to worry about. It was all over Steve's face, and it was more solid proof of the need for my concern than anything that had happened over the past few months. More solid even than the article itself. 'All I'm asking is how you knew he was at the bottom of it.'

A long pause. Outside the windows of our diner, the Missouri plains sank away into the distance, bleak with the flatness of the light, vicious with emptiness.

'I shouldn't have come here,' said Steve. 'Neither of us should have come here. Go home, Dad. It isn't me you need to speak to. It's Cass.'

13

Another plane, another imperceptible transatlantic journey. Since the first time I ever travelled back from America, I have always found these backwards flights disorienting. On the way out, the sun forges a bright path ahead, and the aeroplane hurries behind, as if struggling to keep pace with the headlong expectations of its passengers. But on the way back, though I might leave in the dazzle of a Mid-Western morning, the sun rolls over my head in its hurry to get back to the place I have left, and I am abandoned to darkness.

I remember a time, on Cass's sixth birthday, when she entered a deeply philosophical mood. At around noon she came to me in a panic to point out that it was perfectly possible that it had all been a dream.

I thought it was a return to the fears of homelessness which we thought she'd put to rest a year or more before, but it turned out that her crisis was more existential than that. No, she told me, she didn't mean that she thought that one day she might wake up and find herself back in King's Cross. She might have worried about that when she was little, but she was too old for such nonsense now. What she meant was that *the whole thing* might be a fabrication of her brain. Perhaps she wasn't Cass Bowden at all. One day she might wake up and discover that her entire life was the unbidden fantasy of a completely different little girl. Or perhaps not even a little girl. Maybe an old woman, or a man, or a dog. Or maybe she didn't really live on earth at all, and what she thought now was the human race had been dreamt up by a little green man living on Mars.

I was impressed by her deductions, and all the more so because I had no answer for them. In fact I was entranced.

'Can't you pinch me and prove that I won't wake up?' she pleaded.

'That won't prove anything,' I pointed out. 'How do you know that being pinched works for people who live on Mars? That might be part of the dream too.'

'But *Max*,' she complained. I wasn't supposed to agree with her.

'Look,' I said, 'it's the same for me. I've got no proof that I'm not dreaming either. Nor does anyone else.'

'But it's not the same for you if you're just in my dream!'

I tried not to laugh, because it was a very serious point, and my mind couldn't even grasp it fully. Of course it wasn't quite the same for me anyway, because I had lived a great deal longer, and had two decades more experience of not waking up. At that moment I got my best glimpse of what it was like to be six years old, with a past that had started very recently and of which a third or more was irretrievable. For a six-year-old, half a lifetime had to be taken on the trust of other people's words. If her past was a chimera, why should her present life not be one too?

'Do you want to wake up?' I asked her.

'No!'

'Well, I don't think you will. It'd be a very long time to be dreaming for. *I've* never woken up. And if one day you do, well, you'll have had a lovely dream, and perhaps life on Mars will be just as much fun too.'

Her forehead scrunched with the effort of imagining herself as a Martian, and I could see that her articulation of her thought was already dragging her back to her own life's immediacy. She was incapable of sustaining her disbelief for very long. Suddenly she grinned, having realised that it was just a game. 'Do you think I'd be green?' she asked.

'I don't know. Maybe you'd be orange. What colour would you like to be?'

'Pink,' said Cass, looking down at her new birthday dress, and I knew that she was fine.

I don't think people think like that when they grow to adulthood. As an undergraduate, I'm sure I had all sorts of pretentious conversations about the meaning of life, but they were all theoretical. Young adults may test the limits of their brains, but however much they ponder upon Descartes, few will seriously question those brains' existence. Then, when we finally take up the reins of life, we are too busy carving out careers, running households, bringing up children, to ever have the time or inclination to ask in what sense we exist, because it is all too clear and too pressing that we do. But still there are moments when our stories falter, and with them our sense of ourselves. And when I think of Cass, I falter every time.

When Cass was at the Royal Northern College of Music, I used to travel up to Manchester to see her. In those first years of loneliness, it was heaven to have so far to go and someone so wonderful to see. Because all those years of practice were paying off. It had been an enormous achievement on her part to get there in the first place – RNCM was the most prestigious conservatoire in the country – and despite all her dread and feelings of inadequacy in advance, it had taken her to its bosom. When she was in her final year, she won one of the leading roles in the end-of-year opera, which was the most hotly-contested accolade she'd ever received. I'd watched her in a state of shock, trying to avoid the sight of the rest of my family ten rows ahead, seeing her shimmer before me in purple and hearing the most improbable, immaculate sounds emanating from her head. Afterwards, I took her flowers, which matched her dress. She kissed me lightly on the cheek, and smiled up at me with laughing eyes. I couldn't have been more proud.

Of course, when I went to Manchester, I didn't have much access to her life. It is one of those inevitable things about being a parent, that sometimes you have to sit in the background and just clap. Before her concerts she was rigid with nerves, and afterwards she was whisked off to parties with all her friends. Even on the occasions when I visited her without any particular pretext, there were always lessons to rush off to, hours and hours of study to get through, and singing practice on top of that. Plus the friends rushing in and out, the urgent notes scribbled on the piece of paper attached to the door, and a whole network of relationships to which I just wasn't privy. I didn't mind. It was glorious to see her so happy.

But she was thin. And thinner, as time went on. I wondered at one point whether she might have contracted one of the awful eating disorders which were so much talked about in the press, and even resorted to calling Sally about it.

'No,' said Sally. 'It's nothing like that. She's just working too hard. Far too hard. You know what she was like when she was doing her GCSEs, driving herself into the ground with worry. Well, this is worse.'

But during her GCSEs she'd been a sulky little madam, and now she was a lovely, radiant young woman. I tried to talk to her about it when she was back in London. 'You know, work isn't the only thing in life,' I told her. 'I should know that. You have to look after yourself too.'

'Oh, golly,' said Cass, 'I'm not working half as hard as half of them. You wouldn't believe—'

'And *you* shouldn't believe, either,' I said, remembering the melodramatics of my fellow students at Oxford. 'It can become a competition sometimes. Not just the work itself, but how much of it you're doing, and how stressed out you're getting—'

'I'm not stressed out,' said Cass. 'I'm having a brilliant time.'

And so it appeared. After she left college, she found a job as a member of a small touring opera troupe. This was a huge milestone in itself – the chance to make a living out of performing music is something granted only to a very few – but there seemed little doubt that it was a precursor to bigger and better things. The problem for me was that I saw very little of her after that. It would have been the same for everyone – her schedule quite simply contained no gaps – but I had no-one to talk to about it, no-one to worry with, other than the boys, and I couldn't do that. She sent me postcards regularly, from Taunton, from Lincoln, from Edinburgh, from Amsterdam, from Rome – and my replies chased her around the post office boxes of Europe, some of them probably never received. And I scavenged amongst the radio schedules, in hope of catching her in concert. Even when I did, it was hard to tell which part she was singing.

But when William broke into my house, I needed her. He and Cass might not have been the best friends in the world, but Steve was too young to hear a story involving his brother high on drugs, and she was at least party to the family gossip I didn't hear. I composed a long letter to her, and asked her, both as someone from William's generation and as his sister, for advice. It was the humblest thing I had ever penned to someone so young. I sent it to a post office box in Oslo, and anxiously awaited a reply, as keen to restore meaningful contact with her as I was to make sense of him.

Yet when the reply came, it didn't come from Oslo, and it wasn't really a reply. It was clear that it had been sent without receiving my own letter, and the postmark was Brazil.

'My dearest Max,' the letter said, 'I am here in Rio with work. But I think you can understand that Brazil could never just mean work for me. I know that you always expected me to be curious, and that I always said I wasn't. But of course I was. The reason why I never talked about it was that I was afraid of it. I could never imagine that any other father I could possibly have would be half as nice as you.

'Well, here I am in Brazil, and I'm still afraid. But seeing as I didn't have any choice about coming here, it seems to be about time I faced up to things. Mum put me in touch with his sister, who stayed with him in London for a bit when they were together, and she's sorting everything out. I didn't tell you about it before because I didn't really believe that I'd do it, and I didn't want to disturb you unnecessarily. But now it seems like I will. The company have agreed to give me a few days' break, and I'm setting off for São Paolo tomorrow. The ticket's booked and everything.

'I just want you to know that it doesn't make any difference. Nothing has changed. Oh, this is so hard to write. But I think you know what I'm saying. Please, let me still be your best girl. All my love. Cass.'

I understood, I was glad, I was with her every step of the way. But still the sense of betrayal, of inadequacy, of twenty-five years of my life erased with a few halting words. Like infidelity, except worse. That night I cried myself to sleep, just as I'm sure Cass did, the night she threw my book into the compost heap next door.

After that, all was confusion. I wrote back, but there was no word from her. It seemed intrusive to try and get in touch with her employers, and even worse to bother Sally. I asked William, but though he knew she was in Brazil and that she had gone to visit her biological father, he showed little interest. And whilst I suspected that Steve knew more, he was only eighteen and I couldn't bear to burden him with my worries. Whatever she'd said to him was private between the two of them, and whatever she might want to say to me would have to be said directly.

Another letter. This time, the postmark was miraculously London. 'Max,' it read, 'I daresay you've heard about me from the others, and I'm so sorry about not getting in touch. I'm afraid my head has been in a bit of a mess since I came back from Brazil. I've let the flat go – my flatmate always was a bit of a pain – and I've moved to Bethnal Green, which is cheaper, and also more convenient for work, which is in the City. Just temping for now, while I work out what to do next. I'll ring you soon.'

No address, no telephone number. 'William,' I screeched, because he was the one I saw first, 'what the hell's going on?'

'Oh, yeah,' said William. 'Didn't Mum tell you?'

'Your mother and I don't talk. We're *divorced*.'

'Well, yeah, but—' It was clear from his shrug that he regarded communications between family members as his mother's responsibility.

'What's happened? What's this about temping in the City? What's happened to her career?'

'She gave it up.'

'Gave it up? What do you mean, gave it up? She's been singing since she was a toddler. Why would she give it up?'

'Search me,' said William. 'Too stressful, or something.'

'Is she all right?'

'She's Cass. Cass is never all right.' And in his voice I heard the shadow of decades of concealed sibling rivalry. Of course, William, who was supposed to be the brilliant one, had probably never been very pleased about his sister's hard-won success, and was doubtless more than a little satisfied to have it proved that perspiration didn't necessarily pay off in the end.

'I mean is she ill.'

'Ill? No, she's not ill.'

'And how long has she been back in London?'

'Oh, two months or so. Maybe three.'

'*Three months*?'

'Calm down, Dad. I can't see why you're so bothered anyway. After all, she isn't really your daughter.'

Did he realise how much that would hurt? Probably not. But

it displayed a staggering lack of sensitivity to assume that bringing a child up meant nothing once the job was done. I didn't know which of them to worry about more.

Fortunately, a few days later Cass got in touch properly. 'I'm sorry I put it in a letter,' she said on the phone. 'It just seemed easier to get it all out that way.'

Get it all out? But the letter had said nothing. 'Come round, Cass,' I said. 'Huxley misses you.'

So she came. I laid on the best welcome I could manage, with a bottle of champagne left over from some departmental celebration or other, and a take-away meal wheedled out of the French restaurant on the corner. She did her best to consume both, but her frail body hardly looked up to such a feat of digestion.

I gathered my courage. 'Tell me about Brazil,' I said, as gently as I could.

'Oh, Max.' She laid her knife and fork down, and avoided my eye. 'It wasn't very good, really. It was – I wish I'd had the sense to learn some Portuguese. I mean, my – my biological father spoke some English, but he hadn't used it in so long, and no-one else spoke a word except for his sister. And of course he's got a wife, and his own family, and it was all so strange—'

To my shame, joy surged through me. Schadenfreude is a dreadful thing to feel for someone you love. But she had not found an alternative father to replace me, and that was all I cared about.

'I didn't fit in,' said Cass. Then her chin shot upwards, and she met my eyes at last. 'None of it made sense to me. It seemed as if genes meant nothing at all.'

I didn't know what to say. Her voice was filled with rebellion, as if it was I who thought that genes mattered, as if it was I who wanted that particular connection to count. Then I realised that she probably thought I did. She had not considered for one moment that I might have been lying awake at nights praying that the man who had donated his genes would mean nothing to her in the flesh. All she thought of was my book.

And I couldn't correct her error. To have said 'But genes *do* mean nothing at all' would have been a lie, yet to have addressed the ways in which they did and they didn't would have plunged me into an intellectual quagmire with no bearing on the matter in hand. The matter in hand was how she felt about me, and how I felt about her, and I had no vocabulary with which to talk about that.

'Why aren't you singing any more, Cass?' was all I could manage. 'Was it because of him?'

'It wasn't going anywhere. Oh, God, Max, those people were terrible. They were so driven, they only cared about themselves, and their voices, and about how many people were looking at them. I just – Brazil just brought it all to a head. I was out there, on my own, surrounded by these people who spoke a strange language and wore strange clothes and looked at me as if I was from another planet, and all I wanted was to go home. Not back to the singing. I don't think I'll ever be able to go back to that.'

Home. Which was Edenbridge Terrace, the place I'd never see again. 'Surely you can do something less stressful in music,' I suggested tentatively. 'Like teaching. You don't have to be a secretary.'

'Teaching other people so that they can go through the same thing themselves? I can't do it, Max. I just wouldn't be able to see the point. Anyway, I'm not going to be a secretary all my life. I'll do something else.'

'What else?'

'I don't know. I have to work out what it is first.' She poked at her food, her voice close to tears. 'Can we talk about something else now, please?'

When she left I felt almost sick with distress, for something unnameable, something I didn't understand. I ought to be glad;

she'd rejected her real father and come back to me. But it was all so complicated, and she was so distraught. Then, slowly, I began to identify my misery. It was grief for her forsaken voice. Cass might always have been so fragile that it felt hardly safe to touch her, but there was something within her which transcended all that, something that reached up to the heavens, something unassailable, untouchable, pure. The romance of her progress towards being the greatest opera singer in the world made more sense of my life than perhaps anything else in it. And without it, I felt as if didn't know her at all.

Cass worked out what she wanted to do quite quickly after that. And when she told me, I knew that my main duty was to disguise my discomfort. She was going to work in an old people's home.

'Cass, if you want to train to do something else, money isn't an object, you know—'

'I don't want money. I've always had so much money. Just because I grew up in a lovely house and went to a good school doesn't mean that I should be exempted from shovelling shit. Someone has to do it, and given the mess I've made of my life so far, I see no reason why it shouldn't be me.'

To me, there was something deliberately self-abusive about her whole attitude, and it was very painful to watch. Yet we never argued about it. I did my best to accept her choice, even though I didn't understand it, and visited the home, and was shown around by its manager. I was appalled. The venue for her self-imposed purgatory was an institution at the grimmer end of Shoreditch. I had been familiar with old people's homes ever since my own mother's incarceration, but this place was far more grandiose in its bleakness than the chintz and teacups of Swallowdales. According to Cass, it was part of an organisation founded in the nineteenth century at the behest of a female philanthropist called Mrs Elisabeth Maitland, and its benefactress had harboured ideas of sheltering every needy relic in London. It was not particularly large, but was nevertheless built in the style of a Victorian prison, its grey walls presenting a Bastille to the grubby streets around. Inside, its arrangements were inhuman, blank corridors leading to chilly, high-ceilinged halls, the private rooms of the residents created by subdividing the old dormitories with a material that resembled cardboard. The 'living spaces' were too big and too cold, scattered with heaters and televisions, and the residents huddled around these focal points in clusters, propped up in fraying armchairs and bolstered with innumerable cushions, some of them gurning and dribbling in the general direction of the flickering screens, others with heads lolling in sleep. Further rooms, housing those no longer capable of displaying even such cursory remnants of life, more closely resembled hospital wards. I quitted its shelter with relief, and wandered the grey leaf-stained streets.

To think of my little Cass, the beautiful girl with the golden voice, burying herself in the world of the dying through what should have been the prime of her life was almost unbearable. Yet when I saw her next, I was able at least to agree with her that the work of the home was very necessary. All I disagreed about was that it might as well be her that did it, and I never told her that. At least she was back in London. After a while, she filled out a little, and though her job was clearly both physically and mentally exhausting, she seemed happier.

Until she stopped coming to see me. And since then, it's been impossible for me to know whether she has been happy or not.

It is now two years since I saw her. No, probably more like three. At first it was a gradual sinking away, the sort of accumulating distance which has happened at various points in all the children's lives. It has always been difficult to know how to deal with these changes. My first assumption has been that they are the natural result of growing up and establishing an independent identity, just as I did at the same age. There are some ways in which I am very far from being an evangelist, because I cannot bear the idea of trying to play a larger role in my children's lives than they would have me play. Yet despite this common sense, another thought has always occurred to me. That it is my fault; that I have done something wrong; that in pushing me away, they are punishing me for my sins. What *do* grown-up children want from their parents? When I think about it calmly, I can see that they might want more than one thing at once – to reject me and to keep me coming back, to hide from me and have me want to know, to sever the relationship and blame the severance on me. I would give them all of these things, if I knew they were what they wanted. But I know that if it is that contradictory, then they can never tell me so, and so I persist in thinking – is it me? Have I done something wrong? Can I put it right?

And with Cass it is so much more difficult. To begin with when she was back in London, she used to come round to my place for dinner once a month or so, and she'd curl up with Huxley on the sofa and we'd watch a video. And to begin with, we sustained conversation of sorts, me making those meaningless enquiries one is forced to ask about a working life that one doesn't understand, and her turning the conversation back to the film we were watching. But it wasn't just Cass who found it increasingly hard going. It was me too. As we lapsed into silence and her communications with the dog became more intense and defensive, I watched those videos with a corner of my eye always on her. *I'm not her father. She owes me nothing. It's no wonder if she doesn't want to be here.* Her smiles became wearier and more tearful. The video sessions became fewer and further between. They dissolved eventually into nothing. And I called her.

'Cass,' I said, 'I wonder if you'd like to come over on Sunday.'

'Oh, Max, I'm so sorry. I've just been so busy at work – I'm working on Sunday, as it happens—'

'It doesn't have to be Sunday. Any night next week. Or we could go out. To the cinema. I know, I read a brilliant review of one film. What's it called? It lost out at the Oscars to that Nazi comedy thing – *Central Station*. We could—' I stopped. There was very little I knew about the film, except for what I'd already drivelled at her, and that it was set in Brazil.

'Max, I – I'm really sorry. It's a bit difficult next week. Perhaps I could call you a bit later and fix something up. The week after next.'

I waited for the call all week like a lovestruck teenager. It didn't come. After that, I didn't feel capable of picking up the phone again. I couldn't see how it would end differently. I should see her, I thought. It'll be easier to get things out in the open then. But though I had her address, she'd never invited me to her flat. 'It's fine for me,' she'd always said, 'but it's not exactly suitable for entertaining.' So I went back to the old people's home.

A small fat person with a suspicious demeanour opened the door to me. Just as I was explaining my mission, Cass came round the corner. She was dressed in a pink pinny, sleeves rolled up to accommodate rubber gloves, and her hair was screwed up into a tight knot at the back of her head. When she saw me, she took a step backwards.

'Max,' she hissed, 'you can't visit me here. I'm working.'

'I just wanted to say hello.' The sight of her was a wrench in itself. She was as careless of her looks as she'd once been embarrassed by them. It was as if the intervening time, when she'd been a wisp of loveliness in purple and had clasped my bouquet to her chest, was a fantasy. 'I haven't seen you at all lately.'

'What do you want?'

'To talk. That's all.' The small fat woman was eyeing me up, as if she might try to eject me at any moment. And I could see her point. I was a sad old man clinging to the dream of a beautiful young woman who was no relation of mine and who had no obligation to talk to me, now or at any other time.

'I can't talk to you.' Her voice was a little softer, but her face was still tight with stress. 'It's three hours before I finish my shift.'

I could have just left, had I been another man in another life. 'I'll wait,' I said, hanging on with grim determination, incapable of letting her go.

'You can't wait here.'

'I can. I'll make conversation with the old ladies.'

'Please, Max, you mustn't. You'll confuse them.'

'Well, then, I'll wait outside.'

She sighed deeply and looked down at her feet. Then her head jerked up again. 'All right,' she said sharply. 'I'll meet you at eight. In the pub across the road. But please leave now.'

I wandered the godforsaken streets until eight o'clock arrived. Then we met in the pub. The pink pinny had gone, but it had been replaced with clothes that were no less functional, jeans and a faded blue jumper. Her face was pale and her hair was still knotted tightly behind her head. Behind her were smoke-fugged windows, at which the rain lashed mercilessly. In front of her was a glass of orange juice, the only spark of colour in the whole place, the only reminder of the woman she might once have become.

'I'm sorry,' said Cass. 'But it's been very hard for me since – since I came back from Brazil.'

'I understand that,' I said. 'I know I'm not your real father. But I never tried to replace him. Can't there be a place in your life for the person I always was?'

'It wasn't really him. It's been hard for longer than that.' She didn't seem to be able to say any more.

'How long, Cass? What do you mean?'

The words came out in a sudden rush. 'When I was a little girl I used to have nightmares. I don't know why, but—'

'You thought we'd send you away,' I said gently, trying to prove to her that I'd known what she was going through. 'Cass, surely you stopped thinking that? We talked about it. I thought you were all right.'

'So did I. But then – you see – when I was eighteen, it all came true. You left. I didn't understand why you'd gone, but I did know that I had no choice but to leave too. At the end of that summer Mum put all my belongings in the car and drove me up to Manchester.'

'But Cass—'

She rushed onwards, the colour beginning to return to her cheeks. 'And on the journey Mum told me that there was going to be a divorce. She tried to explain all the reasons, which were all to do with you and her, and she tried to make it better for me. But there was no way she could make it better for me. The point was that you were my stepfather because you were married to my mother. And once you got divorced, you wouldn't even be that any more.'

'I *am* your stepfather. Nothing will ever change that.'

'No you aren't. As far as the facts are concerned, you aren't. You might be something else, but back then I couldn't see what that something else might be. If only there had been a word for it, other than "ex-stepfather", which just sounds awful – it's at two removes, it's about something that's ended, it's as if you'd had a row with *me*. Apart from that, the only word is *father*, and that's never been true. And I was so scared about leaving home. It was as if it wasn't just me leaving. It seemed as if home had gone too.'

'Cass, I'm so sorry. I should have thought.'

'I'm not saying you didn't. I think you did. You were so good to me, writing, coming to see me, everything. And I wanted to cling on to that for as long as I could. So I did. But Max – it seems sometimes as if I've been clinging to things for my whole life. Trying to make up for – I don't know what.'

341

Her whole life? But I thought I'd given her a good life, till now. It was one of the things that was most important to me in the world. 'I thought you were happy at college,' I said. 'You seemed to be having such a wonderful time.'

'I was, in a way. I loved music college, it was amazing, I was surrounded by people like me who wanted to learn to sing. But—'

She was in such misery. I knew I was being selfish, forcing her to talk to me because I couldn't let her go. If being with me made her unhappy, then I should leave her. Yet I simply could not do it. 'But what?' I pleaded.

'It was all such a sham. Oh, God. Max, you mustn't take offence if I tell you this. You see – when you left and started seeing Vicky, the only way I could think of dealing with it was as if you and I were just two adults who were good friends. It's such a funny age, eighteen. You feel as if you're grown up, and in some ways you have all the common sense you'll ever have, but you don't know much about the world. At least I didn't. So I wasn't really sure how an adult would deal with it, except that the worst thing I could think of was losing you, so I tried to see it from your side. As if you were a friend who'd fallen in love. I suppose I made it quite romantic, in a way—'

I tried to gulp down the nausea. 'It wasn't.'

'I know that now. Actually, I knew that pretty soon. Because when I was at college, I met a man.'

'A man? A boyfriend, you mean?'

'Sort of. I suppose so. He was older. Much older. Not – one of the students.'

'Not – a tutor?'

'He was the one I wanted. The boys around me just seemed so young.'

'He didn't—'

'It doesn't really matter what he did. It's what *I* did that counts. You see, I made myself think it was all right, because of you and Vicky. And—'

'Vicky wasn't a student! She was a lecturer!' Yet Vicky's voice boomed in my head. *You toerag. You first-rate bastard. You fuck me around for a year and then you drop me. Well, if you think you can get away with that, you've got another think coming* – I'd thought I had got away with it. Until now.

'I know. It was pathetic. If I'd been half as grown up as I thought I was, I'd have seen straight through it. But young girls can be so silly. Not just me, but I was really silly. I missed out on half the things I should have been enjoying because I spent my whole time mooning over him. Every single taste or opinion I formed after leaving home came from him. And then, of course, when I left college, that was the end of it. His wife – well, he didn't leave her. Which was a very good thing, I don't know how I'd have faced Mum if he had. I couldn't talk to her about it, of course. I couldn't even talk to my friends, because it had been a secret all along. So I was left with nothing. Except for a job, and a huge hole where I thought my heart was supposed to be.'

'You could have talked to me. I would have understood.'

'Yes, well. By that time, Vicky was long gone. I thought you'd see it from his side. That you'd think I was a stupid, annoying little girl, just as he did by then. And you'd have been right.'

'Cass, that's just not true. You were so young. If this man had a relationship with you, he did something very, very wrong. It wasn't your fault. It was his.'

'Did you do something very wrong to Vicky, then? Oh, I know it's not quite the same, but I reckon if you knew how she felt about it, you'd be surprised. I should think she saw it as being more her own fault than you realised. After all, she decided to get into it. And because of that, I should think she was far more hurt by it than you realised as well.'

I was silent. There was nothing I could say.

'Anyway, that's irrelevant. The point is that the way I'd tried to think of you since I'd left hadn't worked. I was wrong about Vicky, and I was wrong about me. I didn't know what to think any more. And work didn't help. I felt like a fraud.'

'You weren't a fraud! You're so talented—' My own actions were too tawdry for me to be able to say a thing about them, but at least I was still sure of her.

'No, Max. I really was a fraud. How do you think I'd have got that part in the end-of-term opera if I hadn't been sleeping with the casting director? And how do you think I'd have got a job like that straight out of college if my tutor hadn't been trying to get rid of me? I *slept* my way into that job. It doesn't get much more of a sham than that.'

'You would have got it anyway. I've never heard such a beautiful voice.'

'No, I wouldn't. Because I wasn't ambitious enough. That became obvious as soon as I started. I mean, singing is wonderful, and so the job couldn't help but be wonderful sometimes. But it was all so political. Closer to warfare than harmony. All anyone cared about was their own career and their own voice. And I found out that I didn't care about those things any more.'

'Are you saying that it was my fault that you gave up singing?'

'No. No, I'm not saying that. I'm just trying to explain.'

'If it was my fault, I'll put it right. I'll do anything you like to put it right. I'm sure you could get your job back if we put our minds to it. Or a better one. I'll—'

'My voice has gone, Max. I destroyed it.'

'*Destroyed it?* You can't destroy a voice.'

'Yes, you can. It's quite easy, when you know how. Just do all the things they tell you not to. Like smoke heavily, and drink whisky, and take drugs—'

'But you don't do any of those things!'

'I did for a month when I got back from Brazil. My flatmate

in those days was a casual heroin user, so it wasn't hard to get supplies—'

'You always said she was a cellist!'

'The two aren't mutually exclusive, you know.'

'You can't have destroyed your voice in so short a time. I'm sure you could still sing beautifully.'

'Not professionally, I couldn't. It's not like singing in the bath. Your voice is your instrument. It needs to be looked after, just as an athlete needs to look after his body. And anyway, you have to realise that I didn't want it any more. I'd been covering up the cracks with music all my life, but now that I was being paid to sing and music was all there was, it just didn't work any more. So I'm afraid it's not a matter of you putting it right by getting me another job or something. I've put it right myself now. By not singing any more.'

There seemed to be no way to staunch the guilt or the pain. 'I don't understand,' I said wretchedly. 'If you were saying that you didn't want to see me because of Vicky, or because of that man you met at college, then I'd understand. But that was a long time ago, and you didn't stop seeing me then. You seem to be saying it's something to do with giving up singing. But I can't see how I've got anything to do with that.'

She was silent for a long time. Then she said, 'The reason I went to find my real father in the end was for your sake, you know.'

'For *my* sake?'

'I wanted to think of you as a father, and yet I didn't have your genes. And genes were so important to you. So I carried on believing in them for as long as I could, because you wanted me to. I thought if I could only find out how my genes worked for me, then I might sort it all out in my head, and find a way to be the right sort of daughter to you. But then I went there, and I was a disgrace. A child conceived out of wedlock, a marriage that should never have happened, a terrible and shameful mistake.

My father barely looked at me the whole time I was there, and his wife just screamed in Portuguese. It wasn't even as if any of them looked like me. They were all huge, like you. And my father was fat, and bald, and he smelt of sausages – I couldn't imagine why Mum ever fell for him. And I couldn't even bring myself to like my aunt, even though she put herself out so much for me. All she ever said was that I wasn't very much like my mother. Which was an insult, really, because she made it quite clear that she worshipped the ground Mum walked on.'

'Oh, Cass. I'm so sorry.'

'That's not your fault. How could it be your fault? But it just made it impossible – to believe in the whole nature and nurture thing, and still have any respect for myself at the end of it. I mean, if it was nature that made me, and my genes were responsible for everything, then I ought to have been able to find some common ground with my father's family, because they were half of what I was. But all they seemed to care about was nurture. I'd come along at the wrong time, I'd been taught to behave in all the wrong ways, and they didn't want me. So if it was nurture that mattered, it should have been fine, and I could have gone back to you. But there you were, still shouting from the rooftops that it was genes that mattered, that everything is inherited from the parents, and I couldn't see a way for you to want me either.'

'I *did* want you. I did everything I could to make that clear—'

'You might want me, as a person. Or as the person you thought I was going to be, when I was a child. But you don't want what I stand for now. Believe me, you really don't. Because it's all nonsense. That's the conclusion I've come to. Nature and nurture mean nothing at all. We have to cast off those kinds of things when we're grown up, and stand on our own two feet.'

'That's fine, Cass. There's nothing wrong with that. I don't have any problem with anything you've said.'

'It doesn't make any difference.' She looked down at the

table. 'When I was a silly young teenager trying to work out why you'd left Mum, I thought it must be because you'd fallen in love. Because those were the sorts of books I read, and that was the way I wanted to see life. But I'm older now, and I know a lot more, and I've realised it wasn't about that at all. You left because you had to. Like me giving up singing. Just because something's awful, and painful, and it seems like it's the worst thing that's ever happened, doesn't mean to say that it's wrong. You were right to leave.'

She looked up at me, and spoke very softly. 'Will you leave now too, please?'

Two weeks later I called her again. But the line was dead. When I called directory inquiries, they told me that the number had been changed, and that the new one was ex-directory.

The last time I saw her was at Steve's graduation. William's had been a difficult occasion, three years earlier – it was the first time I saw Sally with another man – but there'd been my own memories of Oxford to retreat into, the spectacle of the gowns and silly hats, the impenetrable Latin of the ceremony and the gorgeous architecture of the town outside. For Steve's, we met in a windy car park in Hull. Giles looked exactly the same as he had the previous time, and was perhaps the friendliest of the lot towards me. Sally had greyed quite a bit, but was very clearly the same woman. But Cass was a foreign country.

'Dad,' Steve had told me with the utmost gravity, 'Cass doesn't mind that you'll be there, but—'

Mind? That I'd be at my own son's graduation? 'What are you trying to tell me?'

'She'd just prefer that you didn't – try to have a conversation with her.' The sheepishness in his eyes told me that he found this a ridiculous sentence too. 'I mean, obviously, normal things are fine, but – she just thinks that if you try to sort things out or something, it'll just turn into a row—'

'I'll brush up on the long-term weather forecast,' I said gruffly, sure that his worries were unfounded. Of course Cass would speak to me. All she'd have to do was see me and she'd realise the whole thing was ridiculous.

But when I got to Hull I discovered exactly what he was afraid of. Cass avoided meeting my eye, scuttling behind the other members of the party, addressing her replies to my questions to the entire company. I had no choice but to watch her from afar, all my dearest memories polluted by my awareness of how little I knew about her. The last time I'd seen her, she'd told me that she'd got her job by sleeping with her tutor and that she'd binged on drugs to destroy her voice, and nothing could be more alien from my image of the girl I'd thought I knew.

Even Sally was easier to deal with. Our past might be a mountain of lost causes, and our old resentments might be triggered by a single word, but our relationship to one another was neatly encapsulated in the word 'divorced'. It was right that we shouldn't want to talk about anything very important. But Cass – why should I not be able to speak to Cass?

Steve rushed around trying to help us across the minefield of his family, manipulating us into seating plans, keeping Cass and me apart, even if that meant that I ended up next to Giles. Eventually he gave me William as a minder, and we talked rather fractiously about his work, while my younger son, the star of the show, retreated into the bosom of the larger half of the family. When the time came to have dinner, I could take it no more. I sidled up to Steve, and said, 'I think it might be better if I make a move back home now.'

Steve looked at me in confusion, and then his face relaxed involuntarily into a smile. 'All right, then, Dad. Thanks ever so much for coming. See you soon.'

I hadn't thought he'd let me go. Devastated, I stumbled to the station, and tried to block out the pain with the help of the bar on the train. By the time I got back to London in the dead of night, my vision was blurred and my head a throbbing wreck. It was hopeless.

The plane's trail across the firmament is mapped by a little flashing light on the screen on the back of the seat in front of me. It flashes in time with the beat of the cursor on my computer screen. The aeroplane light is imbued with all the knowledge of geometry, geography and aerodynamics that has got us up here, yet it knows nothing. And the cursor marks the track of my thoughts and the route map of my life. And it knows nothing either.

I am suspended in the uncertainty of the worst case scenario. Now I've written it down, it seems feeble that I haven't faced it before. Because it is a fairly plausible answer. But my excuses for having kept it at bay still remain. Why would Cass interfere in my life, when she has struggled so hard to keep me out of her own? What could provoke her into dragging it all up for the benefit of a stranger, when I've made it so clear that I want her to talk to me? And most of all, hasn't her absence itself been punishment enough for one lifetime?

But if Steve says that I must talk to her, then talk to her I must. He, after all, has been punctilious in keeping us apart in the past; and he, by all appearances, knows what I do not. There are so many gaps in my understanding of my stepdaughter. Even if it turns out that she has done this – that her hatred of me is so great that it would extend to deliberate wanton harm – then I don't think I can turn down the chance to find out why.

14

'William. I'm going to have a serious conversation with you.'

'Sure, Dad. Any time you like.'

'I want you to tell me how to get in touch with Cass.'

'Cass? I thought you and she weren't speaking—'

'That's been her choice. But I'm not sure she has the right to make that choice any longer.' It was all bravado, but it was completely necessary, because I knew that if he questioned me there was a danger that I would break down. 'And don't pretend you don't know what I'm talking about, because you do.'

'All right, all right! The thing is, Dad, I wouldn't know. How to get in touch with her, I mean. I haven't got her phone number, if that's what you're asking. I mean, I'm supposed to, of course, but I'm pretty sure I've lost it. You could go and find her at that old people's home—'

So I was right: he did know, even if I didn't. 'That's not appropriate. Look, if you need to, get her number from your mother. You can tell her what it's about, if you like. I'm sure she'll be co-operative.'

An enormous sigh. But total compliance. I found myself wishing I'd played the dictatorial father more often.

When it happened, it could almost have been the closing scene of the corniest movie ever made. All that was needed was a beach at sunset rather than a hillside in the early afternoon, or, if stuck with a hillside, a mass of swaying red poppies. She stood at the top of the hill, arms outstretched, hair loose in the wind, and he ran towards her, faster than he'd ever run before, his little legs lost in a blur of motion, until they were finally united in an embrace.

By the time I reached them the sloppiest of the greetings were over. Huxley lay immobile with ecstasy in her arms, stirring himself only for the occasional adoring lick of her face. She looked up at me, a few strands of hair slipping forwards over her eyes.

'Hello, Max,' she said.

I didn't know whether to kiss her, or shake her hand, or what. 'It's been a long time,' I said feebly.

'I know. I'm sorry. I really do owe you an apology. There were too many things I didn't tell you. But I didn't think you'd want to hear. I thought it would be better for you if you didn't know. I was wrong.'

'What things didn't you tell me?'

'Let's sit down.' She sat on the bench with Huxley still in her arms. When I sat at the other end, the dog eyed me and gave a little growl.

'Oh, you *stupid* creature—' I muttered. How many times had I taken him for walks up this hill? How many times had we sat up here and admired the view together? I stared down at the city of dreams. It shimmered rather feebly below us, awash in a fog of struggling sunshine, pollen and smoke. Down there were the Dickensian turrets of Erasmus College, the beacon that had first drawn me here, still churning out its factory-load of research papers and begowned and hungover graduates. Down there also were the bars that Declan and I had stormed as feckless youths, the bedsits we'd littered with our detritus, and the Fleet Street pub where I'd first met Sally. A mile or so to the north, hidden by distance, haze and the blank brick of the town, was Edenbridge Terrace, the conservatory I'd built with Cass probably long since ripped out by now, the treehouse disassembled, the homely old kitchen replaced by chrome and aluminium. And up here, above it all, was the Heath. We hadn't

351

lived here then – it was somewhere we used to come for days out – and now it had been close to my home for more than a decade. But it was haunted by ghosts all the same, children tumbling through the snow on sledges, strolls down the hill arm in arm with the woman I loved, the cacophony of voices now stilled. Some parts of life are stronger than others. They may fade, but no amount of experience will drown them out.

'He's just overexcited,' said Cass, taking her hands away from Huxley. 'Don't worry, he'll soon remember who feeds him.'

She seemed so composed. And healthy, her cheeks glowing, her hair glossy, her coat lighting up the hillside with pillar box red. 'You look so much happier than you were the last time I saw you,' I said. It was almost an accusation. Because I certainly wasn't.

'Perhaps I am. But I'm not happy about that article, if that's what you mean.'

'Cass, please tell me what happened. Get it over with. I don't think I can bear not knowing for much longer.'

'I will,' said Cass. And she did.

'Do you remember when we built the conservatory?' she said.

We both gazed down the hillside, as if we could see it still. 'Yes,' I said.

'We looked up through the glass, and you told me about the net of numbers which held it all together. Which held the universe together. That was all that was needed, you said, to keep everything going that was in the universe. A net of numbers.'

'I remember.'

'Well, I saw it again one day.'

'Where?'

'It wasn't long after I got back from Brazil. You know what a mess I was back then. Horrible temping job, horrible flat, and no real understanding of why I'd done what I'd done or what

I needed to do next. Well, a friend of mine from college decided I'd been wallowing for too long and forced me to go out with her. She didn't tell me where we were going. I think she was trying to get me to go back to singing, which was the last thing I wanted.'

'Where did she take you?'

'To a concert at St. Martin-in-the-Fields. She was in the amateur choir and she smuggled me in. I was furious when I realised, because I'd started to hate music almost as much as I hated myself. But I sang along all the same. Even then, I couldn't hear a violin striking up without opening my mouth and letting sound come out.'

'But you told me that you'd destroyed your voice.'

'I had, as a professional. But that didn't mean that I wasn't still a darn sight better than the people around me. And Fauré's Requiem is such a lovely tune. I got swept up in it, and found myself looking upwards. That was when I saw it.'

'The net of numbers.'

'Huge lovely equations, supporting all those tons of stone. It was as if they were sheltering the light that streamed in through the stained glass.'

'That's wonderful, Cass.' I couldn't imagine what any of this had to do with Margot Hennessy, or Jeremiah Vernon, or any of the miseries that were tormenting me. But as I watched her and she gazed upwards as if the light shone on her still, the moment was too precious not to be treasured.

'You were right,' she said, and blinked, and I saw in shock that a tear was rolling down her cheek. 'It's the thing that keeps the universe going. There was a shaft of light streaming down on me, and the lumps and crackles fell from my voice. My friend fell silent beside me.'

'You could sing again,' I breathed.

She carried on as if I hadn't spoken. 'Whoever you are,' she said, 'when you sing the earth moves. Not just the air around you, but also the ground beneath your feet. Everything within the range of your song vibrates – and the movement isn't just a reaction to the sound you are making, it's the sound itself. The sound I made that day was stronger and purer and sweeter than I'd ever sung before. I knew the physics of sound and the physiology of singing, and I knew what had happened to my larynx, and I suddenly also knew that this sound wasn't coming from me.'

I had never seen anyone look so beautiful. Not even her mother. But fear was starting to stir within me. I was shivering.

'The air and the ground themselves were picking up the waves, smoothing them out and turning them into something far beyond anything that could have been produced by a messy fragile human heart such as my own. The laws of physics were broken that afternoon. It was a miracle. I heard the voice of God.'

God. And slowly, nauseatingly, the fragments of her life began to crunch into place. My role in her childhood. The older lover who had come to her after she thought I was her father no more. The depression, the drugs, the something missing—

Something missing. Oh, please, please let it not be that.

'And the net of numbers broke, and the walls of the church stood still, as they had since they were built by a thousand peasants a thousand years ago for the glory of God, and I kept on singing. Max, when I was a child you told me that God was something that people invented to stop them from having to see the truth. But he is the truth. He is real. We invent Him, but that can't stop Him from being real. We shield ourselves from Him because we can't cope with that much reality. The song of the universe is singing more loudly than your equations can ever describe.'

'Cass,' I pleaded, 'this isn't you. Whoever's put this into your head—'

'The whoever we're talking about is God.'

'No, this is nonsense. You've got to get a grip. Think about it logically. You—'

Suddenly she was shouting. 'Max, you have to *listen*.'

'I have been listening. Oh, God—' I was shivering uncontrollably. Even that awful conversation in the pub outside her work had been easy to take in comparison. This was something I couldn't even begin to comprehend.

'Now do you see?' she shouted. '*This* is why I didn't tell you. *This* is why I knew you were right to leave us—'

'Right to leave?' The memory struggled up from the depths of the whirlpool in my brain. Yes, that was it. The most hurtful thing she'd ever said to me, and before today, the last.

'It took me a long time to see it from Mum's point of view. Because I didn't think there was a Mum's point of view. I thought that you'd left her for another woman, and that Mum was devastated, and that it was all about you and nothing to do with us. But it was about us. If you couldn't have us think exactly the same way you did, you didn't want us at all. She was *glad* you left. She told me that, when she thought I was old enough. Because if you'd stayed, then none of us could have done anything or thought anything that wasn't what you wanted. She said it was the biggest favour you could have done us, the best and kindest thing you ever did—'

'That's just not *true*.'

'Yes, it is. Remember Christmas in Somerset?'

A lurch of the stomach. 'Yes.'

'When I ran away before lunch. Where do you think I went?'

'I have no idea. You never told me. No-one ever told me.'

'Declan knew straight away. He was thinking about teenage rebellion, and he was right, I was a stupid little teenager, but – what were we all arguing about, all that Christmas?'

I said nothing.

'Christmas carols, Santa and Rudolph – *where do you think I went?*'

How dare Declan have known. And not have told me. So many sorrows could have been prevented if he'd just had the decency to tell me. 'The church.'

'That's right, Max. I went to the church. And Declan found me there, and we made up a story about me collecting mistletoe, and he brought me back. Because I couldn't tell you. I'd felt so safe and peaceful there, and then I felt so guilty. As if you could never love me again if you knew where I'd been. Which was probably true—'

'Stop, Cass. Just stop for a moment.'

She stopped. I tried to sort it all out in my head, and saw the halting, damaged procession of her life as she bounced from father figure to father figure, and finally resorted to the ultimate, the one Father nobody could take away. That was straightforward enough, the almost-logical result of a combination of circumstances whose danger could never have been appreciated until it was too late. But somehow it had become bigger than that; it had stopped being just the story of her life, and had taken over mine too. Everyone I cared about had known about this before me; everyone had lied. I tried to distinguish between the good guys and the villains, divide the people who were on my side from those who weren't. But it was impossible. They were all against me, whether they wanted to be or not.

She began again. 'I'm not saying that you're a bad man, Max. Or that I'm sorry that you were my stepfather. I loved you more than anyone else in the world when I was a child. I still do, in a way. But the way you thought about the world just didn't work for me. And you wouldn't let me think in any other way.'

It was too much. Not just the pummelling she'd just given me, or the months spent torturing myself over Margot's accusations about my family. It was the whole lot of it, the years spent under the cosh of Sally's disapproval, the decades of being vilified by half the civilised world. 'You do think I'm a bad man,' I snarled. 'Because you've joined forces with *them*. The evangelists. The people who think I'm the Antichrist.'

Her self-assurance fell away. And perhaps, a little of her self-righteousness. 'That's different,' she mumbled. 'None of that was supposed to happen.'

'You said when you came here that you owed me an apology. I haven't heard much apologising yet.'

'Oh, Max – you think this is easy for me, don't you? You think it feels all right for me to tell you that I've gone against everything you ever taught me. Well, it isn't easy. I didn't want to turn my back on you. It was the last thing in the world I could ever have wanted. I've so much wanted to tell you every-thing, ever since it happened. I wanted to share it with you, make you happier, make you less lost yourself. Because you are lost, Max. You've banished yourself from the only source of love that can ever sustain you. I don't know what it is in your personality or your life that's made you do it, but that's what you've done. And you're living with the consequences.'

'This is—'

She broke across my words. 'You know, when it first happened, I was as frightened as you are now. Blocking my ears, fighting against it. I walked back along the Embankment after we came out of that church, and looked at the sky, and all I could do was whinge at God. It was like, okay, you've made your point. I could do with a little more information, please. Like, what now? And all I could hear was the noise of the traffic. Complete urban silence.'

She stopped, and a lorry trundled along the road at the bottom of the hill. I opened my mouth to protest once more, but she got there first.

'Knock, and the door shall be opened to you. Even I'd heard that one. But what He didn't point out was that we have no idea how to knock. The door opens an inch and the light's blinding for a moment. But by the time our eyes have adjusted to the brightness, it's gone. The memory of what had happened was still burning me up, but the light was gone, and all I was left with was fear.'

'So you should have been frightened! Cass, you must see that you're talking utter nonsense—'

'Oh, I was just like you, despite what I'd seen. It'll go away, I thought. If I leave it alone, it'll go away. But my brain wouldn't leave it alone and it didn't go away. So, if it wasn't going to go away, where did that leave me? I was afraid because of what I stood to lose. Not much, I suppose. Oh, but it was everything. It was a whole life. It was me. I had to consider my personality being blotted out by an alien force of which I knew almost nothing. Who was he? What did he want with me, shining torches in my eyes and then disappearing? Was I foolish, was I gullible, was I mad? Any of those would have been a comfort. If only it could have been me that was responsible, rather than something from outside.'

Her chin jutted out, and the hair fell away from her face, revealing eyes which were red but blazing. For years I'd thought of her as a child, or, if not a child, someone who needed to be looked after, someone I could heal one day, if she let me. Now the hard lines of her conviction were solid in her face, and she was not a dependant, but an adversary. 'Please, Cass, let me talk for a moment—'

'It's taken me a long time,' she said, ignoring me utterly, 'to come to terms with the fact that He won't be with me all the time. You see, because it was all based on an experience – I suppose you might say it was empirical – I expected to be able to repeat the experiment. Sometimes it came, that warmth again, the sudden glow of certainty, but as soon as I grasped at it, it was gone. Was that all it was, like drugs to an addict, an eternal quest for a feeling that is always in the past?'

'It's *exactly* like that.'

She shot upright in surprise. 'Max – have you – have you ever—'

'Of course I haven't. I mean it's like drugs to an addict.'

'No, but Max, can't you see? Do you remember when we were on holiday in Yorkshire, walking up a hill, and you explained to me what empiricism was? There was this huge swirling fog around us, and you asked me how I knew that the sun was up there somewhere.'

I did remember.

'And I said I knew because the fog might go away in a minute and then the sun would be there. And you said yes, but how did I *know* that, even though there was no proof at the moment? And I said it was because I'd seen it before.'

'Cass, you know there is no empirical proof for God.'

'Yes, there is. In me there is. Empiricism is about experience. I know what I've seen, heard, felt. And I'm learning to trust Him, when he's hidden behind my fog, just as I trust the sun. You think that religion is some sort of tranquilliser, opium for the masses, an easy way out. It isn't. It's infinitely hard. The truth is always hard.'

'The truth is facts. Not – some sort of fuzzy feeling—'

'Max, you know that feelings are truth. I know you know that. But you're scared of them. Very scared. And I understand. It is very frightening. But you must realise that you aren't the only one who's frightened. We all are. In some way you have to give in to this—'

'Cass, just be *quiet*—' I was shouting, and I knew that it was wrong, because I wasn't allowed to shout. Only she was allowed to shout. Because it was I who was the evangelist, I who tried to impose my beliefs on other people, I who was so absorbed in my own view of the world that I was incapable of seeing it from anyone else's point of view. And it was so unfair. How could I have become so tarred with the brush I'd been fighting all my life? 'Stop being such an *evangelist*,' I spat out in the end.

359

'I'm not,' she said.

'Oh, for goodness' sake—'

'Really I'm not, Max. That's why I didn't tell you before. That's why I stayed away. Because it breaks my heart to see you so lonely, when the solution is so close at hand. And yet I knew I could never help you. Because I could never bear to do to you what you tried to do to me.'

I ground my teeth in anger. 'You're trying to do it now,' I said.

'Because I have no choice. It didn't work. I told you, it turned out I was wrong not to tell you I'd found God.'

'In what way was it wrong? Tell me, Cass. Did you go to Jeremiah Vernon, or did he come to you?'

She fiddled with the buttons on her coat. 'Neither.'

'Then what?'

'I met Jerry at a retreat. In London. That's all. We became friends.'

I tried to imagine it. 'You mean it was a concidence? What was he doing in London?'

'He's a missionary. And – well, a lot of missions go to Africa and places, but if you think about it, if you look at William, for instance, London's about as much in need of spiritual help as anywhere on earth. My church helped to fund them. Gave them places to stay, helped out with contacts and practical advice. It was natural that we should meet.'

'And you knew. You knew he was Frank Vernon's son.'

'No, I didn't. I didn't even know his surname for ages. And even when I did, well, it wasn't like it was just this sudden revelation, "Jerry's surname is Vernon." Things don't happen like that. I knew what his surname was without noticing. It's not that weird a name. I didn't think anything of it at all.'

'But he must have known who you were. After all, even if it weren't for his father, if he came here to save Londoners from eternal damnation then I must have been pretty high on his list of enemies.'

'No, of course he didn't. Why would he know that my ex-step-father was an atheist? If you remember, *my* surname is Bowden.'

I was silent for a moment, my sense of righteousness temporarily dissipated. 'Then what did happen?'

'I found a proof copy of the new edition of *Genesis* in his flat.'

'In his flat? What were you doing in his flat?'

'Drinking tea. He started to tell this story. About his father. That was when I realised. I tried to stop him from telling me, but he didn't understand why I didn't want to hear.'

'Presumably because you didn't tell him. There's a lot you haven't been telling, isn't there, Cass?'

'Then he started to talk about the press release. He was sending it out to all the papers, to try to get a debate going. I told him about you then. I' – she faced me for the first time – 'I asked him to stop it, Max. I couldn't bear the thought of him hurting you.'

I wanted to take her compassion and leave all the rest. But it was impossible. 'Can you see now, Cass? How vicious and vindictive and small-minded they are? Can you see the mistake you've made?'

'We tried to stop it. *He* tried to stop it. We rang the church where the envelopes were being stuffed and then we got over there as fast as we could and we destroyed half of the print run. But the other half had already gone. It was too late.' Her eyes confronted me. 'He isn't vicious or vindictive or small-minded, Max. He's just someone who has the courage of his convictions. Like you. But when he realised that it was going to hurt someone he cared about, he tried to stop it. You see, when it gets personal, it's different. That's when it has to stop. And that's what you've never understood—'

A dreadful suspicion entered my mind. 'Personal? How was this personal, for him? Why would he stop the press release, just because you didn't like it?'

She stared at her hands and said nothing.

'You're not saying—'

'It's over now, Max. I sent him away.'

She was indeed saying what I thought she was. 'You were in love with him. He was in love with you.'

'It's over.'

A surge of triumph. 'You chose me over him—'

'*I did not.*' She stumbled to her feet, and I saw that tears were streaming down her face. 'I'm tired, Max. I don't want to marry a man who—'

'*Marry?*'

'—who wants to change the world. Yes, I did fall in love with Jerry. I thought he was like me, and all I've ever tried to do is help myself, and those around me who wanted to be helped. But when I saw that press release I realised he wanted more than that for himself. Which I should have seen before. Because ambition is very attractive. It's probably what made me love him in the first place.'

'You were going to *marry* him?'

'I'm not going to marry him. I'm going to stay right here with my old people and leave you two to fight it out in the limelight.'

'But you were going to marry him. Before you saw what he was really like.'

'Max, you've got to stop thinking that I've chosen you over him. I agree with *him*. And I think he's a better man than you. I told you. When he saw that it was getting personal, he stopped. It's just—' She began to cry properly now.

I wanted to hold her and comfort her as I would have done when she was a child. But I knew that I couldn't. So I sat there, and I thought as hard as I could. 'Why did Steve go to Missouri?' I asked.

'To try to sort things out. To try to find a way for me to make it up with Jerry and for me to make it up with you. But you and I know that isn't possible. Don't we?'

'This is silly. There must be a way.'

'I don't think there can be.'

In the end we each went our separate ways. Huxley was not easily persuaded that he should go with me. But he came in the end. And as I walked back down the hill, just as I did every morning after fetching the paper, the world seemed bleached of anything it had ever held. The ghosts and their laughter were gone; even the bad things were gone. The mystery and the paranoia that had sustained me for months had fallen away, and they left: nothing.

And now, sitting at my computer, still nothing. How ridiculous, that we should both have cared so passionately and have been stirred to such heights of emotion, and be left with so little. Which is like life, in a way. A huge kerfuffle sandwiched by silence.

But I am not dead. And the vacancy within me will not sit still. It will be heard. I will not be defeated by the shouting hordes, the ranks of voices screaming *Be quiet! Say not a word!* I grieve for what I have done, and I grieve for what I have lost. But there has never been a moment when I have been more sure that it is my right to fight back.

I open my internet connection, and log into my email account. Its mindless twittering disguises the truth that is revealed as soon as it flicks to the page which shows me my inbox: I have no messages. Angry now, incensed by its silence, I click on the button that says *Compose*. In the *To* box, I type Margot Hennessy's email address. At the bottom, I attach what exists of this manuscript. And then, in one final, hopeless, defensive act of evangelism, I press *Send*.

Part Four

Revelations

15

'Shit,' said Margot Hennessy.

She turned up on my doorstep two days after I sent the email, bearing a dramatic expression of contrition and a bottle of champagne. I had been in a state of panic and dread ever since I'd pressed that button. The email to her was possibly the stupidest thing I'd ever done in my life. Oh hell, oh Christ, oh Jesus, oh God. I'd sent it to her because I'd wanted her to see what she'd done to me. The article she'd written had shown not a heartbeat of empathy for the decisions I'd been forced to make or the consequences I'd had to live through, and her shallow jibes had poked open a hornet's nest of turmoil and grief. But now that my own version was in her hands, I was afraid that she wouldn't see what she'd done to me at all. She'd see what I'd done to them. She'd see a girl who'd struggled her way free of my evangelistic clutches, who'd fought against the odds to gain command of her own soul, who'd forsaken the man she loved because she was afraid he'd turn out like me and who'd been left stranded on a hillside, fatherless and alone but for the grace of God.

Worse still, the most savage journalist of my acquaintance was now in possession of the most intimate details of my life, from my hard-ons when I first met Sally to the revelation that my step-daughter was a born-again Christian who'd recently conducted a love affair with the son of one of the foremost fundamentalist preachers of the past century. Whatever she'd done to me so far, it was nothing to what I'd given her the power to do now.

So when I saw that champagne and the rueful smile on her

face, at least half of my burden fizzed away. The advantage of fearing the worst is that it is very hard to imagine it taking place in real life. Of course, that wild swing towards optimism was utterly unjustified. She had started her article with the words, 'Max Oldroyd is a man who has failed,' which ought to have been enough to secure my hostility in perpetuity. But it's amazing what the sight of vintage Bollinger can do for a man's mood, particularly when accompanied by a short and highly expressive swear word.

'You were sent a press release,' I said, reaching out for the bottle.

'I was. I would have explained all that in the article if there had been room, but there wasn't, and the editor gave it the chop. I wish he hadn't. It might have saved us all a lot of trouble.' She tucked the bottle under her arm. 'This isn't a gift, you know. It's for us to drink, now. I realise that celebration isn't exactly in order, but I'm not sure I can face talking about something as intense as what you've sent me without the influence of alcohol. And, you know, when you're buying something on expenses, it's never worth skimping unnecessarily.'

She took a decisive step forward, and I took a defensive step back. 'You can't come in here!' I protested. 'You don't like it in here.'

'I'm sorry about that. In the course of this job, there's always the danger of forgetting the basic standards of human courtesy. But if you're still feeling houseproud, we can always go to the pub on the corner instead. It looks rather sweet.'

I watched in horror as the bottle slid smoothly into her large leather handbag.

'Don't worry,' said Margot. 'The drinks will still be on expenses.'

I felt by rights that I ought to grab the champagne and slam the door in her face. But it is unacceptable to stipulate the conditions of another person's generosity, expenses or no expenses. And it is also impossible to turn away from the opportunity to hear the opinion of the one person in the world who's read the riskiest thing that you've ever written.

'All right,' I said. 'I'll just go and get Huxley.'

She raised her eyebrows. 'Surely he can cross his legs for an hour or two. I think it's important to both of us that we make a bit more progress this time.'

It was a fair point. 'Well, I'll get my wallet, then—'

'I've told you, I'm paying. All you need is yourself. Do you have your house keys?'

I took them from the hook on the wall.

'Ready to roll,' said Margot, and it was only from the very slight crack in her voice that I realised that she was at least as nervous as I was.

It is indeed a sweet pub, of the countryside variety, except that in no countryside pubs but those on the wealthier and more bohemian fringes of North London are the regulars a pair of old dears dressed in spotted cravats who brush the lint off one another's sports jackets and address one another as 'darling'.

'Why did you send it to me?' said Margot, once we were settled with our glasses of port by the fireside.

'Because—' I realised that I was about to take a gulp from my glass as if it was beer, and made the necessary adjustments to sip at it delicately. The warm sweet liquid trickled down my throat. 'Because I wanted to show you that you were wrong about me.'

She nodded, and sipped herself. 'Well, I wasn't. You are a failure.'

'But—'

'I know. Declan was right about that one. I was an idiot to define it in those terms. But one should never overestimate the intelligence of one's readership, even in the broadsheets. Subtlety equals instant page turn.'

If she'd felt nervous before, she wasn't betraying it now. 'So you stand by everything you wrote,' I said.

She gave the tiniest of shrugs, and then left a long and elegant pause. 'You know,' she said eventually, 'when I read the first few chapters of your book, I felt immensely flattered. I don't think I've ever prompted anyone to undertake a comprehensive re-evaluation of their life before.'

'Surely you can see why I did,' I said. And then I managed to break free from the hypnotic effect of her composure, and said, 'Margot, what did you know? And how did you know it?'

'I knew about Jeremiah Vernon from his press release, as you already know. The fact that his father was your deadly enemy was completely unknown to me.'

'But the other stuff.'

'There is no other stuff. I have to confess that it wasn't one of my more thoroughly researched articles. You see, I'd spent so much time quoting from *Genesis* in my twenties that I felt I already knew you inside out. Which should be a lesson to me. As you pointed out quite early on, I missed quite a few very juicy stories.'

'But you knew that my children had gone—'

'I knew nothing of the sort. You were a divorcé with an empty house and no photographs in the living room. It doesn't take Sherlock Holmes to make extrapolations from that.'

Photographs. 'You knew what Steve looked like,' I said, in desperate hope of finally catching her out.

'Come on. I wasn't that slack. His yearbook is available at a very modest price from Hull University student union.'

'So you're telling me there was absolutely nothing.'

'Nothing but what I said in the article. I think Declan has told you that I'm not one for holding back.'

I began to be infuriated. 'Are you deliberately trying to behave like that Carolyn woman, or does it come naturally?'

She burst into delighted laughter. 'I knew Carolyn Hillman,

you know! Of course, she was a bit older than me, but – I absolutely pissed myself when I read that bit. You had her spot on.'

I frowned, torn between her praise of my writing skills and her failure to succumb to my insult. 'Answer my question,' I demanded.

'I'm nothing like her. For starters, I lack her physical courage, if courage is what you want to call it. Did you know that she died trying to grab her camera back off one of Pol Pot's militia men in Cambodia? It would have made a bigger splash if she hadn't been such a shit writer.'

'I see.' I tried to feel shocked by her lack of respect for the dead, but it had to be admitted that the news of Carolyn's demise did not affect me greatly, and probably hadn't bothered Declan much either. 'So it was all paranoia on my part.'

'Paranoia is one way of putting it. Though I personally think that's a rather pejorative term for a far broader human characteristic. Early on in your book, you describe the way in which children only slowly learn that there exist people other than them. Well, I suspect that most people never really learn that properly. The world revolves around them, and all roads lead straight back home. If you saw your whole life laid out in my article, why shouldn't you have assumed that that was what it meant?'

'Well, yes, but—'

'Which is all tangled up with the evangelism riff. I admit that it was rather unfair of me to single you out for the exploration of that one. I could have chosen any writer, perhaps any person at all. It's certainly true of me. But it was all the more interesting to use you, with you being a scientist, and having this absolute belief in the *facts* – and of course it was very neat, given that evangelism was what you were supposed to be fighting against. I wish you'd mentioned that it was something to which you'd already given a great deal of thought. We could have gone a lot further with it.'

'I still believe in the facts,' I said fiercely. 'Nothing you could write could make any difference to that.'

'Really? You seem a great deal less sure of them by the end. What about that very important fact about your wife, for instance?'

A wrench at the bottom of my stomach, and suddenly the port tasted sour. 'Of course there were facts behind it. I just don't know what they are.'

'Well, the chances are, as I think you came close to concluding, that nothing happened. Or at least, as Declan so crudely put it, that he didn't fuck her. And as a man, I'm sure that's your main concern. But you'll be quite aware that the denial of that particular exploit can leave room for all kinds of other activities. On top of which, I think you've established fairly securely that he would have done it if he could. He had the desire, and his friendship with you would have been unlikely to have stopped him, because it seems to have been at least partly his jealousy that bound him to you. Which should, in theory, make the salient point not what *he* did, but what *she* did. Yet you seem to have given very little thought to that at all.'

'Well, I can't ask her, can I?'

'You probably could, if you really wanted to. But of course she wouldn't tell you. It isn't just a matter of Declan and Sally. Those are the kinds of things that one never knows. I mean, her relations with Declan may have been quite innocent and yet she could have been having it off with one of your colleagues for years.'

What a complete, top-flight bitch the woman was. 'That's ridiculous. I was married to her. I lived with her for eighteen years. I knew her better than that.'

'The only reason she ever knew for certain about that Vicky creature was that you made sure she did. Wasn't it?'

All the various stories flickered before me. I tried to find some sort of retaliation amongst past and present, truth and fiction, then broke out of the maze and said, 'Margot, what are you actually trying to *say*?'

She grinned. 'Too many things at once, I'm afraid. But mostly that it isn't really relevant what she did any more. If there were any danger of you finding out some empirical truth, then it would be relevant, because you'd be living in fear of having the whole of the past rewritten before your eyes. But given that there's no real chance of that, your suspicions are only relevant in the context of your relationship with Declan. There's no present-day relationship with Sally to undermine. And because you know that he would have betrayed you if he could, the question of whether *she* betrayed you is just a question. The answer doesn't really exist.' She looked at our empty glasses. 'What's your poison this time? I think we should move on from port, or we'll end up like them.' She gestured at the old dears, who'd switched from their positions at the bar to a nook on the other side of the fire, their heads resting against one another as they snored softly.

I scowled. 'Bollinger,' I said.

'No, no, no. All right, I'll decide. Any objections to gin and bitter lemon?'

I grunted, and she went to the bar.

She had not budged an inch. Beyond the first scatological comment she'd made on my doorstep, there had been no hint of apology or even regret. But then why should she come to see me at all, if it wasn't to say sorry?

On the other hand, there was no real reason why I should care what she thought, given how many more important things were hanging in the balance. In comparison with Steve's peace of mind or Cass's future happiness, it was trivial. Yet I did care, immensely. I supposed she would have explained that this was due to my need to evangelise, my urge to fill her head with my own ideas in order to prove to myself that they were true. And it was certainly the case that with each sentence she spoke, I clung on until the end in the hope that she would deliver me some grain of agreement. In fact, that was probably why I'd sent her the manuscript in the first place. There's no point in communicating with a machine. Someone has to read a word, or it's just a mark on a screen. She was, in a way, the reader I'd imagined all along, except without imagining her, so that the inconvenience of her responses was absent. When I was writing, she hadn't existed as a reader, so I'd told her everything; and now she did and had her own opinions, so I wanted to take it all back and have it for myself.

But that wasn't the only reason why I cared. Some of it was much simpler than that. I was spending an evening out with someone I didn't know very well. This was something which rarely happened to me. There were endless collegiate engagements, of course, and drinks parties in the evenings during conferences, and even the Declan-Georgina dinner parties and their offshoots. But the first two were largely professional engagements, and the third so familiar that new people could sit in the same old seats and be heard to say much the same things. This was quite different. Margot didn't talk like anyone I knew. Our professional association had been cast off – at least, I hoped that it had, or I was in very serious trouble indeed – and, as indicated by the champagne, we were free to enjoy ourselves. There was no point in any of it if we couldn't convert at least some of the distance of our unfamiliarity into the intimacy of understanding. It was the same old thing, I realised: that counterpoint between difference and sameness, the drive to cancel out the very separateness which was the spur to attraction in the first place. Good grief.

In confusion, I rearranged my posture. She returned with the drinks, her lips overflowing with the creamy-cat smile I'd noted in her kit-bag of expressions the first time round. As she sat down, I noticed that there was something different about the way she looked from the last time. Had she changed her hair? Done something to her collar? I peered at her in concentration until she peered, enquiringly, back at me.

'You're wearing make-up,' I blurted.

Her eyebrows lifted in slight shock. 'Well, well, Professor Oldroyd, full marks to you. I would have sworn you weren't the kind of man to notice a little detail like that.'

I began to blush. The grin came back and she shoved my glass rather clumsily towards me. 'Coom on, drink oop, lad,' she said.

'Are you from Yorkshire?' I said in surprise.

'Liverpool. But I can't even fake my own accent these days. Yorkshire is safer, when I'm trying to cover my embarrassment. Tell me, Max, do you ever drop into a Plymouth accent? When you're trying to be one of the lads, for instance?'

'I don't think I ever really had one. They tried to knock that sort of thing out of us at school.'

'Declan has one still, and he went to the same school as you.'

'Yes, well, that's a bit different, as you'll have read.' I tasted the drink. It was surprisingly zingy and refreshing, and went rather well with the aftertaste of the port. 'This is nice,' I said.

'Port and lemon are natural partners. I'd have asked for them together, but the barman might have thought I was a whore.'

'Uh?'

'Come on, Max, you're a sailor's son. You must be familiar with the tart's drink of choice.'

'Er, no, I'm not.'

She laughed. 'You really are an almost total innocent, aren't you? That's what I found so fascinating, and what I didn't really manage to capture at all. If only you'd opened up just a little bit more. Then I could have said, this is the man who believes that the universe is morally neutral, but who regards sexual relations with anyone other than the one true love of his life as being a direct route to Hell. This is the man whose guiding principle is that no truth is proven forever, and yet who regards the truth as the lodestone of his life. This is the man who wants to make a world in which the thought of God never passes through a single mind, and yet who spends more time in his contemplation than any priest—'

'Stop it,' I snapped. 'That's just not true. You're twisting me the same way you did in the article, just for rhetorical effect.'

'It *is* true, Max,' she said more softly. 'Or at least, it's true of the character in your book. Or, it's true of my understanding of the character in your book. If you and that character are the same person, you're one of the most spiritual people I've ever met.'

'I don't know what you mean by spiritual, if you're applying it to me. I daresay I've given you plenty of ammunition for saying that there's no such thing as objective reality, because I've written about the disparity between different people's perceptions of the same events. And even about the same people's different perceptions of the same events over time. But they are the same events. This is a table. This is a glass of gin and lemon. You can call it what you like, but it's still the same thing, or at least it was when you called it that. I work in a university, you know, Margot. I have literature and philosophy academics coming out of my ears. I've heard all the bollocks about all our concepts, including the scientific ones, being political and cultural constructions. But what could be more politically or culturally constructed than a philosophy don trying to justify his own employment by claiming that the outputs of all other departments quite literally don't exist? Or' – I made a desperate lunge back towards the original point – 'a journalist who needs a headline saying that a famous atheist is the most spiritual person she's ever met?'

Margot's expression of light amusement hadn't changed. 'It's not a glass of gin and lemon any more,' she said. 'Would you like another one?'

'I said that! I said that it was only the same thing at that particular moment in time!'

She was already behind me. 'Another double coming up,' she said, laying a hand fleetingly on my shoulder.

Was she trying to get me drunk? I didn't care. I was getting closer to the thing I'd been trying to say all along. It didn't matter now whether she opposed me every step of the way. If her opposition got me there, then it was worth it.

She was back faster this time. I felt that it was almost certainly deliberate. Last time she'd been giving me time to think. This time she simply wanted to make sure that I still had a glass of alcohol in my hand.

'You know who it was in the book who most reminded me of you?' she said, and left a pause only long enough for effect, certainly not long enough for me to compose a reply. 'It certainly wasn't William, and it wasn't Steve either. It was Cass.'

Oh, shit. Reality, exploding all over any thoughts about the nature of reality.

'What are you going to do about her?' said Margot softly.

I couldn't think of anything to say. The change in register was too abrupt.

'Because that's the only thing that's really important for you now. Well, one of the two things, anyway.'

'What's the other?'

'We'll come back to the other one. As a moral man in a morally neutral universe, what are you going to do?'

'I—' I had to gulp down my emotion. It was the question I'd been avoiding asking. And I don't usually avoid things at all. 'I could leave it, I suppose. She said there was nothing I could do. I could leave her to live her life, and try to forget about her.' But that just didn't seem bearable, or even possible, and Margot's sceptical expression backed me up. 'Or I could go back to her and apologise. Ask her to forgive me. Admit that I was wrong—'

'You can try that. But I don't think you've really got anything to apologise for. Look, Max. Evangelism works both ways. By the time I'd finished reading about your family, I have to admit that I was rather annoyed by them. They were all so steadfast in blaming you for everything that had gone wrong in their lives. Even *you* stuck completely to their interpretation. I can forgive it in you, because that's another part of the thing we so loosely call paranoia – we'll attribute almost anything that happens around us to ourselves. But I can't forgive it in them. You didn't beat them, you didn't undermine them, you didn't do anything but be yourself. Were you really such a dominant character that they couldn't take any responsibility for themselves? William blames you for the fact that he's a hedonistic arsehole, Steve blames you for the fact that he's left the country, Cass blames you for the fact that she's bloody Christian, for God's sake. What would they do if you weren't around any more? Who would they blame it on then? And what's so wrong with the way they are anyway?'

I stared at her. 'Margot—' I struggled for words. 'You're not supposed to—'

'Not supposed to what? That Sally woman really got her hooks into you, didn't she? I did wonder several times whether it wasn't in fact she who was the dominant one. I can't tell, of course, because she's so shrouded in your picture of her as the perfect, wronged spouse, but if all three of your children have come out thinking the same way about themselves as you think about her, then it must have come from somewhere.'

'I – I'm finding it very difficult to follow what you're saying—'

'Unless it was both of you. Which is the most likely answer, really. She was the person you needed her to be. You were the person she needed you to be. One of you, or both of you, needed your children to be the way she was, not the way you were. It doesn't matter. These things happen in families. You have three brilliant, beautiful children and you don't need to be ashamed of any of it.'

'Margot—' The spotlight was so intensely on me, and I knew that it needed to be shifted. 'You're behaving like Georgina. Giving me a story to make everything all right.'

Her composure dropped. 'I know,' she said. 'I'm sorry. I didn't mean to. But – well – when that's the way you end up going—'

Confusion reigned. I decided to drown it with a large slug of gin and lemon. The hit of alcohol, combined with the release from her pincer-like control of the conversation, gave me the courage to address the original question. 'I'll tell you what I'm going to do about Cass,' I said.

She looked relieved herself. 'What are you going to do?'

'I'm going to tell her to go back to Jerry Vernon.'

'Are you?'

The words were out there now, and would have to be dealt with. I saw Cass. I saw Frank Vernon. Those images had never been allowed to collide until now. Even when Cass was telling me the most intimate details of her relationship with God, I'd been sure that she and Vernon existed in different universes. He'd been a self-interested bigot manipulating the uneducated masses for his own political and financial ends. She was a lovely intelligent confused young girl who'd been driven by her fragmented background to search for higher meaning with humility and hope. But they had existed in the same universe, and it was the same one that I lived in. She believed in God, not only in the way she'd explained it to me, but also in the way she would have explained it to Frank Vernon's son.

And Frank Vernon's son was in love with her. The progeny of that bloated bigot had looked upon my little girl and seen the beauty and light and *sex* that I'd once seen in her mother. His heart had lifted or sunk at her slightest word; he'd been tormented and enraptured by the same thoughts of desecration I'd battled with through the long nights of my pursuit of Sally; he'd wanted to take the purity he adored and debase it to its lowest levels of animal functionality. It doesn't matter how different two men's ideologies are. When it comes to the basic instincts, we're all pretty much the same.

Which is one of the trials of being the father of a daughter. It is one of the things which fathers have had to suppress since long before the emergence of homo sapiens. The facts, however, in this case, were different. Cass had already said that they'd thought of marriage, and their beliefs meant that any reunion was almost certain to result in that. After that, they would be more likely than most twenty-first-century lovers to have children; and it wasn't just that those children would be brought up entrenched in beliefs which were utterly alien to my own, it was that those children would be an actual, physical union of the genes of Cass and Frank Vernon. Every cell in those bodies would be controlled by a genetic code that had been produced by a splicing of the one with the other. Then those children might have children, and the grandchildren great-grandchildren, and so on, stretching to the end of the human race. For all her beliefs, those descendants would be the heaven that Cass's genes went to, and for all Frank Vernon's beliefs, they would be the heaven that his genes went to. Her memorial would be his too. And I would be nowhere amongst it.

I remembered Cass shouting at me about my fear, and she was right, in a way. But I wasn't afraid of God. There is only one thing in the world worth fearing all your life, and it is death. The universe most certainly does not love me, and it will dispose of me quite ruthlessly when the time comes. This does not make it a less remarkable place. I want to live in a world which is infinitely splendid, and such a thing could never shed a tear because Max Oldroyd doesn't talk to it any more. The wonders of the cosmos are just as mighty if they have been achieved by a force devoid of the human need for love. Sometimes I feel that far from placing us at the apex of creation, our self-consciousness marks out the human race as the species which has fallen the lowest. The Bible is a sublime piece of artistry because it screams with our deficiencies. Oh, God, please love me, please need me, please notice what I do and care about it, please write it all down and remember it for eternity, please make me exist when I have gone. And our maker responds in kind, by wanting and needing the same things. Cass was right. God is real enough. It's just that He was made in the image of me.

And so, like God, I have fashioned myself an eternity; and Declan never knew how true his words were when he said that the best things I could rely on were that I'd published and I'd reproduced. I cling on to those minuscule future remnants of myself, even though I know that both the publication record and the bloodline could peter out at any point. I do it even though I know that those aren't the things that matter. Cass has proved that to me absolutely, because I care about her as much as I could about any genetic offspring, and because my books have only done her harm. But still I can't help it. I am afraid.

'Sorry, Max,' said Margot. 'You don't have to answer that question.'

'I have to answer that question.'

'You don't have to answer it – now.' She fidgeted, and now that the parade of carefully-honed expressions had collapsed from her face, I saw once again how pretty it was. There were no arching brows, no curving cheekbones, no elaborate contrast between dark hair and pale skin. Neither the poet's pen nor the pathologist's scalpel could have discovered anything remarkable about that face. But the small traces of colour she'd deigned to touch it up with only emphasised what was already there. Clear skin, round blue eyes, small pointed nose; an approximation of feminine humanity, and a palette for whatever stories she chose to play on it.

Also I noticed how comfortable her body was in its skin. A

lithe, athletic body, neither short nor tall, with all the correct features in all the right places; other women might have displayed such a body in clothes designed to shock or titillate, but this one was not a showcase but a home. Her body confused me, because it was so unostentatious and unselfconscious, and because it made such a contrast with her utterly ostentatious, utterly self-conscious brain.

'I am rather sorry about the article,' said Margot, the voice no longer sounding as if she'd seen it all before. It was small and rather bitter. 'I didn't think I would be. But I think it's a bit unfair to be bombarded with a hundred thousand words telling me just what heartache lies beneath my simple observations. I never thought you'd take the mission to persuade me to quite those lengths.'

'It wasn't you,' I said, backing off from my own thoughts.

'I know it wasn't me. I'm just the anonymous reader, the one who's ill-disposed to hear what you've got to say. Well, what you wrote did affect me. And I stand by what I wrote. I don't know whether I would have written about Sally or William or Steve or Cass if I'd known more about them. You just don't know what you'll do if a situation like that arises. But the fact is that I didn't write about them. I wrote about you. I wrote about you because you agreed to an interview. And the reason you agreed to an interview was because you needed to publicise the reissue of *Genesis*. I've publicised it. We've both delivered our sides of the deal.'

'I never said—'

'It's not my problem if you've got a horrendous situation with your stepdaughter to sort out. I don't think that the situation's particularly your fault more than anyone else's, but I know that it isn't mine. You can't go around doing things like this, Max. What do you intend to do with this book? Publish it?'

'I – no, of course not. You know why I wrote it. You can see why I wrote it. My life was such a mess. I had to sort it out. In my own mind. Not in anyone else's.'

'But you still sent it to me.'

It was the last thing I'd expected, for her to behave as if my moment of stupidity had been an injury to herself. A piece of inspiration struck me. 'Evangelism works both ways,' I said. 'You didn't have to read it.'

She was silent. We sat there for a while, our appraisal of one another hovering between a gaze and an evaluation. The air slowly filled with something I couldn't name, and my body began to stiffen and relax within it.

'You see,' said Margot, her voice recovering just a tiny bit of its previous aplomb, the words popping into the air with both embarrassment and mischief, 'there are some things which are very, very easy to communicate.'

'Um, yes.'

For a second longer, it lasted. Then I had to break the moment. The surrender to non-verbal communication made me feel out of control. 'What drink shall we get now? Let me at least go and fetch them this time.'

Her lips twitched upwards, and she shook her head. 'I've got a bottle of champagne, remember?'

She paused for a moment on the doorstep.

'It's not the dog, is it?' I said in panic.

'I hadn't thought of that. Presumably it sleeps at night?'

'Oh, yes, very soundly.' I didn't care to tell her that he was accustomed to sleeping under my bed. Tonight Huxley would have to put up with a more limited choice of accommodation. 'What is it, then?'

'I just want to say that I don't want to be your sexy psychiatrist at all. I don't want to be put in that box any more than I want to be put in the Sally box. It's just that I'm in the terrible habit of conducting dates as if they were interviews.'

'This was a date?'

'It is now. Isn't it?'

That afterthought of doubt was all I needed to hear. I kissed her.

'I'm going to have to find out more about you some time,' I said as we stumbled together into the dark corridor.

'You might not get the chance. I'm not promising to be your one true love, you know. I might leave you in the morning and never see you again.'

'Do I really have to think like that?'

'Yes. You do.'

'All right, then. I will.'

We drank champagne in bed. It was something I'd never done before, and we giggled like teenagers and sparred playfully to distract us from our lust until, finally, I took her in my arms and forgot all about penetrating her brain.

16

The incompleteness of being a human being is excruciating. Once, very long ago it seems now, Margot asked me whether I was a moral person. And I always thought I was. Oh, I believe absolutely that the *universe* is not a moral thing. Nothing could be more neutral. It is beyond neutrality, because though the laws of physics which govern it contain many balancing positives and negatives, positive does not mean positive and negative does not mean negative in a moral sense when it comes to science. They are just themselves, equal in force, devoid of that thing we impose upon them called meaning. There are only two things which suggest the sort of imbalance which is a requisite for the drawing of moral conclusions. The first is that there is something rather than nothing. The second is that we have something within us with which to witness it. A shiver down the spine as the sun rises over frosted hills. A tremor of the skin as another's lips touch our own. A feeling of rightness in the gut when a girl lets loose the most beautiful sounds that ever were sung. These are the reminders that we exist, and that there exist things outside of us. We shouldn't need goodness in the universe at all. The miracle of existence, however transitory, should be more than enough.

But that thing inside us, our blessing and our curse, our consciousness and our self-consciousness and our consciousness of others, always it cries out for company, always it must be told that it is not alone. Someone like Frank Vernon, or someone like Cass, will demand to see their own mind reflected in every atom of the universe, will depend for their sense of self upon reassurance that the thing in charge is a mind like their own, and that it is on their side. Even someone like me, who is prepared to face the truth, will look for it in the minds of others.

And it is with this reaching out that morality begins. Cass or Frank Vernon might see it prescribed by a spiritual authority, and I might see it purely in my relations with the rest of the universe. But should we expect ourselves to be good? Is it a relevant question, when the workings of a mind outside our own are as unknowable as those of an imaginary Creator? I did my best for Cass, I truly did. Despite all the talk of my evangelism, I don't think I could ever have been accused of being a dictatorial father. I treated her as I would have had my father treat me. And yet if there is one thing she has taught me, it is that I knew not what I did.

She spoke of empiricism, and it reminded me of Frank Vernon, because Vernon used to quote Francis Bacon, the founder of empiricism, to back up his claims about science. Both of them struck at the heart of my own beliefs, because empiricism is the one thing I know which can demonstrably create new realities from what we have learned about the world outside us. We observe that the sun rises each morning, and we predict correctly that it will rise tomorrow too. And whilst, as Vernon pointed out, a scientific proof is never an absolute certainty – the sun can always confound us tomorrow – we can use our predictions to steer a course around the globe, until one day we are proved wrong. Frank Vernon's wriggling fallacies were no more than that, a sleight of hand claiming that empiricism's fundamental openness to that which might disprove its findings actually cancels it out. This is demonstrably false, as long as one has enough time to explain why. But Cass's use of the term was more troubling. She was right when she said that empiricism is about experience. Yet experience is actually the place where it starts to fall down. We can never truly observe what it is like inside someone else's head. All we can record is our observations about the external effects which that experience produces. Our empirical realities remain trapped within our own minds.

Margot left me in the morning. It is all very well rediscovering one's sexuality over gin and lemon and champagne with the words of a lifetime swirling around. But when I woke up and found a woman curled up in my arms, all of that was gone. The half-empty bottle stood on my bedside table, and two glasses lay toppled on the floor. My head ached and my nostrils were filled with the smell of acidifying champagne. Sex is a turmoil, especially if you haven't done it for a while. I felt as if every cell in my body had been rearranged. And then, next to me was this sleeping form, whose insides I had investigated and yet whose skin housed something I would never ever understand.

So I crept from my own bed and cleaned my teeth. And showered. And put all the dirty clothes from the linen basket into the wash. The cleanest shirt and trousers were selected from the only cupboard that is outside my bedroom, and then I went into the kitchen and did the washing up. As I was levering the margarine into the butter dish, she crept up behind me.

'I'll leave now,' she said.

Which was unthinkable. And yet so much the thing she'd warned of, and which I'd confirmed with my behaviour. There was nothing I could do. She left. I prepared my breakfast alone, the margarine spooned with the butter knife from the butter dish, the Marmite delicately implied along the edges of my badly cooked bread. Shit. Shit. Shit.

'That's the only thing that's really important for you now,' Margot had said the night before, referring to my estrangement from Cass, and for all our fine words we had got absolutely nowhere with the one thing that was supposed to be really important. 'Well, one of the two things, anyway—'

The other, presumably, was the liaison with her. Which had been achieved. Had she really had it in mind from so early in the evening? Perhaps she'd thought of it even before that. When she'd bought the champagne. Or when she'd read this manuscript. Or even before any of it, when she'd interviewed me the first time and had gushed in vicious prose about my stunted sexiness, or before that, when she'd been a bright young twenty-something who'd quoted *Genesis* at dinner parties and had thought Carolyn Hillman was an insubstantial adrenaline junkie. What was I doing back then? Rearing children, building a home, prancing around America in headlong pursuit of my own downfall. If I'd met Margot then I wouldn't have looked twice. If I'd met her at any time I wouldn't have looked twice. But for some reason, which was all bound up in her own story, something of which I knew almost nothing, she'd assaulted me with her pen and then had set out with a bottle of champagne and the deliberate intention of bedding me.

And I've felt bereft ever since. As if the loss of the touch of another's hands were the loss of the whole world. Which, in a way, it is. But it seems so wrong to want her back when I don't know who she is. When I was young, I thought that to share my life with a woman would be to understand what it was like to live in another person's brain, yet though Sally and I spent eighteen years together, it turned out that I never understood her at all. It seems so reckless, so masochistic to set off back down a path that I trod with such unflagging belief the last time around and that I now know was doomed to failure.

Yet I am slowly coming to realise that I have to do it. Just the memory of Margot's skin beneath my fingertips is enough to make me sure of it. 'Yes, Max,' she said as I cupped a pale globe of flesh in one of my hands and gazed at it in heady disbelief. 'It's a breast. Is it really so long since you've seen one?'

And even though it hadn't been so very long really, because

I've had to purge my appetites every once in a while, it had been a long time since I'd touched a creature I wanted to know better. It seemed remarkable that she let me see it, let me hold it, and my fingers felt poised on the edge of possession. 'Will you—' I said, and 'May I—' and she didn't even laugh at me, though I know she must have found my tentativeness very funny. She allowed me to proceed at my own pace, which was snail-like, or rather the tortured progress of an object propelling itself in two directions at once. Until I surrendered control, that is, and the desire to extend my state of grace was submerged beneath the desire to lose myself within it. And then it was over, and the last tremors of the explosion died away, and she had to hold me through the storm of tears for everything I hadn't won, and everything I'd lost.

It was good of her to let me cry, and good of her not to ask me what I was crying for. But I'd already told her everything I knew about myself. So perhaps she knew already that I was crying because pleasure doesn't last, and because every culmination dies away. Perhaps she knew I feared the power she held over me, and that I was lost in awe at the damage she might do. But even as I sobbed, and I felt the pulse of her blood in the fingertips on my back and the neck against my lips, I knew that the time had come to face my fear of the unknown. I knew it when I fled my bed in the morning; I knew it when I let her go.

Because the sound of my own voice has drowned out so much these past ten years. They call me an evangelist, but as Margot said, we all want to talk to people outside ourselves. The problem hasn't been that I've talked, it's been that I've had no-one to talk to. My certainty has been an escape from the ravaging uncertainties of communication; perhaps it always was. So I've shouted into the void, as if by shouting alone I could be certain that I was alive; and I was contradicted from a distance, as if distance could protect me from the existence of other minds. Then Margot came close. She scrapped all distance from the minute she took up her pen. And now I know that it's closeness I want, not distance. I'm fed up with shouting; I want her to talk to me about herself. Which she hasn't done, not once, except to confess with reluctance that she was from Liverpool, and to tell me that she didn't want me to think that she was my one true love. So perhaps she's scared of closeness too. Or not; perhaps it's something else that I'll never understand. I don't care. It's too late now. I'm prepared to take the risk. I want her back.

Which is all very well. But I can't escape the past so easily; I can't escape the man I am so easily. Because the other thing I'm starting to realise is that it's happening all over again. Even if the most unlikely thing happens, and I'm saved by the love of a good woman, I will still know that somewhere else, someone else is forsaking communication for the sake of certainty. Someone else is retreating from the fray of love to keep hold of her sense of herself. Someone else is blaming it on what happened to her before; someone else is surrendering herself to the past.

And I can't let it happen. Even though it's Jerry Vernon, I can't stand by and let my best girl send him away. She is sending him away because she thinks the way to live is to be quiet, and help where you can, and to impose nothing of yourself upon others; and whilst that may be true up to a point for her, she is surely wrong to demand an identical attitude from those she loves. If she does that, there will be no love. She said he was like me, but it's she who is behaving like me. Or like her mother; but it's difficult to tell the difference now. I pick up the phone, and it quivers alarmingly as I dial the number William gave me.

'Hello?' says a voice.

'Cass,' I say, 'it's Max.' I don't wait for her to respond. 'About your boyfriend. Or fiancé. Whatever he is. Jerry. You said he was like me. Well, I don't think I'm so bad, really, when you come to think of it. I think you should go back to him.'

Silence. But a good silence. The kind that comes before words; the kind that paves the way for all the words that will make the future.

Acknowledgements

My thanks go to all those who helped me to write this book. In particular, I would like to thank Sophie Petit-Zeman, whose generosity, expertise and enthusiasm were invaluable in enabling me to write about the science, and John Harrison, who kindly provided the biologist I requested! Both my agent, Lizzy Kremer, and my editor, Carole Welch, were wonderful sources of support and guidance, often better at working out what I wanted to say than I was myself. I am also indebted to James McIntosh, with whom I first debated some of the issues raised in this book many years ago, and Arabella Murray, my musical advisor.

The research for this book was conducted over a lifetime's addiction to works of popular science. Amongst those I found particularly useful were *In the Blood: God, Genes and Destiny* by Steve Jones (HarperCollins, 1996); *Consciousness: A User's Guide*, by Adam Zeman (Yale University Press, 2002); *The Creationists: The Evolution of Scientific Creationism*, by Ronald L. Numbers (University of California Press, 1993); *The Selfish Gene*, by Richard Dawkins (Oxford University Press, 1989); *Rocks of Ages: Science and Religion in the Fullness of Life* by Stephen Jay Gould (Vintage, 2002); *Biology: A Functional Approach* by MVB Roberts (Thomas Nelson and Sons, 1986); and *Jesus: Authors Take Sides* edited by Richard Ingrams (HarperCollins, 1999).

Finally, I would like to thank my parents for helping me with what I didn't know, Lynne Stuart for doing a little evangelising of her own, and Edward Paleit for many things, including marrying me in the middle of the editing process.

CLARE GEORGE

The Cloud Chamber

It is 1931, and Walter Dunnachie has arrived at the Cavendish Laboratory after a six-week journey from the other side of the earth. He has fallen in love with Grace, the spirited young adventuress he met on the ship that carried them from Australia to England, and his head is filled with the unshakeable belief that science and pacifism together hold the key to all the riddles of the world.

Fifteen years later Walter's ideals lie in tatters. The wonders he witnessed in Cambridge have led directly to the destruction of Hiroshima, and he cannot forgive his mentors – the charismatic founders of nuclear physics – for this betrayal. Tortured by images of the horrors he has helped to unleash, he struggles to hold together his marriage with Grace, and to come to terms with the arrival in London of his fellow scientist and one-time best friend, Alan Nunn May.

For Nunn-May has returned from Canada, carrying with him a secret as deadly as any that have been kept or betrayed in the six years of the war. And when he tracks down his old friend to ask for his understanding, he unwittingly entangles Grace's and Walter's fates with his own.

'A smartly executed novel, part spy story, part scientific thriller, part romance'
Observer

'This absorbing, ambitious debut . . . has a gift for probing crises of conscience, for the cold, private moments that accompany what President Truman called "a rain of ruin"'
Guardian

'A clever and graceful novel . . . building on the excitement of the search for the atom and conveying the atmosphere of a time when plum pudding was the metaphor of choice for the helium nucleus . . . an ambitious account of scientific enquiry, a spy story and an exploration of the morality of mass destruction'
Time Out

'Compelling and masterful . . . at once a spy story, an exploration of the moral complexity of the Bomb and an engaging reconstruction of an historic era'
Richard Rhodes, winner of the Pulitzer Prize

ς

SCEPTRE